THE JACK REACHER EXPERIMENT

EXPERIMENT

BOOKS 1–7

Jude Hardin

Contents

DEAD RINGER

THE REACHER EXPERIMENT BOOK 1

1

Hundreds of big-rig headlights had whooshed by over the past couple of hours, and there wasn't anything particularly unusual about the pair Wahlman was looking at now.

Except that they were headed straight toward him.

He dove and rolled down the grassy embankment to his left. He half expected the semi to follow him and crush him, but it didn't. It thundered on by, transmitting vibrations all the way down to the bottom of the ditch, tremors that stomped through Wahlman's core like a herd of rhinos. There was no slowing down, no grinding of gears, no screeching of brakes. No indication that a human being was behind the wheel.

Amped on adrenaline, breathing hard, Wahlman clawed his way up the slope, handfuls of slick grass eventually giving way to the gritty pavement at the top.

The massive vehicle continued westward along the shoulder, veering slightly to the right, roguishly, inelegantly, just a stupid machine lumbering through the misty blackness. A machine the size of a house. A machine that would destroy anything in its path.

Wahlman didn't own a cell phone, and there weren't any cars or trucks or motorcycles to flag down at the moment. The interstate had been eerily quiet before the semi approached. No vehicles for several minutes, westbound or eastbound. Wahlman didn't know if it was like that every Sunday at 4:17 in the morning, but he figured it probably was. If you were in Slidell, you probably weren't going to be driving into New Orleans at that hour, and vice versa. You were probably in bed. Maybe one of the lucky ones who could actually sleep through the night every night.

The big truck rolled on. Probably a Freightliner, the way a soft drink is probably a Coke, although it could have been a Kenworth or a Peterbilt or a Mack. Or some other brand. It was pulling a heavy load. You could tell by the hum of the tires on the pavement.

The headlights illuminated a bridge up ahead, a small one built over a canal.

Wahlman figured the truck was traveling at a speed between fifty and sixty miles an hour. Not inordinately fast, but certainly not slow either. Maybe it had been coasting for a while. Maybe the driver had fallen asleep. Or died of a heart attack or something.

Wahlman was standing there wondering exactly what had happened when the semi crashed through the concrete railing that ran along the side of the bridge. The trailer broke loose and toppled cacophonously out into the middle of the highway, showering the pavement with bright orange sparks as the tractor plunged nose-first into the water.

Wahlman wasn't much of a runner. He never had been. He'd played football in high school, but they always put him in a position that didn't require much speed. Offensive line, most of the time. At six feet four inches tall and two hundred forty pounds, there weren't many players who could get past him. In his senior year, a sports reporter at the local newspaper started calling him *Rock*, and the name stuck. He'd been nearly impenetrable on the football field, but he wasn't fast. Not then, not now. He galloped clumsily toward the wreckage, greasy hot steam from the submerged engine rising and meeting him as he finally made it to the edge of the bridge.

The headlight on the driver side was still on, cutting a wedge of brightness into the murky brown canal water. The water wasn't very deep. Eight feet at the most. Wahlman couldn't see into the cab, but he could hear the muffled roar of a classic heavy metal song blaring from the stereo. Nobody could have fallen asleep to that, he thought. Which meant that the driver had lost consciousness some other way. Maybe a cardiac event. Or a stroke. Or something else.

Wahlman pulled his boots off, slid down into the water and peered into the passenger side window. The driver was male, late thirties or early forties, as big as Wahlman, maybe a little bigger. He wore a plaid shirt and a black ball cap. His eyes were closed. There was a thread of blood that started at the corner of his mouth and ended at the edge of his button-down collar. The water inside the cab was up to his chest. Wahlman couldn't tell if he was breathing or not.

Wahlman pounded on the window.

The driver didn't stir.

The music had stopped, and the headlight was getting dimmer by the second.

Wahlman went up for a quick breath of air, and then he dove back down and got on his hands and knees and frantically started searching for something to break the window with. He raked his fingers through the silt, combing a radius of several feet, scooping and grasping at the sandy mud, coming up empty again and again.

He climbed around the engine housing to the other side of the cab, cupped his hands against the window. The water was up to the driver's chin now. Wahlman reared back and hammered the glass with his fist, but it was no use. The resistance from the water prevented the blows from being forceful enough. Maybe he could break through with the heels of his feet, he thought, but he needed to get another breath of air first. He was about to push himself back up to the surface when the driver's eyes opened.

"Help," the guy shouted. "Help me. Please."

Wahlman made a cranking motion with his hand.

"Roll the window down," he said.

Water would flood the cab, violently, like a dam bursting, but then the pressure would equalize and the guy might be able to pull himself out.

"I can't move my arms," the man said.

Every cell in Wahlman's body was screaming for oxygen. He held one finger up to let the driver know he would be right back, and then he surfaced and swam over to the bank. Gasping, coughing, lungs on fire. He grabbed a rock the size of a softball, jumped back into the water and made his way down to the passenger side window. The water was up to the driver's nostrils now. Wahlman started slamming the window with the rock, but the glass didn't break. The water was slowing him down and he was lightheaded and his muscles were starting to fatigue. It felt as though he had been drugged and beaten and thrown into a vat of pancake syrup.

The driver made one last gurgling cry for help as the headlight grew dimmer and dimmer and then went totally black. Wahlman couldn't see anything now. He kept trying to break the window. There was nothing else he could do. He tried several different angles, coming down as hard as he could, gripping the rock with both hands, pounding and pounding and pounding, finally hearing a muffled crack as the safety glass crumpled and folded inward. There was no big gush, as he thought there would be, which meant that the cab was completely full of water now.

Using the rock to grind off any remaining chunks of glass from the window frame, Wahlman managed to climb in and grab the driver by his shirt and pull him out of the truck. The guy was unconscious now. Totally limp. Dead weight. Wahlman struggled to get him into a rescue hold, but it was no use. The man slipped away and sunk to the bottom of the canal like a sack of bowling balls.

Wahlman needed air. He surfaced and took a deep breath, and another, the air warm and wet and heavy, and then he went back down and lifted the driver onto his shoulders, trudged up the slope and heaved the unconscious man onto the rocky bank.

Wahlman was nearly unconscious himself. He coughed out some water and sucked in some air and reached over and pressed two fingers against the side of the man's neck to see if he had a pulse. Nothing. Wahlman struggled to his knees and started chest compressions, noticed right away that the bottom of the man's shirt was soaked with blood.

And then he noticed something else.

The man looked exactly like him.

Same facial features, same hair color, same massive arms and shoulders. The guy had a tattoo on his neck, but otherwise it was like looking into a mirror.

Wahlman continued performing chest compressions.

"Breathe," he shouted.

But the man didn't breathe. And when a thick glob of blackish-red blood oozed out from the center of his mouth, Wahlman decided it was time to stop the resuscitation efforts. He scooted away from the corpse, rolled onto his back, stared up at the diffuse moonlight. A thick blackness engulfed him, and he wondered if he was dying, and he thought he was, and his fingers started tingling and his legs went numb and there was nothing he could do but lie there and let it happen.

2

There was a bright light in Wahlman's face and someone was shaking his shoulder and asking him if he was all right. When he opened his eyes, he saw the silhouette of a police officer standing over him.

He sat up and fought off a wave of nausea.

"I'm okay," he said.

The officer nodded. He slid the flashlight into a compartment on the left side of his belt, between the stun gun and the pepper spray, and then he reached up and keyed the microphone attached to his right epaulet. He announced his unit number and location and told the person on the other end to alert the homicide division and the coroner's office.

"We're going to need a tow truck and a crane and a rescue unit and as many cruisers as you can spare," he said.

The patrolman was young. Twenty-two or twenty-three, Wahlman guessed. Certainly no older than twenty-five. His badge said *NOPD*. New Orleans Police Department. He had pale skin and blue eyes and reddish-blond hair. Five-seven or five-eight, a hundred and fifty pounds at the most. He hadn't been on the job long. Wahlman could tell. He didn't have the air of confidence that came with experience. Maybe this was his first night out in a cruiser by himself. Or maybe this was just the first time he'd worked a major accident.

Wahlman looked up at the bridge. Traffic on the westbound side of the interstate was backed up as far as he could see. A lot of trucks, probably heading into town to make deliveries.

The man who'd been driving the tractor-trailer was still in the same spot on the bank, but he had been covered with a blanket. At least most of him had been covered. The blanket wasn't quite long enough. His mud-caked boots were sticking out of the end closest to the water.

"I tried to help him," Wahlman said to the officer.

"Can you walk, sir?"

"I think so."

"Let's go sit in my car. We can talk there."

Wahlman stood and followed the patrolman up to the shoulder where his cruiser was parked. The officer opened the back door on the passenger side and motioned for Wahlman to get in.

"Why can't I sit up front?" Wahlman asked.

"Against regulations."

"I was an MA in the United States Navy. The only people we put into the backs of cars were suspects. Am I a suspect?"

"I don't know much about the navy," the patrolman said. "But out here in the real world—"

"I was a Master at Arms," Wahlman said. "I was a policeman."

"Then you should know that everyone's a suspect in a situation like this."

"Are you taking me in for questioning?"

"Relax. I just need you to sit here with me until the homicide detective gets here."

Wahlman had an appointment in New Orleans, and he wasn't in the mood to be detained. He knew from experience that these kinds of things could drag on for hours sometimes.

"I'm not getting back there," he said, gesturing toward the back seat of the cruiser. "We can stand out here and talk if you want to."

The officer rested his right hand on the butt of his service pistol. It was a Glock. Probably a .40 caliber. Probably with a 15-round magazine.

"I need you to put your hands on the top of the car and spread your legs apart," the officer said.

"A minute ago we were just going to talk," Wahlman said. "Now you're going to cuff me? Am I under arrest?"

"Hands on top of the car. Now!"

"I haven't done anything wrong. I almost killed myself trying to—"

"Now!"

The officer gripped the pistol and pulled it out of the holster and pointed it at Wahlman's chest. Wahlman glanced down at the barrel, and then he locked eyes with the patrolman.

"What are you charging me with?" he asked.

The policeman's lips trembled.

"Suspicion of murder," he said.

"That's ridiculous. I was just walking along trying to hitch a ride. The truck almost ran me over, and then it crashed through the railing on the bridge. Whatever happened to that driver happened before I ever got to him."

"Either put your hands on the car, or I'm going to add resisting an officer to the charges."

A siren chirped in the distance. Behind the patrolman there was a single blue strobe speeding toward the crash site. Wahlman could see it, but the patrolman couldn't. He was turned the wrong way. He probably didn't hear the siren either. He was too focused on the situation at hand, on what he perceived to be a threat.

"I'm not resisting anything," Wahlman said. "You're nervous and you're not thinking clearly. Pulling your pistol was a mistake. Put it away now and I won't report you for using excessive force."

The patrolman just stood there. He didn't know what to do. Wahlman was obviously unarmed, and he hadn't made any aggressive moves toward the officer. He didn't have any shoes on, so it wasn't like he was going to make a run for it. He hadn't exactly been cooperative, but he hadn't been exceedingly uncooperative either. He just didn't want to get into the back seat of that NOPD cruiser. No door handles, caged off from the front. It was basically a mobile jail cell, and Wahlman hadn't done anything to deserve that sort of treatment, not even for a little while. Not even for one minute.

The car with the single flashing light on the roof steered

in behind the cruiser. It was a black sedan. A Chevrolet, Wahlman thought, although he couldn't tell for sure. One sedan looked pretty much like another these days. A man wearing a wrinkled blue suit climbed out. When he saw what was going on, he dropped to one knee and drew his pistol and aimed it at Wahlman's core.

"On the ground," he shouted. "Hands behind your head, fingers laced together. Do it. Now!"

"There's a dead man on the bank," Wahlman said. "I tried to help him, but—"

Wahlman felt a punch in the gut. A split second later, blue arcs of electric pain shot through every muscle in his body. He collapsed to the pavement. He couldn't move. He couldn't talk.

But he could hear.

"Get a pair of cuffs on him," the man in the wrinkled blue suit shouted.

3

While Wahlman had been talking to the man in the wrinkled suit, the patrolman must have gone for his stun gun. The one with the yellow handle. The one next to the flashlight compartment on his utility belt. Wahlman had been zapped with one before, during a training exercise. It wasn't something you wanted to experience twice. Or even once, for that matter.

When Wahlman was able to stand, the patrolman and the man in the wrinkled suit forced him into the back seat of the cruiser. The man in the wrinkled suit climbed in and sat beside him. He was holding a zippered plastic evidence bag that contained the contents of Wahlman's pockets. The patrolman stood outside the door at parade rest.

"You're making a mistake," Wahlman said. "I didn't kill that guy."

"Someone killed him. I took a quick peek under the blanket. His belly's a mess."

"I saw the blood on his shirt. I figured he must have been shot. Or stabbed."

The man in the wrinkled suit nodded.

"Stabbed," he said. "Multiple times."

"Are you charging me with something?"

"Not yet."

"Then take the cuffs off and let me go."

"What's your name?"

Wahlman glanced out the window. Several other police cars had made it to the scene, along with a fire truck and an ambulance.

"I want my stuff," Wahlman said, gesturing toward the evidence bag.

"What's your name?"

"Wahlman. Now let me out of here."

"Got a first name?"

"No."

The man in the wrinkled suit unzipped the bag, reached in and pulled out Wahlman's billfold. It was dripping wet.

"Rock Wahlman," the man in the wrinkled suit said. "Cute. Your parents must have had quite the sense of humor."

"Either charge me with something or let me out of here," Wahlman said, not bothering to tell the man in the wrinkled suit that *Rock* was not the name he'd been given at birth, that he'd legally changed it during his senior year in high school.

The man in the wrinkled suit slid the billfold back into the bag.

"Detective Collins," he said. "New Orleans Police Department, Homicide Division. This is going to go a lot easier on you if you cooperate with us, Mr. Wahlman."

"I already told you. I didn't kill the guy. And I don't know who did kill the guy. End of story. Take the cuffs off and—"

"I noticed the address on your ID. Are you homeless?"

"Why would you assume that?"

"Not many people live in a post office box."

"Maybe it's a really big box."

The detective laughed. "Or maybe you're a really big smartass," he said. "I think we're done here."

Detective Collins tapped on the window. The patrolman opened the door and let him out. They stood there with the door open, probably hoping to scare Wahlman into being a little more cooperative with talk of jail time and so forth. But Wahlman wasn't scared. He was angry. These guys should have been recommending him for a medal or something. Instead they were treating him like a criminal.

"What do you want me to do with him?" the patrolman asked.

"Maybe we can get something out of him over at the station. He failed to provide me with a proper address, which falls under title fourteen, section one-oh-eight. Resisting an officer. He could do up to six months for that. He's obviously some kind of drifter, which makes him a flight risk, so his bail will probably be set pretty high. He won't be going anywhere for a while. I'm going to make some calls, get a couple of divers over here and—"

"You need to go look at the corpse again," Wahlman said.

"Pardon me?" Collins said.

"The guy looks just like me. He could be my twin brother, if I had one. Don't you think there's something just a little bit odd about that?"

"I think there's something just a little bit odd about *you*," Collins said. "We gave you a chance to cooperate, but—"

"You Tased me and cuffed me and threw me into the back of this car for no good reason. Your rookie friend is wearing a body cam, and both your cars have dash cams. I know a good old-fashioned slimeball lawyer who's going to have a field day with this. You'll be lucky to still have a job when I get done with you."

"Don't threaten me, Wahlman."

"It's not a threat, Collins. It's a promise. Go ahead and take me to the station."

"Give me one good reason not to."

"I'll give you two good reasons."

"I'm listening."

"My boots are over there on the bridge. They're still dry. Not possible if I'd been in the cab with the driver. Whoever stabbed him did it east of here, and then got out of the truck. That's the only way it could have happened. Unless he stabbed himself."

Detective Collins glanced pensively over at the wreckage.

"I figured you might have knifed him right before he got to the bridge," he said.

"Why would I have done that?" Wahlman asked. "It would have been tantamount to suicide."

Collins shrugged. "It would have been a stupid thing to do," he said. "But I don't run across too many geniuses in my line of work. I was thinking our divers might be able to find the murder weapon, and of course that still might be the case. But if your boots are on the bridge, and they're dry, then you're right. You're in the clear. You seemed to have worked that out like a pro."

"Believe it or not, I used to be a pretty good cop," Wahlman said. "I might be able to help you get to the bottom of this thing. But I can't do it from a jail cell."

"You were a cop?"

"I was a Master at Arms in the navy. Twenty years of continuous active duty service."

"You're retired? You don't look old enough."

"I enlisted two days after I graduated from high school."

Collins pulled a handkerchief out of his pocket and wiped his nose. His eyes were bloodshot, and he needed a shave.

"I'm going to need your service number," he said. "I can check it out on the computer in my car."

"Not a problem," Wahlman said.

Detective Collins turned back to the patrolman.

"Got a camera?" he asked.

"Sure. On my phone. You're not going to just let him go, are you?"

"Did he tell you he used to be a law enforcement officer?"

"He might have mentioned it. I don't remember."

"Go take some pictures of the victim's face and email them to me," Detective Collins said to the patrolman. "And grab Mr. Wahlman's boots while you're at it."

4

By the time the patrolman made it back with the boots, Detective Collins had already checked on Wahlman's service record.

"Take the cuffs off," Collins said to the patrolman.

"How am I going to write this up?"

"That's your problem."

Wahlman climbed out of the car. The patrolman took the cuffs off.

"Here's how you're going to write it up," Wahlman said, massaging some circulation back into his hands. "You're going to tell the truth. You're going to admit that you overreacted. It's all on camera anyway, so there's point in trying to deny it. You'll probably get some desk time, maybe some remedial training. I'm not going to pursue this any further, but you need to think really hard the next time you decide to pull your gun out and point it at someone."

The patrolman nodded, but he didn't apologize. Not to Wahlman, or to Detective Collins. He didn't say anything. Collins instructed him to file his preliminary report from the computer in his cruiser.

"After that you can get with your sergeant on what to do next," he said.

The patrolman walked around to the driver side of the NOPD cruiser, opened the door, took his hat off and climbed in.

Wahlman sat down on the pavement and started pulling his dry boots on over his wet socks.

"That could have ended badly for all of us," he said.

Collins nodded. "I'm going to go take a look at those pictures," he said. "You're welcome to join me whenever you're ready."

Wahlman finished tying his boots, and then he walked to the passenger side of the unmarked police car, opened the door and slid into the front seat.

"I'm going to need some dry clothes," he said.

"So here's what I don't understand," Detective Collins said. "You're retired from the navy. You get a paycheck every month. So why are you wandering around with no car, no—"

"Who said I don't have a car?"

Collins looked puzzled. "Don't tell me it's at the bottom of the canal," he said.

"It's parked on the shoulder," Wahlman said. "On the other side of Lake Pontchartrain. Black pickup. It died and I couldn't get it started again. The indicator panel is showing a fault at relay fourteen. I hope that's all it is."

"You left it there and started hitchhiking? Why didn't you call for help?"

"I don't have a phone."

"Why not?"

"I don't usually need to call anyone."

Collins laughed. "Got any more surprises for me?"

"I have a house in Florida. And my application for a PI license is pending approval from Tallahassee."

"You want to be a private investigator?" Collins said. "I'm pretty sure you're going to need a cell phone for that job."

"Maybe."

There was a touch-screen computer monitor mounted on the center of the dashboard, the entire device about the size of a hardcover novel. Collins started tapping and swiping, and a few seconds later an image of the dead driver's face appeared on the screen.

Collins stared at the photo for a few seconds, and then he turned and looked at Wahlman. He went back and forth a few times, the expression on his face changing from neutral to something close to astonishment.

"Unbelievable," he said. "The guy looks just like you."

"Except for this," Wahlman said, sliding his fingers along the curved length of faded scar tissue that ran from his right cheek bone to the bottom of his jaw.

"Yeah," Collins said. "Except for that."

"It's possible that he really is my twin brother."

Collins looked puzzled again. "Okay, so when I asked you if you had any more surprises for me—"

"I grew up in an orphanage," Wahlman said. "I don't remember anything about my mother and father. It's possible that I have siblings that I don't know anything about."

Detective Collins reached into one of his pockets and pulled out a pack of chewing gum, one of the expensive retro brands made from real sugar. He offered Wahlman a stick. Wahlman said no thanks.

"Let's say this guy is your twin brother," Collins said, peeling away the foil wrapper and folding a piece of the chewing gum into his mouth. "What are the odds of something like this happening the way it did? You know? What are the odds?"

"Slim to none, I guess," Wahlman said. "Yet it happened."

Collins scrolled through some more pictures of the deceased truck driver.

"What happened to your parents?" he asked.

"They died in a car accident when I was two."

"You were in the car with them?"

"I was. My face got slammed into the radio."

Collins clawed at the stubble on his chin. "So you don't remember anything about having a brother?" he asked.

"How much do you remember from when you were two?"

"Good point."

"Like I said, I don't even remember my parents."

"Their name was Wahlman?"

"As far as I know."

"Ever try to get in touch with anyone? Grandparents? Aunts? Uncles? Cousins?"

"Why should I? They knew where I was. I spent sixteen years in that shithole. Not one person ever came to see me.

Not a single one. I could have used some family back then. Now I don't care."

Collins tapped on the computer screen.

"I just got an email with some information on the driver," he said.

"Let's take a look," Wahlman said.

"Sorry. It's confidential."

"This guy might be my brother."

"I still can't share his personal information with you. Not yet."

"When?"

"We'll need to notify his next-of-kin. Then we can release the information to the media."

"I have to wait to hear about it on the news?"

"Is there somewhere I can reach you?" Collins asked.

"I have hotel reservations. But I don't have any way to get there."

"Where are you staying?"

Wahlman told him the name of the hotel.

"It's on St. Charles Avenue," Wahlman said. "Near the French Quarter."

"I'll make sure you get a ride," Collins said.

Wahlman climbed out of the car, leaned on the fender and waited. A state trooper pulled up about ten minutes later and drove him into New Orleans, exiting the interstate at Canal Street.

5

Wahlman made it to the hotel a little after seven. He checked in, asked for a toothbrush and a razor and some toothpaste and some shaving cream. The guy at the desk didn't say anything about the way he looked or the way he smelled or the condition of the dollar bills he pulled out of his wallet when he asked for change. He took the elevator to the fourth floor, found his room, unlocked the door and walked inside.

It wasn't a fancy place, but it was nice. There was a king size bed against one wall, and a long wooden unit that served as a desk and a dresser and a TV stand against the other. Bathroom, closet, ironing board, all the usual stuff.

Wahlman peeled off his damp and sticky clothes and took a shower. He shaved and brushed his teeth, and then he took another shower, scrubbing himself until it hurt. He wrapped a towel around his waist, carried his dirty things down the hall to the laundry room, fed some quarters into the detergent dispenser and then some more into the washing machine. He returned to his room and watched the news for a while, and then he went back and loaded everything into the dryer.

As he was turning to leave, a woman carrying a white plastic laundry bag walked into the room. Mid-thirties, long black hair, green eyes, olive complexion. She was very attractive. She seemed startled at first, and then embarrassed.

"Oh, excuse me," she said, keeping her eyes on the bag of dirty clothes as she set it on the shelf beside the washing machine.

"I was hoping nobody would be up this early," Wahlman said. "I don't usually go around with nothing but a towel on."

"I was hoping the same thing," the woman said, picking the items of clothing out of the bag one-by-one and dropping them into the washing machine. "That nobody would be up this early, that is."

"Well, take care," Wahlman said.

He went back to his room, watched the news some more. They were talking about the fatal accident on the interstate, but they weren't giving out any details about the driver. Westbound traffic was still backed up for several miles.

Wahlman decided to close his eyes for thirty minutes or so while his clothes dried. He thought about setting the alarm clock on the nightstand, but he didn't. When he woke up, it was almost one o'clock in the afternoon.

In the distance, someone was pounding on a bass drum. *Boom, boom, boom, boom.* Probably a parade somewhere nearby, Wahlman thought. He'd heard that they have a lot of them in New Orleans.

He wrapped the towel around his waist again and walked

back down to the laundry room. His things were on top of the dryer. Someone had folded them for him. Pants, shirt, socks, underwear. There was a note on top of the stack:

> *I needed the dryer. Your stuff wasn't quite dry, by the*
> *way. You owe me fifty cents.*
> *—Allison, room 427*

Wahlman picked up his things and walked back to his room and got dressed. He looked out the window. He still couldn't see the parade, but he could tell that it was getting closer. *Boom, boom, boom, boom.* After everything that had happened earlier, his body felt a little bit like that. Like something that had been beaten with mallets.

He emptied his wallet and spread some things out on the dresser to dry. Cash, driver's license, bank cards, proof of insurance. There were a variety of business cards that he'd accumulated over the past couple of years, along with dozens of receipts from restaurants and filling stations. Some of the business cards had phone numbers on the backs of them, none of which were legible anymore. He tossed the ruined items into the trash can, feeling like some kind of pathological packrat for hanging onto them in the first place.

He was about to leave the room when the phone started ringing. He picked up and said hello.

"Detective Collins, NOPD Homicide Division. How are you, Mr. Wahlman?"

"Better. I slept for a while."

"Good. I was wondering if you could stop by the station tomorrow morning."

"What time?"

"Nine if you can make it. I'm at the District Seven Police Station on Dwyer Road. I just need to go over a few things with you, and I'm going to need a written statement regarding your involvement with the accident this morning."

"I'll be there," Wahlman said.

"Great. See you then."

Wahlman hung up the phone. He slid his room key and his debit card and two quarters into the back pocket of his jeans, and then he walked down to room 427. He knocked. Waited. Knocked again. The deadbolt clicked and the door opened. It was the woman he'd seen in the laundry room earlier. She was the one wearing a towel this time. Her shoulders were the same shade as her complexion. No tan lines, so it wasn't from the sun. It was just her natural color. She smelled wonderful.

"Sorry," Wahlman said. "I just wanted to pay you back for the dryer."

He reached into his pocket and pulled out the quarters and handed them to her.

"Thanks," she said.

"Thanks for folding my clothes."

"No problem. Is this your first time in New Orleans?"

"It is. Why do you ask?"

"No reason. Just curious. Anyway, maybe I'll see you around."

"Okay."

Allison closed the door. Wahlman stood there for a few seconds, and then he took the elevator down to the first floor and used the ATM to withdraw some money from his checking account. Opposite the check-in desk there was an area with dining tables and booths and a counter where you could order food and drinks, and behind all that there was an alcove with some computers set up for guests of the hotel. Wahlman sat down at one of the computers and searched for automotive repair shops. He wrote down some numbers, went back up to his room and made some calls. The first three places didn't answer their phones. The fourth one did, but it was Sunday and they were closing early, and they asked if he could please call back tomorrow. Wahlman finally found a place that was open until seven, but the guy he talked to said that he would need some kind of guarantee of payment before he could send a tow truck way over to Slidell. Wahlman didn't want to give the guy his credit card number over the phone, so he told him to forget about it.

Wahlman went back down to the first floor and asked the guy at the desk if he knew anyone who worked on cars.

"My brother-in-law might be able to help you," the clerk said. "He has a landscaping business, but he does that kind of thing on the side sometimes."

"I'm pretty sure it just needs a relay," Wahlman said.

The clerk pulled a cell phone out of his pocket and punched in a number. Apparently his brother-in-law's name was Sam, and apparently Sam didn't have a lot going on today. He agreed to pick Wahlman up at the hotel, take him to an auto parts store to buy a new relay, and then take him to his truck. All for a hundred dollars. If it wasn't the relay, he would tie a rope to Wahlman's bumper and tow the vehicle to his place over on the West Bank and try to figure out what the problem was at thirty dollars an hour.

Wahlman agreed to those terms.

As it turned out, Relay 14 was indeed the problem, and two hours later Wahlman was back at the hotel with his truck. He pulled to the curb and climbed out and walked inside and arranged for valet parking, and then he trotted over to the sandwich shop across the street, where he was late for an appointment with a man named Drake.

6

It was almost four o'clock in the afternoon, and there weren't many people in the sandwich shop. Too late for lunch, too early for dinner. There was a middle-aged couple at one table and two women who might have been college students at another. Wahlman didn't see any men sitting alone. He walked to the service counter, where he was greeted by a hairy fellow wearing a red t-shirt and a white apron.

"Can I help you?" the man asked. He had a full beard and forearms that looked like Chia Pets.

"I was supposed to meet someone here," Wahlman said. "Was there a guy here earlier who looked like he was waiting for someone?"

"There were lots of guys here earlier."

"I was supposed to meet him about twenty minutes ago. He said he was going to be wearing a Tulane football jersey."

The man shrugged. "I don't know," he said. "You want something to eat?"

Wahlman looked up at the menu mounted on the wall

behind the counter. It was possible that Drake was running late too, possible that he might show up in a few minutes.

"How fresh are your oysters?" Wahlman asked.

"Pulled out of the Gulf yesterday. Best in New Orleans."

"Let me have an oyster po'boy and a side of fries."

"Anything to drink?"

"I'll try the Abita," Wahlman said.

The man behind the counter reached into a glass-fronted refrigerator, grabbed a bottle of Abita Amber lager and opened it and rang up the order. Wahlman paid him and carried the beer to a table by the window. The middle-aged couple and the college students must have exited the restaurant while Wahlman was placing his order. Now he had the entire dining area to himself.

It was a nice autumn day, and there were quite a few people out on the street. You could spot the tourists by the way they walked along casually and looked around and pointed at things. Some of them were wearing lanyards with nametags attached to them. Probably attending a conference at one of the big hotels, Wahlman thought. Some of them were carrying plastic cups filled with frozen drinks, and some of them were carrying shopping bags filled with who-knows-what. Some of them were eating hot dogs from street vendors. Everyone seemed to be having a swell time and Wahlman was enjoying his beer and the aroma of the oysters frying and he was wondering what had happened to Drake when four shots rang out and four fat holes suddenly appeared in the big plate glass window.

Wahlman hit the deck and started crawling toward the

service counter. People outside were screaming. Panicking. Undoubtedly scurrying in every direction, trying to make it to safety as more bullets whizzed through the sandwich shop and more glass rained down on the floor.

Wahlman made it to the area behind the counter. The hairy man was back there on the floor nervously fiddling with a cell phone.

"Do you have a gun back here?" Wahlman asked.

"Why would I have a gun?"

"Why wouldn't you?"

"This is a good area," the man said. "We don't have no trouble around here."

And yet there was trouble, Wahlman thought. Big trouble. Those first four shots had come within inches of his face. He'd heard the bullets whistle by. It seemed highly unlikely that this was a random attack. It seemed that whoever was doing the shooting had chosen a target, and it seemed that the target was Rock Wahlman.

The hairy man was on the phone with the 911 dispatcher, explaining what had happened. When he finished, he told Wahlman that there were plenty of knives in the kitchen, and that maybe it would be a good idea to arm themselves in case the bad guys decided to come inside.

"Knives won't do us any good," Wahlman said. "Is there a back door?"

"Yes. On the other side of the kitchen."

"Let's get out of here."

"I need to wait for the police."

The shooting had stopped. Wahlman figured the assassin

was long gone by now. You don't shoot up a restaurant and then hang around outside and wait for the police to arrive. And if you're going to come inside to finish the job, you do it quickly. So the bad guy had probably driven off in a hurry. Then again, some very peculiar things had happened over the past twelve hours, so it probably wasn't wise to rule anything out. It was possible that the shooter was out there reloading, that he or she would stroll in any second and blow Wahlman's and the hairy man's brains out.

"We need to leave," Wahlman said.

"Why? It seems that it would be safer to stay inside."

"Maybe. Maybe not."

"But the police are coming. They'll want to talk to me. And they'll want to talk to you too."

"We can talk to them later. Let's go."

"I'm staying."

"I would advise against it."

"I'm staying."

"Okay."

Wahlman crawled toward the beer cooler and then through the swinging door that led to the kitchen. He found the service door, peeked out first and then walked outside to the alley. It took him a few seconds to get his bearings. He noticed another service door on the other side of the alley. Some kind of pizza place. There was a plastic trash can beside the door and a security camera over it and a fat padlock dangling from its metal frame. Canal Street was to Wahlman's right, and Common Street was to his left. A crowd had gathered along Canal Street for another parade.

The band was marching by, along with dozens of other people, some of them waving bandanas and others dancing along with colorful little paper umbrellas. There was the steady thump of the bass drum, like the one Wahlman had heard earlier, along with trumpets and trombones and a tuba and a snare drum. The spectators and the people marching in the parade obviously hadn't heard the gunshots. They were smiling and swaying to the beat and having a good time. Wahlman started toward Common Street, thinking he would try to walk around the block and enter the hotel from the side, but he hadn't gotten very far when he heard an echoing series of blasts from inside the sandwich shop.

Boom, boom, boom, boom.

Four shots, two from one pistol and two from another. One of the guns was probably a .45 or a nine millimeter, the other something smaller. Wahlman could tell by the sound of the reports. Two different weapons, which meant that there were probably two different shooters.

Wahlman turned around and took off running for Canal Street. Best to try to disappear into the crowd at this point, he thought. He was a head taller than most of the other people, so he bent his knees and his neck and tried to keep a low profile as he made his way over to St. Charles Avenue. He took a right at the intersection and jaywalked across the streetcar tracks and pushed his way through the heavy glass doors at the front entrance of the hotel. The doorman said *good afternoon sir* or something like that and Wahlman nodded and made a beeline for the elevators. When he got to the fourth floor, he started thinking about everything that had happened and how close he'd come to dying—twice—and how you might be able to accept that one of those instances was an outlandish coincidence but not both of them. He started thinking that it might not be such a good idea to go to his own room.

So he didn't.

Instead, he trotted down the hallway past the ice machine and the vending machines and the laundry facilities and knocked on the door to room 427.

7

Allison answered the door.

"I'll give you a hundred dollars if you let me borrow your room for a while," Wahlman said.

"Excuse me?"

"Some very bad people are after me. I need a place to hide."

"I'm sorry, but—"

Wahlman moved forward, sidestepped his way past the threshold and closed the door behind him.

"You don't understand," he said. "They're trying to kill me."

"Are you out of your mind? You can't just barge into my room like this."

"I'll make it up to you. I promise. I just need your help for a little while."

Allison's purse was on the bed. She walked over there and unsnapped the front flap and pulled out a cell phone.

"I'm calling the police," she said.

"Good idea. Ask for Detective Collins."

"What are you talking about?"

Wahlman gave her a condensed version of the events that had transpired over the course of the day, starting with the out-of-control diesel rig early that morning and ending with the shooting at the sandwich shop just a few minutes ago.

"So you can see why I didn't want to go to my own room," he said.

"Unbelievable," Allison said.

"I know," Wahlman said.

"No, I mean it's unbelievable that you would slink into my room like you own the place and then try to bullshit me with such a—"

"Call Detective Collins," Wahlman said, stepping toward the window and parting the drapes enough to peek outside. "He's at the Seventh District Police Station. Or maybe he's home by now, but they'll know how to reach him. Collins will verify that everything I've told you is absolutely true."

"What are you looking at?" Allison asked.

"The sandwich shop. It's a crime scene now. Hear the sirens? That's the police and the other emergency vehicles coming. There was only one person working over there when I walked in, one guy ringing up the orders and doing the cooking, one guy taking care of everything while it was slow, between the lunch shift and the dinner shift. I'm guessing he was the owner. And I'm guessing he's dead now."

"If that's true, how do I know you're not the one who killed him?"

Wahlman stood there and stared down at the ruined plate glass window.

"You don't," he said.

And neither would the police, he thought. At least four witnesses—the middle-aged couple and the two college women—had seen him walk through the front door of the sandwich shop, and nobody had seen him walk out of the front door, because he hadn't walked out of the front door. He'd walked out of the back door. He'd walked out and stared straight into the security camera across the alley, and then he'd started running toward Canal Street. Running away like some kind of criminal, like someone who might have just shot the owner of a sandwich shop. He would be a suspect, for sure. And there were no dry boots to get him off the hook him this time.

"I think you better leave my room now," Allison said. "My husband should be back any minute, and—"

"You don't have a husband," Wahlman said. "Or maybe you do, but if so he's not staying here at the hotel with you."

"What makes you so sure about that?"

"I saw you loading your laundry into the washing machine. It was all women's stuff. And there's only one suitcase and one carryon bag over there in the corner. You're here by yourself. Like me."

"You're pretty perceptive," Allison said. "But I really do need you to leave now. I'm going to give you five more seconds, and then I'm calling nine-one-one."

"You don't have a husband here with you, and you're not going to call the police," Wahlman said. "If you were going to call the police, you would have done it by now. My guess is that you have something to hide. I wouldn't want to speculate about what it is, but I'm pretty sure you don't want to talk to the police right now—any more than I do."

Allison sat down on the bed.

"What do you want?" she asked.

"I just want to stay here for a while. I'm pretty sure whoever shot up the sandwich shop was aiming for me. It probably won't take them long to find out my room number. I need to not be there when they come for me."

"Why is someone trying to kill you?"

"That's what I need to find out."

Wahlman was still standing by the window. Two NOPD cruisers were parked in front of the sandwich shop now, blue lights flashing. Allison got up and walked over to the window and peeked out.

"Maybe we should start from the beginning," she said. "Why did you come to New Orleans in the first place?"

"A man named Clifford Terrence Drake contacted me several weeks ago. He wanted me to meet him down there in the sandwich shop at four o'clock this afternoon."

"Why?"

"He's a lawyer. He knew I grew up in an orphanage. Apparently my maternal grandfather passed away recently, and apparently he left me a great deal of money. Drake was in charge of dispersing the funds from the estate."

"You grew up in an orphanage?"

"Yes. My parents died in a car accident."

"I'm sorry."

"It was a long time ago."

"Why the sandwich shop?" Allison asked. "Why didn't Mr. Drake want you to meet him in his office?"

"He said it was being renovated."

"Are you sure he's really a lawyer?"

"I looked him up. He's legit."

"How much money are we talking about?" Allison asked.

"A hundred thousand, according to Drake."

Allison took a deep breath, let it out slowly.

"That's a lot of money," she said.

"It's not exactly life-changing, but it's better than the big fat zero I was expecting."

"But Drake didn't show up for the meeting?"

"He might have. I was running late. He might have given up on me."

Allison walked back over to the bed and sat down. She crossed her legs, laced her hands together, stared down at the gray carpet.

"Maybe Drake was the one who tried to kill you," she said.

"Maybe, but I don't think so. Drake's going to get his percentage no matter how many beneficiaries there are. He wouldn't have had a motive to kill me."

"So it must have been one of your family members," Allison said. "Someone who stood to inherit more money if you were out of the picture."

"That would be the logical conclusion," Wahlman said. "If it was just the incident at the sandwich shop. But it wasn't. Like I told you, a semi almost ran over me this morning. A truck with a driver who looked just like me, a driver who had been stabbed multiple times."

"That's the part that makes absolutely no sense."

"None whatsoever."

"Do you have a phone number for Mr. Drake?"

"I had his cell phone number. It was written on the back of a business card in my wallet. The ink bled when it got wet."

Allison picked up her phone and started tapping and swiping.

"Clifford T. Drake and Associates," she said. "You can use my room phone to make the call."

She told Wahlman the number to Drake's office.

"It's being renovated," Wahlman said. "I doubt if anyone who works in the law office is there. And it's Sunday. So the people doing the renovating probably aren't there either."

"I think most lawyers use an answering service for afterhours and weekends. You could call and leave a message."

"I guess I could. Drake might check his messages from home, or from wherever he is."

"I would think so," Allison said.

Wahlman walked over to the nightstand, picked up the phone and punched in the number, and a recorded voice immediately announced that it was no longer in service.

Drake had told Wahlman that his office was under renovation, but it didn't make sense that his phone had been disconnected. Forwarded to a third-party answering service, perhaps, as Allison had suggested, but not completely disconnected. Most lawyers keep the same office number from the day they hang out a shingle until the day they die. Wahlman had read that in a book one time.

"Let me make sure I dialed the right number," he said.

Allison told him the number again. He punched it in again. Got the recording again.

"Wait a minute," Allison said, staring down at her cell phone. "I think I just found out why Drake's phone was disconnected."

"Why?"

"Because he's dead. I just found his obituary."

"Maybe I talked to his son. Clifford T. Drake Junior."

"He was survived by two daughters," Allison said. "No mention of a son."

She handed her cell phone to Wahlman. He read the first paragraph of the article, and then he noticed the date on it.

"This can't be right," he said. "I talked to Drake two days ago. It says here that he died almost two years ago."

"Maybe he faked his own death," Allison said, her voice taking on a sudden tone of sarcasm. "Sure, that's it. He faked his own death and then he called you out of the blue with promises of great riches. Can't you see that this whole thing was some kind of scam? Clifford T. Drake didn't call you. It was someone *pretending* to be him, someone hoping to scam you out of some money."

"Maybe," Wahlman said. "But the person who contacted me two days ago knew things about me that an ordinary run-of-the-mill con artist just couldn't have known. He knew that I grew up in an orphanage. He knew what kind of car my parents and I were in when we had the accident. He knew what my first name was before I changed it."

"All that means is that he did his research," Allison said. "Some of those operations are incredibly sophisticated these days."

Wahlman walked back over to the window, peeked through the drapes again. Several more police cars had arrived, along with an ambulance and a fire truck. A couple of the NOPD patrolmen were stretching some yellow crime scene tape around the area in front of the restaurant.

"It wasn't a scam," Wahlman said. "Not the kind where someone expects to make some money, anyway. It was a setup. The person pretending to be Drake just wanted to get me inside that sandwich shop at that time of day. It was a hit, pure and simple."

"Shouldn't you be telling the police all this stuff?"

"No. Not until I can prove that I wasn't the one who did the shooting. And the only way to do that is to find the person who *did* do the shooting."

"But if you explain—"

"If I go to the police right now, they'll arrest me. They won't have any choice. Maybe eventually I'll be exonerated. Maybe not. You never know with a case like this."

"So how do you plan on finding the killer?"

Wahlman thought about that for a few seconds.

"Do you have a car?" he asked.

"Yes, but—"

"I'm going to need your help."

Allison shook her head. "No way," she said. "I have my

own problems. I can't just drop what I'm doing and—"

"What kind of problems?" Wahlman asked.

"You don't want to know."

"Maybe we can help each other."

Allison stared down at the floor again. "I don't think so," she said. "Not unless you really are going to inherit that money."

"How much do you need?" Wahlman asked.

"Ten thousand. But it might as well be ten million. I have no way of—"

"Consider it done," Wahlman said. "You help me out for a few days, and I'll give you the money. No questions asked."

"You have ten thousand dollars lying around somewhere?"

"Give or take."

"I need it by Wednesday," Allison said.

"Why Wednesday?"

"I thought you said no questions."

"Fair enough," Wahlman said. "My pension check will be directly deposited into my checking account Tuesday. Once that happens, I'll have a little over ten thousand in the account. I'll pay you Tuesday afternoon."

"How do I know—"

"You don't," Wahlman said. "You're just going to have to trust me."

Allison sat there and stared at the floor some more. Then she looked up at Wahlman and brushed a tear off her cheek and said okay.

8

Wahlman figured it would take the police at least a couple of days to go through all of the video footage from the security cameras in the area, which meant that it would be at least a couple of days before his face was displayed on every news broadcast in the country.

"I'm not too worried about the police seeing me," he said. "They don't know who they're looking for yet. It's the killers I'm worried about. They know what I look like."

"They don't know what I look like," Allison said. "Just let me know what you want me to do."

Wahlman pulled some cash out of his billfold.

"I don't know about you, but I'm starving," he said. "Go out and get us something to eat. And bring back some hair dye and some sunglasses. I need a new shirt and a new pair of pants, and I might want to borrow some of your makeup when you get back."

"Makeup?"

"To cover this scar."

Allison nodded. "I'm going to need some money for gas,

too," she said. "My tank's almost empty, and I maxed out my credit card to get this room for a few days."

Wahlman handed her the rest of his money.

"That should be enough for everything," he said. "I'll hit the ATM again later."

Allison picked up her phone and her purse and walked to the door.

"See you in a little while," she said.

"Okay."

Wahlman secured the deadbolt and the swing bar, and then he walked over to the coffee setup and grabbed the pot and took it to the bathroom and filled it with water. He tore open one of the little packages of coffee and loaded the handy-dandy prefabricated pouch into the filter basket and poured the water into the reservoir. He switched the machine on, and then he walked over to the corner of the room and started inspecting Allison's luggage. It wasn't something that he normally would have done, but he needed to make sure she wasn't hiding something that would put them both in more danger than they were already in.

The big suitcase was empty, and all Wahlman found in the carryon bag was a partial roll of quarters and a bottle of prescription pain tablets and two paperback novels. He fanned through the books to make sure there wasn't anything hidden in the pages, and then he placed everything back the way it was and moved over to the dresser and started opening drawers. He looked through all of them, found nothing out of the ordinary, checked the closet next and found a folded piece of paper in one of the pockets of a brown leather jacket. He carefully unfolded the paper and saw that it was a contract for a loan in the amount of five thousand dollars. If you paid the money back within two weeks, the loan only cost you a grand. Two more weeks and the price went up to twenty-five hundred. And so forth. Allison had been telling the truth about how much she needed. Ten thousand by Wednesday, or the loan went to collections. Maybe a black eye to start with. Maybe a broken bone or two after that. And so forth. Wahlman folded the paper and slid it back into the pocket. He figured it wouldn't be a problem as long as Allison handed over the money in time.

Wahlman walked back over to the coffeemaker and grabbed one of the insulated paper cups from the caddy and unwrapped it and filled it with coffee. He tried to take a sip, but it was too hot. He found the remote and switched on the television, saw that *60 Minutes* was on and realized that it was after seven o'clock and that there probably wouldn't be any local news broadcasts until ten. He tried the coffee again and it was okay and he turned the television off and walked over to the window. Emergency vehicles everywhere. Yellow tape everywhere. There were two police cars parked at the intersection, lights flashing, blocking the traffic turning off Canal Street or coming straight over from Royal Street.

Wahlman finished his coffee, poured himself another cup.

And then the phone started ringing.

Wahlman stood there and stared at it for a few seconds.

Maybe it was Allison. Then again, maybe it wasn't. They should have decided on some kind of code. Ring once, hang up, ring again. Something like that.

Wahlman decided not to answer. He didn't want to talk to anyone. Say it was the front desk, and say a couple of police detectives were down there canvassing for potential witnesses. Allison's room was directly across the street from the sandwich shop, so it was one of the first ones they would call. As long as nobody answered, they would have to assume that Allison was out of the room, and they would have to move on. They would probably try again later, but Allison would be back later and she could tell them she didn't see anything, which happened to be the truth. That was Wahlman's theory—based on his own experience as a law enforcement officer—that the phone would ring eight to ten times and then stop.

But it didn't stop.

It kept ringing.

And ringing.

And ringing.

Then Wahlman remembered. The hair dye. He hadn't told Allison what color to get. Not that it really mattered, but he should have told her something. There was no way for her to know that he didn't care. She was probably calling to ask about that.

Almost certain that a detective working a fresh murder case wouldn't have waited twenty-some rings for someone to answer, Wahlman walked over to the nightstand and picked up the phone and said hello.

"May I speak to Allison Bentley, please?" a male voice said.

Wahlman didn't know which would seem more suspicious—hanging up or talking.

He decided to talk.

"She's not here right now," he said. "Can I take a message?"

"Tell her Mr. Tanner called. Just a friendly reminder."

Dial tone.

Tanner was the name on the loan contract. He was the guy Allison owed money to.

The phone rang again. It was Allison this time, asking about the hair dye. Wahlman told her dark brown, and she was back in the room fifteen minutes later with the dye and a six-pack of beer and the sunglasses and the clothes and a big bag of fried chicken.

Allison opened two of the beers, loaded the others into the little dormitory-style refrigerator by the window. She put a clean bath towel on the center of the bed and spread the food out and they sat there and ate picnic-style. Chicken, slaw, mashed potatoes, biscuits.

"This is good," Wahlman said.

"Have you given any thought to how you're going to go about finding the people who shot up the sandwich shop?"

"They didn't just shoot up the sandwich shop. They killed the owner."

"You know that for sure?"

"I heard four gunshots soon after I exited the building."

"Maybe they were just trying to scare the guy."

"Are you always so optimistic?" Wahlman asked.

"Are you always so pessimistic?"

"Not always. Anyway, we'll know for sure at ten o'clock when the news comes on."

"You never did answer my question. Have you given any thought—"

"Someone called here a while ago," Wahlman said. "A man named Tanner. He said something about it being a friendly reminder. Then he hung up."

"I'll call him back later. You still didn't answer my question."

"I need to sleep on it."

"Which brings up another subject," Allison said. "I hope you don't think—"

"Don't worry," Wahlman said. "I'll sleep on the floor."

"I guess I could ask for a rollaway bed."

"I would prefer to keep our little arrangement a secret. Eventually the police will be over here conducting interviews, so it's best that the management doesn't know you have a guest."

"Okay. Whatever you want."

They finished the chicken and opened two more beers and looked out the window for a while. Wahlman decided to go ahead and dye his hair and try some of Allison's makeup on his face. He took his shirt off and walked over to the vanity in the little alcove that led to the bathroom and emerged an hour later looking like some kind of department store mannequin. Extra- large, extra-creepy.

"What do you think?" he asked, laughing. "Tell the truth now."

"I think maybe I better help you," Allison said.

She went to the vanity with him and washed the makeup off and scrubbed some of the dye out of his hair. She toweled him off and put him in the desk chair and sat on the edge of the bed and reapplied the makeup.

"I feel like I'm getting ready to go on TV or something," Wahlman said.

"This is the first time I've ever put makeup on someone else. I'm sure I'll get better with practice. Anyway, this is better than it was. Want to take a look?"

Wahlman got up and walked to the vanity and looked in the mirror. The transformation was remarkable. He barely recognized himself.

"I think you did a great job," he said.

"Thanks. It's almost ten o'clock. Did you want to watch the news?"

"Yes."

Allison turned the television on, and a few minutes later they learned that the man who'd been working alone in the sandwich shop was indeed the owner.

And they learned that he was in the hospital in critical condition.

9

Wahlman woke up at 5:27 a.m.

He always woke up at 5:27, regardless of the time he went to bed. It was the time he'd always set his alarm clock for when he was in the navy. The last several years, anyway, after he'd been promoted to Senior Chief and didn't have to work any of the night watches anymore.

He put his new clothes on, khaki pants and a striped polo, made sure the makeup Allison had applied last night was still covering the scar, left the room and took the stairs down to the first floor. He exited the hotel through the side door, hoping to avoid any contact with the staff.

One of the housekeeping associates was out on the sidewalk smoking a cigarette, but she was busy thumbing a text message into her cell phone and didn't seem to pay any attention to Wahlman as he sauntered by and made his way out to the street.

It seemed to Wahlman that for the past few decades a good percentage of the world's population had been injected with a toxic dose of distraction. *Amazing technology*, they called it. Cell phones, tablet computers, navigation systems. Eyeglasses with holographic video displays. Wrist watches that monitored everything from your heart rate to your sleep cycles—and even your thoughts, according to some of the wilder conspiracy theories. Wahlman doubted that the technology was quite that advanced yet, although it was probably only a matter of time. At least the ubiquitous electronic devices made it relatively easy to walk around and not be noticed, he thought.

Allison had set her alarm clock for seven, and Wahlman figured it would be at least eight before she was ready to do anything. He found a coffee shop on Canal Street, used the ATM by the door to withdraw some money, ordered a large cup to go and asked the barista how to get to the hospital.

"You mean University?" she asked.

"Yes."

"It's about a mile up that way. Just past the interstate on the left."

"Will the streetcar take me there?"

"Sure."

Wahlman paid her, walked up to the next corner and waited for the streetcar. The first one that came by was full, but the one behind it had plenty of space. Wahlman climbed aboard and paid the driver and found a vacant seat near the back. Solid wood benches, naked light bulbs, cords you pulled when your stop was coming up.

Windows that you could lower if you needed some fresh air.

Point A to Point B with no air pollution and very little noise.

Engineering that had been around for almost two hundred years.

Wahlman wondered why more cities didn't use streetcars. He guessed they weren't amazing enough.

He got off and crossed the street and made his way through the revolving glass door at the front entrance of the hospital and stopped at the information desk. A woman wearing a navy blue dress and an expensive set of fingernails asked how she could help him this morning.

"I wanted to check on a patient named Walter Babineaux," he said.

"Are you family?"

"Just a friend."

The woman clicked her mouse and tapped her keyboard, the fake nails adding a whispery plastic-on-plastic sound that Wahlman found incredibly attractive for some reason.

"He's in the Intensive Care Unit on the eighth floor," she said. "All I can tell you right now is that he's stable."

"Would it be possible for me to go up and visit him?"

"Sorry. Family only. Anyway—and I really shouldn't be telling you this—he hasn't regained consciousness yet. So I'm afraid it wouldn't be much of a visit, even if you were allowed."

"Okay. Thanks."

Wahlman walked over to a gigantic window that overlooked Canal Street, sat on a padded bench and sipped his coffee, which had finally cooled off enough to drink. He had wanted to ask Babineaux if he had seen the people who shot him. A physical description would be useful in identifying them if they happened to show up in the area around the hotel again.

And Wahlman was almost certain they would.

The local news channels were calling the attack on the sandwich shop an armed robbery. Addicts desperate for a fix, maybe. But Wahlman knew better. They might have taken some money on the way out to make it look like some kind of heist, but their primary purpose had been to eliminate Rock Wahlman.

And leave no witnesses.

Which meant that Walter Babineaux was still in great danger.

Wahlman wondered if the police department had posted a guard outside his room. If not, they needed to. Family only, the woman at the desk had said, but hired assassins probably weren't overly concerned with hospital rules. They would find a way to get to Babineaux, to make sure he never woke up.

Wahlman walked around the first floor of the hospital until he found a payphone. He asked the operator for the non-emergency number for the New Orleans Police Department, dropped some money into the slot and made the call. The officer who answered identified himself as Sergeant Dobbs.

"There's a man named Walter Babineaux in ICU at University," Wahlman said. "I have reason to believe that the people who put him there still pose a threat. He needs a guard outside his room around the clock."

"Your name, sir?"

"This is an anonymous call. I just wanted to make sure you know what you're dealing with."

"We appreciate your concern, sir. Thanks so much for calling."

Sergeant Dobbs hung up.

Wahlman called the number again. Dobbs answered again.

"You shouldn't blow me off," Wahlman said. "I know what I'm talking about."

"Sir—"

"I know. It's an ongoing investigation, and you can't discuss any of the details over the phone. But here's the thing: the media's calling it an armed robbery. It wasn't. It was an assassination attempt. I know this because I was the intended target. I was sitting there looking out the window when four bullets whizzed by my head. Walter Babineaux had nothing to do with anything. I just happened to walk into his sandwich shop instead of someone else's. But he's a witness now, and the people who shot him aren't going to be happy that he's still alive. He needs protection."

"If what you're saying is true, it sounds as though you might need protection as well," Dobbs said. "Come to the station and identify yourself, and—"

"I can't do that," Wahlman said. "Not right now. But if you give Babineaux the protection he needs, he can verify my story when he wakes up."

Dobbs started saying something about how much the department depended on ordinary citizens to come forward in cases like this, started rambling on and on about it, kept talking while Wahlman wiped his fingerprints off the receiver and left it dangling and walked back out to the streetcar stop. As he was boarding for the ride back to the hotel, he saw two NOPD cruisers pull to the curb in front of the hospital.

Probably sent by the suddenly-talkative Sergeant Dobbs to apprehend him, he thought.

10

Allison was already downstairs when Wahlman got back to the hotel, sitting at a booth in the little bistro opposite the front desk. There was a crumpled copy of the *Times-Picayune* on the seat beside her. Wahlman could see that she had been working on the crossword puzzle.

"So what's on the agenda for today?" she asked, stirring some creamer and artificial sweetener into her coffee.

"I'm supposed to meet with Detective Collins at the District Seven Police Station," Wahlman said.

"I thought you were avoiding the police."

"I'm avoiding them in regard to the shooting yesterday. There's no way for Collins to know I was involved in that, not until the detectives working the shooting go through all the video, which should take at least a couple of days. Collins is in charge of the case involving the murdered truck driver."

"The one who looked just like you."

"Yes. The one who was stabbed to death, undoubtedly by the same people who tried to shoot me at the sandwich shop. If I can learn the driver's identity, it might help in establishing a motive, which eventually might help in tracking down the killers."

"Have you thought about trying to get in touch with someone from your biological family? You know, to see if you had a twin brother?"

"That's next on the list. First I need to talk to Collins. My appointment's at nine o'clock, so we need to get going."

They left the hotel, made it over to Dwyer Road a little before nine. The police station looked like something a kid had put together with blocks. Some of the big concrete cubes had been painted a color that might have looked good on a 1956 Ford or the walls of a nursery when you knew it was going to be a boy. Allison parked the car in the visitors' lot and waited there while Wahlman climbed out and headed toward the front entrance. He was a little nervous about the meeting, because it was possible that the security videos from the area around the sandwich shop had been circulated already, possible that the desk sergeant would activate some kind of alarm as soon as he walked in the door.

But that didn't happen.

"Can I help you?" the sergeant asked.

"I have an appointment with Detective Collins," Wahlman said. "I'm a little early."

"I'll see if he's in yet."

The sergeant lifted the receiver from a phone base with a bunch of buttons on it, punched in a four-digit number and notified whoever answered that Mr. Rock Wahlman was out in the waiting area. A couple of seconds later, he hung up and instructed Wahlman to push on the solid metal door to his right when the buzzer sounded. Wahlman did that, and then he followed the uniformed officer waiting on the other side down a long hallway to a door that said *HOMICIDE.*

"You can go on in," the officer said. "Detective Collins is in the first office on your left."

"Thanks."

Wahlman pushed the door open and entered the common area of the office suite. There was a young lady sitting at a desk with a computer and a phone and a little sign that said *Tori Moore, Administrative Assistant.* Short brown hair, civilian business attire, stylish eyewear. She didn't look up from the work she was doing when Wahlman walked in. Probably accustomed to the door opening and closing every five minutes. Probably so accustomed to it that she completely tuned it out most of the time.

Wahlman looked around. There was a copy machine and some bookshelves and a long table with a chrome coffeemaker the size of a beer keg on it. Collins was over there filling a ceramic mug that looked like it had been dredged out of the Mississippi.

"Want some coffee?" he asked.

"Does the percolator get washed any more often than the cups?"

Collins laughed. "I brought this in the day I got my gold shield," he said. "These layers of grunge represent nine years of hard work and untold gallons of Hills Brothers."

"You never clean it?"

"Never. And everyone around here knows not to touch it. Help yourself if you want some coffee. It's not bad, especially this time of morning. It starts to get pretty stout after lunch."

Wahlman had been around lawmen long enough to know that many of them developed peculiar little habits along the way. Brown socks on Friday. Whatever. Everyone knew that these idiosyncrasies were supposed to keep bad things from happening, although nobody ever actually said that out loud. You go thousands of days without washing your coffee mug, and you go thousands of days without ending up in the emergency room or the morgue. You know that it's totally irrational to think that there's a correlation between this thing and that thing, but you continue the behavior anyway. Just in case.

Wahlman grabbed a paper cup from a stack on the table. He filled it and took a sip and followed Collins into his office. There was a small wooden desk with a computer and some pictures on it and a steel file cabinet and a corkboard and some chairs, everything crammed into a space about the size of a station wagon.

Wahlman took a seat in one of the wooden chairs in front of the desk, Collins in the padded vinyl one behind it. The desk and both of the wooden chairs had been coated with the same shade of blue that had been used on the exterior of the building. Wahlman figured the paint must have been on sale, or maybe even free.

He took another sip of the coffee.

"This is good," he said.

Collins nodded. "You might need something a little stronger when you hear what I'm going to tell you," he said.

"First of all, our divers didn't find a knife or any other kind of weapon down there in the canal."

"I knew they wouldn't," Wahlman said. "The assault must have taken place a mile or two before the truck went off the highway. No reason for the killer to leave the weapon behind."

"Right. So now I'm wondering how the assailant managed to get out of the truck while it was still moving. It had to have been going sixty or seventy miles an hour. Maybe even faster than that."

"The bridge over Lake Pontchartrain," Wahlman said. "You could jump out of the passenger side of the truck, land in the water and then swim ashore."

"Sure," Collins said. "If you're in a James Bond movie or something. That shit doesn't happen in real life."

"Depends on how desperate you are to get away. I cuffed a sailor to a drainpipe one time while I chased his friend down a fire escape. Two bricks of heroin on the kitchen table. They were breaking it up and weighing it and spooning it into smaller bags for distribution. The guy cuffed to the pipe cut his own hand off with a broken beer bottle. Never did find him or the dope."

"What about the friend?"

"He's doing twenty in Leavenworth. Hard to say which one of them got the worst end of the deal."

"I guess we could check the lake," Collins said. "But I really don't think that's how it happened. Anyway, I wanted to let you know that we identified the victim. What was the name of the orphanage you grew up in?"

"Fine Place West. A misnomer if there ever was one. It was in the western part of Tennessee, so I guess that part made sense. They shut it down a few years ago. What's the vic's name?"

"Darrell Renfro. He also spent some time in an orphanage, but not that one. He was in a place in Illinois for a while, but apparently he was adopted when he was six."

"What was his name before he was adopted?"

"I don't know. The person I talked to said his records were archived years ago. We'll probably have to get a court order if we want to pursue that angle any further. Anyway, you and Renfro look almost exactly alike, and you were both orphans, and your name came up as a possible match when we ran his fingerprints."

"So that's it," Wahlman said. "He's my twin brother."

"Different date of birth, so I don't think he's your twin. But it certainly would appear that the two of you are related. We'll have to run a DNA test to know for sure."

"It blows my mind that we were both on the same stretch of highway the other night, and that I was the one who ended up trying to rescue him. It's either the most bizarre coincidence in history, or someone—"

"Set it up," Collins said, finishing Wahlman's thought for him. "And believe it or not, we discovered something even stranger than all that. We got a second possible match on the prints."

"A second possible match?"

"Guy named Jack Reacher."

"Never heard of him."

"I did a little research," Collins said. "He was an officer in the army. Special Investigations. Served thirteen years. Apparently he was involved in some questionable activities after he got out."

"What kind of questionable activities?"

"Some vigilante stuff. I haven't read through everything, but it seems that for quite a few years he had a habit of showing up in places where trouble was brewing."

Wahlman looked down at his own fingertips, thinking about the day he was sworn in at the United States Armed Forces Processing Station in Memphis, the day his prints were added to the FBI database.

"So I might have two brothers," he said.

"No. Reacher was born in nineteen-sixty."

"So he's—"

"Yeah. A long time ago."

"And he was related to Renfro and me?"

"I don't know. The only thing we can say for sure right now is that the three of you have similar fingerprints. Not identical, but similar enough for the computer to flag them as possible matches. Which is rare. I've been in law enforcement quite a few years, and I've never seen that happen. Fingerprints are usually unique enough for the computer to distinguish one family member from another, even with identical twins."

Wahlman nodded. "Now that you mention it, I remember reading about that one time. Something about various environmental factors in the womb affecting the grooves and ridges. So how is it even possible that Renfro and Reacher and I have prints that are so close to being the same?"

"I don't have an answer for that," Collins said. "I'm just as baffled as you are. We have an expert coming from Baton Rouge to take a look, but it's probably going to be tomorrow before she can make it down here. In the meantime, I have some paperwork I need you to fill out. And a nurse is supposed to stop by in a little while and swab your cheeks for the DNA test."

11

It was almost noon by the time Wahlman made it back out to the parking lot. Allison was sitting there with the windows open, doing some more work on the crossword puzzle she'd started earlier.

"You're not finished with that thing yet?" Wahlman said.

"I took a short nap."

"Must be nice. I had to wait for a nurse to come and jam some cotton-tipped sticks into my mouth. She drew some blood, too."

Wahlman showed her the square of gauze taped to the inside of his left elbow.

"You poor thing," Allison said. "Did she at least give you a lollipop?"

"It was a he," Wahlman said. "And no he didn't. Which is pretty infuriating, now that you mention it. This is the last time I'll ever come *here* for DNA testing."

Allison laughed. Wahlman filled her in on everything he'd learned from talking to Detective Collins.

"Sounds to me like you've found your great-great-grandfather," she said, referring to the man named Jack Reacher.

"Sounds to me like a glitch in the computer system," Wahlman said. "There's no way the three of us really have such similar fingerprints. It just doesn't happen."

"Can't the police examine them the old fashioned way? With a magnifying glass or whatever?"

"They've called in an expert. So we'll see what happens. Right now I need to find out who killed Darrell Renfro and put Walter Babineaux in the hospital. I need to do it before the police find the video of me running away from the sandwich shop, and I need to do it before the same people try to kill me. Again."

Allison started the car, rolled the windows up, switched the air conditioner on.

"Want to go back to the hotel?" she asked.

"I need a gun. Any idea where I can get one?"

"Why would I have an idea about that?"

"Just asking."

"You think I'm some kind of criminal, don't you?"

"Actually, I don't know anything about you," Wahlman said. "Which doesn't seem quite fair, since you know so much about me."

"What do you want to know?"

"I want to know why you need ten thousand dollars by Wednesday."

Allison stared through the windshield. The sunlight reflecting off the dashboard made her eyes glow aquamarine.

"Ask me about something else," she said. "Anything else. I don't want to talk about that."

"Do you know where I can get a gun?"

Allison sighed. "I know a place," she said. "But I don't want to go there."

"Because it's the same people you owe money to?"

"Yes."

"You can park a block away and stay in the car," Wahlman said. "I'll go in by myself."

"Can't we wait until tomorrow? That way I can go ahead and pay them and be done with it."

"I need a gun today. I want to go to my room at the hotel and fish the business card with Clifford T. Drake's cell phone number on it out of the trash can. The man pretending to be Clifford T. Drake, that is."

"Fake Drake," Allison said.

"Right. I need a gun in case the guys he sent to kill me are watching the room."

"I thought you said you couldn't read the number on the back of that card. I thought you said the ink bled."

"It did. But your comment about a magnifying glass gave me an idea. Maybe the pen left enough of an indentation for me to make out the number."

Allison put the car in gear.

"I can't believe I'm doing this," she said.

She steered out of the police station parking lot, got back on the interstate and took the Pontchartrain Expressway across the river. A few minutes later she exited on Belle Chase Highway, following signs that said *NAVAL AIR STATION, NEW ORLEANS.*

"We're going to the base?" Wahlman asked.

"We're going to an ice cream store in a strip mall. It's not far from NAS."

"I met some guys from one of the squadrons there when I was stationed in Spain. VP Ninety-Four, I think. They were on deployment. They kept telling me I should pick New Orleans for my next duty station."

"But you didn't?"

"I made it my first choice. But the navy doesn't always give you your first choice. They sent me to San Diego."

"I've heard it's nice out there," Allison said.

She turned down a residential street, pulled over to the curb, gave Wahlman directions to the ice cream place. She told him what to say when he got there, and how much money he would need for the purchase. He took three crisp one hundred dollar bills out of his wallet and folded them into one of his back pockets, climbed out of the car and started walking.

The strip mall was about half a mile from where Allison had parked. It was a warm day and Wahlman had worked up a sweat by the time he got there. Hardware, pharmacy, auto parts, grocery. Two vacant storefronts, and then a narrow one in the corner with a pink and white striped awning and a sign that said *DENA JO'S OLD FASHIONED ICE CREAM.*

Business was not booming. Only one vehicle in the designated parking lot, no customers at the tables.

A bell jingled as Wahlman pushed his way through the door and stepped up to the counter. A slender young man wearing a spotless white shirt and a paper hat asked him how he was doing.

"Fine," Wahlman said. "How about you?"

"Great. What can I get for you today?"

"One scoop of almond-raspberry in a cup," Wahlman said.

"Sorry, sir. We're all out of that flavor."

"You don't have any in the back?"

The man gestured toward a door that said *EMPLOYEES ONLY.*

"See for yourself," he said.

Wahlman opened the door and walked into a room lined with steel storage shelves. It was freezing in there. Literally. Giant cardboard containers had been placed in rows on the shelves, each tubular box labeled with the flavor of ice cream that was inside it. Wahlman counted nineteen different varieties, none of which were almond-raspberry. There was an insulated suit hanging on a hook in the corner. It looked like something you might see on an arctic explorer. Or an astronaut.

Wahlman waited.

And waited.

A digital thermometer hanging from one of the shelves said that it was minus five degrees Fahrenheit in there. Wahlman's teeth were chattering and his fingertips were turning blue. He was about to retreat back to the front of the store when a door on the other side of the room swung open and a man wearing a black leather jacket and a ski mask walked in carrying a briefcase.

"Show me the cash," the man said.

Wahlman pulled the money out of his back pocket and

handed it to the man, who smelled strongly of tobacco. The man set the briefcase on the floor, and then he turned around and left the room without saying another word.

Wahlman picked up the briefcase and exited the freezer, nodding to the man in the paper hat as he jingled through the door and made his way out to a very welcome change in temperature.

12

Wahlman didn't open the briefcase until he was back in the car with Allison.

The .38 revolver had cost double what it was worth, but that was the price you paid for convenience.

For not having to wait a week for the paperwork to go through.

"Now all I need are some shells," Wahlman said, spinning the cylinder and viewing the unimpeded daylight beaming through all six of the chambers.

"You're kidding," Allison said. "They didn't put any bullets in the gun?"

Before Wahlman could respond, someone started tapping on the window on Allison's side. Someone with an enormously large belly and a baseball bat.

"Start the car," Wahlman said. "Let's get out of here."

But Allison didn't start the car. She rolled the window down and asked the man standing there what he wanted.

"What do you think I want?" the man said. "I want my money."

"It's not due until tomorrow," Allison said.

The man stepped to the front of the car and smashed the driver side headlight with the baseball bat. He pounded the front fender on that side a couple of times, and then he waddled back over to the window and looked at his watch.

"Tomorrow starts at midnight," he shouted. "About ten hours from now. What difference is ten hours going to make? Either you have the money, or you don't. And since you obviously don't—"

Wahlman climbed out and slammed the door. He walked around to the driver side and inspected the broken headlight and the dents in the fender, told Allison to roll her window up and lock the doors. He was downwind from the man with the bat, and he could smell the odor coming off of his body—a putrid mixture of whiskey and rotting fish guts.

There was a silver SUV with tinted windows parked about twenty feet behind Allison's car. It was the single vehicle that had been parked in the lot at the ice cream place. Wahlman had seen it drive by him a couple of times after he left. At first he was concerned that it might be the people who were trying to kill him. Now he knew it was Tanner. The loan shark. Apparently Tanner had followed him after the transaction at Dena Jo's, maybe suspicious because he was on foot. Maybe suspicious that he was a cop or something. Selling any kind of firearm without a license was a serious offense. Hence the coded language and the long wait in the walk-in freezer. No telling what kind of shady business went on in there. Money laundering came to mind.

Maybe some crystal meth packed in with the mint chocolate chip.

Tanner was about six feet tall and six feet wide. He was one of the fattest people Wahlman had ever seen. He wore yellow pants and a yellow shirt and a black sports jacket that could have doubled as a boat cover. He looked like a gigantic bumble bee.

"Leave her alone," Wahlman said. "She'll have your money for you tomorrow afternoon. I guarantee it."

"Where's my briefcase?" Tanner asked.

"That's why you followed me?"

"You were supposed to put it in the trash can by the hardware store."

Allison rolled her window down and handed the briefcase to Wahlman, who then whizzed it toward Tanner like some kind of aerodynamically-challenged Frisbee. It landed on the gritty pavement, skidded and came to a rest at Tanner's feet.

"There you go," Wahlman said. "Hope the asphalt didn't scar it up too bad."

"You should probably get back in the car," Tanner said, tapping the head of the baseball bat against the palm of his hand. "As of now, this is none of your business."

"Allison's my friend," Wahlman said. "So I'm making it my business."

Tanner laughed. "Well, it's nice to have friends, isn't it? Especially ones as loyal as you seem to be. I have friends, too. And believe me, mine are *incredibly* loyal."

Two guys climbed out of the SUV. They walked up to

where Tanner was standing. One of them was a little taller than Tanner, the other a little shorter. Both of them had square jaws and broad shoulders and thick corded necks. They wore tailored black suits and black ties and white shirts. Military buzz cuts, wraparound shades. Goon A and Goon B, Wahlman thought. From central casting. They didn't say anything. They just stood there with their hands behind their backs.

"I need the money now," Tanner said. "She's already way behind, and she hasn't returned any of my phone calls. I'm a reasonable man, but—"

"You got shit in your ears?" Wahlman asked. "You'll get your money tomorrow. Now tell your guys to get back in the truck before they break a nail or something."

Goon A took a few steps forward.

Goon B followed.

Now they were standing several feet in front of Tanner. Several feet closer to Wahlman. They didn't have their hands behind their backs anymore. They had them at their sides.

And Wahlman could see that each of them was wearing a set of brass knuckles.

"The only thing we're going to break is your face," Goon A said.

"You need to get back in your vehicle," Wahlman said. "Your fat boss might have a heart attack if he has to carry you over there."

Goon A took another step forward, reared back and took a roundhouse swing, aiming for the left side of Wahlman's jaw.

Wahlman had never been hit with brass knuckles before, but he knew what kind of damage they could do. He'd seen an x-ray one time. Sailor in a bar fight up in Philadelphia. The guy's skull had been cracked like an egg.

The roundhouse from Goon A came fast and hard. Wahlman ducked, felt the cold metal graze his left ear, went down dizzily and caught himself with his palm and jammed the sole of his foot into the center of Goon A's knee. He struck the joint squarely, the ligaments snapping like dry twigs as the newly-ruined extremity crumpled in the wrong direction.

Goon A screamed and fell to the pavement while Goon B moved in and kicked Wahlman in the back of his ribcage. Viciously. Repeatedly. Arcing back and following through, swinging the boot like the weight on a pendulum, again and again and again, heaving and grunting, snarling and snorting, pouring everything he had into a stupid slobbering anger-fueled frenzy that left his incredibly loyal ass almost totally exhausted after about thirty seconds.

Wahlman knew that his back would be extremely sore tomorrow, but he also knew that Goon B hadn't done any lasting damage. He hadn't broken any ribs. The latissimus dorsi muscles on Wahlman's back were much thicker than most people's. This was partly due to some of the exercises he did when he played football, but it was mostly due to genetics. By the time Wahlman turned fifteen years old, his body looked like something out of a comic book. Pecs like blocks of concrete, biceps the size of cantaloupes. All without lifting a single dumbbell. Everyone assumed that he spent a lot of time at the gym, but he didn't. It was just the way he was built. The massive layers of muscle tissue provided him with great strength, and they also protected his bones and internal organs against the kind of blunt trauma Goon B had been delivering so enthusiastically over the past half-minute or so.

Wahlman was still lightheaded from being clipped with the brass knuckles, but he could tell that Goon B was getting tired. He could tell that the intensity of the impacts had started to wane. As Tanner edged a little closer to the ruckus, Wahlman rolled over and grabbed the boot Goon B had been kicking him with and twisted it clockwise. Goon B lost his balance, fell and landed right on top of Goon A, and—based on the guttural string of shrieks and expletives that ensued—reignited the pain in the part of his leg that had once been a knee.

Wahlman didn't wait for Goon B to get up. He was on him in an instant. He grabbed his skinny black tie and yanked upward on it, causing his chest to rise and his head to tilt back, and causing another series of agonized cries from Goon A, who now had two people on top of him. When Goon B instinctively straightened his neck in an effort to correct the awkward and uncomfortable position, Wahlman met him with an elbow to the nose. There was a sickening crunch and a shower of bright red blood and some coughing and gurgling, followed by a sudden unsettling silence as both of the injured men apparently lost consciousness.

Tanner took a step backward, toward the SUV. He still had the bat, but he wasn't holding it in a threatening manner anymore.

"This isn't over," he said.

"Looks over to me," Wahlman said.

"I'm going to get my money, one way or another."

"You'll get it tomorrow. Like I told you before. Minus whatever the damage to Allison's car adds up to. Right now you should probably get in your truck and call whoever you need to call to come and scrape these unfortunate gentlemen off the asphalt."

"I could have busted your head open with this bat," Tanner said.

"And I could have shoved that bat up your ass," Wahlman said. "Sideways."

Tanner turned around and started walking toward the SUV.

Wahlman walked around to the passenger side of Allison's car and climbed back into the front seat.

"I guess I forgot to tell you to put the briefcase in the trash can," Allison said.

"Yeah," Wahlman said. "I guess you did."

13

A box of .38 shells purchased legally at a sporting goods store cost almost as much as the revolver had cost in the freezer over at Dena Jo's. Wahlman didn't need a whole box of bullets, but you couldn't just walk in and ask for half a dozen. It didn't work that way. You had to buy the entire sealed box and you had to sign for it and you had to pay the tax. You could buy single rounds on the black market, but Wahlman didn't have any of those kinds of connections in New Orleans.

Tanner was the only person Allison knew who sometimes dealt in undocumented merchandise, but of course he wouldn't have sold Wahlman a water pistol after the incident over on the West Bank.

So Wahlman had to buy the entire box of .38 caliber cartridges, and he had to pay a lot of money for it. Not to mention that by law every such transaction had to be conducted in front of a video camera, which meant that the police could eventually obtain even more incriminating evidence to use against Wahlman if they picked him up for the sandwich shop shooting. Which they would, eventually, unless he found the real shooters first.

Allison parked her car in the hotel's garage. Wahlman broke the seal on the box of bullets and started loading the gun.

"Sorry about all the trouble," Allison said.

"Me too. But I feel better now that I have a weapon and some ammunition."

Allison started massaging her temples with her fingertips.

"I'm glad someone feels better," she said.

"You have a headache?"

"I'll be okay. I have some pills in my carryon bag. Are you going to your room now?"

"My truck is parked somewhere in this garage. I'm going to try to find it so I can get my luggage. Then I'll go to my room and take a look at the business card with the cell phone number on it. Then I'll come to your room and try to call the guy."

"Don't you think the maids have emptied your trash cans by now?"

"I left the *DO NOT DISTURB* sign on the door," Wahlman said. "So the room should be just as I left it."

"Okay. Is there anything I can do to help you right now?"

"Just go to your room and wait. I'll be there in a little while."

Wahlman stuffed some extra shells into the right front pocket of his jeans, climbed out and slid the revolver into his waistband and walked around the garage until he found his truck, careful to stay in the shadows until he was relatively certain there weren't any assassins in the vicinity.

Level 5, Section H, Space 14. Right where it was supposed to be, right where his valet parking receipt said it would be. He hadn't wanted Allison to drive him there, because he didn't want her to know where the vehicle was parked. She seemed to be all right, but he had been hurt more than once by people who seemed to be all right. There was only one person in the world he fully trusted, and Allison Bentley wasn't that person. Especially since the goof-up with the briefcase. Wahlman believed that it had been unintentional, but still. Those were the kinds of mistakes that got people killed.

Wahlman's suitcase was in the back, zippered into a weatherproof vinyl cover. He pulled it out and carried it to the elevator, and then he decided that the stairs might be safer. He walked down to the first level and out to the street and around to the hotel.

He climbed the stairs to the fourth floor, went to his room and promptly discovered that his key didn't work anymore. It had worked just minutes ago when he'd entered the hotel through the side door, but it wasn't working now. He tried the card several times, kept getting the red LED on the electronic indicator at the front of the slot.

He looked around, saw a housekeeping cart outside a room down at the end of the hallway. He walked down there and asked the woman pulling sheets off the bed if she could let him into his room.

"Which room?" she asked.

"Four sixty-two. I have my key, but it's not working for some reason."

The woman looked at her clipboard. "Says here that room's vacant. I was going to clean it after I clean this one."

"It's not vacant," Wahlman said. "It's my room. I don't want it cleaned right now."

"I'll have to get with my supervisor on that," the woman said.

Wahlman nodded. The elevator bank was right around the corner and his suitcase was heavy and he was tired of taking the stairs. He made it down to the first floor, trotted over to the front desk, waited for a man wearing an off-white linen suit and an off-white straw fedora to ask a million or so questions before deciding on a double with two queens, and then he stepped up to the counter and asked the guy standing behind it why he couldn't get into his room. The guy did his thing on the computer, and then he told Wahlman that the account that he had used to check in with did not contain sufficient funds to cover the hotel's standard hold on incidental charges.

"That's impossible," Wahlman said. "I have over seven thousand dollars in that account."

"Not according to the statement we received from your bank," the clerk said. "If you would like to provide an alternate form of payment, I would be happy to—"

"Use this," Wahlman said, sliding his Visa card across the desk.

Wahlman didn't like to buy things on credit. He believed in paying as he went. He'd opened the account as an emergency backup, kept a zero balance and a low limit.

He reckoned this qualified as an emergency.

The clerk ran the card and handed over a fresh set of room keys, apologized for the inconvenience and told Wahlman to have a great day.

By the time Wahlman made it back up to his room, the *DO NOT DISTURB* sign on his door handle was gone and the housekeeping cart was nowhere in sight. He opened the door and walked in and saw that the bed had been made and the trash had been emptied.

He set his suitcase down, stepped over to the phone and called the front desk.

"May I help you?"

"I need my garbage back," Wahlman said.

"Excuse me?"

"Would it be possible for me to speak to the housekeeping supervisor?"

"I'll try to transfer you. Hold on just a second."

Wahlman held on for way more than a second. More like two minutes. Finally, the jazzy rendition of a twentieth century song Wahlman couldn't remember the name of stopped abruptly and was replaced by the voice of a man who sounded as though he might have just gotten up from a nap.

"Housekeeping," the man said.

"This is Rock Wahlman in four sixty-two. My trash was emptied a while ago, and I need it back."

"You need your trash back?"

"I accidentally threw something away. A business card. It has a very important phone number on it. I need to get it back."

There was a long pause.

"That's going to be a problem," the man said. "All the trash gets loaded into big plastic bags, and then it's dropped down a chute that empties into a bin in the basement. It's not separated by which room it came from, or even which floor. We're talking half a ton of garbage every day. There's no way you're going to find a business card in that mess."

"I need to try," Wahlman said.

"I can't let you crawl around in that bin. It's not safe. Broken glass, razor blades. Who knows what might be in there. You know what I'm saying?"

"Sure. I know what you're saying. I guess I'll just have to forget about finding that card. I guess it's gone forever. Thanks anyway."

"Sorry I couldn't be of more help."

Wahlman thanked the man again, hung the phone up, walked downstairs and out the side door, headed up to Canal Street to buy some goggles and rubber gloves.

And a magnifying glass, which he'd somehow forgotten to stop for on the way back to the hotel with Allison.

14

It wasn't quite as difficult as the housekeeping supervisor had thought it would be for Wahlman to determine which of the big white plastic bags contained the trash from his room. It only took him about five minutes to find the bag from the fourth floor. The plastic was translucent, and he could see the logo on the box from the chicken place Allison had gone to last night to get their dinner.

He tore the bag open and started ferreting through the nastiness. No broken glass or razor blades, but plenty of stuff that probably should have been sealed into a container with a biohazard stamp on it. There was a dirty diaper that probably should have been sealed in lead and buried deeply in the ground. Half-eaten hamburgers, dental floss, candy wrappers. Someone had discarded a sizeable wedge of birthday cake. Chocolate with chocolate frosting. It said *PY BIR*, and below that, *JA*. Maybe the person's name was Jane. Or Jason. Or Jack. With the hefty tax on sugar these days, Wahlman wondered why so much of the cake had been thrown away. He didn't wonder about it long, though, because right underneath the circular piece of cardboard it had been mounted on was the business card he was looking for.

He reached down and picked up the card, slid it into his back pocket, climbed out of the bin and brushed himself off. He tossed the goggles and the rubber gloves and took the stairs back up to the fourth floor and went to his room.

The clothes he was wearing were filthy from fighting in the street and digging in the trash. He opened his suitcase and set out some clean things—Levi's and socks and boxers and an undershirt, and a blue oxford button-down with tails that could be left out to conceal the revolver—and then he shaved and took a shower and transferred everything from the pockets of his dirty clothes to the pockets of his fresh clothes and made a pot of coffee and looked at the business card with the magnifying glass. He'd used a ballpoint pen to write Fake Drake's number on the card, and the pressure from the point had indeed left an impression, albeit a very faint one. He could make out every number except the second to the last.

The phone started ringing. The only person Wahlman wanted to talk to right now was Allison, and there was no way to be certain that she was the one calling. So instead of answering the phone, Wahlman turned the coffee pot off, stuffed the clothes he'd been wearing earlier into the trash can, slid the .38 into his waistband, zipped up his suitcase and left the room.

As he made his way down the corridor, it occurred to him that maybe he didn't even need his own hotel room anymore. Now that he'd gotten the business card back, the room wasn't much more than a liability. He'd initially hoped to use it as a lure for the assassins, but now he was concerned that the detectives investigating the shooting at the sandwich shop would show up first.

He knocked on Allison's door. She opened it and let him in. The drapes had been closed, and all the lights were off except for the shaded lamp on the nightstand.

"Why is it so dark in here?" Wahlman asked.

"I told you I have a headache," Allison said.

"Did you take something?"

"I did. But it hasn't kicked in yet."

"I need to borrow your cell phone," Wahlman said.

"Did you find the card?"

Wahlman nodded. He pulled the crumpled and stained business card out of his pocket and handed it to her, along with the magnifying glass.

"See if you can make out the second to the last number," he said. "In the meantime, there's another call I need to make."

Wahlman actually needed to make two other calls before he tried Fake Drake. One to the front desk to check out of his room, and one to his bank to see why the hotel had rejected his debit card.

Allison handed him her cell phone, and then she walked over to the nightstand to examine the business card under the lamp.

Wahlman punched in the number for the front desk.

"Guest services. May I help you?"

"This is Rock Wahlman, four sixty-two. I've decided not to take the room after all."

"Is there a problem, sir?"

"There's no problem with the room. I have some urgent business back home, and I'm going to have to leave town sooner than expected."

"So you want to check out right now?"

"Yes."

"You realize that your card will be charged for the full—"

"I know," Wahlman said. "That's fine. Just go ahead and close everything out."

There was a pause and a flurry of keyboard clicks, and then the clerk cheerfully informed Wahlman that he had been checked out of the room and to please visit again soon and to have a nice day.

Wahlman disconnected and punched in the 800 number for his bank. A robot asked him for his account number and personal identification number and gave him a list of things he could do over the phone, including the option to hold for a period of time that might exceed thirty minutes in order to speak to a real live human being.

Wahlman didn't feel like waiting. He felt like slamming the phone down on the floor and stomping it into a million pieces.

Allison must have sensed his frustration.

"What's wrong?" she asked.

"They want me to stand here with my thumb up my ass for half an hour. This is why I usually do all my banking in person."

"If you want, I can put it on speakerphone while you wait."

He walked over to where she was standing and handed her the phone. She tapped the display screen a couple of times, activating a built-in stereo speaker system that you probably could have carried around on a dime. This time, Wahlman remembered the name of the song playing, a country blues number called "A Tomorrow Like Yesterday." It was one of his favorites.

"Thanks," he said. "Were you able to make out that second-to-the-last digit on the back of the business card?"

"I think it's a two. But I'm not sure. Anyway, there are only ten possibilities. You can try one at a time until the guy you want to talk to picks up."

"Fake Drake."

"Yes. Fake Drake. You can use my room phone if you want to."

"I'm afraid the hotel will show up on his caller ID. I went ahead and checked out of my room, by the way. So I'll need to stay here again tonight."

"Okay. Why are you calling your bank?"

"There was a problem with my debit card. Don't worry. I'll get it straightened out."

"You're still going to be able to pay me tomorrow, right?"

"I hope so."

"What do you mean you hope so? You saw the kind of people I'm dealing with. I have to have that money."

"What were you planning to do before I made the offer to pay you?" Wahlman asked.

"Beg for more time. But after what happened a while ago—"

"Tanner's not going to give you more time. Does he know where you're staying?"

"I don't think so."

"Good. Anyway, there's no reason to start panicking yet. I should be able to give you the money tomorrow. Then you can pay Tanner and be done with him."

"That's what I thought was going to happen," Allison said. "Now I'm getting nervous again."

The music coming from the phone stopped abruptly, replaced by a woman who apologized for the wait. She identified herself as Brenda and asked how she could be of assistance today.

Allison tapped the speakerphone off, picked up the device and handed it to Wahlman.

He put it to his ear.

"I had some trouble with my debit card a while ago," he said.

"What kind of trouble?"

"Insufficient funds. Which doesn't make sense, because I know for a fact that there's plenty of money in the account."

"What's your account number?"

Wahlman gave her the number, and a few seconds later she told him his balance.

"That's not right," Wahlman said. "It's off by about seven thousand dollars."

"I'm showing an online transfer of exactly seven

thousand dollars at five-fourteen this morning."

"Transfer to where?"

"Looks like a business account. It's at another bank."

"I never authorized a transfer," Wahlman said. "Someone stole my money."

"The only way that's possible is if they knew your user name and password and the answers to your security questions. Do you know of anyone who might have had access to that information?"

Wahlman did in fact know of someone who had access to that information. Mike Chilton. His best friend. The one person in the world he trusted unequivocally. House keys, passwords, insurance policies. He and Mike Chilton had each other's back on all that stuff.

Wahlman was still concerned about the money, but more than anything he was concerned about Mike. His immediate thought was that Fake Drake had gotten to him somehow.

"I'm going to have to call you back," Wahlman said.

"That's fine," Brenda said. "I'll be here until nine tonight."

She gave Wahlman her personal extension, told him that he still might have to wait on hold for a while, but that at least he wouldn't be routed to a different representative.

"Thanks," Wahlman said.

He disconnected and immediately tried to call Mike Chilton.

No answer.

He left a message, clicked off and handed the phone to Allison. She set it on the nightstand and plugged it into its charger.

"What's going on?" she asked.

"I need to go to Florida," he said.

"Why?"

"Someone transferred most of the money out of my account. I need to find out about that, and I need to make sure my friend Mike is okay."

"Why would your friend Mike not be okay?"

"He's the only person besides me who knows my password. I'm afraid—"

"Maybe someone hacked into the account," Allison said.

"It's possible. And Mike does have a habit of turning his phone off sometimes, so I'm not ready to go into panic mode just yet. Whatever the case, I need to go home and straighten everything out."

"Where in Florida do you live?"

Wahlman told her the name of the town.

"It's inland," he said. "Between Jacksonville and Gainesville."

"How far is that from here?"

"About ten hours."

"What about me?"

"I was thinking you might want to come with me."

Allison glanced toward the window. She took a deep breath.

"Will we be back by tomorrow?" she asked.

"I don't see how."

"I need to give Tanner that money tomorrow."

"He might have to wait another day or two. Go ahead and get your stuff together. I'm going to walk downstairs and use one of the desktops to change my password."

Wahlman left the room and took the stairs down to the first floor. While he was down there, he used the payphone to call Detective Collins. He wanted to let him know he was leaving New Orleans for a couple of days, and he wanted to give him Allison's cell phone number in case there were any new developments he needed to know about.

He was especially interested in the results of the DNA tests. With recent advances in processing, preliminary results were usually available within twenty-four hours, and Wahlman was anxious to find out how he and Darrell Renfro—and Jack Reacher—were related.

15

Collins wasn't in, so Wahlman left a message with the administrative assistant there in the office suite. The one with the short brown hair and the stylish glasses. Tori something or another.

"I'll be sure he gets the message," she said.

"Thanks," Wahlman said.

"No problem. Have a good one."

Wahlman disconnected, took the stairs back up to the fourth floor. As he approached Allison's room, he noticed that the door was ajar. Not much, just a crack. Just a razor-thin slit, but enough to allow a wedge of light to spill out into the hallway, enough to subtly announce that the door had not been properly secured.

Wahlman knew for a fact that he hadn't left it that way.

And he was fairly certain that Allison wouldn't have left it that way.

Which meant that there was a good possibility that someone else had been in the room.

Or that someone else was still in the room.

There was no way for Wahlman to know for sure who the *someone else* was, but three distinct possibilities immediately came to mind: NOPD detectives investigating the shooting at the sandwich shop, in which case Allison was probably very nervous but still physically okay; some more of Tanner's hired muscle, in which case Allison was *definitely* very nervous and maybe *not* physically okay; assassins sent by Fake Drake, in which case Allison was dead.

Wahlman pulled the .38 from his waistband, tiptoed to the threshold, leaned in and cupped his free hand against the painted steel door, hoping to hear the calm and reasonable voices of police detectives out searching for potential witnesses.

Nothing.

Total silence.

Which meant that it wasn't the cops. If it had been the cops, there would have been voices. Cops don't hang around when there's nothing left to say. Not in Wahlman's experience. When there's nothing left to say, cops leave. Every time. No exceptions.

Which narrowed the distinct possibilities down to two: Tanner's guys, or Fake Drake's guys.

Wahlman stepped back and pushed the door open a few inches with his finger.

"Allison. You in there?"

Nothing.

Total silence.

And then a click. Metallic. Like maybe a switchblade opening or a pair of handcuffs locking, or the hammer of a pistol being pulled back.

Wahlman pushed the door all the way open with his foot, walked into the room with his arms outstretched, both hands wrapped tightly around the grips of the revolver, sweeping left and then right and then left again, sweeping past the drapes and the bed and the long wooden unit that served as a desk and a dresser and a TV stand, sweeping past the framed prints bolted to the walls and the vanity and the mirror in the little alcove that led to the bathroom, unable to determine the origin of the click, seeing nothing out of the ordinary except that Allison wasn't there.

Unless she was in the bathroom.

Wahlman walked to the alcove and knocked on the door.

"Rock? Is that you?"

A sense of relief washed over Wahlman like a warm breeze.

"Why was your door open?" he asked.

"My door was open?"

"Yeah. So instead of *me* moseying on in, it could have been—"

"I can barely hear you. I'll be out in a minute."

Wahlman slid the gun back into his waistband, walked over to the bed and sat down. Then he noticed that the door to the room was still open, so he got up and closed it. Remembering that there were still a couple of beers in the refrigerator, he walked over there and got one out and twisted the cap off and chugged about half of it on his way back to the bed. He sat down again and grabbed Allison's cell phone from the nightstand and tried to call Mike Chilton. Still no answer.

Allison walked out of the bathroom with a towel around her head.

"I figured you'd be ready to go by now," Wahlman said.

"I've been feeling kind of icky since this morning, when I had to sit out in the car all that time. I thought I better take a shower before we hit the road."

"How's your headache?"

"Better. Thanks."

"Why was your door open?"

"I don't know. You must not have closed it all the way when you left the room a while ago."

"I closed it all the way."

"You're sure about that?"

"Yes."

"Then I don't know. Maybe the maid came by while I was in the—"

Before Allison was able to finish her sentence, before she was able to say *shower*, the drapes parted and a man with a sound-suppressed semiautomatic pistol stepped forward and drilled two rounds into her chest.

Wahlman rolled off the bed and hit the floor a split second before two more bullets thudded into the mattress. He grabbed the revolver from his waistband and raised it over the edge of the bed like a periscope and started firing in the general direction of the assailant, the reports from the .38 booming out like cannon fire in the enclosed space. Wahlman squeezed off all six rounds, reached into his pocket and pulled out a handful of shells, thinking it was useless, almost certain that he was going to die before he had a chance to reload, but doing it anyway, because there was no point in not doing it, no point in just lying there and waiting for the assassin to step around the corner of the bed and finish him off.

Wahlman pushed the cartridges into the chambers one-by-one, his heart thumping like a boxer on a speed bag. He managed to load all six of the bullets, and then he waited and wondered why he wasn't dead yet. A few seconds ticked by, and then a few more, and then Wahlman leaned up and peaked over the top of the mattress and saw that the bad guy was on the floor next to Allison and that the top of his skull was missing.

Wahlman stood and walked over to Allison and checked her for a pulse, knowing just by looking at her that she didn't have one but checking anyway, also knowing that the six shots he'd fired had made a lot of noise and that he needed to get out of there in a hurry.

He took a deep breath, trying to think everything through, trying not to panic. The digital clock on the nightstand said 2:47. Which meant that there probably weren't many people around. Especially on a Monday. The weekend crowd was long gone and the housekeeping associates had finished with their cleaning duties and the people checking in for the night weren't in their rooms yet. The tourists in town for the week were out and about doing touristy things, and the business people were out and about pitching their crummy little products that nobody needed or sitting around bored out of their minds in a meeting somewhere or out doing whatever else those kinds of people did all day. The rooms seemed to be pretty well insulated, so it was possible nobody had noticed the six earsplitting shots from Wahlman's gun.

Possible, but there was no point in sticking around to find out.

Wahlman grabbed Allison's cell phone and charging cable and the business card with Fake Drake's number on it from the nightstand and jammed it all into his pocket. He kicked the pistol away from the bad guy's hand, bent over and picked it up and wiped the blood off with some tissues from the little chrome dispenser on the front of the vanity. He unzipped his suitcase and tossed the pistol in there and zipped it back up and grabbed it by the handle and walked to the door. He looked out the peephole, and then he opened the door and stepped out into the hallway and headed for the stairs.

16

It was almost two o'clock Tuesday morning by the time Wahlman made it to his house in Florida. He usually referred to the little place as a *cabin*, which he thought sounded marginally better than *shack*. Five hundred square feet, board-and-batten siding, metal roof. There was one small bedroom and a small living room and a small kitchen, and a bathroom with an enormous cast iron claw foot tub that was probably two hundred years old and probably weighed five hundred pounds. The exterior was situated so that the back of the house faced the road. There was no back door, but there was a window on the back side of the house, and Wahlman could see that the kitchen light he'd left on was still on.

He stopped and got his mail out of the box, steered into the gravel driveway and around to the wooden deck in front. Switched the engine off and the headlights and sat there for a while and stared down the slope toward the lake, which was glistening calmly in the moonlight.

For ten and a half hours he'd been wondering why the

assailant had waited for Allison to come out of the bathroom before he attacked. At first Wahlman thought the guy must have been one of Fake Drake's hit men, maybe part of the same team that had tried to kill him at the sandwich shop, maybe part of the same team that had been successful in killing Darrell Renfro out on I-10. But if that was the case, the way it went down didn't make much sense. Why didn't the assassin step out from behind the drapes and finish his business as soon as Wahlman walked into the room?

So maybe it wasn't one of Fake Drake's guys after all. Maybe it was one of Tanner's guys, out for revenge. But that didn't make much sense either. Why kill Allison? Why kill someone who owes you money? Seemed like a good way to never get paid.

After turning it over in his mind a thousand times, it seemed to Wahlman that he should be the one lying in a puddle of blood on the hotel room floor right now and that Allison should be the one still breathing. That was the way it seemed, but of course that wasn't the way it was.

He decided not to think about it anymore right now. He was exhausted. He needed sleep. Maybe he would be able to think a little more clearly in the morning.

He got out of the truck and grabbed his suitcase from the back, climbed the four wooden steps and crossed the deck, unlocked the nice set of French doors he'd installed two years ago and walked inside. The cabin had that strange feel to it that all houses have after you've been away for a while, quiet and still and kind of foreign.

Wahlman set his suitcase down and turned some lights

on. There was a loveseat in the living room and a wingback chair and a small folding table that you could put your drink on while you were watching television. Pine planks overhead, exposed beams and a ceiling fan that wasn't much to look at but helped move the air around, helped with the heating and air conditioning costs, which were minimal in such a small space anyway but every little bit helped.

Wahlman had driven by Mike Chilton's place on the way home, hoping that Mike might still be up, hoping to find out why he wasn't answering his phone. It was late and the house was dark and he knew that Mike might be asleep, but he'd walked up on the porch and knocked anyway. Mike never came to the door. Which didn't necessarily mean that anything was wrong, because Mike was the soundest sleeper Wahlman had ever known. The shrillest of alarm clocks were of no use to him, and he'd even slept through a hurricane one time. You pretty much had to grab him and shake him to wake him up. So Wahlman wasn't terribly worried that he hadn't answered the door. His car had been in the garage and the house had looked okay. No mail in the mailbox, no circulars littering the driveway. Wahlman had driven away, planning to check again in the morning but figuring that Mike was just being Mike.

Wahlman walked to the bathroom, peeled his clothes off and took a long hot shower. He put on a fresh pair of boxer shorts and nothing else and went into the kitchen and made a peanut butter sandwich and opened a bottle of beer. He sat down and looked at his mail. Phone bill, electric bill, a credit card offer, sales papers from some of the local stores.

And a letter from Clifford T. Drake, Attorney at Law.

Fake Drake.

Wahlman hadn't tried the number on the business card yet. He hadn't wanted to mess with it while he was driving, because there was still a digit he was unsure of.

He tore the envelope open and read the letter, which was nothing formal, just a handwritten note.

Dear Mr. Wahlman,

I'm sorry you were unable to make it to our appointment Sunday afternoon. I've tried calling several times, but there was no answer. Please call me at your earliest convenience.

Thanks,

C.T. Drake

There was a phone number at the bottom of the note. Wahlman checked it against the one on the business card. It was the same. Allison had been correct. The illegible digit on the business card had been a two.

Wahlman used Allison's phone to make the call.

Four rings, and then a sleepy male voice picked up and grunted hello.

"This is Wahlman."

Silence for a beat.

"Where are you?" the male voice asked, sounding a little perkier now, undoubtedly noticing the incoming area code and thinking the call had originated in New Orleans.

"It's none of your business where I am," Wahlman said.

"You sound angry. If anyone should be angry, it should be me. Do you have any idea what time it is?"

"This was my earliest convenience."

"I see. Well, if you wouldn't mind—"

"Why did you kill Darrell Renfro? Why are you trying to kill me?"

"What?"

"A woman named Allison Bentley is dead now too. I guess you're going to tell me you don't know anything about that either. I guess you're going to stick with your story about the inheritance. I did a little research. Once upon a time there was indeed a lawyer in New Orleans named Clifford T. Drake. He even specialized in estate planning. But—"

"He was my father," the male voice said. "My full name is Clifford Terrence Drake Junior."

"You're lying," Wahlman said. "There was no mention of a son in the obituary."

"My father and I had a falling out about ten years ago. He sort of disowned me. Cut me out of his will, the whole nine yards. I can tell that you're really upset, Mr. Wahlman, but I can promise you I had nothing to do with the things you're talking about."

"How do I know you're telling the truth?"

"Well, you could check my Louisiana Bar credentials. It's all a matter of public record."

"Maybe I'll do that," Wahlman said.

"Good. Call me back in the morning and we'll talk some more."

The man claiming to be Clifford Terrence Drake Junior hung up without saying another word.

Wahlman set the phone down, ate the rest of his sandwich and drank the rest of his beer. He put his dishes in the sink and walked to the bathroom and brushed his teeth, and when he finished he stood there and looked at his reflection in the mirror.

"That guy's full of shit," he said, staring into his own tired eyes. "Even if his name really is Clifford Terrence Drake Junior, and even if he really is an estate attorney, and even if his office really is under renovation. Even if all that's true, it doesn't mean that he's not responsible for what happened on the interstate and in the sandwich shop and in Allison's hotel room. Right? Because someone's definitely trying to kill me. There's no doubt about that. Someone who knew exactly where I was supposed to be Sunday afternoon and exactly when I was supposed to be there. It had to be Drake. It had to be. The only other person who knew about that meeting was Mike Chilton. So it had to be Drake, right?"

Wahlman's reflection said nothing.

17

Wahlman woke up at the usual time Tuesday morning.

5:27.

Which meant that he'd only slept about two hours. Which meant that he should have been dragging ass. But he wasn't. He felt energized, ready to go. Only not in a good way. More like a mechanical toy that had been wound too tightly, torqued to the breaking point and then pointed toward the edge of a table.

He couldn't find a clean pair of jeans, so he put on the same pair he'd worn yesterday, along with a white t-shirt and a striped button-down. He drank a pot of coffee and watched some news on television, and then he grabbed Mike Chilton's spare set of keys and left the cabin.

Mike lived in a nice big house on the other side of the lake. He'd done well for himself after the navy, finishing his master's degree and starting a software consultant company. He spent sixteen hours a day in his office sometimes, seven days a week sometimes, but he always said he enjoyed the work, and he certainly was raking in the dough. Wahlman wasn't jealous of Mike's success. Not even a little bit. Mike was his best friend, and he was happy for him.

Wahlman steered into Mike's driveway, cut the engine and climbed out of the truck and mounted the porch and knocked on the front door.

No answer.

It was a little after nine, and Mike was usually up by eight. His car was still in the garage, so it didn't seem likely that he'd gone anywhere.

Of course it was possible that he was still in bed.

Wahlman didn't usually enter Mike's house without being invited, but the intrusion seemed warranted under the circumstances. He slid the key into the deadbolt and opened the door and stepped into the foyer. To his right there was a set of stairs that led to the bedrooms on the second floor. He shouted Mike's name, waited a few seconds, climbed the stairs and walked to the master bedroom. As he reached to open the door, Allison's cell phone trilled.

Wahlman looked at the display, saw that it was Detective Collins.

Collins.

With everything else that had happened over the past twenty-four hours, Wahlman had kind of pushed Collins to the back of his mind. He pretty much knew what was coming, knew that it wasn't going to be good, but he figured there was no escaping it now. Best to just go ahead and deal with it.

He tapped the screen and answered the call.

"This is Wahlman," he said.

"Collins, NOPD Homicide. I need you to come to the station as soon as possible."

"I drove home," Wahlman said. "I'm in Florida."

Collins sighed. "There was a double homicide in the hotel you were staying at," he said. "A man and a woman. The coroner thinks two different guns were used, neither of which were found on the premises. The cell phone you're talking on is registered to the woman."

"You guys work fast," Wahlman said.

"I need you to come to the station."

"I didn't shoot her."

Collins sighed some more. "I also received some footage from a security camera this morning," he said. "It shows you exiting the back door of the sandwich shop across from the hotel, and it shows you running up the alley toward Canal Street. This was right around the time the owner of the restaurant was shot. Man named Walter Babineaux."

"I didn't shoot him either."

"I want to believe you, Wahlman. I don't think you had anything to do with Darrell Renfro out there on the interstate, and I want to believe you didn't have anything to do with Babineaux in the sandwich shop or the man and the woman in the hotel. I want to believe you, but—"

"Is Babineaux still alive?"

"Last I heard."

"Is he conscious? Has anyone talked to him yet?"

"I'm not going to sugarcoat this," Collins said, ignoring Wahlman's questions. "We have a warrant for your arrest. Assault with intent to kill. We're working on a second warrant, and that one's going to be for first degree murder. I need you to drive to the nearest sheriff's department substation and turn yourself in. They'll get the extradition process started, get you transferred back to New Orleans before the end of the week. Otherwise, we're going to have to initiate a—"

"Who do you think I murdered?" Wahlman asked.

"The woman in the hotel room. The man too. But you have the woman's phone, so it's going to be—"

"Her name's Allison."

"Right. So you knew her. I can go ahead and take a confession over the phone if—"

"I didn't kill her," Wahlman said. "I killed the man, but not Allison. It was self-defense. He shot her, and then he started shooting at me. I know the scene is still fresh, but eventually you're going to find two nine millimeter rounds in the mattress, and six thirty-eights elsewhere. One of the thirty-eights just happened to plow through the top of the guy's head."

"We're going to sort it all out when you get back to New Orleans."

"I'm not turning myself in," Wahlman said. "Not yet."

"You have to. The warrant's out there. You're a fugitive. You're considered armed and dangerous. Every law enforcement officer in the country is going to know what you look like in a matter of hours. There's nowhere to hide. Might as well make it easy on yourself."

Wahlman took a deep breath. "Did you get the DNA results back yet?" he asked.

"Irrelevant."

"But did you?"

"Yeah. But something's wrong. We're going to have to redo the whole thing."

"Some sort of mistake in the lab?"

"Had to be," Collins said. "Because according to the results, you and Darrell Renfro and Jack Reacher are all the same person."

"What does that even mean?"

"We'll talk about it when you get to New Orleans. Right now you need to drive to the substation and turn yourself in."

"I can't do that."

"Then you're in for a world of trouble, my friend."

"Talk to Babineaux," Wahlman said.

And then he hung up.

He figured it was a good time to get rid of Allison's cell phone. The whole lack of privacy thing was one of the reasons he didn't own one. He didn't like the fact that anyone with a computer could track his whereabouts twenty-four hours a day. The only reason he'd taken the phone in the first place was so he could keep trying to call Mike Chilton on the drive back to Florida.

He reached for the doorknob to Mike's master bedroom again.

The phone trilled again.

It wasn't Detective Collins this time. It was Clifford Terrence Drake Junior.

Wahlman clicked on. "I was going to call you later," he

said. "I haven't had a chance to do the research I need to do yet."

"There's been a change of plans," Drake said. "I'm going to give you an address in Jacksonville. I want you to go there and meet with one of my associates."

"I'm not going anywhere until—"

"I'm going to switch over to a conference call. Don't hang up, okay?"

There was a series of clicks and a short period of static, and then a very familiar voice came on the line, a voice that was somehow hoarse and weary and frantic at the same time.

It was the voice of Mike Chilton.

"Rock, you need to run. Just run, man. Don't worry about me. You need to get out of the country. Today. Get the cash out of my safety deposit box and—"

Click.

Silence.

And then Drake came back on.

He told Wahlman to be at the address in Jacksonville in exactly one hour.

Or else.

18

Wahlman crossed the Buckman Bridge and exited on San Jose Boulevard. He had the .38 with him and the 9mm, minus the silencer, which he'd removed to make the gun easier to carry. Clifford Terrence Drake Junior had arranged for Mike Chilton to be kidnapped, which meant that Clifford Terrence Drake Junior was going to die. Maybe not today, or tomorrow, but soon. That was for sure. As soon as Wahlman could get back to New Orleans, Drake was a dead man. In the meantime, anyone who worked for him was going to get a good old-fashioned Master-at-Arms ass kicking.

At the very least.

Wahlman sped through four yellow lights and one red one, took a right and covered several more blocks in a matter of seconds, driving the pickup like some kind of racecar, downshifting into the curves and flooring it on the straightaways, finally veering into an industrial loop and steering into the abandoned factory where the meeting was supposed to take place.

He got there with about ten minutes to spare.

He climbed out of the truck, stuffed both guns into the back of his waistband, covered the grips with the tails of his shirt. He was supposed to walk to the gate and press the big red button and wait for an escort. But that was not what he did. There were no rules in a situation like this, as far as Wahlman was concerned. His best friend had been abducted, and was being held against his will. All bets were off. No holds barred. So instead of pressing the button and waiting for someone to come, he climbed the fence and walked up a set of concrete steps to the loading dock and entered the factory through one of the big rollup doors, which had been left wide open.

There was a guard standing about five feet inside the door. Average height, average weight, gray coveralls, black ball cap.

Twelve-gauge pump.

"You here to see Mr. Nefangar?" the man asked.

"Maybe," Wahlman said.

"You were supposed to wait outside the gate."

"Yet here I am."

"I'm authorized to shoot you if you give me any trouble."

"You're not going to shoot me. If you were going to shoot me, I'd be dead already. Take me to Nefangar."

"I was supposed to call him when you sounded the buzzer."

"So call him."

"You didn't do what you were supposed to do."

"Want me to climb back over the fence and start over?" Wahlman asked.

"You're a smartass, you know that?"

"Better than being a dumbass, like you."

The guard chuckled. "Just wait," he said. "In less than an hour, you're going to be begging me to shoot you. That's how much pain you're going to be in."

He leaned the shotgun against the wall, pulled a cell phone out of his pocket and punched in a number. While he was waiting for an answer, Wahlman reached around and pulled the .38 out of his waistband, aimed and fired and blew the guard's right kneecap off. The cell phone skittered across the concrete floor as the guy collapsed in a screaming heap.

Wahlman walked over and grabbed the shotgun, and then he picked up the phone and pressed it against his ear.

"Anyone there?" he asked.

"Who is this? McNeal? Was that a gunshot I just heard? Where are you? Where's Wahlman?"

"Who's McNeal?" Wahlman asked. "The guy in the gray coveralls? I'm afraid he's not feeling very well right now. Can I take a message?"

"Wahlman?"

"Nefanger?"

"You just signed your friend's execution order. I hope you know that."

"Let him go," Wahlman said. "Drake doesn't care anything about him. Drake wants me. For whatever reason. I really don't even care anymore. If he's determined to kill me, then he's going to kill me. That's the way it works in the real world. But I'm not going to turn myself over until I know that Mike is safe."

"You're in no position to be making demands," Nefangar said. "I'll kill your friend, and then I'll kill you."

"No you won't. Because like I told McKneeless over there, if you'd wanted to kill me, then I never would have made it through the door. You want to keep me alive for some reason. For a while, anyway. It doesn't really matter why, but I can promise you one thing: I'm going to keep doing a whole lot of damage until you let Mike Chilton go."

Nefangar laughed. "What kind of damage?" he asked.

Wahlman walked over to McNeal, who now seemed to be in shock. Maybe from the blood loss, maybe from the excruciating pain. Maybe from both. Wahlman pressed the barrel of the shotgun against his chest.

Wahlman had never shot a man at point blank range before.

And he'd never shot an incapacitated man at any range.

But then there was a first time for everything.

"This kind of damage," he said, and pulled the trigger.

19

Partially deafened from the blast, Wahlman stood there and fiddled with the phone until he figured out how to turn up the volume.

"What did you do?" Nefangar asked.

"I killed your sentry. Go ahead and send more. I'll kill them too."

"Are you out of your mind?"

"Plenty of places to hide in this building. I'll pick your guys off one at a time until there's nobody left. Then I'll come after you."

Silence for about ten seconds.

"I'm going to call Mr. Drake and ask him how he wants to proceed," Nefangar said. "I'll call you back."

"Try to make it quick," Wahlman said. "I'm starting to get impatient."

Nefangar disconnected.

There were two stainless steel tanks at one end of the room, massive cylindrical things about twenty feet tall and as big around as bedrooms. Above the tanks, and leading down into them, were a pair of motorized mixing blades, huge steel shafts mounted on tresses that had been bolted to the ceiling. There was a stretch of scaffolding along the rear edge of the tanks, with a portable set of stairs pushed up against each side. Above the scaffolding Wahlman could see electrical conduit and copper plumbing, everything caked with grime and exposed in a tangle, like some kind of filthy industrial spaghetti, as if the infrastructural components of the operation had been installed as an afterthought, as if the pipes and valves and wires and junctions had been utilized for a short period of time and then abandoned and left to decay.

Wahlman started walking toward the tanks. He figured if you got both of those things humming real good you could crank out about a hundred and sixty thousand margaritas in no time. Assuming the tanks were five thousand gallons each, and assuming you used eight ounce glasses for the drinks.

Wahlman was good at calculating things like that in his head. In school he'd sometimes been suspected of cheating on math tests, because he always finished quickly and rarely needed to work anything out on paper. He would look at the problems and write down the answers, and then he would spend the rest of the period doodling or daydreaming. It drove his teachers crazy.

He stayed close to the wall as he approached the tanks, trying to keep a low profile in case any more guys in gray coveralls were lurking about. He made it to the mobile steel staircase on the right, tested his weight on the first couple of risers and then climbed up to the catwalk and peered down into one of the tanks through an access hatch. The shiny steel floor was dry, but the air smelled faintly of vinegar. Maybe this had been a salad dressing factory, he thought. He envisioned automatic chutes and conveyor belts and plastic bottles and hoses and nozzles and cardboard boxes stacked on wooden pallets.

And then he wondered why the factory wasn't here anymore. People still ate plenty of salad dressing, so it had to be coming from somewhere. But then maybe something else had been produced here, something that had become obsolete. He was staring down into the tank and thinking about that when the phone trilled again.

"What did he say?" Wahlman asked, assuming it was Nefangar.

"By *he*, I suppose you mean *me*," an unexpected male voice said.

It was Drake.

"I suppose I did," Wahlman said. "I'll tell you the same thing I told Nefangar. I'm not turning myself over until I'm a hundred percent certain that Mike Chilton has been set free."

"I'm on a jet to Florida right now," Drake said. "My clients have insisted that I tend to this matter myself."

"Who are your clients?"

"You wouldn't believe me if I told you."

"Try me."

"Let's just say they're quite perturbed that this situation wasn't taken care of Sunday at the sandwich shop. But it's going to be taken care of today. Definitely."

"Who are your clients?" Wahlman asked again. "I think I have a right to know who's trying to kill me."

"We'll discuss that when I get there. Then again, maybe not. Seems kind of pointless, if you want to know the truth."

Wahlman did want to know the truth, but it seemed increasingly unlikely that Clifford Terrence Drake Junior would ever deliver it in any sort of meaningful way.

"Where's Mike?" Wahlman asked. "I want to see him. Or at least talk to him."

"Your friend is being driven to a different location as we speak. He was Special Forces in the navy, right?"

"Yes. He was a SEAL."

"Then he shouldn't have any problem finding his way out of the Okefenokee Swamp. It might take him a day or two, but he will survive."

"That's your idea of setting him free?"

"I'm afraid that's the best I can do. I can't just take him back to his house, now can I? He might come back to the factory and attempt some kind of daring rescue."

Drake seemed to be enjoying himself. He was having a little fun at Wahlman's expense. His vocal inflection on *daring rescue* made it sound like a melodramatic and silly thing to try.

"How will I know that you really let him go?" Wahlman asked, keeping his own tone serious, refusing to take the bait.

"We'll transmit satellite images to your phone. You'll be able to see the beads of sweat on your friend's face as he tries to make his way out of the swamp."

Live images from cameras in outer space. Close-ups. High-resolution. Ordinary citizens didn't have access to that kind of technology. Which told Wahlman that Drake's clients were not ordinary citizens.

"You're not a lawyer," Wahlman said. "You're some kind of mercenary."

"Who says I can't be both? Now listen very carefully. I'm going to give you some information you'll need to gain access to the satellite feed."

Drake spelled out a user name and a password.

"Who hired you?" Wahlman asked again.

"This thing is bigger than you, or me, or Darrell Renfro, or Allison Bentley. This thing is bigger than big. You need to wrap your head around that, Mr. Wahlman. And you need to wrap your head around the fact that you're going to die today."

Wahlman wanted to wrap Drake's head around something. Maybe one of the steel mixing blades he was staring down at.

"When will I be able to see the pictures of Mike out in the Okefenokee?" he asked.

"Check your phone in about an hour."

"Then what?"

"Then I'll call you and instruct you on exactly what to do next. In the meantime, you should stay where you are, there on the catwalk behind the mixing tanks."

"How did you know—"

"See you soon," Drake said, and disconnected.

20

Drake hadn't given Wahlman much information, but he'd given him some. And along with the other things Wahlman had learned over the past two and a half days, it was enough to piece some things together and formulate a loose hypothesis.

A United States government agency, or a branch of the military, or a foreign government agency or military, had hired a team of mercenaries to kill Renfro and Wahlman, who somehow shared similar fingerprints and the exact same DNA as a former army officer named Jack Reacher. That was it in a nutshell. Which meant that the United States government, or a branch of the military, or a foreign government or military, had something to hide regarding Reacher and Renfro and Wahlman, something that possibly involved some sort of genetic research.

Because according to the results, you and Darrell Renfro and Jack Reacher are all the same person.

Human cloning.

As insane as it sounded, Wahlman couldn't think of anything else it could be.

Detective Collins had said that the lab results were an obvious mistake, but Wahlman didn't think so.

The technology had been around for a long time, and it had been illegal for a long time. Most mainstream scientists considered it unethical, for a variety of reasons. But the fact that it was illegal and unethical didn't mean that it wasn't happening, and it didn't mean that it hadn't been happening back around the time Wahlman was born. There were conspiracy theories to such effect. The tabloids were full of them. Wahlman had never put much stock in those kinds of things, but he supposed it was within the realm of possibility that some of the theories were true.

Clifford Terrence Drake Junior—maybe his real name, maybe not—was the leader of the team of mercenaries. The team had been hired to kill Wahlman and Renfro, and maybe dozens of other clones. Hundreds? Thousands? It sounded improbable and outrageous, but then this whole thing sounded improbable and outrageous. Human duplicates? Why would a government have done such a thing? And why would they have chosen this Jack Reacher fellow as a donor? Was it a random choice, or was there some sort of reasoning behind it?

Those were some of the questions rattling around in Wahlman's brain, although he was doubtful that he would live long enough to find the answers.

But maybe he would. The team of mercenaries had probably only originally consisted of five guys: Drake and Nefangar, the first and second in command; the guy behind Allison's drapes and McNeal, the first and second to die; and one other guy, who was currently transporting Mike Chilton to the Okefenokee Swamp.

Five to start with.

Three remaining.

That was Wahlman's guess, based on his experience with similar groups on similar missions. If you were putting a crew like that together, you didn't want too many people on the payroll, and you didn't want too many people who could testify against you if things went bad. The fewer the better. Drake and Nefangar probably could have handled the job themselves, but they'd chosen to hire the other guys, for whatever reasons.

Five to start with.

Three remaining.

Wahlman's estimate was also based on the fact that nobody else had come after him yet. If there had been more hired guns hanging out somewhere in the factory, they would have come and tried to kill him by now. Two, three, a dozen, it didn't matter. If they had been here, they would have come.

Which meant that Nefangar was probably alone right now.

Wahlman thought about going after him, decided not to. Mostly out of concern for Mike. Also, it was indeed a big building, and there were indeed plenty of places to hide. And Nefangar was probably monitoring Wahlman's movements. Wahlman hadn't been able to spot any security cameras yet, but he knew they were there. It was the only way Drake could have known that he was on the catwalk behind the tanks.

Which was the safest place for him to be right now.

Wahlman hadn't climbed up there out of curiosity. He'd chosen the position as a tactical defense strategy. If his estimate regarding the number of mercenaries was wrong, or if Drake and Nefangar somehow managed to call in some reinforcements, at least he would have a fighting chance from the elevated position. Maybe more than a fighting chance, considering the assortment of weapons he'd accumulated over the past twenty-four hours. The .38 and the 9mm and the shotgun. He wasn't equipped to fend off an army, but he wasn't exactly helpless either.

The phone made a little tinkling sound that Wahlman hadn't heard before. He looked at the display and saw that Drake had sent him a text message. No correspondence, just a link to a website. When Wahlman tapped on the link, a login window popped up. He entered the user name and password Drake had given him earlier, and the next thing he saw was a wide grassy area flanked on each side by small ponds and massive oak trees. He zoomed in. A little black dot appeared to be moving slowly across the grassy area. He zoomed in some more, closer and closer, zeroing in on the little black dot, which turned out to be a man, but not the man Wahlman had been expecting to see. Not Mike Chilton, his best friend in the world, but someone else, someone he'd never seen before. The man was running, sweating, grunting, seemingly on the verge of collapse, pushing himself forward as if someone was chasing him, someone who meant to do him great harm. Then, suddenly, something swooped in behind him, a flying object, a helicopter, a very small one, the rotors churning in an arc no bigger than a pizza pan. The man started zigzagging toward the tree line in one last frantic effort to survive, but it was no use. The copter dove down a little closer to the ground and leveled out directly behind the man and there was a short burst of gunfire and that was it.

The display went dark for a few seconds, and then another scene appeared. Another man running, sweating, grunting. This time it was Mike Chilton. Wahlman recognized him, even though his head had been shaved completely bald. Mike was wearing the shirt Wahlman had given him for his birthday a couple of years ago. It was torn and dirty and soaked with sweat. The miniature helicopter was no longer visible, but Wahlman could hear the motor whirring somewhere in the distance, perhaps just out of camera range.

The phone made the little tinkling sound again.

It was another text message from Drake:

Just wanted to show off our handy-dandy little drone. Just so there's no misunderstanding, just in case you were thinking you might be able to escape now that Mike Chilton has been set free. From this point forward, if you do anything other than what we tell you to do—and I mean exactly what we tell you to do—your friend will die.

The phone trilled. It was Nefangar.

"Did you get the message from Mr. Drake?" he asked.

"I got it," Wahlman said.

"Good. I want you to climb down the set of stairs to your right. You'll see a door that says AUTHORIZED

PERSONNEL ONLY. Open the door and walk all the way to the end of the hallway and take a left."

"Then what?"

"Don't worry about *then what*. Just do as you're told. And leave your weapons there on the catwalk. The twelve-gauge and both of the handguns. Any sort of failure to cooperate will result in the immediate execution of your friend."

"We're kind of back to square one, aren't we?" Wahlman said. "Even if I do cooperate, how do I know you're not going to—"

Nefangar hung up.

Wahlman thought about staying on the catwalk and trying to fight it out. But if he did, Mike would die for sure. Going along with Drake and Nefangar wouldn't guarantee a better outcome, but it would give Mike some time to think. He was a SEAL. He was an expert at surviving, even when the odds seemed insurmountable. And maybe Drake and Nefangar would keep their word and let him live. Or at least not gun him down with the drone. At least give him a chance to navigate his way out of the swamp.

With that in mind, Wahlman set all three of his guns down on the steel platform and headed toward the stairs.

21

When Wahlman got to the end of the hallway and took a left, a man was standing there waiting for him.

A small man with a large gun.

A .44 magnum.

Nickel plated with black grips. Barrel as fat as a soup can.

"Nefangar?" Wahlman said.

"Don't talk. Drop the phone. I want you face down on the floor with your hands laced behind your head. Do it. Now."

"You sounded bigger when I talked to you earlier. Is Drake a pipsqueak too?"

Nefangar reached into his pocket and pulled out a cell phone.

"I have a text ready to be sent out," he said. "All I have to do is tap the *SEND* button, and your friend is dead."

Wahlman weighed his options. He could go for the gun and hope Nefangar didn't have the presence of mind to send the text, or he could go for the phone and hope Nefangar didn't have the presence of mind to blow his brains out.

Then he remembered something Mike Chilton had told him one time: *when an opponent has the upper hand, sometimes you just have to play it cool for a while. Sometimes you just have to wait for the right opportunity to present itself. As long as you're still breathing, there's a chance the tables will turn. When they do, don't hesitate. Strike fast. Strike hard. Get out.*

It wasn't anything you were going to find in any sort of field manual. It was something Mike had learned from experience. From being in situations that seemed hopeless.

In his formal training, Wahlman had been taught to avoid capture at all costs.

But this time the cost was just too high.

Wahlman dropped Allison's cell phone, heard the display window crack when the device hit the concrete. He got down on the floor and laced his hands behind his head, immediately felt Nefangar's knee come down hard on the lower part of his back. Nefangar dug his bony little thumbs into some pressure points on Wahlman's hands and forced them down to the center of his ribcage and secured them at the wrists with nylon zip ties.

"Seems like you might have done this kind of thing before," Wahlman said.

"Get up."

Wahlman rolled over and rose to a standing position, again noticing what a small man Nefangar was. Five-five, maybe five-six. Skinny and pale. He wore an outfit identical to McNeal's. Gray coveralls and a black hat.

"You look like you could use some vitamins," Wahlman said. "Or a blood transfusion or something."

Nefangar pointed the .44 at Wahlman's chest. "Turn around and start walking," he said. "Slowly. All the way to the door at the end of the hallway."

"You're pretty tough with a gun in your hand. Put it down and see if I don't kick your ass all the way to the door at the end of the hallway."

"Move!"

Wahlman turned around and started walking. When he got to the end of the hallway, Nefangar instructed him to step to the right and place the toes of his boots against the baseboard and his forehead against the wall.

"So you can shoot me in the back of the head?" Wahlman asked. "So you don't have to look into my eyes when you do it?"

"You're starting to get on my nerves."

"That's okay. You're starting to get on mine too."

"Mr. Drake will be here shortly. Then you will die. Slowly and painfully, if I have anything to say about it. In the meantime, I need you stand against the wall while I open this door. Then I'm going to follow you into the room on the other side of it. That's one way we can do it. The other way is for me to shatter the bones in your feet with a couple of .44 slugs and drag you into the room."

"I guess I'll go for Option One," Wahlman said.

"Good choice."

Wahlman turned and edged his toes up against the baseboard, and then he leaned in and pressed his forehead against the painted sheetrock. Nefangar's keys jingled as he pulled them out of his pocket, and they jingled some more as he turned them over in his hand and searched for the one that would open the door.

Which presented a potential opportunity.

One of Nefangar's hands was busy fumbling with the keys, and the other was busy holding the unwieldy handgun, which meant that the cell phone with the fatal *SEND* button was out of the picture for the moment. Probably in a pocket. Within reach, but it would take some time to fish it out. At least a couple of seconds.

As long as you're still breathing, there's a chance the tables will turn. When they do, don't hesitate. Strike fast. Strike hard. Get out.

Wahlman waited until he heard the key slide into the slot and the deadbolt click open, and then he pivoted ninety degrees and lowered his left shoulder and rammed into Nefangar's right arm, hammering him with tremendous force, tenderizing him like a piece of raw meat. The keys tinkled brassily to the concrete floor, Nefangar's left ribcage slammed crunchily against the steel doorframe, and the .44 magnum discharged harmlessly into the section of sheetrock Wahlman had been leaning against.

Wahlman got down on the floor and arched his back and bent his knees and wriggled his restrained hands to the front where he could use them. He grabbed the keys and stuffed them into his pocket, and then he stood and pressed his boot against Nefangar's wrist and bent over and pried the revolver out of his fingers. Nefangar tried to resist, but it seemed that the little bit of strength he had left was being used to draw air into his right lung—the only one that was still functioning at full capacity.

Wahlman reached into Nefangar's left front pants pocket and carefully pulled out the cell phone.

"You're going to die," Nefangar grunted.

"We're all going to die," Wahlman said. "Some of us sooner than others. You sooner than most."

He pressed the barrel of the .44 against Nefangar's forehead.

Cocked the hammer back.

"Wait," Nefangar said. "I can arrange it so you'll know for sure that Mike Chilton is safe."

"How can you do that?"

"I'll show you how to disable the drone. Then you can pinpoint Mike's exact location and send some cops or whoever out there to help him."

"Okay. Show me."

"First you have to promise that you're not going to shoot me."

"Who was the guy running from the drone earlier?" Wahlman asked. "The one who got shot in the back."

"That was our man," Nefangar said. "He drove Chilton out to the swamp."

"Why did you kill him?"

"He made a stupid mistake. He was a liability."

"Show me how to disable the drone."

"First you have to promise that you're not going to—"

"Okay. I promise."

Wahlman gently released the hammer and slid the humongous revolver into his waistband. Nobody needed a gun that big, he thought. It was like carrying an anvil.

"Use my cell phone to access the satellite site," Nefangar said. "But don't log in. I'm going to give you a special user name and password."

"I'm going to need my hands," Wahlman said. "Do you have something I can cut these ties off with?"

Nefangar nodded. He slowly and painstakingly slid two fingers into his pocket and pulled out a small lock-blade knife. He tried to open it, didn't have the strength. He finally gave up and tossed the knife on the floor near Wahlman's feet.

Wahlman bent over and picked it up.

Opened it.

Examined it.

Noticed that there were some tiny blackish-red flakes where the blade locked into the handle.

Blood, he thought. Most likely from Darrell Renfro's abdomen.

He sawed the zip ties off and folded the blade back into the handle and slid the knife into his pocket. Then he pulled out Nefangar's phone.

"The first thing you need to do is retract the kill command," Nefangar said.

"How to I do that?"

"See the button that says *SEND*?"

"Yes."

"If you tap it two times in quick succession, your friend will die in a matter of seconds."

"I obviously don't want that to happen."

"Right. So what you need to do is tap the button *three*

times in quick succession. That will cause the drone to return to its base to wait for further commands."

"I thought you said I could disable the drone completely," Wahlman said.

"You have to send it back to its base first."

"How do I know you're telling the truth? How do I know that tapping the button three times won't dial in the kill command?"

"I'm trying to save my own skin," Nefangar said. "That's what this is all about, remember? Why would I lie?"

Wahlman nodded.

He looked down at the display screen.

Stared at the *SEND* button.

Thought about it.

Thought about it some more.

And then he tapped the button three times.

22

Nothing happened.

"How do I know Mike's okay?" Wahlman asked. "How do I know the drone went back to its base?"

"Go to the website," Nefangar said. "There's a link in my bookmarks."

Wahlman found the link and accessed the website for the satellite feed.

"I'm looking at the login window," he said. "I need the special user name and password you told me about."

Nefangar started laughing. "There's no special user name and password," he said. "I made that up. Why should I help you get what you want? I was dead the second you took my gun. Look at me. I need a doctor. I'm going to need to be hospitalized. Drake's not going to let me live. I'm of no use to him now."

"What are you saying?"

"I'm saying that your friend Mike Chilton is dead. And I'm saying that you're the one who killed him. If you had cooperated, everything would have been all right. We would have let Chilton go. But you had to be the big hero, didn't you? My life is over now, Mr. Wahlman, but so is yours. There's no escape. Even if you manage to get away from Drake, there's still no escape. Our clients aren't the kind of people who give up. Ever. They'll hire someone else to track you down, or maybe they'll do it themselves this time. They'll find you. Tomorrow, next week, whenever."

Wahlman reared back and threw Nefangar's cell phone toward the end of the hallway. He threw it hard, overhand, like a baseball, and then he pulled the .44 from his waistband, cocked the hammer back, aimed the barrel at Nefangar's face.

"Who are your clients?" he asked.

"Seems like you have some anger management issues. You might want to see someone about that."

"Who are your clients?"

"I'm sure you have a lot of questions," Nefangar said. "Like how it went down with Renfro. Like how we placed one of our guys in Allison Bentley's hotel room. Like how we drained your bank account, or why any of this is even happening. With Renfro, it was supposed to look like an accident. McNeal and I followed—"

Wahlman jammed the barrel of the revolver into Nefangar's mouth, breaking several of his front teeth in the process.

"I don't care about any of that shit," Wahlman said. "Not anymore. You think I'm going to stand here and listen to you talk until Drake gets here? I'm going to ask you one more time. Who are your clients?"

Nefangar started gagging. Wahlman pulled the gun out of his mouth. Nefangar turned his head to the side and coughed out some blood and tooth fragments.

"You want to know who hired us?" he said, his speech wet and garbled and nearly incomprehensible. "Why? So you can go after them? It's not going to work. They're too big. The issue they're trying to keep secret is too big. You don't have a chance."

"As long as I'm still breathing, I still have a chance," Wahlman said.

And then he took two steps backward and emptied the revolver into Nefangar's chest.

Which he knew right away was a big mistake. He had allowed his emotions to get the best of him. He should have kept at least one bullet for contingencies.

Because when he turned to run back out to the tanks, to retrieve the weapons he'd left on the catwalk, he saw a man with an Uzi standing at the end of the hallway.

"Allow me to introduce myself," the man said. "Clifford Terrence Drake Junior, Attorney at Law."

Wahlman didn't know what was behind the door Nefangar had opened a few minutes ago, but he knew it couldn't possibly be any worse than what he was facing now. He dropped the .44 and dove toward the door and rolled into the room on the other side of it, barely beating a short burst of rounds from Drake's machinegun. The bullets pinged off the concrete and thudded into the wood and drywall as Wahlman scurried back to the threshold and slammed the door shut and secured the deadbolt.

There was another door on the other side of the room. Two entrances from two different hallways. Typical for this kind of setup, Wahlman thought. A common area for staff meetings and educational presentations and whatnot. He'd seen plenty of similar arrangements on naval bases, and even on ships.

Drake was still on the other side of the door that Nefangar had opened with the key. Wahlman could hear him over there ramming it with his shoulder, trying to bust through the frame. Maybe he had never been to the factory before. Maybe he didn't know about the double entrance. Wahlman hoped he didn't, because the second door represented his only chance of getting out of there alive. He stayed low, belly-crawling past a conference table and a file cabinet and a small steel safe, almost making it to the door before looking back and noticing that he was leaving a trail of blood.

He'd been hit.

Left hamstring, several inches above the knee joint.

The extreme adrenaline rush from the fight-or-flight response must have kept him from feeling the bullet as it went in, but he could certainly feel it now. Like someone holding a soldering iron to the back of his leg. He reached up and unlocked the deadbolt, opened the door and crawled out into the hallway.

Drake was still trying to break through the door on the other side. Wahlman could hear him. Banging with his shoulder, kicking with his foot. Probably thinking that he had plenty of time. Probably thinking that he had Wahlman trapped.

Drake could have tried blasting the lock off with the Uzi, but Wahlman supposed he was too smart for that. It was highly unlikely for a bullet to strike a lock mechanism in the precise manner it would need to in order to break it open. What was more likely was that one or more of the rounds shot at the lock would ricochet back and hit the shooter. Not to mention the ammunition that would be wasted. Trying to blast a lock with a gun was an all-around fail most of the time, a notion that was dispelled during the first week of any sort of serious firearms training.

Wahlman stood and started limping toward the end of the hallway, toward the turn that would lead him back to the production area, warm blood from the gunshot wound trickling down the back of his leg in a steady stream. The injury was serious, but it could have been a lot worse. If the bullet had clipped his femoral artery, he probably would have bled out by now. The hole in his leg hurt like crazy, but it didn't present an immediate threat to his life.

He made it to the end of the hallway, took a right down a shorter corridor, pushed his way through the heavy steel door, out into the big room where the big tanks were. Now it was just a matter of getting over to the stairs and climbing up to the catwalk and retrieving the weapons he'd left there. Easier said than done when it felt like a handful of razorblades were being jammed into the back of his leg. He hobbled along the edge of the factory floor as fast as he could, losing a few more drops of blood with every excruciating step.

By the time he got to the portable steel staircase on the

right side of the tanks, the one he'd used previously, the pain in his leg had subsided some, which was good, but then he saw that the staircase had been pulled away from the catwalk, which was not good. Now there was a gap between the top step and the horizontal platform. Ten feet or so. Too far to jump, especially with a shredded hamstring. Wahlman backed up far enough to see that the staircase on the left had been moved as well. He figured Drake must have pulled the units away from the platform on his way in. Motivation unknown. Maybe he'd thought that Wahlman was still up there. Or maybe he'd planned ahead, envisioning the possibility of the scenario that was playing out now. Smart. And if that was the case, it probably wouldn't be long until he came out to the production area to take a look, regardless of whether or not he managed to break through the door to the conference room.

Which meant that Wahlman needed to hurry.

He tried wheeling the staircase back into position, quickly realized that there was a braking mechanism on it somewhere that needed to be released. He found the lever and yanked it back and scooted the stairs closer to the catwalk. Not quite flush, but close enough. He mounted the first step and immediately fell back and landed on his ass.

The pain in his leg had subsided because his leg had gone numb.

No longer able to stand on two feet, Wahlman started crawling up the steps, gripping the back of each riser with his fingers and pushing himself upward with his right leg. His heart was racing and he felt weaker than he'd ever felt in his life. He was dizzy and he couldn't remember what day it was and he knew that he was going to die if he didn't get medical attention soon. Just a few more feet, he thought. Just a few more feet to the top of the stairs. Then he could defend himself. It was just Drake now. Just one guy. No problem. All he needed to do was make it up to the catwalk.

And then, suddenly, he was there.

And just as suddenly, a familiar voice echoed from the other side of the production area.

"Now I've got you," Drake said.

23

A deafening barrage of automatic rifle fire blasted through the cavernous space, a staccato series of earsplitting explosions, like a brick of firecrackers linked with a single fuse. Wahlman scrabbled toward the section of the catwalk where he'd left the guns. The .38 and the 9mm and the twelve gauge pump.

But they weren't there.

They were gone.

Drake must have done something with them before he moved the staircases.

Wahlman pulled himself up to the lip of the tank and peered down into the same access hatch he'd peered down into earlier, thinking the enormous container would have been a convenient place for Drake to ditch the weapons.

Same faint smell of vinegar, same shiny steel floor.

No guns.

They weren't at the bottom of the tank, because they were on top of the tank. Near the edge, in front, about twelve feet from where Wahlman was standing. Drake had probably tossed them out there, thinking he would come back for them later. Which made sense. The fewer pieces of evidence left behind, the better. And it would be much quicker and easier to retrieve these particularly incriminating items from the top of the tank than it would from the bottom.

Thinking ahead again.

Smart.

But not really. Arrogant was more like it. Drake had never anticipated Wahlman escaping and getting enough of a head start to be in the position he was in right now.

He'd underestimated his opponent.

A big mistake, and now he was going to pay for it.

Wahlman had been on the verge of passing out, but a fresh surge of adrenaline had brought him back to a high state of alertness. He felt reenergized, but he knew it wouldn't last. He'd lost a lot of blood, and the only way to fix that was to replace it. He needed someone to dig the bullet out and stitch the wound and transfuse him with two or three units of packed red blood cells.

But first things first.

The top of the tank was filthy, coated with the same greasy dust as the plumbing and electrical conduit. Wahlman climbed up there and started crawling toward the edge, his numb left leg and the slimy black film on the tank making it ten times more difficult than it should have been.

Somewhere around the halfway point, Drake opened up with the Uzi again. Bullets drum-rolled off the upper part of the tank, leaving trails of bright orange sparks as they tore through the ceiling.

Wahlman was hesitant to proceed toward the edge of the tank now. Toward the weapons that represented a potential way out of this, but also toward the hailstorm of machinegun rounds that represented potential instant death. He was hesitant to proceed, but he knew it was the only possible way he was going to survive. If he stayed where he was, he would die. He would eventually lose consciousness from the blood loss, or Drake would eventually climb up to the catwalk and finish him off with the Uzi. One of those two things would happen if he stayed where he was. It was only a matter of which would happen first. So he had to continue moving forward, even though it went against his instincts. He figured his odds of making it out of the factory alive were about a million to one at this point, but a million to one was better than a million to zero.

He kept inching toward the edge.

Grunting.

Sweating.

Wheezing.

And then the fingers on his right hand closed around the grips of the 9mm semiautomatic pistol. Finally. Now he could defend himself. He waited for another short burst from Drake's Uzi, aimed toward the muzzle flash and pulled the trigger.

And nothing happened.

He turned the gun over and stared into the hollow space where the magazine was supposed to be. No magazine, no bullet in the chamber. He tossed the pistol aside and grabbed the shotgun, checked it over and saw right away that the ammunition had been ejected from it as well.

Which left the revolver.

The .38 he'd bought in the freezer at Dena Jo's.

He grabbed the gun and aimed it down toward the area Drake had been shooting from and squeezed the trigger.

Nothing.

The .38 was empty too.

Drake had removed the ammunition from all three guns.

Thinking ahead.

Smart.

He hadn't underestimated his opponent after all. He'd done everything just right.

And now the only thing Wahlman could do was lie there and wait.

But maybe not.

He still had the folding lock-blade knife he'd taken from Nefangar.

It wasn't much, but it was better than nothing.

He reached into his pocket to get it as Drake's footsteps creaked rhythmically up the staircase.

24

Drake was moving slowly, cautiously. It took him a minute or so to make it to the section of the catwalk behind the tank on the right. Now he was standing directly across from Wahlman, who was still lying on top of the tank, near the edge.

Drake slammed a fresh magazine into the Uzi, and then he aimed the barrel at Wahlman's core.

"You win," Wahlman said. "You killed Darrel Renfro, and Allison Bentley, and your own man out in the swamp, and Mike Chilton. Now you're going to kill me, and there's nothing I can do to stop you. All I want to know is why."

"There's no short answer for that," Drake said.

Wahlman kept his eyes glued to Drake's right index finger. The one on the trigger.

"Then give me the long answer," he said.

"What's the point?"

"At least tell me who hired you. At least give me that."

Drake looked at his watch.

"My plane back to New Orleans isn't scheduled to take

off for another couple of hours," he said. "I suppose I could stand here and chat for a while. Watch you slowly bleed to death. Or I could finish you off right now. I'll get paid the same regardless, so it really doesn't matter to me. What do you want to know?"

"Everything."

Drake laughed. "If I were in your position, I suppose I would want to know everything too. Delay the inevitable for as long as possible. Maybe the cavalry will show up just in the nick of time. Maybe I'll drop dead of a heart attack. Anything could happen, right? But we both know that nothing like that is going to happen. And we both know that the little knife in your left hand isn't going to do you any good, and that the thirty-eight revolver in your right hand isn't going to do you any good. Or maybe you haven't tried the gun yet. Maybe you don't know. Go ahead. Aim it at me and pull the trigger. There aren't any bullets in it. I threw them away. All six of them. I discarded the ammunition from the other guns up there beside you as well. So all you really have is the little knife. Which isn't going to help you, no matter how long I stand here and talk. What are you planning to do? Throw it at me? Hope it sticks in my throat or something? Get real."

"Like I said, you win. I'm not delusional, Drake. I just want to know why all this had to happen."

Drake nodded. "Fair enough," he said. "Okay. Everything. Well, believe it or not, it all started in nineteen eighty-three, at Ramstein Air Force Base in Germany. Quite a few American soldiers and officers were there being treated for injuries sustained during an attack in Beirut, Lebanon. During one of the routine a.m. blood draws, an army general called in an order for forty extra vials to be taken from forty of the American patients. Nobody's sure exactly why he called in the order, but he did. The vials were labeled and shipped to the States, where the cells were analyzed and then cryogenically preserved in a secret underground laboratory in Colorado. Fast forward seventy-four years. Two thousand fifty-seven. A lot of things had changed by then. Politically. Financially. Technologically. An independent group of scientists petitioned the United States Army for funds and a venue to conduct a series of experiments on human cloning. It was illegal, of course, just as it is now, but the army said they would go along with it—in an unofficial capacity—as long as no living person was used as a donor. One of the scientists did a little research and discovered that the preserved samples from nineteen eighty-three were still in the deepfreeze, right there in the lab they wanted to use. Long story short, a total of eighty fetuses were produced, two from each specimen. Out of those eighty, only two survived. Both from an officer named Jack Reacher."

"So I was one of the two," Wahlman said. "And Renfro was the other."

"Correct. Two surrogate mothers were hired, strict non-disclosure agreements and all that, but at some point during the pregnancies, the army decided to bail on the experiment, leaving the independent group of scientists with no funding and no venue. You and Renfro were given fake identities and fake histories and sent to orphanages in different states. That should have been the end of it. You should have been left to live out your lives. No harm, no foul. Happily ever after. Unfortunately, the army recently discovered that an electronic file containing a thousand or so pages of classified data might have been hacked into. They're not sure, but they think some of the correspondence between the geneticists and the officer in charge of the clandestine funding might have been included in that data. So they're basically trying to cover their tracks, trying to eliminate any sort of evidence that would link them to the illegal study."

"Why don't they just kill the hackers?" Wahlman asked.

"That would be one way to approach the problem. Unfortunately, they have no idea who the hackers are. In fact, they don't really know if there *are* any hackers. It's just a strong suspicion, based on—"

"So they hired you to kill Renfro and me as a precautionary measure? Just in case some of that classified data was breached? That's insane."

"What can I say? It's the army. They pay well, I can tell you that. And now that Nefangar and the other three guys are gone, I'll get to keep it all for myself. One squeeze of the trigger, and I get to retire. In style."

"One squeeze of the trigger," Wahlman said.

And as he was saying it, he discreetly flicked his wrist and whizzed the little lock-blade knife off the side of the tank. It toppled down through the dirty pipes and the electrical conduit, making enough noise to create a momentary diversion. When Drake turned his head slightly to the right, the barrel of the Uzi shifted slightly to the right as well.

Which gave Wahlman just enough time to aim the .38 and blast a hole through the left side of Drake's jaw.

One bullet was all it took. Which was a good thing, because one bullet was all Wahlman had. He'd found it in the bottom of his pocket a few minutes ago, when he'd reached in for the knife, leftover from the extras he'd taken out when he first opened the box of shells in Allison's car.

An extremely expensive box of shells, but worth every penny.

Strike fast.

Strike hard.

And now it was time to get out.

Wahlman crawled back over to the catwalk and used Drake's cell phone to call a friend—a retired navy surgeon who owed him a favor.

25

Four days later, Wahlman was sitting on a bus, traveling on I-75, somewhere between Atlanta, Georgia and Chattanooga, Tennessee, staring out at the rural landscape and wondering what he was going to do, how he was going to live.

Our clients aren't the kind of people who give up. Ever. They'll hire someone else to track you down, or maybe they'll do it themselves this time. They'll find you. Tomorrow, next week, whenever.

Nefangar was right. They weren't going to give up.

The United States Army. Not the entire branch of the service, of course. Probably some sort of special research division. Isolated. Rogue. Working in their own little bubble. Trying to cover their own little asses, conspiring to conceal the division's involvement in an experiment that took place decades ago.

Which didn't really make sense.

Wahlman was doubtful that it was just a matter of eliminating a pair of lookalikes who'd grown up in separate orphanages. Maybe there were more clones running around somewhere. Maybe it was something else. Drake had said that this thing was bigger than all the people involved. Bigger than big, he'd said. And if that was the case, there had to be more to it. Way more. The cover-up had to involve something that was happening right now. Something that would jeopardize the careers of the personnel working on it right now. Wahlman figured that he and Renfro were just the tip of the iceberg. He had no idea how deep it all went, but he intended to find out, and he intended to use the information as a bargaining chip. Maybe threaten to take it all to the media. The people who were trying to kill him obviously wanted to play hardball, but that was okay. He would give them a game. At the very least, he would go down swinging. He figured it was the only potential pathway back to any sort of normalcy.

Not that things would ever return to the way they were before all this happened. He knew now that his entire life had been a lie. No mother, no father, no car accident. He'd been produced in a lab, grown inside a woman who'd rented her body to the army for nine months. A woman who had probably never been allowed to hold him after he was born. His entire life had been a lie, but he could deal with that. In a way, it eliminated some of the bitterness he'd held onto since childhood. Since there never were any actual grandparents or aunts or uncles or cousins, there were no reasons for Wahlman to be angry at them. So the whole bogus personal history thing wasn't bothering him much. It was the loss of Mike Chilton that he was having a problem dealing with. It never should have happened. It was a totally unnecessary tragedy, and it was a weight that Wahlman would carry around for the rest of his life.

He had convalesced at the surgeon's house for two days, and during that time he'd made some phone calls. He'd spoken to Detective Collins, who told him that Walter Babineaux had regained consciousness and had given the department detailed descriptions of the men who shot him, neither of whom looked anything like Wahlman.

"So we've dropped the charges on that one," Collins had said. "But we still need to talk to you regarding the shooting at the hotel."

"I already told you what happened. It was self-defense."

"You left the scene in a hurry. You took the woman's cell phone with you. We can't just let it go. You know that, as well as I do. We need you to come in and make a formal statement. We'll have to book you, but if everything points toward self-defense, then naturally we'll drop those charges as well. And we're still waiting for—"

"I'm going to have to disappear for a while," Wahlman said. "But not because of that. Get with the Jacksonville Sheriff's Office. Three men were found shot to death in an abandoned factory day before yesterday. Bad guys. Assassins. The guy you found in Allison Bentley's hotel room was working with them. I was the target. I'm pretty sure Allison was involved too. I'm pretty sure she sold me out."

"What are you talking about?"

"She owed a guy ten thousand dollars. She was desperate to get her hands on the money. The guys who were trying to kill me might have found out about that, might have offered to clear the debt in exchange for a quick favor. All she had to do was let one of them come into her room and hide behind the drapes for a while. I've thought about it, and I'm pretty sure that was the only way it could have happened. Maybe Allison didn't know the guy was planning to kill me. Maybe they told her he was just going to rough me up or something. I don't know."

"Who did she owe money to?" Collins asked.

"Guy named Tanner. He's a loan shark. He also runs a business called Dena Jo's Old Fashioned Ice Cream. It was where I bought the .38 that I killed the guy in Allison's room with."

"Tanner. I'll check him out."

"Also, I think I have the knife that was used to kill Darrell Renfro. I'm going to overnight it to you in a padded envelope. It belonged to one of the guys at the factory. Guy named Nefangar. I don't know if that's his real name. Get your forensics team to check it out."

Wahlman had disconnected then. He hadn't been able to think of anything else he needed to talk to Collins about. The results of the repeated DNA tests weren't especially important anymore. Not to Wahlman. He knew for sure now that the initial results had been correct, that he was an exact genetic replica of a man named Jack Reacher. *He was an officer in the army. Special Investigations. Served thirteen years. Apparently he was involved in some questionable activities after he got out.* Wahlman had been thinking about that, thinking he might like to learn more about Jack Reacher someday, maybe take the time to research some of those questionable activities—if anything had ever been written about them.

A rectangular green sign with reflective white letters said *CHATTANOOGA, 46 MILES*. Wahlman was hungry, and his leg was hurting. The surgeon had given him some pain pills, but they didn't help much. Mostly they just made him feel groggy, and he didn't like that. He needed to stay alert while he was traveling. He needed to be aware of his surroundings. His life depended on it.

He had a little over three thousand dollars in his pocket, but he knew it wouldn't last long. Maybe a month. Cheap hotels, diners, fast food joints. Bus tickets, train tickets, maybe thumbing it sometimes. His retirement check had been credited to his checking account on Tuesday, as scheduled, and he'd managed to close the account and withdraw the balance, but there was no way he could continue receiving the direct deposits every month. No way to do any sort of business that would leave a paper trail. No way to have a permanent address or an automobile.

No way to do anything except run.

And keep running.

Maybe forever.

And try to find out what Drake had meant by bigger than big.

MOVING TARGET

THE REACHER EXPERIMENT BOOK 2

1

The money ran out in Barstow.

Wahlman got off the bus at 10:37 a.m. He randomly chose a direction and started walking. Fifteen minutes later, he pushed his way through a swinging glass door and entered a place called The Quick Street Inn. It was a diner. It was on Main Street. So the name made no sense. It was eight blocks from the depot. Quite a little walk in the desert sun, even in January when the daytime temperatures usually maxed out at around sixty. There was a hardware store on one side of the diner and a pharmacy on the other. Storefronts with awnings and plate glass windows and welcome signs. Old-fashioned. Retro. Like a scene from an old movie. Like the days before strip malls and discount superstores. The electric vehicle charging ports mounted to the bottoms of some of the parking meters—and of course the cars themselves—were the only visual indications that it was 2098, and that Wahlman hadn't actually traveled back in time.

As you walked into the restaurant, there was a long counter on the left with a long row of chrome and vinyl stools in front of it. A guy was sitting on the fourth stool from the door. Collarless knit shirt, dark glasses. There was a cup of coffee on the counter in front of him, and a plate with a slice of apple pie on it. He was reading a newspaper. A coat had been draped over the stool to his right. Black leather. Long. Like a trench coat. Behind the counter a man wearing jeans and a t-shirt and a white apron was scraping down the flattop grill with a broad steel spatula, and a woman wearing a crisp blue-and-white-striped dress was rattling some ice cubes around in one of the glass coffeepots. Wahlman guessed the woman to be in her mid-thirties. Medium-length black hair, shiny and silky, pulled back from her face with plastic tortoise shell barrettes. She moved with a certain kind of poised confidence and balance. Like a dancer. Or a circus performer, maybe. Wahlman could see her in one of those skimpy little sequined bathing suits walking a tightrope or swinging from a trapeze.

Five booths lined the wall on the right, and then the room doglegged around the counter to an area with several freestanding tables. All of the tables were vacant, and only one of the booths was occupied, the one furthest from the entrance. Three guys were sitting there drinking coffee. One facing the front of the restaurant, and the other two with their backs to it. The guy facing the front of the restaurant was wearing a red ball cap. Pale skin, dark circles under his eyes. He was holding a short yellow pencil. The kind you use at a golf course. He was showing the other two guys something on the back of a paper placemat.

The restaurant looked safe enough for the moment. The

breakfast crowd was long gone, and it was still a little early for lunch. Wahlman's disguise had held up so far, the wraparound shades and the ball cap and the beard, but he still tried to avoid people as much as possible. He ate at odd hours and took buses to unusual locations and never stayed in one place for more than a few days.

He walked past the center point of the counter, set his backpack down on the waxed rubber tiles and sat on the tenth stool from the door, leaving five stools between him and the guy with the newspaper. Four stools between him and the leather trench coat. The woman in the crisp dress walked over and smilingly asked if he would like to see a menu. Her nametag said Kasey.

"Why the ice cubes?" Wahlman asked.

"Pardon me?"

"Why were you shaking ice around in that coffeepot?"

"I was cleaning it. You sprinkle some salt in there, and then you swirl the ice around, and it gets all the residue off the inside of the pot."

"Why not just wipe it out with a towel?"

"The ice and salt works better. You need a menu, or—"

"What can I get for two dollars?"

Kasey looked at her watch. "You can get the breakfast special if you order in the next thirty seconds," she said.

"What's the breakfast special?"

"Coffee, one egg, and a slice of toast, all for a buck fifty."

"I'll take it."

"Great."

Kasey hurriedly punched the order into the computer,

and then she asked Wahlman how he wanted his egg.

"Over easy," he said.

The guy with the newspaper grabbed his coat, got up and exited the restaurant. Abruptly. As if some sort of urgent situation had been brought to his attention. He left a five between his cup and his plate, the bill weighted down with a bottle of hot sauce.

"Such a waste," Kasey said, walking toward the spot where the man had been sitting. "Why order a piece of pie if you're not going to eat it?"

Wahlman was hungry. He wanted the pie. But he didn't want to look like some kind of bum. He sat there and watched Kasey scrape the untouched dessert into the trashcan.

She pocketed the five, walked back to where Wahlman was sitting and poured him a cup of coffee.

"Did you know that guy?" Wahlman asked.

"The guy who left the pie?"

"Yeah."

"Never saw him before."

"He left in kind of a hurry," Wahlman said. "Like maybe he was running late for something."

"I didn't really notice."

"Did he order anything other than the pie?"

"Just coffee."

"How many refills?"

"No refills. I offered a couple of times, but—"

"He paid for the pie and the coffee up front, right? The five dollar bill he left on the counter was a tip."

"Why are you so curious about that man?"

Wahlman was curious because the man had obviously walked into the diner just to kill some time. He'd been staring at a newspaper and waiting for eleven o'clock. Not one minute before. Not one minute after. Eleven. On the dot. Maybe he was supposed to meet someone at that time. But if that was the case, why not leave the diner a few minutes early? Why wait until the last second?

It was probably nothing. Wahlman knew that. But twenty years as a master at arms in the navy had taught him to notice unusual circumstances. Curiosity and suspicion had saved his life more than once.

"Why do they call this place The Quick Street Inn?" he asked, changing the subject.

Kasey shrugged. "I really don't know," she said. "That's just what it's always been called. I'll be back in a minute, okay?"

She grabbed a pot of coffee and carried it to the back booth. Refilled the three ceramic mugs in front of the three guys sitting there. Asked them if they needed anything else. They didn't. She carried the coffeepot back behind the counter and set it back on its burner. Poised. Confident. Balanced.

Wahlman's food was ready. He could see it on the section of stainless steel countertop beside the flattop. Kasey picked it up and brought it over and set it in front of him. One fried egg, one slice of toasted white bread.

And two strips of bacon.

"I didn't order any bacon," Wahlman said.

"I know. I thought you might like some. It was left over from the breakfast rush."

"Thanks."

Wahlman sprinkled some salt and pepper on his egg. He took a bite of the bacon and a sip of the coffee, and then he buttered his toast.

"One of the guys sitting over there wants to talk to you," Kasey said.

"Which one?" Wahlman asked, not bothering to turn and look toward the booth where the three men were sitting.

"The one in the red hat."

The one on the very back seat, Wahlman thought. The one facing the front of the restaurant. The one Wahlman had pegged as the boss of the little crew as soon as he'd walked into the diner.

When you see three guys hanging out together, one of them is usually the leader. Maybe not officially, but that's the way it usually works out. When you see three guys hanging out in a booth in a restaurant, the leader is usually going to be the one who gets a seat all to himself. The one with the highest rank, if they're in the military. These guys weren't, but same principle. And when you see three non-military guys in their mid-to-late twenties hanging out in a booth in a restaurant at eleven o'clock on a sunny Friday morning, you have to wonder what the three guys are up to.

Wahlman picked up his fork and cut into his egg.

"Did the one in the red hat happen to mention why he wants to talk to me?" he asked.

"No. He just told me to send you back there so he could have a word with you."

"Do you know those guys?"

"I don't know their names or anything, but they come in here all the time. Sit in the same booth, drink coffee for a couple of hours, hardly ever order anything to eat."

"Good tippers?"

Kasey laughed. "What do you think?"

"I think I'm going to finish my breakfast," Wahlman said.

Kasey poured some more coffee into his cup.

"So what brings you to Barstow?" she asked.

"How do you know I don't live here?"

"I saw the backpack. Just figured you were—"

"A lot of people carry backpacks," Wahlman said.

"Sorry. I didn't mean anything by it."

"Anyway, you're right. I don't live here. I'm looking for work. Any idea where I might be able to find some?"

"What kind of work do you do?"

Before Wahlman had a chance to answer, he felt a tap on his right shoulder. He set his fork down, turned and saw the man in the red hat standing there chewing on a toothpick. The other two guys were standing a few feet behind him.

"How's it going?" the man in the red hat asked.

"Great," Wahlman said.

He picked up his fork and turned back toward his food, hoping that the man in the red hat and the other two guys would mosey on out of the restaurant. They didn't.

"You're not very friendly, are you?" the man in the red hat said.

"Just trying to finish my breakfast."

The man in the red hat reached over and picked up the salt shaker. He screwed the top off and dumped the entire contents onto Wahlman's plate.

"There," he said. "Now you're finished."

Wahlman stared down at the ruined food. Half an egg, one strip of bacon, half a slice of toast. And the yolk. He'd been planning to sop it up with the remaining piece of bread.

Wahlman was six feet four inches tall, and he weighed two hundred and thirty pounds. Biceps the size of footballs, hands big enough to palm dinner plates. He'd received extensive training in several different fighting disciplines, but all of that invariably went out the window during actual confrontations. When another man was trying to hurt you—or kill you—there was only one technique that mattered: winning. He could have taken the man in the red hat with no problem. One quick pivot on the stool, one quick swing of an elbow. Instant pulverized nose. The other two guys would probably take off running at that point, at the sight of the eyes rolling back and the knees buckling and the blood gushing, but if they didn't, Wahlman could handle them as well. No problem.

But he didn't want to fight these guys. Not here. Not now. Kasey, or the guy back there cooking the food, would undoubtedly call the police, and Wahlman would undoubtedly be arrested and charged with assault and battery. Or manslaughter, if the elbow just happened to crack the nose just right. Wahlman didn't want to kill anyone, not even the punk in the red hat, and he certainly didn't want any trouble with the police. As far as he knew, a New Orleans homicide detective was still actively searching for him, in regard to the fatal shooting of a man and a woman in a hotel room, and he knew for sure that someone in the army was still actively searching for him, in regard to being born.

Best to just lean over and pick up his backpack and walk away.

Which was what he intended to do.

Until the man in the red hat reached into his pocket and pulled out a switchblade.

2

Wahlman swiveled around and stood up and faced the man in the red hat. The man with the knife. He still didn't want to fight. But if he did, and if the police came, at least it would be an obvious case of self-defense now. He probably wouldn't be arrested, unless he killed one or more of the guys. Which was always a possibility.

"You should go on home and drink a beer or something," Wahlman said.

"At least I have a home to go to."

"Is that what this is about?"

"We have enough dirt bags around here already," the man in the red hat said. "We don't need another one."

"So you're telling me I need to get out of town? Who are you, the sheriff? Aren't you going to give me until sundown, like they do in the movies?"

"You got a smart mouth."

The cook appeared from behind the counter then, holding a kitchen knife, the kind you use to chop things with. Onions and whatnot. The shiny stainless steel blade was fat by the handle, and it gradually narrowed to a point at the end. Nine or ten inches long, Wahlman guessed, and heavy enough to cut a watermelon in half with a single downward swing.

The cook was probably about forty-five years old. Black hair, graying at the temples, long, pulled back into a ponytail. He was taller than the man in the red hat, but not nearly as tall as Wahlman. Probably around six feet. Earrings in both ears, acne scars, faded tattoos on both arms.

"I don't want any trouble in here," he said.

"We were just leaving," the man in the red hat said.

He folded the switchblade and slid it into his pocket, turned and headed toward the exit. The other two guys followed.

"Wait a minute," Wahlman said. "You still owe me for the breakfast."

"That's right," the cook said. "You need to pay him for the food you ruined."

The man in the red hat turned around and walked back to where Wahlman was standing.

"How much do you figure I owe you?" he asked.

"Ten bucks should cover it."

"Ten bucks? There was hardly anything on the plate."

"It's past eleven now. I can't get the special anymore. Bacon, eggs, toast. Maybe throw in a glass of juice for the emotional stress I endured. And of course I'll want to leave a nice tip."

The man in the red hat took a deep breath, exhaled incredulously from the side of his mouth. He had a black leather wallet in his back pocket with a chain on it that hooked onto one of his belt loops. He fished out a five and five ones, but instead of handing the bills over nicely, he threw them down on the floor near Wahlman's backpack.

"Don't let me catch you out on the street," the man in the red hat said. "Things might not work out so well for you next time."

"Just make sure you bring more money," Wahlman said.

"And why is that?"

"Boots. I'll need a new pair after I ram one of these up your ass."

The man in the red hat pulled the toothpick out of his mouth and flicked it toward the pile of money. Then he turned around and left the restaurant without saying another word.

"Thanks for not taking those boneheads apart in here," the cook said. "Whatever you want to eat is on the house."

"Tell you the truth, I don't have much of an appetite anymore," Wahlman said. "But thanks."

"Come on back later today. Lunch, dinner, whatever you want. It's on me."

Wahlman picked the money up and stuffed it into his pocket.

"You own this place?" he asked.

"Bought it two years ago. Just now starting to turn a profit."

"Why is it called The Quick Street Inn?"

"I don't know. That was the name of the place when I bought it. I'm not from here, and none of the locals seem to remember it ever being called anything else."

"Ever think about changing the name?"

"Not really. People like what's familiar. Plus I would have to pay for a new sign."

Wahlman nodded. "I appreciate the offer for a free meal," he said. "But what I really need is a job."

"I don't have any openings right now. What kind of job are you looking for?"

"The temporary kind. Cash daily. No paperwork."

"I'll check around. If you want to come back later this afternoon, I might have something for you."

"Okay. I'll do that. Thank you."

"What's your name?"

"Tom," Wahlman lied.

"I'm Greg. Come on back around four or five."

Wahlman lifted his backpack, slid it onto his shoulder and exited the diner.

There was a park bench on the sidewalk outside the pharmacy. The man in the red hat and his two friends were sitting on it. Each of them had a cigarette going. Wahlman decided to walk the other way. He made it past the hardware store, and the barber shop, and then he heard footsteps coming up from behind him at a trot. He looked over his shoulder and saw a crisp blue-and-white-striped dress heading his way. Kasey. He wondered what she was doing. Then he remembered that he never had paid her for the breakfast special.

He stopped and waited for her to catch up.

"Sorry," he said, reaching into his pocket and pulling out

his wallet, intending to give her the original two dollars he'd come to town with.

"Don't worry," Kasey said. "Greg took care of it."

"Oh. I thought—"

"You thought I was chasing you down to pay your tab?"

"Yeah. So why are you chasing me down?"

"I remembered something after you left. I know a guy who's involved in a research study. I mean, we're not great friends or anything, but he comes in the restaurant sometimes."

"What kind of research study?" Wahlman asked.

"You can make two hundred dollars a night just for sleeping. That's what he told me, anyway."

"Two hundred dollars a night just for sleeping," Wahlman repeated. "Are they testing a new drug or something?"

"I don't really know all the details, but I can give you the guy's number if you want to talk to him."

"I don't know. There must be some kind of catch. Why aren't you doing it?"

"Because I'm divorced and I have a kid at home and—"

"Sorry," Wahlman said. "I didn't mean to be nosy."

"Anyway, it wouldn't hurt to talk to the guy."

Kasey reached into her purse and pulled out a business card. She looked it over, front and back, and then she handed it to Wahlman.

Dr. William Surrey
Department of Psychology
D.U. Coffee University, Barstow, CA

There was a phone number printed on the bottom of the card, along with Dr. Surrey's office hours.

"Do they have a football team?" Wahlman asked.

"It's just a small liberal arts college, so—"

"If they had a football team, they could call them The Tables. The Coffee Tables. Go Tables!"

"Shut up," Kasey said, Laughing. "Dr. Surrey wrote his cell number on the back."

Wahlman flipped the card over. "Are you sure this wasn't about something else?" he asked.

"What do you mean?"

"Maybe he wants to go out with you."

"I don't think so," Kasey said. "He's older. In his sixties, probably."

"That doesn't mean anything."

"It does to me. Anyway, he didn't act like he was hitting on me or anything. Are you going to call him?"

"Maybe. I want to talk to Greg later, see if he comes up with anything."

"Okay. Well, if you do call Dr. Surrey, tell him Kasey at the diner sent you. He said he would give me ten dollars for every referral. You know, for the ones who actually sign up to participate in the study."

"If I call him, I'll tell him you sent me," Wahlman said.

"Great. I hope it works out for you."

Kasey folded her arms over her chest. The wind had picked up, and she wasn't wearing a coat.

"Shouldn't you be getting back to work?" Wahlman asked.

"I was just scheduled for the breakfast shift today," Kasey said. "You were my last customer."

"Oh. You want my jacket? You look cold."

"I have one in my car. But thanks. I guess I better get going."

"Is there a public library around here anywhere?" Wahlman asked.

"Take a right at the light. The library's four blocks down on the left."

"Okay. Thanks."

Kasey lowered her head into the cold breeze and headed back toward the restaurant. There was something heartbreakingly sad about watching her walk away, something Wahlman couldn't quite put his finger on. Maybe he would see her again at the restaurant, he thought. Maybe not. He needed to keep moving. He couldn't stay in Barstow for more than a few days. As soon as he made enough money for another bus ticket, he would have to leave. And if he didn't make enough money for another bus ticket, he would have to leave anyway. He would have to walk. Or hitchhike. Destination unknown, and not particularly important. As long as it was somewhere else.

He gazed down the sidewalk and wished things could be different.

He was about to step off the curb and cross the street when Kasey stopped in front of the barber shop and turned around.

"I could give you a ride," she shouted.

"You could?"

"Sure. Come on. My car's parked behind the diner."

3

Annex Two Support Team Manager, All-Source Intelligence Division 1030B.

That was Major Stielson's official title.

His unofficial title was *Colonel Dorland's Stooge.*

He didn't much care for being Colonel Dorland's Stooge, but there was nothing he could do about it. He was stuck out here in the Mojave Desert for seventeen more months—unless he failed to carry out the unofficial duties that Colonel Dorland had assigned to him, in which case he would probably be stuck out here for the rest of his life, however brief a period that turned out to be.

The duties surrounding his official title aside, Major Stielson currently had exactly one job: kill Rock Wahlman.

Which sounded easy enough, but had turned into a logistical nightmare over the past few months.

Stielson didn't know exactly why Wahlman had been targeted, just that he had. A matter of national security, Colonel Dorland had said. No specific details. Which was somewhat annoying, but that was just the way it worked sometimes.

Orders were orders. You either followed them, or you risked being court-martialed and sent to Leavenworth. Or worse, where Colonel Dorland was concerned.

The original plan should have worked. Wahlman should have been eliminated in New Orleans, along with the other target, a long-haul trucker named Darrell Renfro.

Remarkably, Wahlman had managed to escape, and even more remarkably, he had managed to leave the team of assassins, the team that Major Stielson had unofficially commissioned with unofficial funds, shot to death in a variety of locations.

Renfro was dead, but his body had been recovered, which was never supposed to have happened. If Renfro had simply disappeared from the face of the earth, then Wahlman never would have been curious about why the two of them looked almost exactly alike, and a New Orleans homicide detective named Collins never would have sent blood specimens that eventually confirmed a genetic connection.

In essence, the fact that Darrell Renfro's body had been recovered was the main reason Major Stielson presently found himself in such a predicament. Of course it wasn't his fault that the body had been found. The assassins had been careless. They'd failed to follow his precise instructions, leaving him holding the overstuffed, flimsy-bottomed bag. Idiots. At least they were all dead now. If one or more of them had been captured by the police, Stielson probably wouldn't be breathing right now, and he definitely wouldn't be parked outside an abandoned filling station waiting to meet with their potential replacement.

Not a team this time.

Just one guy.

But he was supposed to be the best. A bona fide hit man with over one hundred successfully completed assignments to his credit.

They called him Mr. Tyler.

He didn't come cheap, that was for sure. But according to one of Stielson's most trusted sources, he was worth every penny. There were some things you just didn't skimp on, the source had said, and hiring a man to kill another man was one of those things.

Stielson certainly couldn't argue with that. Not after his experience with the first people he'd hired. He supposed the old saying, that you get what you pay for, was true most of the time, although it had taken quite a bit of effort to convince Colonel Dorland to let go of the additional funds. If things weren't taken care of this time, the current sling Stielson's ass was in would seem like biscuits and gravy compared to what would come next. Another old saying— that failure was not an option—was true in a way that couldn't be stressed strongly enough.

As the digital clock on Major Stielson's dashboard changed from 11:29 to 11:30, a car skidded up beside him. The driver side door swung open and a man climbed out. Average height, average weight, dark glasses, thick wavy hair the color of the desert sand. He was wearing a black leather coat. Long. Like a trench coat. He opened Stielson's front passenger side door and slid into the seat.

"Are you Mr. Tyler?" Stielson asked.

"Who else would I be?"

Stielson's heart did a little flip-flop in his chest. Mr. Tyler's voice was deep and flat, and there was something about him that made Stielson immediately uncomfortable. Like being out in the middle of a lake in a leaky rowboat with dark swollen thunderheads approaching. Exactly like that. An overwhelming urge to be somewhere else as quickly as possible.

"I had to ask," Stielson said. "There's always a chance that—"

"I checked my account on the way out here," Mr. Tyler said. "There hasn't been a deposit."

"It should go through sometime early this afternoon."

"Should?"

"It will."

"Tell me about the job."

Stielson handed him a nine-by-twelve envelope.

"Everything you need to know is in there," he said.

"Photographs?"

"Of course."

"What's the target's name?"

"Everything you need to know is in the—"

"What's the target's name?"

"Rock Wahlman. Although he's probably using aliases."

"Why would he do that?"

"He closed his bank accounts and abandoned his home in Florida about three months ago," Stielson said. "We haven't been able to establish his whereabouts since then."

"You don't know where he is?"

"No. He could be anywhere, although we're pretty sure he hasn't left the country."

Mr. Tyler laughed. "Do I look like a bloodhound?"

"I thought—"

"You thought wrong. I have other jobs. I don't have time for this."

"What if I offered to increase your payment?" Stielson asked.

"I'm listening."

"You tell me. How much would it take?"

"Ten."

"Ten million dollars?"

"That's my price. I'll stay on it for as long as it takes. Satisfaction guaranteed."

Ten million. Dorland was going to blow a gasket.

"I don't have the authorization to go that high," Stielson said.

"Are you interested in my services or not?"

"I am, but—"

"Then get the authorization."

Stielson reached into his pocket and pulled out his cell phone. He punched in Colonel Dorland's unofficial private number, the one that only a handful of people knew about, a line secured with scrambling software for voice and encrypting software for text, a device to be accessed only during otherwise unsolvable situations surrounding unofficial clandestine activities.

The connection went through.

One ring, and then Stielson heard a squeaky little thud to his right. A bright squeal and a hammering throb. Two distinctly different sounds, but in unison. As if a sneaker had stopped hard on a basketball court as the ball simultaneously got slammed against the backboard. The unusual noise was followed by a pinch somewhere deep in his gut, followed by the realization that he was bleeding profusely.

He glanced to his right and saw the sound-suppressed semi-automatic pistol.

Mr. Tyler reached over and gently removed the phone from his hand.

"I always prefer to deal directly with the person in charge," Mr. Tyler said.

A second or two later, Stielson felt the barrel of the pistol being pressed against the side of his face. It was still warm from being fired.

He thought about the first time he'd held a girl's hand. It was at the roller rink, the summer between sixth and seventh grade. He'd looked for her that next Saturday. And the next. He never saw her again. He wondered what had happened to her.

Then he heard the squeaky little thud again.

4

Kasey steered into the parking lot, pulled around to the front entrance and stopped at the curb.

"It's not a very big library," she said.

"That's okay," Wahlman said. "I just want to use one of the computers for a while."

"Let me guess. You're going to look Dr. Surrey up and make sure he's not some kind of mad scientist."

Wahlman laughed. "That's not what I had in mind, but it's not a bad idea. You'd have to trust someone quite a bit for something like that."

"Something like what?"

"Watching you sleep. Especially if there's some kind of drug involved."

"I don't think there is. It's the psych department. They probably just hook some wires up to your head or something."

"That's comforting."

"It's two hundred dollars a night," Kasey said. "Just for sleeping. I would do it in a heartbeat if I could."

"I'm thinking about it," Wahlman said.

"Are you going to call him?"

"Probably."

"Don't forget to tell him I sent you."

"I won't."

"And let me know how it goes."

"How can I do that?"

"You can call me."

Kasey started digging around in her center console. Wahlman figured she was looking for a pen.

"You don't have to write it down," he said. "Just tell me. I have a good memory."

She told him the number.

"You can call me even if you don't participate in the study," she said. "You know, if you just want to hang out for a while or something."

"You're very nice," Wahlman said.

"Not everyone in Barstow is like those three guys at the diner."

"Good to know."

"Call me."

"I will."

Wahlman climbed out of the car and walked into the library. He stopped at the circulation desk and got a guest pass, and then he sat down at one of the desktop computers and logged on to the internet. He'd been trying to gather some information on a former army officer named Jack Reacher—who probably wasn't the actual reason he'd been targeted, but whose history might provide some clues as to why, and some clues as to who exactly might have ordered the hit.

That was what he was hoping for, anyway.

Someone was out to get him. That was for sure. Someone in the army, supposedly. Probably not just one person. Probably a rogue outfit led by a rogue colonel or general. That was his guess, and he figured that exposing the culprits and blowing the whole thing wide open in the media would be his best chance of putting a stop to it.

But first he had to find out who the culprits were, and why they were trying to kill him. He couldn't just call one of the major newspapers and tell them that some people in the army were trying to kill him. They probably got dozens of calls like that every day. The more persistent callers probably ended up in nice restful rooms somewhere. He couldn't go to the police, because of the arrest warrant in Louisiana. If he went to the police, a different kind of room would be waiting for him. One with bars.

So he needed information.

Which, so far, had been hard to come by.

According to one of the assassins who'd tried to kill him three months ago, his entire life had been a lie. His parents hadn't died in a car accident when he was two, as he'd always been led to believe. Instead, he had been produced using a vial of cells taken during a routine hospital blood draw way back in 1983.

According to the assassin, Wahlman was an exact genetic duplicate of this Jack Reacher fellow. A clone. Grown in a laboratory for a few days, and then implanted into a surrogate mother for the gestation period.

Supposedly, a total of eighty fetuses were produced, from a variety of unwitting donors, and only two survived—both grown from cells that had been harvested over a hundred years ago.

Both grown from cells that had been harvested from Jack Reacher.

It was an outrageous claim, and Wahlman might have dismissed it as such if not for a DNA test performed by the New Orleans Police Department. The NOPD detective who ordered the test had assumed that the lab had made an error, but Wahlman knew better. He'd seen the other surviving clone, a man named Darrell Renfro—had watched him die, in fact—and a few weeks ago he'd finally found a picture of Jack Reacher online.

Physically, Wahlman, Renfro, and Reacher were nearly identical. Same hair color, same eyes, same facial features. Same extreme musculature. Reacher was listed as being six feet five inches tall, and Wahlman was only six-four, but environmental factors could have accounted for the difference. Wahlman had smoked cigarettes for a while when he was a teenager. Maybe they had stunted his growth.

He smiled. It amused him that anyone might think of six-four as being stunted.

Through previous searches, he'd learned that Reacher had once been assigned to an elite military police outfit called the 110th Special Investigations Unit. The unit no longer existed, and some of their files had been declassified over the years.

Thousands of them, actually.

More pages than one person could read in a lifetime.

Wahlman had started skimming through the documents a couple of weeks ago in Tucson, Arizona, which was the last place he'd taken the time to visit a library. He looked around now to make sure nobody was watching him, and then he accessed a search engine and found the appropriate website and went back to where he'd left off.

Most of the cases he'd read about in Tucson were routine, and none of them had been relevant to his current situation. Which was to be expected, on both counts. Wahlman knew enough about military life and law enforcement to know that there were thousands of hours of thumb-twiddling boredom for every minute of pulse-pounding excitement, and he knew that finding a connection between the army of Reacher's day and the army of 2098 was going to be like finding a needle in a haystack.

Still, he felt like he needed to keep trying. He felt like it was his only chance of getting out of this thing alive.

He clicked on a file.

United States Army Court Martial 18793-15B. National Archives, War Department, Office of the Judge Advocate General. This case was tried in Rock Creek, Virginia, with Colonel Harrison Lee Whitmore presiding. Primary investigator: Major Jack (none) Reacher.

A non-commissioned officer had been suspected of smuggling automatic weapons from one Central American country to another. The non-com, whose name had been blacked out in the public version of the file, was being tried on a variety of charges, the most severe of which was treason against the United States of America.

Wahlman read through the file. The proceedings did not go well for the non-com. Not well at all.

Major Reacher had been a good detective, Wahlman thought.

Better than good.

Great.

Maybe one of the best of his day.

Solid groundwork, exceptional deductive skills, ducks in a row on the day of the court martial.

Reacher had been a great detective, and he had been a great soldier. Highly decorated, including the Silver Star Medal for valor in combat.

Wahlman started thinking about his own military career. Maybe it wasn't a coincidence that he had chosen law enforcement. Maybe he had inherited some of Reacher's aptitude for that kind of work. He'd been enlisted, of course, whereas Reacher had been an officer, but still. Cops are cops, and it appeared that Reacher had done his share of work out in the field. He didn't seem like the kind of guy who would be happy sitting behind a desk all day, dealing with the bullshit those kinds of guys had to deal with. He seemed like the kind of guy who liked to get his hands dirty. Which was something Wahlman could appreciate, because he was the same way.

He clicked back to the homepage of the website, scrolled down and found another document with Reacher's name on it, but before he had a chance to open the file, a woman who smelled like cinnamon walked up behind him and reminded him that there was a waiting list and that his time was about to expire. He exited the internet and cleared the browsing history and dropped his guest pass back at the circulation desk.

He browsed the stacks for a while, and then he decided to call the number on the business card Kasey had given him.

Dr. William Surrey

Department of Psychology

D.U. Coffee University, Barstow, CA

He wasn't crazy about the idea of someone watching him sleep, but he also wasn't crazy about the idea of spending the night on a bench or under a bridge. Especially with temperatures forecasted to dip into the thirties. He was still planning on talking to Greg at the diner later, but maybe this research thing would be okay for a night or two.

Wahlman didn't own a cell phone. They were too easy to hack, too easy to track, and the taxes on usage had gotten out of hand back when he was a kid. In his current situation, one of those things would have been nothing but a boatload of potential trouble. He didn't want one, even if he could have afforded one.

And a lot of people felt the same way. Payphones had made a comeback. They were almost as ubiquitous in 2098 as they were in 1958. There was one just outside the front entrance of the library. Wahlman had noticed it on his way in. He walked out there and fed some coins into it and dialed Dr. Surrey's office number.

One ring.

Two.

Wahlman smelled cinnamon again. A group of young ladies had set up a folding table and some folding chairs on the side of the library entrance opposite the payphone. There was a large poster board taped to the front of the table. Apparently the young ladies were band members from one of the local high schools. They were having a bake sale to help pay for new uniforms. The woman who'd reminded Wahlman about the waiting list must have bought a cookie or something.

After eight rings, a robot voice announced that Dr. Surrey was currently out of his office and to please leave a message after the beep. Wahlman hung up and tried the cell phone number written on the back of the card.

One ring.

Two.

"Hello?"

"Is this Dr. William Surrey?"

"Yes. May I ask who's calling, please?"

"My name's Tom. I'm interested in participating in your research study."

"Which one?"

"There's more than one?"

"We have one we're doing right now, and two more we're starting next month."

"I'm interested in the one you're doing right now," Wahlman said. "The sleep thing."

"Are you a student?"

"No."

"What kind of work do you do?"

"I'm retired," Wahlman said.

He heard some papers shuffling. Dr. Surrey checking to see if there were any available slots, he supposed.

The girls sitting at the bake sale table looked bored.

"We had a cancellation for tonight," Dr. Surrey said. "So if you're available, we could certainly use you."

"Are there any drugs involved?"

"No. In fact, if you normally take any sort of medicine to help you sleep—"

"I don't," Wahlman said.

"Good. We'll need you on campus no later than ten tonight. Social Sciences building, third floor. You'll be meeting with Belinda. She's one of the graduate students working on the study with me."

"I'll be there," Wahlman said.

"Great. I'll tell Belinda to be expecting you."

"Thank you. By the way, a waitress over at The Quick Street Inn gave me your card. Her name's Kasey. She said that you'd offered her a referral fee."

"I know who you're talking about," Dr. Surrey said. "I'll take care of her."

"Thanks."

Wahlman hung the receiver back onto its hook and walked over to the bake sale table. He bought a brownie. The girls didn't say much. They still looked bored. There was a convenience store across the street from the library. Wahlman trotted over there and bought a cup of coffee, and then he started making his way back toward Main Street.

5

The talk with Colonel Dorland had gone well.

Mr. Tyler slid his key card into the slot and opened the door to his hotel room. He planned to drive his rental car back to L.A. in the morning. From there, he planned to fly to Florida and begin his search.

Ten million dollars, half of which had already been transferred to his account. Dorland had also agreed to pay for his expenses. Which was nice. Like a bonus. Mr. Tyler planned to pass the other two jobs he had lined up on to some B-list assassins who needed the work. He figured he could spend up to a year on this Wahlman thing and still come out way ahead.

He tossed Major Stielson's cell phone and the nine-by-twelve brown envelope on the bed.

Colonel Dorland hadn't seemed particularly grief stricken over Stielson's untimely demise. Mr. Tyler got the sense that Stielson's days had been numbered anyway. Which meant that Mr. Tyler had sort of done Colonel Dorland a favor. A freebie, as it turned out. Maybe that was why Dorland hadn't tried to haggle over the price for the Wahlman job. He'd gotten the two for one special.

Mr. Tyler took his coat off, walked to the bathroom and splashed some cold water on his face. He patted himself dry with a towel, and then he went back to the bed and picked up the envelope and carried it over to the cheap little wooden desk in the corner. He switched on the cheap little lamp and sat down in the cheap little chair and opened the envelope.

There were four eight-by-ten photographs of Rock Wahlman, each taken from a different angle.

Mr. Tyler wondered why this man looked so familiar.

And then it hit him.

He used Stielson's special cell phone to call Colonel Dorland's special number.

"I saw Wahlman," he said. "This morning. Downtown. At a diner called The Quick Street Inn."

"You're kidding," Colonel Dorland said. "Are you sure it was him?"

"I do this for a living. Remember?"

"Okay, but—"

"It was him. He might have caught a train or a bus by now, or he might have hitchhiked to Vegas. Who knows? But maybe he's still here."

"So what's the plan?"

"I booked a flight to Jacksonville a while ago. I'm going to cancel it. I'm going to stay here for another day or two and see if I can close this thing out for you."

"Don't forget I'm going to need proof," Colonel

Dorland said. "Blood and tissue samples for DNA analysis. And then—"

"I know," Mr. Tyler said. "And then you need for the body to disappear. I'm a professional. You only have to tell me things once. Understand?"

"Listen, I'm paying you a lot of money, and I really don't appreciate—"

"You're going to get what you paid for," Mr. Tyler said. And then he hung up.

6

Wahlman walked around town for a while, making mental notes of the street names and the stores and the bus stops. He made it back to the diner a little after five. Greg was sitting at the counter eating a hamburger. Otherwise, the place was empty.

Greg turned toward the door as Wahlman walked in.

"Hello, Tom," he said.

"Hey. How's it going?"

"Just taking a little break. Can I get you something?"

"Maybe just a cup of coffee."

Greg got up and walked behind the counter and poured some coffee into a cup. He set the cup on the counter, along with some sugar in a glass-and-chrome shaker and some cream in a miniature stainless steel pitcher, and then he returned to the stool where he'd been eating.

Wahlman set his backpack down and saddled into the stool where Greg had left the coffee.

"I made a couple of calls," Greg said. "I know a guy who's trying to restore an old railroad caboose, and he could use some help with scraping and sanding. It's dirty work, but it pays twenty an hour and you won't have to fill out any paperwork or anything."

"Sounds good," Wahlman said.

"The only thing is, he needs someone who can stick around until the job is finished. The last guy he hired cut out without any notice. Took a few of my friend's tools with him, too."

"How long does he figure the job will last?"

"A month or so. Apparently the old caboose is in pretty rough shape."

Wahlman took a sip of the coffee, which was also in pretty rough shape. Probably left over from lunch, he thought. He stirred some cream into it.

"I can't stay here a month," he said. "But I could work double shifts, maybe finish up in a few days."

"I'll see what he thinks."

"Tell him I work way faster than that other guy."

Greg laughed. "Okay, I'll tell him. Sure you don't want something to eat?"

"I'm all right. I had a brownie a while ago."

"Well, let me know if you need anything."

Greg turned back to his hamburger. Wahlman took another sip of coffee, which was slightly more tolerable now that it had been heavily diluted with cream.

Wahlman knew something about scraping and sanding. He'd been temporarily assigned to a corrosion control detail soon after he joined the navy. Right after boot camp, a few weeks before entering the Master at Arms training program that the recruiter had promised him. It was sweaty and dirty and boring. You had to wear goggles and a respirator and long sleeves and gloves, and a week after you were done with it all, everything you ate still tasted like rusted steel and paint chips.

Never again, he'd told himself at the time. But of course there was no way he could have anticipated his current situation. Twelve dollars to his name, on the run from some people who didn't want him to exist. Some people with great resources and great determination. Some people who, for whatever reason, would do whatever it took to get rid of him.

"Is there a payphone in here?" he asked.

"In the back," Greg said. "By the restrooms."

"How much for the coffee?"

"Don't worry about it."

"Thanks."

Wahlman walked to the back of the diner and called Kasey.

"I just wanted to let you know that I decided to participate in the sleep study," he said. "I told Dr. Surrey about the referral. He said he would take care of you."

"Great. When are you going to do it?"

"Tonight. I'm supposed to be there by ten."

"Let me know how it goes."

"I will."

"So what are you doing until ten?" Kasey asked.

"Just hanging out, I guess. I'm at the diner right now. Maybe Greg can give me directions to the college."

"It's about ten miles from there," Kasey said. "Too far to walk."

"I can catch a bus," Wahlman said.

"Or you could come over to my house for dinner, and then I could drive you over to the campus later."

"That would be great. Why are you being so nice to me?"

"Maybe I'm just a nice person," Kasey said. "Or maybe I have ulterior motives."

"What kind of ulterior motives?"

"You'll have to come over for dinner to find out."

"I'm really curious now. How can I say no?"

"Good. I'll pick you up in a few minutes."

Wahlman hung the phone up and walked back to the counter. A waitress he hadn't seen before was over by the drink station rolling silverware into paper napkins. Greg was gone. Probably in the back room, Wahlman thought. Doing prep work or whatever.

The waitress looked up from the pile of knives and forks and spoons she was working on.

"Can I help you?" she asked.

"When you see Greg, tell him I'll check with him tomorrow about the job."

"What's your name?"

"Tom."

"Okay. I'll tell him."

Wahlman exited the diner and sat on the bench outside the pharmacy, the one the man in the red hat and his friends had been sitting on earlier. There was an empty cigarette package on the sidewalk. He noticed the brand name. It was the same kind he'd smoked when he was a teenager.

7

Mr. Tyler walked into the diner. A few early birds were there for dinner already. A man and a woman were sitting across from each other at one of the booths. Older. Probably retired. Probably married for decades. How could they not be sick of each other after all that time together? It was something that Mr. Tyler had often wondered about, how two people could meet each other at a young age and then spend the rest of their lives together. It was something totally foreign to him. Beyond the realm of his personal experience, and beyond the scope of his understanding.

A much younger man and a much younger woman and a baby in a highchair were at one of the freestanding tables around the bend. Just starting out, their whole lives ahead of them.

Astoundingly, the older couple actually seemed happier than the younger couple. They were talking and laughing about something, whereas the younger couple just sat there staring at their menus. Interesting.

Mr. Tyler took his coat off. He draped it over a stool and

sat on the one next to it. Different stools than he'd used earlier. He was wearing different clothes this time, and he didn't have a newspaper with him, and he wasn't wearing his sunglasses.

A waitress walked over and asked him if he needed a menu. Her nametag said Marta. She was a few years younger than the one who'd been working earlier. But the one who'd been working earlier had been prettier, in Mr. Tyler's opinion. He couldn't remember her name. Something that started with a K, he thought.

"Just coffee," he said.

"Cream and sugar?"

"No. Just black."

She brought the coffee.

He handed her a ten dollar bill.

She brought him his change.

"Let me know if you need anything else," she said.

He wanted to ask her if she'd seen a tall muscular guy carrying a backpack. But he didn't. Best to just hang around and wait to see if Wahlman showed up for dinner. It would probably be dark outside by then. Mr. Tyler could follow him out of the restaurant and drop him on the sidewalk. One quick shot to the back of the head. Then he could cut one of his ears off and put it in the zippered plastic storage bag that was currently in his coat pocket. For the DNA test. To make sure that the other five million got transferred to his account.

The baby was crying and the young couple looked miserable. Marta was over there taking their order. She wrote it all down, and then she walked over to the drink station and scooped some ice cubes into two humongous plastic tumblers. She filled the glasses with tea from a pitcher and dropped a lemon wedge into each one and a long skinny spoon. She delivered the drinks, and then the mother got up and lifted the baby out of the highchair and headed toward the restrooms.

The old man in the booth was working on a plate of meatloaf and mashed potatoes. The old woman sitting across from him must not have been very hungry. All she'd ordered was some soup.

Mr. Tyler sipped his coffee. It was good. Fresh. Flavorful. Marta walked over and poured some more into his cup.

"Is there a waitress working here whose name starts with a K?" he asked.

"Kasey?"

"Yes."

"She's off tonight."

Mr. Tyler remembered that Wahlman had spoken to her. A little more than just the usual back and forth between a customer and a food server. Something about the way she was cleaning a coffeepot. They'd seemed friendly toward each other. Maybe even a little flirtatious.

Kasey. Yes, that was it.

"Would you happen to know when she's working again?" Mr. Tyler asked.

8

Kasey's house wasn't far from the diner. She steered into the driveway, set the emergency brake, switched off the engine.

"What do you think?" she asked.

Stucco exterior, low roof, decorative gravel and cacti. Similar structures with similar landscaping lined both sides of the narrow street.

"Looks nice," Wahlman said.

"Thanks. Wait until you see the inside."

Wahlman climbed out of the car and followed her to the front door. She slid her key in and opened the deadbolt and stepped inside.

Wahlman wiped his boots on the welcome mat. They were dusty from all the walking he'd done earlier.

"Maybe I should take my shoes off," he said.

"You're fine. Come on in."

He went on in. Hardwood floors, low ceilings, textured walls painted white. The living room was sparsely furnished, just a couch and a coffee table and a television. There was a stone fireplace on one side of the room with a rustic wooden mantle. No pictures hanging on the walls, but there were some framed photographs on the mantle, along with some candles and a small trophy topped with a pair of shiny golden music notes.

"Nice place," Wahlman said.

"Thanks. I just moved in a few weeks ago. That's why there's not much furniture here yet or anything."

"I like it like this. I guess I'm a minimalist at heart."

Kasey glanced around. "Come to think of it, maybe I am too," she said. "Anyway, have a seat. I'll get us something to drink. Want a beer?"

"I have that research study thing tonight, so I better not. They might consider alcohol a sedative."

"You don't have to be there until ten, right? That's almost five hours from now. I don't think one beer is going to hurt anything."

"Okay. You talked me into it."

"Be right back."

Kasey walked into the kitchen. Wahlman took his jacket off and sat down on the couch.

It was nice being inside an actual house. Wahlman had abandoned his residence in Florida three months ago, and since then he'd been living in one cheap hotel room after another. He'd met some kind people along the way, but none as kind as Kasey.

She walked into the living room carrying two cans of beer. She handed one to Wahlman.

"Thanks," he said.

Kasey sat down on the couch. Middle cushion. Her right

leg was touching Wahlman's left leg. He liked that. He liked her beside him. It felt right.

"I thought we could order a pizza," she said. "If you want to. Or I could go to the store and get something to cook."

"Pizza's fine. Didn't you say you have kids?"

"I have a daughter. Ninth grade. She's over at a friend's house right now doing something for school. She's going to eat dinner over there."

Wahlman took a sip of beer. Amber lager. Good and cold.

He took another sip.

"So tell me about these ulterior motives," he said.

Kasey leaned in and rested her head against his shoulder. She didn't say anything. She didn't have to. Wahlman set his beer on the coffee table. Then he took Kasey's beer from her hand and set it next to his. He put his arm around her, leaned over and kissed her on the lips. It was a good first kiss. Soft, warm, and gentle. He started to tell her how nice it was, but before he could say anything, she pressed her hand against the back of his neck and opened her mouth pulled him in eagerly. It was a good second kiss. It went on and on. When it ended, Kasey moved in even closer, kissing Wahlman's neck just below his right ear. She was breathing very heavily. So was he. She started unbuttoning his shirt with her free hand. He wondered if it had been as long for her as it had for him.

"Want to see the rest of the house?" she asked.

"I would love to," he said.

"Let's start down at the end of the hall."

She led him to the end of the hall and showed him the

master bedroom. She showed him the antique dresser, and the full-length mirror, and the king size bed. Especially the bed. Every square inch of it.

Forty-five minutes later, he still hadn't seen the other bedrooms or the kitchen or the dining room.

"Is this what they call the grand tour?" he asked, collapsing back onto a pillow.

"Disappointed?"

"Not at all. I think it's a splendid house."

She kissed his chest. His heart was still pounding from the intensity of their lovemaking session. He wondered if she really had worked for the circus at one time.

"Want me to go ahead and order the pizza?" she asked.

"Sure. Mind if I take a shower?"

"I don't mind. There's a little closet in the bathroom, with towels and washcloths and all that. You need soap and shampoo?"

"I have some in my backpack."

"But your backpack's out in my car."

"Good point. So I guess I need soap and shampoo."

Wahlman took a nice long shower. Hot and steamy at first, cold and bracing at the end. He smelled like cocoa butter and kiwi fruit when he came out.

His backpack was at the foot of the bed. Kasey must have brought it inside while he was in the shower. He put some deodorant on and some clean clothes, and then he sat on the edge of the bed and wiped the tops of his boots off with a damp paper towel. Kasey walked into the bedroom as he was tying his laces.

"I hope you like pepperoni," she said.

"I hate pepperoni."

"What?"

"Kidding. I like everything. Anyway, I'm hungry enough to eat the box."

She walked over and sat on his lap and kissed him.

"I could get used to this," she said.

Wahlman thought about the sanding and scraping job. He could stretch it out for a month if he wanted to. It was what Greg's friend expected, and a month with Kasey sounded wonderful. Then, if everything was still going well, maybe he could find something else nearby.

Only he knew that wasn't going to happen. He couldn't let it happen. It was too risky. In a few days he would have to leave. He would have to start over with a different name in a different town, and he would never see Kasey again.

And it wouldn't be fair to pretend otherwise.

Not even for one night.

"I could get used to this too," he said. "But I'm afraid it's just not possible."

"You're in some kind of trouble, aren't you?"

"Why do you say that?"

"I heard you talking to Greg. The whole no-paperwork-cash-daily thing."

"Yeah. I'm in some kind of trouble."

Kasey climbed off of his lap.

"I'm not going to bug you about it," she said. "I don't even want to know. Unless you want to tell me."

"I can't," Wahlman said.

The doorbell rang.

"That must be the pizza," Kasey said.

She took a step backward and looked Wahlman directly in the eyes, and then she turned around and exited the bedroom. Poised. Confident. Balanced.

Wahlman zipped up his backpack and slung it over his shoulder.

It was going to be hard to say goodbye.

9

After numerous refills on his coffee, and several trips to the restroom, Mr. Tyler had decided that Wahlman probably wasn't going to show up for dinner at The Quick Street Inn. It was almost nine o'clock, and there weren't any other customers in the restaurant, and the waitress named Marta had been sent home, and the pedestrian and vehicular traffic on Main Street had gone from what you might call bustling to what you might call sparse. For the past forty-five minutes, the guy in the apron, the one who cooked the food, had been tending to the counter, and he didn't seem very pleased that Mr. Tyler had been sitting around drinking coffee for hours without ordering something to eat. Maybe he owned the place, Mr. Tyler thought. That must be it. Otherwise, why would he care?

The guy in the apron carried one of the glass coffeepots over to where Mr. Tyler was sitting.

"More?" the guy in the apron asked.

Rudely.

Aggravatedly.

"I'm fine," Mr. Tyler said. "I need to get going. What time do you close?"

"Ten. And I lock up early sometimes if the place is dead."

"Well, I certainly wouldn't want to keep you. I was hoping to see Kasey tonight. I guess she was off, huh?"

"Yeah. She a friend of yours?"

"A potential client, actually. I seem to have misplaced the referral card I had on her, and I was trying to remember her last name so I could look her up and give her a call."

"What kind of business are you in?" the guy in the apron asked.

"Insurance," Mr. Tyler said.

Which was a lie, of course, but one that Mr. Tyler could have backed up with several forms of identification if he'd been challenged.

"If you want to leave a business card, I'll be sure she gets it," the guy in the apron said.

"Couldn't you just tell me her last name?"

"Sorry. It's a security issue. Not that I don't trust you, but—"

"I understand," Mr. Tyler said. "You can't be too careful these days."

The guy in the apron nodded. He seemed annoyed. He obviously wanted to finish up and close the place so he could go home.

He set the coffeepot back on its burner.

"So you want to leave a number where she can reach you, or what?" he asked.

Rudely.

Aggravatedly.

Mr. Tyler reached for his coat. A special pocket had been sewn into the lining to accommodate his semi-automatic pistol and the sound suppressor attached to the barrel. He thought about pulling the gun out and drilling a nice fat 9mm hole into the guy in the apron's forehead.

But he didn't.

He hadn't risen to his current status by being impatient.

"I just remembered where I left that referral card," he said. "I'll give her a call tomorrow. Have a great night."

"Thanks," the man in the apron said. "You too."

Mr. Tyler put his coat on and exited the restaurant. As he was leaving, three guys walked inside. One of them was wearing a red hat. Mr. Tyler guessed the guy in the apron wouldn't be able to close early after all.

Which meant that there was still a chance that Wahlman might stop in for a bite to eat.

Mr. Tyler had parked his car in the lot behind the restaurant, but there were plenty of open spots along the curb now. He drove around the block and parked directly across the street from the pharmacy, giving him a nice view of the entrance to the diner.

He found a radio station that played the kind of soft and soothing music he liked, and then he killed the engine and sat there and waited.

10

Kasey was angry.

But not at Wahlman.

After dinner, she'd called the friend's house that her daughter was supposed to be doing something for school at, only her daughter wasn't there. According to the friend's mother, the girls had gone out for ice cream and should be back any minute.

"Where do they usually go for ice cream?" Wahlman asked.

"There's a place right up on the corner of Main," Kasey said. "It's only a couple of blocks away. But that's not the point. When she left here to go work on her project, I specifically told her to call me if she was going to go anywhere else. I tell her that every time she leaves the house. She's supposed to ask permission. I've told her that about a million times. She's fourteen, you know? I need to know exactly where she is twenty-four-seven."

"I could go for a caramel sundae," Wahlman said. "Want to ride up there?"

Kasey raked her fingers through her hair. "I do, but—"

"You don't want her to see me?"

"I would rather avoid it if possible. She knows I go out with guys sometimes, but I don't usually do the whole introduction thing unless it's someone who might be around for a while. Does that make sense?"

"Sure," Wahlman said. "I understand completely. I probably still have time to catch a bus out to the campus. You go ahead and take care of your family matters."

"I'm sorry."

"It's no problem. Really. Are you working tomorrow?"

"Breakfast shift again. I have to be there at six."

"I'll probably stop in for a cup of coffee."

Kasey's cell phone trilled. She looked at the caller ID, and a puzzled expression washed across her face.

"I'm going to take this back in the bedroom," she said.

"Want me to leave?" Wahlman asked.

"No. Don't leave. I'll be right back."

Wahlman sat on the couch and waited. About thirty seconds later, Kasey came running back into the living room. She was frantic. She grabbed her jacket and her purse and bolted out the front door.

Wahlman followed.

"What's going on?" he asked.

"My ex was supposed to be at a meeting this evening," Kasey said. "He didn't show up. The last time this happened, he ended up going to San Diego for three days, and he took Natalie with him."

"Natalie's your daughter?"

"Yes."

"He kidnapped her?"

"I have full custody, so technically, yes, he kidnapped her. I dropped the charges, but he still got into trouble for being AWOL. Not as much as you might think, but—"

"He's in the military?"

"He's in the army. And he's an idiot. I have to find my daughter. Right now."

"I'm coming with you," Wahlman said.

"Okay."

Kasey's hands were shaking so badly she was barely able to open the zipper on her purse to get her car keys.

"Want me to drive?" Wahlman asked.

"Would you?"

"Sure."

Kasey handed him the keys. He clicked the doors locks open with the remote. Kasey ran around to the passenger side and climbed in while Wahlman slid in behind the wheel and adjusted the seat. He started the engine and backed out of the driveway and headed toward Main. When he got to the light, he could see that the police had pulled someone over down at the next block. Two cruisers, blue lights flashing. More than a routine stop. The driver who had been pulled over was sitting on the curb with his hands behind his back while one of the cops searched his car with a flashlight.

"The ice cream place is right over there," Kasey said, pointing toward the other side of Main.

Wahlman waited for the light to turn green, and then he crossed over and found a place to park on the street.

"Want me to wait here?" he asked.

"You can come in with me if you want to."

Wahlman climbed out of the car and followed Kasey into the ice cream place. There were two young girls sitting at a table by the window. One of them had long blond hair and the other had short brown hair. Wahlman figured they'd been sitting there watching the drama unfold down the street. He figured they'd probably lost track of time.

"Mom, what are you doing here?" the one with the short brown hair asked.

Natalie. Kasey's daughter. Wahlman could see the resemblance.

"Get up," Kasey said. "Let's go."

"But Mom—"

"Now! We'll talk about this at home."

Wahlman walked over and handed Kasey her car keys.

"I should be going," he said.

"Okay. Sorry about all this. It's just—"

"No need to apologize. I'll probably see you tomorrow."

As Wahlman was walking out the door, he heard Natalie say, "Who was that?"

He didn't pause to hear Kasey's explanation. He kept walking.

He needed to go east on Main, toward the flashing blue lights, but he didn't. He tried to avoid law enforcement as much as possible. He was a wanted man, after all, and he wasn't sure his fake ID would hold up under any sort of intense scrutiny. Not that the officers down there would have any reason to stop him, but it was always best to keep a distance.

So he walked in the opposite direction, up to the next corner, and sat at the bus stop there, instead of the one down by the diner, which would have put him three blocks closer to the campus. No big deal, except that it felt sort of like backtracking, which went against his nature.

It was chilly, probably in the low forties, and he wished there was somewhere up on this stretch of Main to get a cup of coffee. But there wasn't. He thought about risking it and walking on down to the diner. But he didn't. He reached into his backpack and pulled out his old navy watch cap and stretched it over the top of his head and waited for the bus.

11

A campus security guard stopped Wahlman on his way to the Social Sciences building.

"My name's Tom," Wahlman said. "I'm here to participate in a research study."

"Where's your lanyard?"

"My what?"

"They're supposed to give you a lanyard with a temporary student ID card."

The guard was about six inches shorter than Wahlman. Twenty-two or twenty-three years old. His shoes were scuffed and his uniform was wrinkled and he needed a haircut and a mustache trim. A navy drill instructor would have made him do pushups.

"It was a last minute thing," Wahlman said. "Dr. Surrey approved it over the phone."

"Can I see your driver's license?"

"I don't have a driver's license."

"Do you have any sort of identification with you, sir?"

"Yes."

Wahlman pulled out his wallet and produced the phony state ID card he'd bought in Texas. The officer looked it over, and then he scanned it with a cell phone. Which was one of the things Wahlman had wanted to avoid. Now he was going to be in the university's security database. Or at least his alias was.

"You can proceed to Social Sciences," the officer said. "But make sure they give you a temporary ID card and a lanyard if you plan on returning to campus after hours again."

"I'll make sure," Wahlman said.

He followed the signs to the Social Sciences building, entered through the glassed-in atrium and climbed the stairs to the third floor. Dr. Surrey hadn't told him which room to report to, and he hadn't thought to ask. He wandered around for a couple of minutes, and then a female voice from behind him said, "Excuse me, are you Tom?"

He turned around. "You must be Belinda," he said.

She was petite, not more than five feet tall, with long dark hair and blue eyes and a medium skin tone that might have been Eastern European. She was wearing glasses and a white lab coat, and she was carrying a clipboard in her left hand. She looked very scientific.

"You're late," she said.

"One of the guards stopped me."

"Because you don't have a lanyard. Sorry about that."

"He said I should get one for next time."

"We'll only be needing you for one night," Belinda said. "Did Dr. Surrey tell you anything about the study?"

"Not really."

"Well, there's really not much to tell. I'm going to place a couple of electrodes on your forehead, and then you'll be on a bed in a room by yourself until you fall asleep. Eight hours later, I'll wake you up and ask you some questions designed to test your mental acuity. Have you taken any sort of medication in the past twelve hours?"

"No."

"Alcohol?"

Wahlman thought about the sips of beer he'd taken at Kasey's.

"No," he said.

"Great. I just need you to sign our agreement form, and then we can proceed."

She handed Wahlman the clipboard. He skimmed through the form and signed it at the bottom. He almost signed his real name, but he caught himself in time.

"You're not going to hypnotize me and make me do the Watusi or anything, are you?" he asked.

Belinda laughed. "No, nothing like that. Follow me to the sleep lab and I'll get you set up."

"What if I'm not able to fall asleep?" Wahlman asked.

"There's no time limit. So if you fall asleep four hours from now, that's when the study will begin."

"What if I don't stay asleep for eight hours?"

"Eight hours is the goal, but anything over five will work for our purposes."

"Okay."

Belinda pulled a zippered plastic bag out of her lab coat pocket.

"I'll need to lock all your valuables in our storage room," she said.

Wahlman handed her his wallet.

"What about my backpack?" he asked.

"I'll put that in the storage room too. Are you wearing any jewelry?"

"Just a watch."

She opened the zippered bag and held it out in front of her. Wahlman took his watch off and dropped it into the bag. He followed her down the hallway, and then through a door that led to an office suite. Inside the suite there were a bunch of desks separated by a bunch of three-sided partitions. A couple of guys were sitting at a couple of the desks, staring at computer screens. Probably other grad students working on other projects, Wahlman thought. He stayed behind Belinda as she wove her way through the maze of cubicles. The sleep lab was located at the very back of the suite. The section where the actual sleep took place was a twelve-by-twelve room with thick carpeting on the floor and acoustic tiles on the walls and ceiling. No windows. Everything in there was the same medium shade of blue, including the clock on the wall and the linens on the bed.

"Did you bring pajamas?" Belinda asked.

"I didn't know I was supposed to."

"Do you normally just sleep in your underwear?"

"Yes."

"That's fine. Go ahead and take your clothes off and get in bed, and I'll be back in a few minutes."

"Okay."

Belinda exited the room. Wahlman took his clothes off and climbed into the bed. It was a good mattress. Not too soft, not too firm. The sheets were cool and clean and it was quiet in there and Wahlman felt himself getting sleepy right away.

Belinda came in and tore open a plastic package and pulled out a pair of insulated wires with electrodes attached to one end and USB connections attached to the other. She instructed Wahlman to lie flat on his back, and then she peeled the plastic film off the backs of the electrodes and pressed the sticky little squares onto his forehead.

She plugged the USB connections into a black metal box about the size of a deck of cards.

"There's a bathroom right outside the door if you need it," she said.

"I think I'll be okay."

"Great. Well, goodnight."

"Goodnight."

Wahlman glanced up at the clock. It was 10:42. Belinda turned the light off on her way out of the room. Wahlman took a deep breath and closed his eyes and thought about the wonderful afternoon and evening he'd spent with Kasey. He liked her a lot, and he wished he could stick around and get to know her better. Maybe they could stay in touch. He was trying to think of a way for that to happen when he drifted into a dream about Mike Chilton. His best friend. The best friend he'd ever had. The only person in the world he'd ever loved unconditionally. The only person in the world he'd ever trusted unequivocally. In his dream, Mike was sitting across from him at a small round table. They were at a bar. Drinking beer. A jazz trio was playing in the background. Wahlman could see the moon and the stars above, and he could see traffic moving on the street a few stories below. They were outside. Some kind of rooftop bar.

"It's my fault," Wahlman said.

"What are you talking about?"

"I clicked on the SEND button three times."

"Yet here I am."

"How is that possible?"

"You've been watching too much television," Mike said, and then he started laughing, that crazy infectious laugh of his, as if *you've been watching too much television* was the funniest thing ever uttered by a human being. Wahlman started laughing along with him, because it really was the funniest thing ever, and then the lights went out and there was blackness for a while and the jazz trio got louder and Wahlman was trying to find a classroom and he was late for a test that he hadn't studied for and he knew he was going to fail and he knew that Mr. Moben at the orphanage was going to be very displeased and he knew that he wouldn't get any sugar with his cornflakes in the morning for at least a month. More blackness, deeper and deeper, and then Wahlman was at the bar with Mike again but there wasn't any moon and there weren't any stars and the traffic was gone.

"You've been watching too much television," Mike said again, only this time he didn't laugh.

This time he cried.

And Wahlman cried too.

Then Mike reached across the table and put his hand on Wahlman's shoulder and started nudging him gently and telling him it was time to wake up.

Wahlman opened his eyes and saw Belinda standing there by the bed.

The clock on the wall said 6:47.

Which was wrong.

Wahlman knew it was wrong, because he always woke up at 5:27, no matter what time he went to bed—the result of setting an alarm clock for that time back when he was still in the navy. He didn't know exactly what time it was right now, but he knew it wasn't 6:47. He knew it was way earlier than that.

He didn't say anything. Manipulation of the clock—and the participant's perception of how much sleep he or she had gotten—was obviously part of the experiment, and he didn't want to risk losing his payment by letting on that he'd figured it out.

"How do you feel?" Belinda asked.

"Fine. I could use some coffee."

"I'll get you some in a little while, but first I want you to go through the little test I told you about."

"Okay."

"I'm going to leave the room so you can get dressed. I'll be right outside the door whenever you're ready."

Wahlman climbed out of bed and put his clothes on. He made a quick trip to the restroom, and then Belinda led him out of the sleep lab and over to one of the cubicles out in the office suite. She gave him a brief set of instructions, and then she left him there alone while he sat at the desk and worked on the test. He was to finish as much as he could in fifteen minutes. It was mostly about memory. Lists of random words and then questions to see how many of the words you could remember. Wahlman guessed they were trying to see if the participants who *thought* they had gotten eight hours of sleep performed as well or nearly as well as the participants who actually had gotten eight hours of sleep. He read through the lists of words and answered as many questions as he could as fast as he could.

Belinda brought a cup of coffee with her when she returned.

"Has it been fifteen minutes already?" Wahlman asked.

"Yes. Here's a cup of coffee for you, and here's your payment for participating in the study."

She set the coffee and the money on the desk.

"Thank you," Wahlman said. "Am I free to go now?"

"You are. But I need to tell you something first."

"Okay."

"You didn't really sleep eight hours."

"I didn't?" Wahlman asked, playing along.

"You only slept two."

"But the clock in the room—"

"It's wrong. We intentionally misled you to believe that you got way more sleep than you actually did."

"Amazing," Wahlman said. "So what time is it?"

"Almost one-thirty. The purpose of the study is to see if the effects of sleep deprivation can be significantly altered by distorting one's perception of how much sleep was gotten."

"So how did I do on the test?"

"I'm not allowed to share those results with you. Sorry. How do you think you did?"

"I think I aced it," Wahlman said. "And I didn't even study."

Belinda laughed. "I'll get your things out of the storage room," she said.

Wahlman folded the money and slid it into his pocket. Now he had two hundred and twelve dollars. Enough to live on for a few days.

He drank some of the coffee while he waited for Belinda to return. He stared at the blank computer screen and thought about Kasey, suddenly realizing that he didn't even know her last name. And of course she didn't know his real name. To her, he was Tom. He wondered if he would ever be able to trust anyone enough to divulge the facts pertaining to his past, and the total uncertainty of his future. He needed a friend. An ally. Hard to come by when you drifted around the country under an assumed name, traveling from town to town on buses and trains, staying at cheap hotels and eating cheap food, living out of a backpack and saving your quarters for the next depressing little coin laundry in the next depressing little strip mall. With a lifestyle like that, it was practically impossible to form bonds and establish trust.

But that was what Rock Wahlman needed. Maybe there was a way to have that with Kasey, he thought. He didn't really know her, but she seemed smart and responsible and trustworthy and conscientious. Maybe he would tell her the truth someday. Maybe someday soon. Maybe he would tell her that he was the result of an experiment that started over a hundred years ago, an exact genetic duplicate of a man who lived back when Mars was a place that people only dreamed about going to, and maybe he would tell her that someone in the army was determined to make him disappear for some unknown reason.

And maybe she would even believe him.

Belinda was wearing a nylon ski jacket and a knit scarf when she carried his backpack and his other things into the cubicle.

"I was hoping you might let me go back to bed," Wahlman said.

"Sorry. I need to lock everything up when I leave. I know it's not the most convenient time to be going home, but—"

"Do the buses even run this late?"

"They run all night," Belinda said. "I took a late one a while back when my car was being worked on. I was the only passenger for several miles. Just me and the driver. Which was kind of creepy, if you want to know the truth. Anyway, you don't have to take the bus. I can give you a ride home if you want."

Wahlman thought about that. There was no *home*, of course, and he didn't want to spend money on a hotel room, not when checkout time would only be a few hours away. He couldn't go to Kasey's. Not that she would turn him away, but he didn't want to impose, especially with her daughter there at the house. *I don't usually do the whole introduction thing unless it's someone who might be around for a while.*

And Wahlman wasn't a *be around for a while* kind of guy.

Not because he didn't want to be.

Because he couldn't be.

"Could you give me a ride to The Quick Street Inn?" he asked.

"I'm pretty sure that place is closed right now," Belinda said.

"They open at six."

"You're going to wait that long?"

"I'm staying with a friend who lives over that way," Wahlman said, hoping to avoid the need for any further explanation.

"Okay, then," Belinda said. "Sure. I'll give you a ride."

Belinda switched the lights off on the way out of the office suite. Wahlman followed her down the stairs and into the atrium and out the door, and then he strolled along beside her on the sidewalk. The disheveled security guard gave them a little wave as they passed the Humanities building.

It had gotten colder outside and the wind had picked up.

Wahlman reached into his backpack and pulled out his watch cap.

Six o'clock suddenly seemed a long way off.

12

Wahlman sat on the bench outside the pharmacy. He'd decided to take the caboose job, and he wanted to talk to Greg about it as soon as the diner was open for business. He turned his collar up and pulled his cap down as far as it would go and closed his eyes.

Just four hours, he told himself. He actually had a fairly high tolerance for uncomfortable weather conditions. It was one of the skills he'd developed in the navy. Four hours was nothing. He'd spent four *months* in Alaska one time, out in the middle of nowhere, standing watches for sixteen hours at a time sometimes, in subzero temperatures. Four hours was a cakewalk. He could have done it standing on his head. He would have preferred to have been in a nice warm bed somewhere, of course, but it wasn't that big of a deal.

Only it was that big of a deal. This was the first night he'd spent outside since he left his home in Florida. He didn't want this to be the new normal. He refused for it to be the new normal. This would be the one and only time, he told himself. From now on, he would find a decent place to sleep at night, no matter what.

He felt himself dozing off, and then he heard footsteps approaching.

More than one set.

He opened his eyes and glanced over toward the diner. It was the man in the red hat and his two friends. Wandering the streets at two o'clock in the morning. Wahlman wondered when they slept and what they did for money.

They walked over to the bench and stood there and stared down at him, the man in the red hat flanked by the other two guys. The other two hadn't been wearing hats earlier, but they were now. The guy on the left was wearing a white one, and the guy on the right was wearing a blue one. Red, White, and Blue. The colors of our great nation, Wahlman thought. The colors he'd spent twenty years of his life defending. It didn't seem quite right for these punks to be wearing them.

"Why are you still here?" Red asked.

"It's a free country," Wahlman said.

"The bus depot's right up the road. Go exercise your constitutional rights somewhere else."

Silence for a few beats, and then the guy in the white hat spoke up.

"This is our spot," he said.

"I don't see your name on it," Wahlman said.

"We always sit here. It's our spot."

"We could *make* you get up," Blue said.

"You could try," Wahlman said.

The three of them moved in closer. Wahlman took a

deep breath, and then he rammed the bottom of his right boot into Red's solar plexus. As Red was stumbling backwards and gasping for breath, Wahlman stood and clocked White in the jaw with a left hook. It was a vicious blow, one that landed squarely, one that immediately put White out of commission for the rest of the morning.

Or maybe for longer than the rest of the morning.

Wahlman didn't want to kill these guys, but he wasn't going to pull any punches. Not when it was three against one. Not when at least one of the three was carrying a deadly weapon. The pearl-handled pocketknife Wahlman had seen yesterday morning at the diner. The switchblade. Which Red produced a couple of seconds after White collapsed on the sidewalk. He came at Wahlman with the knife, charging toward him recklessly, swinging the blade in a figure-eight, nostrils flared, breath steaming, eyes as red as his hat. As he moved in with the knife, Blue stepped behind Wahlman and clouted him in the back of the head with something that felt like the butt of a pistol or a baseball bat. Everything went black for a second and Wahlman's knees got weak and the next thing he knew Blue was holding him from behind and Red was pressing the blade against the side of his throat.

"You're not so big and tough now, are you?" Red said.

"Do it," Blue said. "Cut him."

Wahlman didn't want to kill these guys, but they weren't giving him much of a choice. He spun away from Red and backed Blue into the parking meter at the edge of the curb. Blue grunted loudly as the mechanical knob on the front of the meter dug into the flesh on his back. When his grip loosened, Wahlman turned and brought an elbow down on the top of his nose. There was a crisp snap as bone met bone, a sound something like that of a pencil being broken in half, followed by copious streams of bright red blood from both nostrils.

While Blue was staggering across Main Street, maybe trying to escape from the pain and the dizziness and the bitter taste of blood and defeat, maybe trying to remember his own name, Wahlman squared off against Red, who was still holding the knife.

"You should back off now, while you still have a chance," Wahlman said. "You should help your friends. They're in desperate need of medical attention."

Red didn't say anything. And he didn't back off. He was hyped up on something. Some kind of drug. Wahlman could see it in his eyes. Crystal meth, maybe. Or something similar. Which meant that he wasn't thinking clearly. Which made him twice as dangerous as someone who was. He started doing the figure-eight thing again, slashing the air with the shiny steel blade as he slowly moved closer to where Wahlman was standing. There was no real defense against such a maneuver, other than running away or obtaining a superior weapon. A gun would have been nice. Or a sword. Or even a two-by-four. But Wahlman didn't have any of those things. The only thing in reach was the bench he'd been sitting on. It was six feet long. Solid oak slats on a steel frame. It probably weighed two hundred pounds. Or more. Wahlman reached around and picked it up and advance toward Red in a single relentless forward motion, like a locomotive pulling out of the station, driving Red backwards into the same parking meter his friend had been slammed against a couple of minutes earlier.

If the meter had been a brick wall, Red would have been crushed against it. From the weight of the bench, and from Wahlman's forward momentum. Broken ribs, massive bruising, internal bleeding. Death, maybe. Hospitalization for sure. But the meter wasn't a brick wall. It was a coin-operated steel and glass timing mechanism called the *head* mounted onto a steel pipe called the *stem*. A long time ago, insurance lobbyists had convinced lawmakers that the pipes should be designed to break at the base if hit with enough force, thereby avoiding the potential vehicular damage and personal injury that might result otherwise. It was a lot cheaper to replace a parking meter than it was to replace a car, and nearly everyone agreed that the infrastructural makeover was a good idea as far as public safety was concerned—and a good talking point for when election year came around. So it became a law, and every parking meter in the country was fitted with a shiny new breakaway stem, including the one the guy in the red hat was being backed into on this chilly January night in Barstow, California.

There was only one problem. The lawmakers who had mandated the nationwide change in parking meter stems hadn't anticipated the high consumer demand for electric vehicles that had occurred during the energy crisis of the mid-2080s. There was no way for them to know that by 2090 one in three American automobiles—one in three of the everyday passenger vehicles parked along the thoroughfares in the business districts of cities large and small coast-to-coast—would be powered solely by batteries. And since they didn't know that, there was no way for them to know that approximately one third of their ingenious new parking meter stems would be retrofitted with ingenious new charging ports.

The subject of parking meter safety was once again being discussed in Washington, and a bill had been drafted that would require expensive underground motion-sensitive circuit breakers to be installed at every charging port—digital ground fault interruption modules to augment the mechanical ones already in place, which had been shown to be ineffective under certain conditions.

But the law hadn't been passed yet.

Which meant that a fancy new circuit breaker hadn't been installed under the meter that the man in the red hat was being backed into.

The stem broke at the base, just as it was designed to do, and the weight of the bench came down hard on the man in the red hat, trapping him against the pavement. The power cables attached to the charging port were uprooted, and apparently the jagged end of the pipe sliced through the insulation enclosing one of them. The live wire started dancing around at the edge of the curb, humming its high voltage tune and showering the area with bright orange sparks.

"Get this thing off of me," Red said, referring to the heavy steel and wood bench parked on his chest.

"Don't move," Wahlman said. "There's a hot power line about six inches away from your left foot."

Red didn't listen. He moved. And it wasn't the fearful kind of movement you make when you're trying to wriggle away from certain death. It was the aggressive kind of movement you make when you're still determined to win.

Somehow, he'd managed to hold onto the switchblade. As a young master at arms pulling shore patrol duty from time to time, Wahlman had seen his share of them. The ones he'd confiscated were cheap and ugly and sharp as a razor. Good for street brawls and not much else.

But then Red probably wasn't planning on peeling an apple.

He propped himself up on his left elbow, reared back and threw the knife overhand, whizzed it through the air with perfect aim, the blade and the handle whirring end-over-end directly toward Wahlman's heart.

Instinctively, Wahlman raised his elbows and closed them together at the front of his core, using his upper extremities as sort of a shield, his massive forearms pressed together like two books on a shelf. The knife could have thudded into his lower abdomen, or his thighs, or the muscles in his arms, but it didn't. It bounced off his left sleeve and skittered harmlessly into the gutter.

Harmlessly for Wahlman.

Not for the man in the red hat.

As it turned out, the open knife, which happened to be just long enough to span the area between the sparking wire and the man's left foot, was an excellent conductor of electrical current.

Wahlman couldn't watch. And he couldn't wait around

for the police to show up. Which meant that he couldn't wait around for The Quick Street Inn to open. Which, among other things, meant that he couldn't even tell Kasey goodbye.

He turned and started walking east on Main, toward the bus station.

Eight blocks, if he remembered correctly.

13

Mr. Tyler was having a very good dream when his bedside alarm clock started wailing. He briefly considered hitting the snooze button and trying to go back to sleep, but he didn't. He had work to do.

He climbed out of bed and took a shower and got dressed, and then he drove back over to Main Street. To the diner. He wanted to be there when it opened, to see if Rock Wahlman showed up for breakfast.

He parked across the street from the pharmacy again, set the radio to a station that played soothing music again. Then he noticed that one of the parking meters in front of the pharmacy was missing. Some idiot must have jumped the curb and run into it, he thought. Sometime after the diner closed last night, after he went back to the hotel.

He climbed out of his car and walked over there to take a look. The entire meter was gone, and someone had already capped the hole where the stem had been set into the concrete.

And something else was missing. The nice long park

bench that had been on the sidewalk. That was gone too. Which was interesting, because there was no other evidence that a motor vehicle accident had occurred. No skid marks, no damage to the storefront. Just a missing meter and a missing bench.

Interesting indeed.

Mr. Tyler looked at his watch. It was a few minutes after six. He walked over to the diner and cupped his hands against the glass door and peered inside, saw nothing but darkness. He was about to walk back across the street to his car when the lights came on and the door opened and the guy in the apron stepped out to the sidewalk.

"Sorry," the guy in the apron said. "Running a little late this morning. Come on in if you want to."

"I was just going to get a cup of coffee," Mr. Tyler said.

"I'll get a pot going right away. Takes about five minutes."

Mr. Tyler followed the guy in the apron into the diner. The guy in the apron hurried behind the counter and grabbed a stainless steel filter basket and a paper filter and started scooping some coffee out of a can.

Mr. Tyler took his coat off and sat on one of the stools at the counter.

"Here by yourself this morning?" he asked.

"Kasey should be here any minute," the man in the apron said. "We're usually pretty busy by seven, so I'm definitely going to need the help."

"You get customers in here that early on weekends?"

"You'd be surprised. Anyway, sorry I was late opening up. We had a little excitement outside earlier this morning."

"What kind of excitement?" Mr. Tyler asked.

"Some local guys got beat up pretty bad. By a homeless person. A transient. The local guys are all in the hospital right now. All three of them. One of them is in critical condition. They're not sure he's going to make it."

"What happened?"

"Well, I got a courtesy call from the electric company around three this morning, letting me know that the power to the restaurant was going to be off for at least a couple of hours. I wasn't sure I was going to be able to open at all this morning. Which concerned me, of course. Anyway, long story short, I drove over here to see what was going on, and I ended up getting some of the details from one of the cops working the scene. Apparently the three local guys were walking along minding their own business when this drifter came running out from the alley and attacked them in front of the pharmacy."

"Just one guy?"

"Yeah. But they said he was really big."

"Did the police catch him?" Mr. Tyler asked.

"No. But I think I know who it was. The cop I talked to said to call the station if I see him again."

"Big guy, huh? Was he carrying a backpack? Was he in here eating breakfast yesterday morning?"

"You saw him?"

"I think he came in right before I left. If it's the same guy."

"Sounds like it," the guy in the apron said. "He ordered breakfast, and then he had some words with some guys who come in here all the time. I don't know if it was the same guys who got beat up last night, but it probably was. That would make sense. And of course it's possible that the guys who got beat up are lying. They might have started the fight. They're not exactly what you would call upstanding citizens, if you know what I mean."

"Did you happen to catch the homeless guy's name?" Mr. Tyler asked.

"Tom. Seemed like a nice enough guy. I even offered to set him up with a job, but I guess—"

"I'm going to have to take a rain check on that coffee," Mr. Tyler said.

He got up from the stool and put his coat on and walked out of the diner. Crossed the street and climbed into his car and sped toward the bus station. He wanted to get there before they changed shifts. He wanted to talk to the person at the ticket counter. It was possible that Wahlman had used some other mode of transportation to get out of town, but the bus station seemed like a good place to start.

14

Wahlman got off the bus at 6:27 a.m. Downtown Bakersfield. He didn't plan on staying there for any length of time, but he was hungry and he wanted to talk to Kasey before it got busy at The Quick Street Inn. He found a payphone and punched in the number for her cell. When she answered, he could tell that she had been crying.

"What's wrong?" he asked.

"I got a call about an hour ago," she said. "My ex isn't AWOL. He's dead."

"What?"

"I don't have all the details yet. I just know that he was shot."

"In combat?"

"No. He was murdered."

Wahlman's stomach lurched. Like the first big downhill plummet on a rollercoaster. Innocent people had died because of the mess he was in. One in Louisiana, one in Florida. The one in Louisiana had been the other surviving clone. The one in Florida had been his best friend.

Kasey's ex-husband had been shot. Kasey's ex-husband was in the army. Someone in the army was behind everything that was happening. Probably just a coincidence, Wahlman thought. He hoped that was the case. He hoped it with all his heart.

"Did it happen somewhere here in the states?" he asked.

"Yes. He was stationed at a temporary post not far from here. He's been picking Natalie up every other weekend and taking her to his place. They found him in his car. I just can't believe this is—"

She broke off then. Wahlman could hear her crying. Muffled. From a distance. He stood there and stared at the payphone's keypad for a few seconds, trying to wrap his head around what she had just told him.

"Are you at work?" he asked.

"*Work*," she said. Sighing, sniffling, making an effort to compose herself. "I forgot all about work. I need to call Greg."

"I just wanted to let you know that I had to leave town this morning," Wahlman said.

"Why?"

"I told you I was going to have to leave."

"But I didn't know it would be this soon."

"I know. I'm sorry."

There was a long pause.

"I need to go," Kasey said.

"Listen, this is not how I wanted to—"

"I'm going to have to wake my daughter up in a little while and tell her that her daddy's dead. Do you have any idea how difficult that's going to be?"

"I'm sorry. I wish there was something I could do to help."

"Just being here would help," Kasey said.

Wahlman stared at the keypad some more.

"I would like to stay in touch," he said. "Is it all right if I call you sometimes?"

"What's the point? I'm in Barstow, and you're wherever. I just don't see how—"

"Maybe we could meet somewhere," Wahlman said. "I'll get some money together and buy you a plane ticket. We could spend a whole weekend together. Or a whole week. And I don't plan on living like this forever. I just need some time to sort some things out."

"I need to go," Kasey said.

Wahlman didn't want to say goodbye. He didn't want this to be the end.

"Can I call you?" he asked again.

Another long pause.

And then a click.

Followed by a dial tone.

Wahlman wasn't hungry anymore. He bought another ticket and got back on the bus. He rode it all the way to Atascadero this time. He ate lunch and walked around for a while, and then he checked into a hotel. He took a shower and climbed into bed and turned the television on, hoping to hear some news about the recent homicide near Barstow. Hoping that it had been the result of an argument in a bar, or a drug deal gone bad, or a robbery, or a case of road rage, or whatever. Hoping to rule out what he feared the most.

That it might have had something to do with him.

And that the killer might be hot on his trail.

NO ESCAPE

THE REACHER EXPERIMENT BOOK 3

1

Rock Wahlman was digging a post hole twenty miles east of downtown Seattle, and he was thinking about telling Kasey everything.

He'd been thinking about it for a few weeks. Kasey was the kind of woman you couldn't get off your mind, even if you tried. And Wahlman hadn't tried. He liked having her on his mind.

Maybe it was unwise to trust her. After all, he'd only known her for a short time, and he hadn't even talked to her since the day he left Barstow. And maybe she didn't even feel the same way. Maybe she hadn't fallen for him the way he had for her.

But maybe she had.

He needed to know.

He'd discovered some things about himself over the past few months, some things that were nothing short of mind-blowing. Like the fact that he was an exact genetic duplicate of a former army officer named Jack Reacher. Like the fact that someone in the army was trying to kill him, trying to cover up a cloning experiment that had started over a hundred years ago.

Maybe telling Kasey all that would be a huge mistake.

But he had to do something. He needed to find out why all this was happening, and he needed to find out who was responsible.

And he couldn't do it alone.

He dug some more dirt out of the hole, thought about it some more. One tiny misstep could cost him his life. One slip of the tongue. One wrong turn. One misplaced scrap of paper.

Should he trust her?

Joe walked over and asked him if he was ready to break for lunch. Joe was the owner of the fence company. *Joe's Fence Company*, it was called, written in fancy letters on both sides of the company truck. It was a nice red truck, brand new 2098, all electric, with a nice hydraulic flatbed that tilted like the bed on a dump truck if you needed it to. There was a keypad on the dashboard. You punched in a code and the motor started. Wahlman knew the code. There had been times when he had needed to drive the truck for one reason or another, and Joe had told him the numbers, making it clear that the truck's GPS tracking system was being monitored by a private security company twenty-four-seven, making it clear that anyone who even thought about going for a joyride would be dealt with in a manner that included the destruction of certain delicate anatomical features. Joe was a little overprotective when it came to his truck, but he was a good guy. He paid cash daily and he always paid for lunch. This was the fourth day Wahlman had been working for him. As far as Joe knew, Wahlman's name was Calvin.

Joe was friendly and informal, and he'd been calling Wahlman *Cal* since day two.

"Let me just finish this last hole," Wahlman said.

He'd used a solar-powered auger to dig most of the holes, but there was a tough tree root where this one was supposed to go, so he'd been forced to dig it out the old-fashioned way, with posthole diggers and a long steel tool called a root bar.

"Finish it later," Joe said. "I'm hungry."

Wahlman left the diggers sticking out of the hole and followed Joe to the truck.

"What time are the posts supposed to get here?" Wahlman asked.

"One o'clock. That's why I wanted to go ahead and get lunch out of the way."

Joe had arranged for one of the local home supply centers to deliver the four-by-four wooden fence posts today, and the eight-by-six wooden shadowbox panels tomorrow. The plan was to get all of the posts tamped in today, as long as the weather held out.

"I think I just felt a raindrop," Wahlman said.

"Shut up, Cal. It was just your imagination."

"If you say so."

"I say so. And I say it's your turn to drive."

Joe pitched Wahlman the fob that controlled the truck's door locks.

"Where to?" Wahlman asked.

"Jimmy's."

There was a restaurant called Jimmy's Ringside not far from the jobsite. It was a burger place. The owner was a former heavyweight boxing champion. The only thing on the menu that remotely resembled a vegetable was something called the TKO, which was basically an enormous order of deep fried onion rings, seasoned with cayenne pepper and served on a dish the size of a turkey platter. It came with a bowl of creamy dill sauce for dipping, just in case you still had one or two coronary arteries that weren't clogged.

Wahlman steered the truck into the parking lot. The sky had gotten a little darker on the way to the restaurant, and a light mist had started coating the windshield. Just enough to activate the automatic wipers every few seconds.

Wahlman liked burgers, but he wasn't really in the mood for Jimmy's. Not after eating there Monday, Tuesday, and Wednesday.

"What about that place across the street?" he said. "Might be good for a change."

"Who paid for lunch yesterday?" Joe said.

"You did."

"That's right, Cal. I paid for lunch yesterday. *And* day before yesterday. *And* the day before that."

"But this is going to be the fourth day in a row that we've—"

"I don't care if it's going to be the millionth day in a row. He who pays gets to choose, and he who pays chooses Jimmy's."

Wahlman felt like asking if he who pays also got to

choose the physician for the eventual bypass surgeries, but he didn't. He followed Joe inside and sat across from him at a booth by the window.

As always, Wahlman paid close attention to his surroundings, scanning the dining area and the parking lot for anyone or anything that looked even remotely suspicious. It was a habit that he'd picked up as a master at arms in the navy, a habit that was more important than ever now that someone was actively trying to find him and kill him.

The food servers at Jimmy's wore extremely short cutoff jeans, black t-shirts, and sneakers. Every one of them was female, and most of them were blonde. Early twenties, fit, shapely. Some of them liked to roll the bottom hems of their t-shirts up a few inches, exposing their piercings and tattoos and store-bought tans. The one who came to the booth where Joe and Wahlman were sitting had eight gold studs in each ear. Which seemed excessive, in Wahlman's opinion. Then again, maybe he was just old. He wondered if she could pick up shortwave radio signals with those things. He decided not to ask.

Joe ordered a glass of iced tea. Wahlman ordered coffee.

"Do you guys know what you want to eat?" the waitress asked. "Or do you need a few minutes to look at the menu?"

"I'll take the Down-For-The-Count platter," Joe said. "And I want the burger really well done this time. Yesterday it was still pink in the middle."

"Well done," the waitress said, writing the order down on a pad of guest checks. "Will this be together or separate?"

"Together," Joe said.

The young lady turned to Wahlman.

"I'll take the roasted chicken breast and a side salad," he said.

"Sir?"

"Scratch that. I want the grilled salmon with steamed broccoli."

"Sir, if you need a few minutes to look at the menu—"

"Never mind. I guess I'll take that Down-For-The-Count thing too."

"You want the burger well done?"

"Medium," Wahlman said.

The waitress scribbled down the order, and then she slid the pad into her back pocket and walked away.

"She must be new," Joe said.

"Why do you say that?"

"Most of them don't bother writing down the orders. Which means that the orders are wrong about half the time."

"So why do you keep coming here?"

"Jimmy's an old friend of mine. I used to spar with him sometimes."

Wahlman nodded. "I'm going to the restroom," he said.

He slid out of the booth and walked back toward the entrance. On the wall behind the cashier's counter there were dozens of framed photographs, pictures of Jimmy back when he was still fighting. At the center of the display, there was a large chrome and glass frame with a championship belt mounted inside it. The gold buckle was about the size of a paperback novel. It was engraved. It said *Heavyweight Champion of the World*. Wahlman was impressed. He wondered if Jimmy ever came into the restaurant.

Past the cashier's counter there was an alcove that led to the restrooms. At the center of the alcove, between the door that said *Men* on the left and the door that said *Women* on the right, there was a water fountain and a payphone. Wahlman stepped up to the payphone, lifted the receiver from its hook, and pressed zero to speak with an operator. He told her that he needed to make a long distance call, and that he wanted to pay for it with cash. She took the number he wanted to make the call to and told him that ten dollars would buy him five minutes. He inserted a ten dollar bill into the paper money slot at the bottom of the payphone. The operator said thank you, and a few seconds later Wahlman heard Kasey's phone ringing.

"Hello?" she said.

"It's Tom," Wahlman said, using the name he'd been using in Barstow.

There was a long period of silence. Several seconds. Wahlman wondered if Kasey was going to hang up on him. She didn't.

"Well, hello there stranger," she said. "Where are you?"

"I'm in Seattle. Sorry I haven't called. I need to talk to you. I need to tell you some things."

"Like what, Tom? What could you possibly tell me that's going to—"

"My name's not Tom, for one thing."

"Oh, really? What should I call you, then? Shithead? Works for me."

"I'm using aliases because I have to. If we could meet somewhere in person—"

"I really wasn't expecting to ever hear from you again," Kasey said.

"It's only been a few weeks."

"Yeah, well, a lot has happened in those few weeks."

"I'm in trouble, Kasey. You know that. And it's really not my fault. If you could just give me a chance to explain everything—"

"I'm late for work. Some of us have actual responsibilities, you know? You're going to have to come to Barstow if you want to talk to me in person."

She hung up.

The payphone gave Wahlman two dollars and thirty-five cents of his money back. He stuffed the coins and the bills into his pocket and returned to his seat across from Joe, where the Down-For-The-Count platter he'd ordered was waiting for him.

"She never brought my coffee?" Wahlman asked.

"Waiting for a fresh pot to brew," Joe said. "You should have ordered tea. Who drinks coffee for lunch?"

"Lots of people."

"Not at Jimmy's, obviously. Hurry up and eat your food. We need to be back at the jobsite in about twenty minutes."

"Just let me know when you're ready," Wahlman said. "I'm not that hungry anyway."

He took a bite of his burger. It was good, in the way that hot greasy meat and cheese and onions and lettuce and tomatoes and pickles and mayonnaise and a bun grilled in butter always is.

"Let me see that," Joe said.

"What?"

"Let me see your burger where you bit into it."

"Why?"

"Just humor me for a minute," Joe said, making a circular motion with his index finger.

"Whatever," Wahlman said.

He rotated the burger so Joe could see where he had bitten into it.

"That burger's well done," Joe said.

"So?"

"So mine's pink in the middle again. She must have gotten our orders mixed up when she delivered the plates to the table. She must have given me your plate, and she must have given you my plate."

Wahlman sighed. "You want this burger?" he asked.

"Not after you already ate on it."

Wahlman shrugged. He took another bite of the burger, thought about what Kasey had said on the phone. *You're going to have to come to Barstow if you want to talk to me in person.* Wahlman had learned some things about himself since he'd been on the run, and one of the things he'd learned was that he disliked backtracking. After he'd been to a place once, he didn't want to go back to that place again. And it wasn't just because people were trying to find him. It wasn't because of the arrest warrant in Louisiana, or even because of the contract on his life. It was something in his nature. Something he had been born with. He'd felt it to some degree in the navy, but he'd never realized the full extent of the aversion until he'd abandoned his home in

Florida and started traveling around the country. He had no desire to return to Chattanooga, or Louisville, or Quincy, or Dallas, or any of the other cities he'd spent time in over the past few months. He didn't want to go back to any of those places.

But Barstow was a different story.

The exception to the rule.

Wahlman did want to go back there. Because of Kasey. He wanted to go back, but there were reasons why he couldn't. Three of them, to be exact. Three boneheads who'd challenged him out on the street one night. Three boneheads who'd lost. Severely.

Barstow was off limits now. Forever. Kasey would just have to agree to meet with him somewhere else. He would have to convince her, somehow. He planned to call her tonight from his hotel room and give it a try.

He glanced toward the drink station, to see if the coffee he'd ordered might be coming sometime before the turn of the century, and when he did he noticed a man sitting alone at a booth on the other side of the dining area. The booth had been vacant earlier. The man must have entered the restaurant while Wahlman was on the phone. There was something familiar about the man, something Wahlman couldn't quite put his finger on.

Then he noticed the leather coat that had been draped over the padded bench seat directly across from the man.

It was long.

Like a trench coat.

2

Wahlman had seen the man weeks ago. At the diner in Barstow. The Quick Street Inn, where Kasey worked. Now the man was in the Seattle area, at Jimmy's Ringside, looking at a menu at 12:37 on a Thursday afternoon, the exact same time that Wahlman was in the Seattle area, at Jimmy's Ringside, swallowing a bite of a cheeseburger. What were the odds?

"I'm going to the restroom," Wahlman said.

"Again?" Joe said. "Are you all right?"

"I'm all right."

Wahlman slid out of the booth and started walking, kept his eyes straight ahead, focusing on the trophy display against the front wall. When he passed the cashier's counter, he didn't take a right, toward the alcove that led to the restrooms. He took a left, toward the exit. Joe's back was to him. Joe couldn't see what he was doing. But the man with the leather trench coat could see what he was doing just fine. The man with the leather trench coat had a clear line of sight all the way to the front of the restaurant. Acutely aware of the man's position—and that his presence probably wasn't a coincidence—Wahlman made an effort to keep his movements smooth and ordinary. Just a casual little stroll to get something out of the truck. Maybe he'd forgotten his wallet. Or his reading glasses. Or whatever. He pushed his way through the swinging glass door and sauntered across the concrete sidewalk that lined the perimeter of the building, out to the slightly damp asphalt of the parking lot, walking a little faster as he went. Which, as it turned out, was a natural thing to do, because of the drizzle, which had gotten a little heavier over the past fifteen minutes or so.

When he got to Joe's truck, he opened the driver side door and slid in behind the wheel and punched in the code to start the motor. Now was the time to drop the act of casual indifference. Now was the time to get out of there. Fast. He slammed the truck into gear and weaved his way out of the parking lot, out to the four-lane highway that led back to the subdivision where he and Joe had been working. Only he didn't turn into the subdivision. He drove past the gated entrance and took a right at the next light. Toward the interstate. Toward wherever. He couldn't go very far north, because that would put him in Canada, and he didn't have a passport, or even a driver's license. He couldn't go very far west, because that would put him in the Puget Sound, and as nice as Joe's truck was, it didn't have the amphibious capabilities that some of the more expensive models on the market were equipped with. Wahlman was trying to decide between south and east when he glanced into the rearview mirror and saw a pair of headlights. They were about a hundred yards behind him and closing in fast.

Wahlman floored the accelerator. There was a traffic signal just ahead. It turned yellow. Wahlman sped through it. The light turned red, but the car behind Wahlman didn't stop. Now it was only about twenty yards away.

Ten.

Five.

Wahlman could see the car clearly in his rearview mirror now. It was a two-seater. Some kind of sports car. Dark gray, about the same shade as the pavement. And the sky. Thick billowing clouds the color of molten lead now, rolling in from the west, reflecting off the little car's windshield, making it impossible for Wahlman to see the driver's face, making it impossible to see whether or not anyone was in the passenger seat.

Wahlman didn't think so. The man with the leather trench coat had been alone at the diner in Barstow, and he'd been alone at Jimmy's Ringside. Maybe he was a private investigator, hired by the New Orleans Police Department, hired to find Wahlman and alert the nearest law enforcement agency for temporary detainment pending extradition back to Louisiana. But if that was the case, why hadn't Wahlman been taken into custody in Barstow? He'd been sitting five stools away from the man. Four stools away from the man's coat. The man could have easily phoned the police, and the police could have easily come and taken Wahlman away. But that didn't happen.

Which meant that the man was probably not a private investigator.

Which meant that things were probably about to get a lot worse for Rock Wahlman.

There was a loud pop, like the sound of a hammer slamming into a tray of ice cubes. It occurred in conjunction with the appearance of a hole about the size of a quarter in Joe's windshield. Just below the rearview mirror. Just to the right of Wahlman's head.

Wahlman didn't turn around to look, but he figured that there was a similar hole in the truck's back window, and he figured that the holes, front and back, had been bored by a single slug, and that the slug had been fired from a large-caliber handgun, probably a .45 or a 9mm. He knew that such projectiles traveled at a high velocity, faster than the speed of sound, and he knew that this particular one had come very close to gathering some blood and bone and brain tissue on its way out of Joe's cab.

He also knew that it's extremely difficult to drive a vehicle and effectively shoot a gun at the same time. You have to steer with your right hand, stick your left arm out the driver side window, find your target and take aim, hoping all the while that your vehicle, or whatever you're aiming at, doesn't move a fraction of an inch to the left, or a fraction of an inch to the right, hoping that there's not a slight dip in the pavement, or a slight rise, or that any number of other factors that *could* adversely affect the trajectory of the bullet when you pull the trigger *don't* adversely affect the trajectory of the bullet when you pull the trigger. Wahlman knew from experience how difficult it was to drive a vehicle and effectively shoot a gun at the same time, especially when the vehicle was traveling at a high speed—one hundred and eighteen miles per hour, to be exact—which made him think that maybe the man with the leather trench coat wasn't working alone after all. It's somewhat easier to shoot from a car if you aren't the one driving it. You can steady the gun with both hands, and you can focus entirely on the target. It's still something of a crapshoot, but if you have the right training, and if you squeeze off enough rounds, there's a fairly good chance that at least one of your bullets will hit what you want it to hit.

And one is usually all it takes.

With those things in mind, Wahlman was thinking that the man with the trench coat probably had a partner, and that the partner, who was obviously a highly skilled marksperson, was probably doing the shooting. Wahlman was thinking that, and he was pretty sure of it, until he glanced up at the rearview mirror and saw a muzzle flash coming from the driver side of the sports car and heard another loud pop as another slug drilled its way through the windshield.

No partner.

The guy was just good.

A third bullet punched its way through the glass, and this time Wahlman actually heard the projectile whistle past his right ear.

Joe was probably aware by now that his nice red truck was not in the parking lot anymore, and that the guy he'd hired named Calvin hadn't really gone to the restroom. Someone at the private security company that monitored the nice red truck's GPS tracking system twenty-four-seven was probably watching a nice red luminescent dot move at a fairly fast clip on an electronic map right now, and a call would probably be going out to the police soon, if it hadn't already. Somehow, Wahlman needed to abandon the truck and get far enough away from it to avoid being captured by the police, and at the same time he needed to get far enough away from the assassin in the car behind him to avoid being dead.

He opened Joe's glove compartment and started ferreting through the papers in there, hoping that Joe wasn't really the straight-laced law-abiding citizen that he seemed to be, hoping to find something to defend himself with. A pistol would have been nice. A hand grenade would have been better. All he found was a bunch of receipts and some paper envelopes and a package of cheap cigars and a lighter and a bottle of cheap cologne and two condoms in a little box that had contained three before it had been opened. Wahlman thought about pulling the items out onto the seat and trying to assemble some sort of explosive device with them. The cologne probably had a good amount of alcohol in it. You could soak a strip of paper from one of the cigars with some of the cologne, and then you could stuff the paper down into the bottle and light it with the lighter, and then you could chuck your miniature Molotov cocktail out the window, and then it would smash through the little gray sports car's windshield and blow the little gray sports car and the driver to smithereens, and then you could hide the truck in the woods and hike on up to the interstate and hitch a ride to

Portland or somewhere. You might be able to do all that if you weren't traveling at speeds in excess of a hundred miles an hour, and if you didn't need at least one hand on the steering wheel at all times, and if you weren't whizzing past a sign that said ROAD CONSTRUCTION 2 MILES AHEAD BE PREPARED TO STOP.

Wahlman took his foot off the accelerator.

Slowed down to eighty.

Another bullet whistled past his head.

There had to be a way out of this. There had to be a way to survive. Only there wasn't. Wahlman was going to die, and there was nothing he could do about it.

Then he remembered that the bed of Joe's truck was equipped with a tilting mechanism. Like a dump truck. He flipped the toggle switch on the right side of the dashboard, the one directly beneath the radio. He'd activated the mechanism once before. Yesterday, when he'd needed to drop off some rolls of barbed wire at Joe's storage lot. So he knew what was supposed to happen. The bed was supposed to start rising away from the frame. It was supposed to tilt at an angle that would allow the cargo to slide off. The only thing back there at the moment was a crate of decking screws, purchased at the home supply center that morning when Joe had arranged for his deliveries, meant to be used tomorrow, to attach the wooden panels to the wooden posts. The crate would probably split open when it hit the pavement, and the decking screws would probably go everywhere, and some of them would probably end up under the little gray sports car, and there's nothing quite like a tire blowing out at eighty miles an hour to totally ruin an assassin's day.

But when Wahlman flipped the switch, nothing happened. The bed didn't tilt, and the crate of screws didn't slide off, and the man with the leather trench coat didn't lose control of the car he was driving.

Wahlman figured that the truck had been equipped with some sort of safety device that prevented the bed from tilting while the truck was moving. He glanced down at the dashboard. There was a square button to the left of the steering wheel. It was about the size of a Scrabble tile. The letters *KMO* were printed underneath it, and underneath the letters there was a little red lens that probably had a little light bulb behind it.

Wahlman had no idea what the *K* stood for, but he hoped that the *M* stood for manual and that the *O* stood for override. He pressed the button in with his left index finger. The little red light started flashing and a buzzer started sounding and the bed started tilting. Wahlman stopped the mechanism before the front edge of the bed rose to the level of the roof of the cab, thinking that the safety device had been installed for a reason, thinking that if the bed rose too high it would act as sort of a wing at these speeds, creating lift that could potentially flip the truck over backwards. Which might or might not ruin the assassin's day, but would definitely ruin Wahlman's.

The rear window was blocked now, but Wahlman could still see behind the truck, using the big rectangular mirrors that were bolted to the front fenders, just in front of the top door hinges. The wooden crate slid off the bed and smashed into the pavement and splintered into a million pieces. The decking screws went everywhere, just as planned, but none of the tires on the little gray sports car blew out, and the man with the leather trench coat didn't lose control. Maybe some of the screws had punctured some of the tires, causing slow leaks that would be a nuisance later on. But slow leaks didn't do Wahlman any good at the moment. He needed slow leaks like he needed a hole in the head. Which, unfortunately, was exactly what he was going to get if the man with the leather trench coat had his way.

At least the rear window was shielded now. Wahlman heard a couple of bullets ping off the heavy steel bed as he tried to think of what to do next.

He needed to do something.

And he needed to do it fast.

Because half a mile ahead there was a guy in an orange vest holding a portable stop sign.

One way or another, this thing was going to end in a matter of seconds.

And Wahlman couldn't imagine how it could possibly end in his favor.

3

Kasey wasn't really late for work. She'd called in sick. Again. Seven times in the past five weeks. Four times in the past two. She'd been waiting tables at The Quick Street Inn for a little over two years, and she considered Greg, the owner, to be her friend as well as her boss, but she knew that he wouldn't be able to keep her on the schedule if she continued missing shifts. He would have to fire her. She knew that, but she didn't really care.

She poured herself another glass of vodka and stared out the dining room window, noticing the weeds in her back yard and not really caring about those either.

Her cell phone trilled. It was Natalie. Her daughter.

"Why aren't you at school?" Kasey asked.

"I am at school," Natalie said. "I'm waiting for you to pick me up."

Natalie was in the ninth grade. School let out at three o'clock. It wasn't even one yet.

"What are you talking about?" Kasey asked.

"We got out early today. Remember? I told you last

night. You said you'd pick me up and take me shopping for some new jeans."

"That's right," Kasey said, although she didn't actually recall the conversation. "I am so sorry, honey. It totally slipped my mind. Go ahead and take the bus home. I'm not feeling very well today, but maybe we can—"

"The buses are gone already, Mom. I need you to come and get me."

"The buses are gone already?"

"We got out at twelve. Everyone's gone. Even the teachers."

Kasey tried to think of someone she could call to go pick up her daughter, but everyone she knew was either at work or out of town.

Or dead.

Kasey's ex—Natalie's dad—had been found dead in his car a few weeks ago. Murdered. Shot to death outside an abandoned filling station twenty miles west of town. That was when Kasey had started drinking heavily. That was when her life had started spiraling out of control. It was when the bills had started piling up, bills that she would never be able to pay, not on what she brought home from the diner, even if she worked triple shifts seven days a week. She hated that she'd become dependent on the money her ex had been contributing toward Natalie's upbringing, but she had, and now that it was gone she didn't know what she was going to do.

She walked to the kitchen and dumped the vodka into the sink.

"I have to take a shower," she said. "But I'll be there, honey. Soon as I can. Okay?"

"I'm sitting on the bench outside the gym," Natalie said.

"Okay. I'll see you in a little bit."

Kasey disconnected. Her phone trilled again. She picked up, thinking it was probably Natalie again, but it wasn't.

"If you value your life, and your daughter's life, you'll stay away from him," a male voice said.

Kasey's heart started beating faster. The adrenaline rush was like a slap in the face. It was the first time in weeks she'd actually felt sober. It was the first time in weeks she'd felt much of anything.

The emotions pulsed in like an electrical power surge. Fury. Outrage. Fear. Nobody was going to get away with threatening her daughter.

Nobody.

"Stay away from who?" she asked. Fiercely. Aggressively. A tigress ready to fight to the death to protect her young.

But the caller had already hung up.

4

Wahlman slammed on the brakes.

At the same time, he pressed the KMO button, causing the truck bed to tilt back further, causing the rear edge of the flat steel platform to scrape against the pavement. It was an abrupt and desperate maneuver, instinctive, spur of the moment, with absolutely no forethought, which was a good thing, as it turned out, because it took the man with the leather trench coat totally by surprise. He didn't react quickly enough. He didn't hit the brakes in time, and the little gray sports car rolled up onto the bed and shot over the top of the truck like a little gray rocket. Wahlman saw the undercarriage as it flew past his windshield. He saw the tires and the oil pan and the dual exhausts. The car was airborne for three or four seconds. It landed about fifty feet in front of where Joe's truck had skidded to a stop. It landed with exactly the kind of explosively harsh crunching thump you would expect to hear when a ton or so of metal and rubber and glass slams into a nice fresh stretch of asphalt. It landed and went spinning counterclockwise toward the shoulder, toward the guy in the orange vest holding the portable stop sign, all four tires screaming, greasy hot smoke spreading and mingling with the misty Seattle haze, smoke so thick you could taste it, the man with the leather trench coat desperately trying to regain control of the vehicle and failing fabulously.

The guy in the orange vest let go of the sign and darted out of the way, narrowly avoiding being flattened and crushed as the car careened nose-first into the roadside drainage ditch.

Wahlman was still about fifty feet from where the road construction started. Fifty feet from where the guy in the orange vest had been standing. The guy shouted something that Wahlman couldn't make out and started running toward the little gray sports car. A few seconds later more guys in orange vests started running that way. Wahlman grabbed his jacket from the seat and climbed out of the truck and crossed the ditch and ran into the woods and hiked on up to the interstate and hitched a ride to Portland. It was about five o'clock in the afternoon when he got there. He bought a bus ticket, and fifteen hours later he was in downtown Bakersfield. He called Kasey on the same payphone he'd used to call her the day he'd left Barstow. A robot voice told him that the number was no longer in service. He called the operator to get the number for The Quick Street Inn. The operator told him to deposit some money into the payphone and then she made the connection for him. The phone at The Quick Street Inn rang four times. A man picked up. Wahlman recognized the voice. It was Greg, the owner.

"Quick Street," Greg said. "May I help you?"

"May I speak to Kasey, please?"

"May I ask who's calling?"

Wahlman didn't want to identify himself, not even by the fake name he'd used in Barstow previously.

"She reported a problem with the cable TV at her house," he said. "She listed this number as an alternate. I tried to call her cell, but—"

"Hold on," Greg said.

Wahlman held on.

"Hello?" Kasey said.

"It's me," Wahlman said. "I'm in Bakersfield."

"Unreal," Kasey said.

"Please don't hang up. I need to—"

"No, I mean it's unreal that you caught me here. I just came by to hand in my time card and my uniforms."

"You're quitting your job?"

"What kind of trouble are you in, Tom? Or whatever your real name is. I need to know. I need to know right now, because—"

"Meet me somewhere," Wahlman said. "I'll tell you everything."

Silence for a few beats. Wahlman thought she was going to hang up on him again, but she didn't.

"There's a shopping center in Bakersfield called the Uptown Center," she said. "Meet me at the bookstore in three hours."

"I'll be there," Wahlman said.

"I have a new cell phone. It's one of those cheap things you can buy at a discount store and add minutes to with a credit card."

She told him the number, and then she disconnected.

5

Mr. Tyler's ass was bruised because his rental car had gone airborne and then bottomed out on the highway, and his ego was bruised because the target he'd been commissioned to eliminate had somehow managed to get away. Of course it could have been a lot worse. He could have been unconscious when the four road construction guys ran over to the car to check on him. They would have called an ambulance and the police would have come and it would have been hard to explain the 9mm semi-automatic pistol in his hand and the box of shells in the glove compartment and the holes in the windows of the truck he'd been chasing. But he hadn't been unconscious, and the construction guys hadn't called anyone, and he'd made certain that none of them would ever call anyone ever again.

He didn't like that it had gone down that way, and he didn't like that he'd been forced to shoot the woman whose car he'd hijacked, but the only alternative was getting caught and spending the rest of his life behind bars, and that just wasn't going to happen.

Now, almost twenty-four hours later, he was standing naked in front of a full-length mirror in a hotel room in downtown Seattle, assessing the damage and waiting for Colonel Dorland to return his call. There were the bruises on his buttocks, all shades of purple and yellow and gray, and there were the tiny cuts on his arms from the tiny chunks of safety glass that had showered him when his car had slammed into the ditch, and there was the abrasion on his right elbow, an injury that he couldn't explain but that was bothersome nonetheless. More bothersome than all the others combined, really, because the elbow was extremely sore and stiff now, and the soreness and stiffness would affect his ability to aim and shoot from that side. He was just as good from the left—a little better, actually—but the limitation made him uncomfortable, in the same way that the owner of a delivery service would be uncomfortable if half his vans broke down. You get used to operating a certain way, and anything less than what you're used to becomes substandard and unacceptable. Maybe the elbow would loosen up in a day or so. Mr. Tyler hoped that it would.

His cell phone was on the dresser, between the television and the ice bucket. It started vibrating and he walked over there and lifted it off its charging mat and answered the call.

"I trust you have some good news for me," Colonel Dorland said, cheerfully.

"Unfortunately, I do not," Mr. Tyler said.

"What? I thought you had his location pinned down. I thought you were on him. Like stink on shit. That's what you told me when we talked yesterday morning. Like stink on shit. Those were your exact—"

"He got away," Mr. Tyler said.

"Got away? How is that even possible?"

Dorland didn't sound very cheerful anymore.

"He was in a restaurant," Mr. Tyler said. "I couldn't just walk in there and blow his brains out, right there in front of the lunch crowd. I had to wait for the right opportunity. I had to wait until he left the place or went to the restroom or something."

"So what happened?"

"He must have sensed that something was going down."

Mr. Tyler explained what had happened at Jimmy's Ringside, and the high-speed pursuit that had followed.

"I thought you were supposed to be the best," Colonel Dorland said. "That's why I'm paying you so much money. I don't have time for mistakes. Do you understand that? I don't have time to be worrying about—"

"Listen, I've been busting my ass on this job," Mr. Tyler said. "Literally. I told you I would get it done, and I will. What I *won't* do is take any shit from you, or from anyone else. Do *you* understand *that*? I hope so, Colonel. I really hope so."

Mr. Tyler clicked off. He put the phone back on its charging mat and eased himself down onto the bed and stared at the ceiling. He put a pillow under his sore and stiff right arm, and then he switched on the television and fell asleep watching a very old movie about a very large shark.

6

There were two entrances to the bookstore in the Uptown Center. Or two exits, depending on your perspective. Depending on whether you were coming or going. One of them was on the mall side of the store, and the other was on the street side. There was a small coffee shop wedged into the corner by the one on the mall side. Wahlman walked over there and sat on a stool and ordered a large black coffee and a bagel with cream cheese. The barista asked him if he wanted the bagel toasted. He said yes. The barista cut the bagel and slid it into a shiny chrome toaster oven. She brought the coffee. There was steam rising from the cup. It smelled delicious.

Wahlman was early. Kasey wouldn't be there for another hour. If she even showed up. He hoped she would, but he wasn't counting on it. He'd learned not to count on anyone but himself. He wasn't happy about that, but he wasn't sad about it either. It was just the way it was.

He drank the coffee and ate the bagel, and then he decided to walk around the mall for a while. He'd hitchhiked to Portland, and he'd been on a bus for fifteen hours after that. He needed to wash up, and he needed a fresh set of clothes.

The backpack he'd been carrying around for the past few months was still in Seattle, in the hotel room where he'd been staying. Actually, it probably wasn't in the room anymore. He'd been paying for one night at a time, so another hotel customer was probably in the room now, and the backpack, which contained all of his pants and shirts and socks and underwear and his shaving kit and his navy watch cap and half a bag of pistachios and some other odds and ends, had probably been picked up by someone on the housekeeping staff and carried to wherever things that got left behind were carried to. The lost-and-found, or whatever they called it. At any rate, it was doubtful that he would ever return to Seattle, which meant that it was doubtful that he would ever see that backpack or its contents again. Which was okay. It was time to get some new things anyway.

He walked out into the mall and found a store that he was familiar with. It was a store that sold durable and reasonably priced clothes for outdoorsy types and for a certain set of young adults who wanted to sport that sort of look at the clubs they frequented. He bought a new backpack and two pairs of khaki work pants and two black pullover knit shirts and a package of socks and some boxer briefs and a pair of leather work boots that were approximately the same color as the pants. He paid at the register, and then he walked back out into the mall and found a discount pharmacy and bought some soap and shampoo and deodorant and a razor and some shaving cream and a pair of scissors to trim his beard with and some toothpaste and a toothbrush. He thought about buying one of those nifty folding toothbrushes, but the regular ones were cheaper and there was plenty of room in the backpack, so he picked out a nice blue one that came with a free spool of floss and dropped it into the basket with his other things and stood in line at the only register that was open.

While he was standing in line, he looked past the exit and noticed the gym on the other side of the walkway. There was a sign on a post that said FREE ONE-DAY MEMBERSHIP! TODAY ONLY! Wahlman paid for the things at the pharmacy and walked over there to see about signing up.

The young lady at the desk might have been old enough to order a drink at a bar, but if so only barely. She had blonde hair pulled back and pinned up and a blue spandex outfit and an expensive smile. She wasn't wearing any makeup, and she didn't need any. Her nametag said Ashley.

"What's the deal on the free one-day membership?" Wahlman asked.

"All you have to do is fill out one of our index cards," Ashley said. "Then you're free to use the facility for the rest of the day."

"What's the catch?"

"No catch. Of course we're hoping you like our state-of-the-art, top-of-the-line equipment enough to sign up for one of our premium packages. Which are on special right now, by the way. Where do you usually work out?"

"I don't," Wahlman said.

She looked him over. Head to toe. Then she actually reached over the counter and felt his biceps, which were approximately the size of soccer balls.

"But seriously," she said. "Where do you go?"

"I work outside a lot," Wahlman said. "Keeps me in shape."

"If you say so. Anyway, want to fill out one of our cards?"

"Sure."

He filled out one of the cards, using a fake name and phone number and email address. Ashley took the card when he was finished and slid it into a plastic file box and told him to give her a holler if he needed help with any of the machines. He said thanks and walked back to the men's locker room and took all his clothes off and wadded them up and stuffed them into a trashcan. He tied a towel around his waist and stood at one of the sinks and dabbed on some shaving cream and used the razor to shape his beard and then used the scissors to trim it. He climbed into one of the shower stalls and turned the water on and got it nice and steamy in there and soaped himself up and worked some shampoo into his hair. He rinsed and then he turned the hot water off and stood under the bracing cold spray for about thirty seconds and stepped out and used three more of the gym's towels to dry himself. He put on a pair of the boxer briefs he'd bought and a pair of the khaki pants and one of the black knit shirts and a pair of socks and the boots and zipped everything else into the backpack and exited the locker room.

"Leaving already?" Ashley said as he walked past the front desk.

"I'm meeting someone," Wahlman said. "Maybe I'll come back after a while."

"We're open until ten."

"Thanks."

He walked back to the bookstore and navigated past the display tables in front and sat on the same stool he'd been sitting on earlier and ordered a cup of coffee. The barista did a double-take when she saw him. She must have been wondering how he'd gotten all shiny and new. She brought the coffee. There was steam rising from cup again. It smelled delicious again. Wahlman paid her and they both said thank you and then the barista walked over to the other end of the counter to take care of an attractive middle-aged woman sitting next to a very large shopping bag.

Wahlman took a sip of the coffee.

Then he felt something hard and circular being pressed against his back, just below his right rib cage, something that felt very much like the barrel of a handgun.

7

Wahlman didn't move.

"What do you want?" he said.

"You're coming with me," a male voice said.

"Why would I do that?"

"Because I have the gun. That's the way it works. I'm going to tell you what to do, and you're going to do it."

"Or what? You're going to shoot me right here in the bookstore? With all these people around?"

"You need to come with me," the man said.

"Am I under arrest?" Wahlman asked.

"Not exactly. Not right now. But you're going to be."

"Are you a private investigator?"

"You're smarter than you look."

"Working for a homicide detective in New Orleans named Collins?"

"You're *way* smarter than you look," the man said. "Let's go."

"Private investigators can't arrest people," Wahlman said. "You don't have the authority. You can't make me do anything I don't want to do. That being the case, I would suggest that you put the weapon away and turn around and walk out of here. Otherwise, I'm going to put the weapon away for you, and you're not going to like where I put it."

"I already called the state police," the man said. "They should be here any minute. They'll book you and get the extradition process started. I was hoping we could wait outside in my car, thereby avoiding a big scene in this very public place."

"It's good to know that you have my best interests in mind," Wahlman said.

"Collins told me you could be a smartass," the man said. "If you want to sit right there until the cops come, that's fine with me. As far as I'm concerned, we can wait here all day."

Wahlman still had his fingers hooked into the handle of the coffee mug he'd been sipping from. In one swift motion he slung the steaming hot liquid from the mug over his right shoulder, splashing it directly into the private investigator's face, and he pivoted on the stool and grabbed the man's right wrist and twisted it with a quick jerk and planted the sole of the nice new work boot on his left foot into the man's left knee. The private investigator went down and the gun skittered across the floor and the attractive woman sitting on the other end of the counter started screaming. Wahlman picked up his backpack and grabbed the gun and trotted down the aisle to the street side exit and stepped outside and took a quick look around to see if any police cars had showed up yet. He didn't see any. There was a passenger van parked at the curb with the name of a car dealership painted on the side of it. Some kind of shuttle, Wahlman supposed. You take your car in to get it worked on and the dealership gives you a complimentary ride to the mall so you don't have to sit around in a plastic chair and watch TV for several hours. The van was empty, except for the gray-haired guy behind the steering wheel, who appeared to be either asleep or dead. Wahlman was thinking about using his newly-acquired revolver to persuade the elderly gentleman to let him borrow the vehicle for an hour or so when he saw a car that he recognized. It was Kasey, looking for a place to park. Wahlman ran that way. Kasey braked to a stop when she saw him coming. She unlocked the passenger door and he climbed in and told her not to panic but that they needed to get out of there right away.

She looked him directly in the eyes.

Then she glanced down at the gun in his hand.

"What's going on?" she asked.

"Please. Just drive."

She put the car in gear and weaved her way through the parking lot, out to a traffic signal that allowed customers exiting the mall to turn left or right or continue straight across to a cluster of boutiques and restaurants.

"Which way?" Kasey asked.

"Left," Wahlman said. "Get on the interstate."

"Should I run the red light?"

"No. And don't speed, either. Just drive like you normally would."

"Normally I would speed," Kasey said.

"Just go with the flow of traffic. Not too fast, not too slow."

"Are we in danger?"

"Not at the moment."

"Why do you have a gun?"

"It's a long story."

The light turned green and Kasey steered out into the intersection and merged over into the far right lane and took the ramp to the interstate.

"East or west?" she asked.

"East," Wahlman said. "Don't stop until you get to Vegas."

8

Kasey stopped for gasoline about ten miles from the Las Vegas city limits. There was a shabby little motel across the street from the filling station with a marquis that said FREE CONTINENTAL BREAKFAST and some fast food joints and a Mexican restaurant with some dusty pickup trucks with big tires parked near the entrance.

"I'll go inside and pay for the gas," Wahlman said. "Want me to get some snacks and drinks while I'm in there?"

"I'm hungry," Kasey said. "I want a proper meal."

"You like Mexican?"

"Yes."

"We can eat across the street after I get the gas."

"Okay."

It was almost four o'clock in the afternoon. On the drive to Nevada, Wahlman had told Kasey his real name, and he'd told her about his ordeal in New Orleans a few months ago. He'd told her about almost being run over by a semi, and about the driver of the truck—a man named Darrell Renfro, who looked almost exactly like him—dying from multiple stab wounds, and he told her about a homicide detective named Collins coming to the scene. He told her about the DNA tests that followed, tests indicating that Wahlman and Renfro were exact genetic duplicates of a former army officer named Jack Reacher. He told her about the woman he'd met named Allison, and about narrowly escaping the assassin who killed her, and about getting into a gunfight with the guy and blowing the top of the guy's skull off. He told her about the subsequent warrant issued for his arrest and about going back to Florida and about his best friend Mike Chilton being abducted and murdered. He told her about the team of assassins in Jacksonville, and about being shot in the leg, and about learning that the cloning experiment had actually started way back in 1983, and that now, over a hundred years later, someone in the army was trying to eliminate any evidence that it had ever happened. He told her about the guy in the little gray sports car who'd tried to kill him just yesterday afternoon, about how it was the same guy he'd seen at The Quick Street Inn that first morning in Barstow, and he told her about the private investigator who'd tried to detain him just before he'd come running out of the bookstore. When he finished telling Kasey about all of those things, she told him about the threatening phone call she'd gotten and about putting her daughter on a plane to her parents' house early that morning and about being afraid to go back to her own house.

Wahlman was thinking about all of that as he pumped the gasoline into Kasey's car. He was thinking about all of it, but he was especially thinking about the threatening phone call Kasey had received, about how such a thing could have happened, and about why it had happened. It seemed that the people who were after him had somehow discovered that he'd made contact with her. Maybe they'd tapped into her cell phone signal, or maybe they'd planted a listening device in her house. He wasn't exactly sure why they would have done any of that, but he'd started formulating some ideas, some sketchy hypotheses that kept circling back to Kasey's ex-husband, who'd been shot to death in his car outside an abandoned filling station out in the desert.

Whatever the case, it was good that Kasey had terminated her phone service, and it was good that she'd gotten her daughter and herself away from Barstow.

He finished pumping the gas and climbed back into the car. Kasey drove across the street to the Mexican restaurant and they got out and walked inside. A hostess led them to a table and gave them menus and asked if they would like something to drink. Wahlman ordered a bottle of Mexican beer, and Kasey ordered a margarita with an extra shot of tequila on the side. The hostess told them that their server would be there shortly, and then she walked over to the bar to put the drink orders in.

"An extra shot of tequila?" Wahlman said.

"Don't worry," Kasey said. "I'm not planning on driving anymore today."

"So you want me to drive?"

"No. I've decided we're going to stay here tonight."

"Here?"

"Sure. Why not?"

"I have some money," Wahlman said. "We can ride into town and stay at a decent hotel."

A skinny young man with dark hair and a dark complexion brought the bottle of beer and a frosted glass and the margarita and the extra shot of tequila, along with a basket of tortilla chips and two saucers and two small crocks filled with salsa.

"My name is Rey," the skinny young man said. "I'll be your server today. Would you like to order something from the appetizer menu?"

"Do you have quesadillas?" Kasey asked.

"Yes, ma'am. Excellent choice. Anything else?"

Kasey looked at Wahlman.

"That's fine," Wahlman said. "Just the quesadillas for now."

"Okay, I'll be back around with those shortly. If you would like to go ahead and order dinner, the stuffed flounder is on special this evening and it's really, really good."

"I think we'll take a few minutes to look at the menu," Kasey said.

"Take as long as you like. I'll be right back."

Rey smiled and walked away. Wahlman spooned some salsa onto his saucer and tried one of the tortilla chips.

"These are good," he said. "They taste really fresh."

Kasey took a sip from the shot glass, and then she knocked it back and chased it with a long pull from the margarita.

"That phone call wasn't the only reason I sent Natalie to her grandparents' house," she said. "I've been having some personal problems."

"Anything you want to talk about?" Wahlman asked.

"Well, I told you about my ex-husband being murdered."

"Yeah. And then I saw it on the news. His name was Stielson, right?"

"Right. And I kept his name after we got divorced. It's Natalie's last name, and I just didn't want to—"

"I understand," Wahlman said.

"Anyway, I've been having some problems since then, just trying to keep it together, if you know what I mean."

"Were you still in love with him?"

Kasey almost choked on the sip of margarita she'd just taken. She coughed into a napkin, and then she reached into her purse and pulled out a tissue and wiped the tears from her eyes.

"No," she said. "In fact, just the opposite. I didn't even cry at the service they had for him. I think that's part of the problem. The guilt I'm feeling for not feeling anything. I had a child with the man, you know?"

"Of course," Wahlman said.

"So there's that, but it's mostly about the money he was sending me every month. On the first of February, when the money didn't come, it became glaringly obvious that I wasn't going to be able to keep making a car payment and a house payment and a payment to the school Natalie was going to. I started feeling like a complete failure and I started drinking a lot, and then I finally heard from you after weeks of waiting, and then I got that other phone call—which was a death threat, there's really no other way to put it—and that's kind of where I am right now. I'm kind of a mess."

"I would love to tell you that everything's going to be all right," Wahlman said.

"And I would love to hear that everything's going to be all right," Kasey said.

Wahlman took a drink of the Mexican beer, not bothering to pour it from the bottle into the glass.

"For what it's worth, I don't think you're nearly as much of a mess as you think you are," he said. "I think you're keeping it together incredibly well, considering the circumstances."

"Thank you."

"I think you did the right thing by sending Natalie to your parents' house. Since she had to fly there, I'm assuming it's a fairly good distance from Barstow."

"Oh, it's way far away from Barstow," Kasey said. "But I'm not going to tell you exactly where. I'm not going to tell anyone."

"That's fine. I don't need to know where your daughter is. All I need to know is that she's safe. And I need to know that you're going to be safe too. Are you planning on joining Natalie there at your parents' house?"

"I don't know what I'm planning to do," Kasey said. "Right now I'm just planning to order another shot of tequila."

Rey brought the quesadillas and asked if they were ready to order dinner yet.

"We need a few more minutes to look at the menu," Wahlman said.

"No problem," Rey said. "How are you doing on the drinks?"

Kasey ordered another shot, and Wahlman decided to have one as well. They looked at the menu while Rey walked up to the bar, and when he returned they ordered dinner. And more shots. Rey brought the drinks, and then he delivered the food a few minutes later. Wahlman had the chili rellenos with refried beans and Kasey had the tamales with Mexican rice, and they shared portions from each other's plates. They sat there and ate and talked, and they laughed some and they cried some and they drank tequila until it wasn't a good idea for either one of them to drive.

9

"He was a Military Policeman," Wahlman said.

He and Kasey had decided to stay at the shabby little motel, which wasn't all that shabby once you got to your room. It was as clean and comfortable as any of the chain places Wahlman had been staying at, and the nightly rate was about half what those places usually charged. He and Kasey had decided to stay in the same room, and they had decided to sleep in the same bed. They hadn't actually done any sleeping yet, but they had done just about everything else a man and a woman can do on a king size mattress in a motel room ten miles west of Vegas between seven and nine o'clock on a Friday evening, including at least one thing that you weren't likely to find in any sort of manual or magazine.

Kasey snuggled in close and rested her head on Wahlman's shoulder.

"Who was a Military Policeman?" she asked.

"Jack Reacher. He was a lawman. Like me."

"You were an MP?"

"Master at Arms. That's what they call it in the navy, but it's basically the same thing."

"Do you think about him a lot?"

"Reacher?"

"Yes."

"I do," Wahlman said. "I've been doing some research online, trying to gather as much information as I can, thinking that maybe something he did or said might provide some insight into my current predicament. Apparently he'd been involved in what Detective Collins referred to as *some questionable activities* after he got out of the army, some vigilante justice stuff and whatnot, but I haven't been able find any details on any of that yet."

"What have you been able to find?" Kasey asked.

"Mostly records from court martial proceedings that he'd been involved in. He was a good cop. And a good guy, all-around, as far as I can tell. Which makes me happy, since he's the closest thing to a biological father I'll ever have."

"Remarkable that they were collecting cells for a future cloning experiment way back in nineteen eighty-three," Kasey said.

"Yeah. So far, there's no indication that Reacher was aware that he'd been chosen as a donor. Supposedly there were forty of them. American Soldiers. They had been injured during an attack in Beirut, Lebanon, but I'm guessing that they were healthy otherwise, and I'm guessing that they weren't chosen at random. I'm guessing that there was something about their physical and mental attributes that the army wanted to copy. Supposedly there were two fetuses produced from each donor. And supposedly, out of the eighty fetuses produced, the two from Jack Reacher were the only two that survived."

"Darrell Renfro and you," Kasey said.

"Right."

"Which means that you and Renfro were the strongest. The crème de la crème. The baddest of the badasses."

"I guess so," Wahlman said. "Assuming all that stuff about the experiment is true. Right now I'm just going on the word of a man who was trying to kill me. But he was convincing. He sounded like he knew what he was talking about. And of course the DNA tests that Collins ordered confirmed the genetic connection."

"There's something I don't understand," Kasey said. "If that guy with the leather trench coat was trying to kill you, why didn't he kill you in Barstow? You were sitting five stools away from him that first morning you came into the diner. You and I started talking about how I was cleaning the coffeepot, I think. He was sitting right there. Why didn't he just wait until you walked out of the diner and then—"

"He left abruptly," Wahlman said. "At exactly eleven o'clock. I think I mentioned that at the time. Like he had somewhere to be. The only thing I can figure is that he didn't know who I was yet. Maybe he had a meeting set up with the people who hired him. Maybe they told him my name at the meeting and gave him photographs and everything. Maybe he looked at the photographs and realized he'd seen me earlier that day right there in Barstow. He couldn't have known for sure that I was still in town, but he probably stuck around for a while, thinking that I probably was. He probably stuck around until he was certain that I was gone, and then he probably started working on finding out where I'd gone to. You never saw him come into the diner again?"

"No. I was off that night, and then the next morning I got the call about my ex."

"When you first told me about your ex being murdered, I was hoping that it didn't have anything to do with me. I didn't see how it could have, until the guy with the leather trench coat showed up at Jimmy's Ringside yesterday afternoon."

"You think that guy killed my ex-husband?"

"I don't know," Wahlman said.

"Why would he have had a reason to do that?"

"I don't know. You said your ex was assigned to a temporary post there near Barstow. What kind of work was he doing for the army?"

"Intelligence. You know, classified stuff. He never talked about it much. Are you implying that—"

"It's possible," Wahlman said. "It's possible that your ex was involved with the people trying to cover up the cloning experiment. It's something I've been thinking about for the past day and a half."

Kasey rolled away from Wahlman's shoulder and stared at the ceiling.

"Why am I getting the feeling that Barstow was never just a random choice of destinations for you?" she asked.

"I knew that the United States Army maintained a strong

presence in the area," Wahlman said. "So that part of it wasn't random. But I had no idea that there was some sort of temporary intelligence unit out there somewhere, the exact kind of unit that could be behind the nightmare that has become my life. And when I started talking to you, and when we got together that first night, I had no idea that your ex was even in the army. I didn't know he was active duty military until you told me about the time he went AWOL and took your daughter with him."

"I think I need some more tequila," Kasey said. "Or maybe not. I almost called you Tom. I have to keep reminding myself that your real name is Rock. Which I like, by the way."

"Was your ex an officer?" Wahlman asked.

"He was a major."

"Do you know who he reported to?"

"What do you mean?"

"His immediate supervisor. It probably would have been a colonel or a lieutenant colonel."

"I don't know. Like I said, he never talked much about his work."

"Did he know where your parents live?" Wahlman asked.

"We were married for seven years," Kasey said. "He was Natalie's father. Of course he knew where—"

Kasey sat straight up in bed. She reached over and grabbed her purse from the nightstand and pulled her cell phone out and frantically started punching in numbers.

10

The digital clock on the dashboard said 9:12 p.m. Mr. Tyler had slept a few hours, and then he'd checked out of the downtown Seattle hotel where he'd been staying. He'd rented a car, and he'd started back toward California.

He knew that Wahlman had called the Barstow waitress named Kasey from the payphone at Jimmy's Ringside. He knew this because he'd followed Wahlman toward the restroom, thinking he would ace him in there—two quick shots to the back of the head if he used a urinal, two quick shots to the heart if he used a stall. When Wahlman stopped at the payphone, Mr. Tyler edged past him and continued on into the men's room. He stood just inside the door, where he could clearly hear Wahlman's side of the conversation.

I'm in trouble, Kasey.

Trouble indeed. There would be no escape this time, Mr. Tyler thought. He would make sure of that.

He doubted that Wahlman would actually go into Barstow, not after what had happened with the three guys outside the pharmacy on Main Street. But Wahlman obviously had a thing for Kasey, so maybe he would arrange for a meeting somewhere nearby. Kasey would eventually return to her workplace, and when she did, Mr. Tyler would persuade her to give up boyfriend's location. Of course he would have to kill her then, but that's just the way it went sometimes.

Mr. Tyler's cell phone trilled.

It was Colonel Dorland.

Odd for him to be calling this late, Mr. Tyler thought. Especially on a Friday. He hoped that Colonel Dorland wasn't going to give him another round of verbal counseling, or whatever they called it in the army. There was only so much he could take, and the needle on the Bullshit Tolerance Meter had been jittering dangerously close to the red zone when he'd talked to the colonel earlier.

"Yes?" Mr. Tyler said.

"I wanted to apologize for what I said the last time we spoke," Colonel Dorland said. "Or, more specifically, the way that I said it. I wanted to let you know that I'm one hundred percent confident that you're going to wrap this thing up soon."

"Believe me, Colonel, nobody wants to wrap this thing up more than I do."

"And I also wanted to let you know that my unit is pulling out of California."

"Any particular reason?"

"Stielson."

"Stielson?"

"We have reason to believe that he was involved in a breach of security."

"He was a spy?"

"He was a bonehead. The breach was probably unintentional. We're still checking into it. Regardless, we can't take any chances."

"How soon will you be leaving California?" Mr. Tyler asked.

"As soon as possible," Colonel Dorland said.

"And where will you go?"

"That's still to be decided."

"Okay. Well, thanks for letting me know."

"There's something else," Colonel Dorland said.

"I'm listening," Mr. Tyler said.

"I'm afraid I won't be able to pay you the amount we agreed on earlier."

"What?"

"I'm going to be able to pay you more. An additional five million if the target is eliminated in the next seven days."

"Sort of like a bonus," Mr. Tyler said, relieved that he wasn't going to have to hunt the colonel down and take any sort of monetary shortage out of his verbal-counseling ass.

"My superiors have elevated the urgency status on this particular part of our mission," Colonel Dorland said. "It's now considered Priority One. It has to be done, and it has to be done quickly."

"Understood," Mr. Tyler said.

"If there's anything I can do to help you, just give me a call."

"Okay. I will."

Colonel Dorland disconnected.

An extra five million. Mr. Tyler's bruised ass didn't feel

quite as sore as it had a few minutes ago. It was nice to be appreciated. It was nice when the people you worked for recognized you for what you were: the best hit man on the planet.

And that's exactly what Mr. Tyler was.

The best.

Nobody else even came close.

He set the cell phone down on the center console and turned the radio on and listened to a lovely orchestral arrangement of a song that was popular when he was a teenager. They just don't write them like that anymore, he thought.

11

Kasey's mother answered the phone.

"Where's Natalie?" Kasey asked.

"She's watching television. Do you want to talk to her?"

"Listen to me, Mom. Are you listening?"

"Yes."

"I want you and Dad to take Natalie to the lake house. I want you to go tonight."

"I don't think she would have much fun there right now. I'm pretty sure the lake is frozen."

"This isn't about fun," Kasey said. "I think we might be in danger. All of us. Remember what I told you about the threatening phone call?"

"Yes."

"Well, it's worse than I thought. Henry might have been involved in all this, somehow."

"Your ex-husband Henry?"

"Yes. And of course he knew where you and Dad live. It might be on his army record somewhere, and someone in the army might have made that phone call, and—"

"You're making me nervous, Kasey."

"It's complicated, Mom. I really can't go into it over the phone. You need to get Natalie out of that house as soon as possible. Is Dad there?"

"He drove up to the store to get some things. It's supposed to snow later tonight. Up to eight inches, they're saying."

"Tell Dad to call me when he gets home. The new number I gave you, okay?"

"I'll tell him."

Kasey disconnected. She slid the phone back into her purse, climbed out of bed and started putting her clothes on.

"Going somewhere?" Rock asked.

"We need to go back to California. We need to find out exactly what's going on, and we need to put a stop to it."

"We?"

Kasey sat on the edge of the bed.

"This is not just about you anymore," she said. "I was threatened. My daughter was threatened. My ex-husband was murdered. Maybe you don't care about any of that, but—"

Rock sat up and scooted over and sat beside her. He was still naked. In the amber glow of the bedside lamp his arms and chest and torso looked like something that had been painted or sculpted. He put his arm around her and held her close to his side.

"I care," he said. "Very much."

"We need to go."

"We need to sleep. Neither one of us is in any shape to drive tonight."

Kasey took a deep breath.

"I guess you're right," she said. "But first thing in the morning, we're going straight back to California."

Her phone trilled. It was her dad. She told him everything she'd told her mother. He wanted details. He wanted to call the police. Kasey finally convinced him that there wasn't really any concrete evidence to go to the police with yet, and she finally convinced him to get everyone out of the house, at least for the night. She said she would call him back in the morning to let him know if anything had changed.

She plugged her phone into its charger and set it on the nightstand.

"I heard you talking to your parents about a lake house," Rock said. "Is that something your ex didn't know about?"

"Mom and Dad bought the place back in November. Natalie's their only grandchild, and they were planning to surprise her with it this summer. Swimming, skiing, barbecues, fishing, all that kind of stuff. I don't think they told my ex about it. In fact, I'm sure they didn't. As far as I know, they hadn't had any contact with him since the divorce."

"It sounds like a good place for your daughter to be right now," Rock said. "And a good place for you to be as well."

"No. I'm in the thick of this now. I'm not going anywhere."

"I could definitely use the help, but—"

"As of this morning, I'm unemployed," Kasey said. "My house isn't in foreclosure yet, but it will be. Natalie might have to go to summer school this year, but at least I know she's going to be safe there at the lake house with my parents. In short, I'm free as a bird, and you're stuck with me until we get this thing resolved."

"I can't think of anyone I would rather be stuck with," Rock said.

He kissed her on the lips and they eased back onto the bed together and kissed some more and made love some more and fell asleep in each other's arms.

12

Wahlman woke up at 5:27. He climbed out of bed and took a shower and put some clothes on and walked outside. The air was cool and dry, and the smell of it reminded him of the freshly-laundered linens that always seemed to be pinned to the clotheslines at the orphanage where he grew up.

He walked across the parking lot to the office. A fat man with thinning black hair was standing behind the desk thumbing through a magazine. There was a small television on a table behind the desk. It was tuned to a news channel. They were talking about four road construction men who were shot and killed near Seattle following an accident on the highway Thursday afternoon. Wahlman had been wondering if the man in the little gray sports car had survived the crash. Now he knew. A woman was also found shot to death nearby, and then her car was found later, parked miles away.

"Can I help you?" the fat man said.

"I was looking for the free continental breakfast," Wahlman said.

The fat man pointed to a table in the far right corner of the room. There was a toaster and a loaf of white bread and some little plastic tubs of margarine and a jar of grape jelly with a spoon sticking out of it. There were two coffeemakers on a separate table. One of them had a little sign taped to it that said DECAF.

"We're out of cups for the coffee," the fat man said. "Marla's supposed to be bringing some in. She'll be here at seven."

Wahlman didn't say anything. He turned around and exited the office and walked over to the burger place next door. He bought two large coffees and two sausage and egg biscuits and carried everything back to the room. Kasey was still asleep. Wahlman set the cardboard drink holder and the bag containing the biscuits on the little round table by the window, and then he sat on the bed and lightly stroked Kasey's back with his fingers.

"Something smells good," she said.

"You can sleep some more if you want to."

"What time is it?"

"A little after six."

"We should get going."

"Checkout time isn't until eleven," Wahlman said.

"But we should get going."

Kasey got up and took a quick shower, and then she sat at the table and drank some of the coffee and ate part of a biscuit and asked Wahlman if he wanted the rest of it.

"No thanks," he said. "I'm not very hungry."

"You need to eat something," Kasey said.

"There's another biscuit in the bag. Maybe I'll eat it later."

"You should eat it while it's still warm."

"The guy who was chasing me ended up shooting some road construction workers," Wahlman said.

"He killed them?"

"Yeah. And it looks like he hijacked a car and killed the woman who was driving it too."

"That's terrible."

"Yeah."

"So the guy with the leather trench coat is still out there somewhere," Kasey said.

"He is," Wahlman said.

"Still trying to find you."

"No doubt."

"And when he finds you, he will try to kill you."

"Yes."

"So what's the plan?"

"I'm going to let him find me," Wahlman said. "And then I'm going to make him wish he hadn't."

13

Mr. Tyler walked into The Quick Street Inn at 10:07. It was crowded in there and it smelled like coffee and fried potatoes and maple syrup. Knives and forks were clinking against plates and people were talking and laughing. A guy in a white apron—the same guy Mr. Tyler had talked to several weeks ago—was standing at the flattop, rolling some link sausages around with a long fork. There were two waitresses working the dining area and one working behind the counter. None of them was Kasey.

The waitress working behind the counter had short blonde hair with bright blue streaks dyed into the strands that framed her face. She was young and petite and perky and she had a nice smile. Mr. Tyler figured she made a lot of money in tips. He took his leather coat off, folded it in half and placed it on one of the chrome and vinyl stools bolted to the floor, and then he sat down on the stool next to the one he'd put his coat on. The guy to his left was wiping the egg yolk off his plate with a half a slice of buttered toast. When he finished doing that, he stuffed the bread into his mouth and noisily slurped some of the coffee from his cup. Mr. Tyler thought about finding another place to sit. He didn't. The perky young waitress came and asked him if he wanted coffee. He did. She brought it and asked him what he would like for breakfast this morning. Her nametag said Sally.

"Is there some sort of breakfast special today?" Mr. Tyler asked.

"Sorry. Not on weekends. But I think you'll see that our prices are really reasonable anyway."

"What would you suggest?"

"Do you like biscuits and gravy?"

"Yes. That sounds good. With two eggs. Scrambled."

"Coming right up," Sally said.

"Can I ask you a question?"

"Sure."

"Do you know a young lady named Kasey who works here?"

Sally thought about it for a few seconds.

"Kasey Stielson?" she said.

Stielson. Her last name was Stielson?

Mr. Tyler felt as though he'd just won the lottery.

"Yes, that's her," he said.

"She doesn't work here anymore," Sally said. "She a friend of yours or something?"

"Just an acquaintance," Mr. Tyler said. "Hey, could you add some hash browns to my order?"

"Not a problem."

"And could you make that order to go?"

"Of course."

Ten minutes later, Sally brought a brown paper bag containing the food Mr. Tyler had order. He paid her and gave her a nice tip and walked out of the diner and called Colonel Dorland from his car. Dorland was in transit to his new headquarters, and it took him almost an hour to get back to Mr. Tyler with Kasey Stielson's home address.

Yes, there was a connection to Major Henry Stielson.

She was his ex-wife.

And they had a child together.

Colonel Dorland had been a wealth of useful information, and Mr. Tyler was confident that he would be able to put this matter in the scrapbook—and the remaining payment from it into the bank— within the next day or two.

The gravy from The Quick Street Inn had been a little too salty for Mr. Tyler's taste, but otherwise this was shaping up to be one of the most delightful mornings he had ever experienced. He started his car and pulled away from the curb. He momentarily considered stopping and getting a haircut, but he didn't. He drove on past the barber shop and took a left at the light.

14

Mr. Tyler parked across the street from Kasey Stielson's house. There was a car parked in the driveway. Mr. Tyler ran a search on the tag number and saw that the car was registered to Kasey. Which meant that she was probably home.

This day just kept getting better and better.

Mr. Tyler climbed out of his car and walked up to the porch and rang the bell. When the door swung open, Mr. Tyler pointed his sound-suppressed semi-automatic pistol at Kasey's face and told her not to scream.

Her eyes got wide and her fingers started trembling and her lips tightened and arched into an extreme frown.

"What do you want?" she said, her voice quivering and tears welling in her eyes.

"I want you to stop talking and back away from the door," Mr. Tyler said.

Kasey stopped talking and backed away from the door. Mr. Tyler entered the house. He kept the pistol pointed at Kasey's face. One squeeze of the trigger and her brains would be splattered all over the wall behind her.

"I don't have any money," she said.

"Is anyone else in the house?"

"No."

"Where's your daughter?"

"She's not here."

"Will she be coming back in the next thirty minutes or so?"

"No."

"Sit down on the couch," Mr. Tyler said.

Kasey sat down on the couch. Mr. Tyler remained standing. He lowered the gun to his side.

"Please don't kill me," Kasey said.

"That's not my intention. I just need some information from—"

Before Mr. Tyler could say *you*, something that could have been a fist or a lead pipe came down hard on the back of his neck. The world went black and his body went numb and when he opened his eyes there was a very large boot on his chest with a very large man attached to it.

The very large man was Rock Wahlman.

He was aiming Mr. Tyler's sound-suppressed semi-automatic pistol directly between Mr. Tyler's eyes.

"Who are you working for?" Wahlman said.

Mr. Tyler looked over at the couch. Kasey was still sitting there. She had a gun too. A revolver. Her fingers weren't trembling anymore. No tears. It had all been an act. Mr. Tyler felt stupid for allowing himself to fall into their little trap. He'd been too eager, too excited by the information he'd received from Dorland. He should have handled the whole thing differently. He should have been more patient.

"Mind if I take my coat off?" he said. "It seems to have gotten terribly warm in here over the past few minutes."

"Don't worry," Wahlman said. "You're not going to live long enough for it to bother you much."

Inside the right cuff of Mr. Tyler's leather coat there was an electronic switch, a tiny computerized device that could only be activated by a certain series of sounds. The switch had been tuned to recognize Mr. Tyler's voice and Mr. Tyler's voice only. The switch was connected to a two-minute delay circuit, which was connected to a long thin tube, which had been sewn into the bottom hem of the coat. The long thin tube had been filled with a highly explosive putty-like substance. Enough to destroy a room or two with the initial blast. Enough to reduce a human being to itsy bitsy pieces.

Every time Mr. Tyler contracted a job, he guaranteed that the intended target would be eliminated. Colonel Dorland was going to get what he paid for. Rock Wahlman was going to die. The exploding coat was something of a last resort, of course, because while it would certainly take care of the target, it would also take care of any other living beings in the vicinity, including Mr. Tyler himself.

That was where the timer came in. The idea was to activate the switch and then skedaddle. Two minutes was plenty of time to get far enough away, even on foot.

Plenty of time if you weren't staring at the barrel of your own pistol.

Escaping unharmed was clearly a long shot at this point. A million to one. Mr. Tyler knew that, but he figured he might as well give it a try. The target was definitely going to be eliminated—obliterated, as it turned out—in a few minutes, along with the pretty young lady who'd been stupid enough to get involved with him. Mr. Tyler still had a chance to get away, but first he needed to convince Rock Wahlman to let him take the coat off.

"Please," Mr. Tyler said. "I'm sweating."

"Who are you working for?" Wahlman said, scooting the sole of his boot away from Mr. Tyler's chest and pressing it against his throat.

"Let me take my coat off and I'll tell you everything," Mr. Tyler said.

"Let him take it off," Kasey said. "It's worth some money. Probably two hundred dollars or more at a pawnshop. It would be a shame to get blood all over it."

"Guys like this don't walk into situations like this without some kind of backup plan," Wahlman said. "He probably has a weapon he's trying to get to. Maybe another pistol. Maybe something else. I'm not going to give him the opportunity to make a move."

"How is he going to make a move?" Kasey said. "If he tries anything, I'll shoot him."

"You can pat me down if you want to," Mr. Tyler said. "You're not going to find another weapon."

Kasey got up from the couch. She walked over to where Mr. Tyler was lying and searched him, starting at the ankles and ending at the shoulders. She found a cell phone and a wallet and a set of keys. She tossed everything onto the coffee table, looked at Wahlman and shrugged.

Wahlman took his foot off Mr. Tyler's throat and backed away a couple of steps

"Go ahead and take the coat off," Wahlman said. "Slowly."

Mr. Tyler wriggled out of the sleeves.

"Thank you," he said. "That's so much better."

"Who hired you?" Wahlman said. "I want names."

"I need to use the restroom," Mr. Tyler said. "I drank about ten cups of coffee a while ago, and—"

Wahlman fired a round into Mr. Tyler's right thigh. The pain was immediate and intense. It felt as though someone had driven a railroad spike into his leg with a sledgehammer.

"Go ahead and piss your pants," Wahlman said. "You're not getting up from that floor until you tell me what I want to know."

Mr. Tyler turned his head and retched.

"I guess I'm not getting up at all now, am I?" he said, trying to fight the continuous waves of nausea washing over him.

"So much for not getting blood on the coat," Kasey mumbled.

"Who are you working for?" Wahlman said.

"You're persistent, aren't you?" Mr. Tyler said.

"Tell me."

"I was contacted by a man named Stielson," Mr. Tyler said. "He was a major in the United States Army. He gave me an envelope that contained—"

"I already know about Stielson," Wahlman said. "Who

was his supervisor? Who was calling the shots?"

"Colonel Dorland. I don't know his first name."

"Where can I find him?"

"There's a cluster of singlewide trailers out in the Mojave Desert," Mr. Tyler said. "Not far from where the police found Major Stielson. Just south of there. A little southwest, I think. Not more than a couple of miles. It seems to be the command center for whatever they're doing out there. I would guess that everything you want to know is inside those trailers."

"Tell me how to get there."

"It's off the beaten path. I wasn't even supposed to know about it. I don't know if I could find it again, but I could try."

Kasey was on the couch again. Wahlman glanced that way.

"Sounds like our best chance," Kasey said.

Wahlman nodded in agreement.

"I need to put a pressure dressing on his leg," he said. "I need some tape and some sort of absorbent padding. Gauze, washcloths, whatever you have."

"The only kind of tape I have is duct tape," Kasey said.

"That's fine. I'll use it to tie his wrists together while I'm at it."

Mr. Tyler turned his head away from them and smiled.

So far, so good.

Maybe this was going to work out after all.

15

The assassin's name was Mr. Tyler.

Kasey had asked while Wahlman was bandaging his leg. There were two wounds. An entrance wound, and an exit wound. The bullet had lodged into one of the oak floorboards beneath the assassin.

Mr. Tyler.

Just a regular name.

Like a regular human being.

Only he wasn't a regular human being. He was a predator. A killer. He did it for money. He stayed alive by seeing that other people didn't. Wahlman's plan was to leave him out in the desert and then make an anonymous call to the police. Maybe a cruiser and an ambulance would get out there before the vultures picked him apart.

Wahlman looked out the living room window.

"Is that your car parked across the street?" he asked.

"Yes," Mr. Tyler said. "It's a rental."

"How much gas is in it?"

"Three quarters of a tank."

"Good. We'll take your car and leave Kasey's here."

"Do either of you have anything I could take for pain?" Mr. Tyler asked.

"I could put a bullet in your skull," Kasey said. "That would take care of it for you."

"I'm trying to cooperate here," Mr. Tyler said. "The least you could do is—"

"Shut up," Wahlman said. "I'm going to go get your car and back it up to the door. Then I'm going to open the rear hatch and load you into the cargo area, like the sack of shit that you are."

"What if someone sees him back there?" Kasey asked. "What if a cop sees him?"

"Nobody's going to see him," Wahlman said. "I'm going to cover him with this."

Wahlman picked up the leather trench coat, and then he grabbed Mr. Tyler's keys off the coffee table. As he headed out the front door, Mr. Tyler uttered something in a language Wahlman wasn't familiar with. He turned around and looked the assassin directly in the eyes, and then he continued over the threshold.

He trotted across the street, opened the rear passenger side door and draped the coat over the back headrest on that side, where it would be easy to grab and pull over Mr. Tyler once he was in the cargo area. He walked around the front of the car, opened the driver side door and climbed behind the wheel and adjusted the seat. Before he slid the key into the ignition, he looked in the rearview mirror and noticed something odd about the coat. There was a slight tear along the bottom hem. The bullet he'd fired into Mr. Tyler's leg must have grazed the coat on its way out.

But that wasn't the odd thing.

Something was showing through the tear in the hem.

Something that looked like modeling clay.

Wahlman had spent several weeks studying explosive ordnance during his training to become a Master at Arms in the United States Navy. He knew what plastic bonded explosives looked like. And now he knew why Mr. Tyler had been so anxious to get the coat off.

He started the car and slammed it into reverse and squealed up onto Kasey's yard, spraying the stucco on the front of the house with landscaping pebbles and destroying a few decorative cacti as he fishtailed his way to the porch. He skidded to a stop about four feet from the front door, climbed out of the car and ran inside and picked Kasey up and held her in his arms and started running toward the rear of the house.

Mr. Tyler was still on the living room floor. He started shouting, pleading for help as Wahlman twisted the knob and slung the back door open and ran outside.

Then there was a great big boom.

Then there was silence.

16

Kasey had packed a suitcase, and she'd loaded it into her trunk before Mr. Tyler had come to her house. The explosion hadn't done much damage to her car. Just some scratches and small dents from the debris that had fallen on it.

Wahlman was sitting in the passenger seat, checking the 9mm semi-automatic pistol he'd taken from Mr. Tyler. He pushed the magazine into position and jacked a round into the chamber as Kasey steered into the driveway of the abandoned filling station where her ex-husband had been murdered.

"So this is the place," she said.

"This is the place," Wahlman said. "Supposedly, the cluster of singlewide trailers Mr. Tyler told us about is just southwest of here."

"Which way is southwest?"

"That way," Wahlman said, pointing toward an area between the setting sun and a large cactus plant in the distance.

"There's no road," Kasey said. "I'm not sure how well my car is going to do on this terrain."

"I want you to wait here," Wahlman said. "I'm going to walk the rest of the way."

"Two miles? It's going to be dark in an hour."

"That's why we stopped and bought flashlights."

"I didn't know you were planning to walk all that way."

"I wasn't. But you're right. Your car's not going to make it."

The revolver Wahlman had taken from the private investigator in Bakersfield was in the glove compartment. Kasey reached over and unlatched the door and pulled it out.

"I want to go with you," she said.

"You should wait here."

"Why?"

"You haven't been trained for this kind of thing."

"So?"

"It might get ugly."

Kasey took a deep breath.

"A guy got blown to bits inside my house a while ago," she said. "I think I can handle ugly."

"Have you ever killed a person?" Wahlman said.

"Of course not."

"If you come with me, you might have to."

"My daughter was threatened," Kasey said. "She's basically in hiding right now. I want this thing to be over as much as you do."

"You want your daughter to be an orphan?"

"No, but—"

"Stay here."

Wahlman climbed out of the car, slid the 9mm into his waistband, and started walking. He had one of the flashlights they'd bought in his backpack, along with a bottle of water and a black ski mask and a compass and the partial roll of duct tape from Kasey's house.

It took him about forty minutes to find the complex. He was about a quarter of a mile away when he spotted it. There were four identical singlewide trailers arranged in a square, sealed off from the rest of the desert by a chain link fence. The fence was eight feet tall. It was topped with barbed wire and razor ribbon. There was no light coming from any of the windows of the trailers, but that didn't mean anything. The glass might have been painted. Or blacked out with static film.

Wahlman put the ski mask on and got down on his belly and crawled closer to the complex. There was a sentry by the gate, an enlisted man wearing desert cammies. The guy was sitting on the ground with his ankles crossed, leaning back against the fence and smoking a cigarette. That was when Wahlman knew for sure that there weren't any senior officers around. The guy should have been standing at parade rest. He was in charge of granting or denying access to the complex. That was his job. The fact that he was treating his duty so casually meant that the brass had secured for the day. Or maybe for the week. It was Saturday. Maybe intelligence officers posted out in the middle of nowhere only worked Monday through Friday.

Whatever the case, the sentry was a total slacker. If he'd

been caught sitting on his ass smoking a cigarette while standing a quarterdeck watch—or any watch—in the navy, he would have been dealt with severely. Wahlman figured the army had similar standards. He waited until it got completely dark, and then he snuck up beside the guy and grabbed him by the collar and forced his face into the sand.

"What's your name, soldier?" Wahlman said, planting his right knee between the guy's shoulder blades.

"I can't breathe, sir," the guy said.

"What's your name?"

"This is a restricted area, sir. I'm going to have to ask you to identify yourself, and I'm going to have to ask you to—"

"It's a simple question," Wahlman said. "Tell me your name and maybe I won't have you court-martialed for dereliction of duty."

The sentry coughed. His lips were caked with sand.

"Pickerman, Arnold," he said. "Private First Class. It's my duty to inform you—"

"What kind of outfit is this?"

"Sir?"

"What's your mission out here?"

Pickerman coughed some more.

"Permission to speak freely, sir?" he said.

"Permission granted," Wahlman said.

"I'm just out here on temporary duty. It's not my unit. They bugged out. I'm not supposed to talk about it."

"When did they leave? Where did they go?"

"Sir, I have orders to—"

"Forget about your orders. You need to talk to me."

Pickerman reached for his pistol. Before he could unsnap the holster, Wahlman clubbed him in the back of the head. Turned him over, pressed a strip of duct tape across his mouth, wrapped some around his wrists and ankles. Took his gun and his wallet and his walkie-talkie. The fact that he was communicating by radio meant that there was at least one other person in the vicinity. Maybe someone inside one of trailers. Maybe someone in a truck, patrolling the area or watching from a distance with binoculars. Wahlman kept that in mind as he opened the gate and trotted over to the nearest trailer and tried the door. It was locked. He tried the doors on the other three trailers. They were locked too. He walked through the gap between two of the units and saw that a courtyard had been fashioned back there. Concrete pavers, picnic tables, fifty-five gallon drums cut in half lengthwise and topped with steel grates for barbecuing. He also saw that there weren't any generators back there, and that the ports on the electrical boxes had been covered with steel caps and tagged with laminated cards that said ARMY.

Which meant that Pickerman had been telling the truth. The personnel who'd been posted there were gone now.

Wahlman sat down at one of the picnic tables and went through Pickerman's wallet and found nothing of interest. There was a half-eaten hotdog under the table. Wahlman picked it up and examined it. The mustard on it hadn't completely dried out, and the bread was still soft. Which meant that it was probably less than a day old.

The walkie-talkie chirped.

"Rover One radio check," a male voice said. "Over."

317

"Radio check loud and clear," Wahlman said. "Over."

"I need to log a report for eighteen hundred. Over."

"All secure. Over."

"Get your head out of your ass, Pickerman," the male voice said. "Over and out."

Wahlman pitched the hotdog back under the table where he'd found it, and then he used the butt of Pickerman's pistol to break one of the windows on the trailer that was facing west. He climbed inside and used his flashlight to look around. All of the desks were bare, and all of the file cabinets were empty. The rubber tiles on the floor had a fresh coat of wax on them, and there wasn't a speck of dust on any of the surfaces. The place had been vacuumed and wiped down and shined and scrubbed and polished. It had been left exactly the way that a well-disciplined military outfit should have left it, and Wahlman knew that the other three trailers would be the same.

He decided to exit through the front door. As he was heading that way, he noticed something on the floor, a tiny strip of paper, partially hidden under one of the legs of a portable metal shelf unit. He crouched down and tilted the shelf unit and aimed the flashlight at the strip of paper and picked it up. It was about three inches long and about as wide as a cocktail straw. Wahlman figured it had fallen on the floor while someone was emptying a paper shredder. There was something printed one side of it, but the shredder blades had lopped off the tops and bottoms of the letters, making them extremely difficult to decipher. Wahlman stood there and studied the mutilated text for a couple of minutes, finally managing to fill in the missing pieces imaginarily.

acher and backorder another bat

The first word could have been *Reacher*, but it also could have been *teacher*. Or maybe it was the tail-end of some other word that Wahlman couldn't think of at the moment.

Considering the number of documents that probably got destroyed when an intelligence unit relocated, it was highly unlikely that a single miniscule strip of paper contained anything that would ever be useful.

Wahlman slid it into his pocket anyway.

Because you never know.

He exited the trailer. Pickerman was still in the same spot, just outside the gate. He was still breathing. Wahlman figured Rover One would come and see about him when he failed to respond to the next radio check. Wahlman pitched his things into the sand a few feet away, and then he started walking back toward Kasey's car.

If he'd only gotten to the complex a day sooner, he thought. Now he would have to keep running, keep searching. There would be more assassins. More hotel rooms and diners and stretches of highway that seemed to go on forever. There would be no peace of mind until this matter was completely resolved.

Which was discouraging, to say the least.

But he was alive, and Kasey was with him, and he knew the name of the intelligence unit's commanding officer—Colonel Dorland, if Mr. Tyler had been telling the truth.

And he had a strip of paper that said *acher and backorder another bat*.

And that was something.

KILL SHOT

THE REACHER EXPERIMENT BOOK 4

1

Bees buzzing, flowers blooming, not a cloud in the sky.

It was a fine day for a man to hire an assassin.

Colonel Dorland took his coffee and his cell phone out to the deck. He was working from home today. Or, more precisely, from the personal quarters the United States Army had assigned him to, a one-room cabin on the edge of a cliff, somewhere between Mont Eagle, Tennessee and the middle of nowhere.

Not that he was complaining. His staff—the officers and the enlisted guys—had been crammed into an open bay barracks over at the new headquarters complex, all nine of them sharing a space about the size of a two-car garage. They ate together and showered together and their beds were exactly two feet apart. Less than optimal accommodations, for sure, especially for an elite intelligence unit, but then this was the army. At least they weren't digging latrines behind a row of tents somewhere.

Dorland tapped in the telephone number he'd been given. A woman answered on the second ring.

"Sun River Disposal, Nashville Satellite Office," she said.

"Sorry," Dorland said. "I must have the wrong number."

"Who were you trying to reach, sir?"

"A man named Waverly."

"I'm Mr. Waverly's administrative assistant. My name is Brenna. How may I help you today?"

Sun River Disposal. Administrative assistant. Not what Dorland had been expecting.

"I need to speak with Mr. Waverly," he said.

"Mr. Waverly is in a meeting right now. Would you like to leave a message?"

"I need to speak with him now. Tell him it's Colonel Dorland. United States Army."

"Please hold."

There was a click, followed by silence. Dorland sipped his coffee. Waited. Two minutes. Three. Another click.

"This is Waverly."

"I was told you might be able to help me with a problem," Dorland said.

"What kind of problem?"

"The kind people don't talk about over the phone."

"Could you be a little more specific, sir?"

"No."

"Then I'm afraid—"

"What kind of outfit is Sun River Disposal?" Dorland asked.

"We handle all types of hazardous materials," Mr. Waverly said. "Removal and disposal. We have facilities coast-to-coast. No job too big, no job too small."

Dorland thought about that for a few seconds.

"The problem I'm dealing with is definitely hazardous," he said. "And I would definitely be interested in removal and disposal."

"I see," Mr. Waverly said. "And would this hazard happen to be of an organic nature?"

"Yes."

"I think I understand. I would be happy to meet with you in person to discuss the particulars and provide you with a free estimate."

"Great," Dorland said. "Just tell me where you want to meet. I can be in Nashville in two hours."

Mr. Waverly told Colonel Dorland where he wanted him to be, and when he wanted him to be there, and then he hung up.

2

The sign out front said *USED BOOKS*.

The sign on the door said *OPEN*.

Rock Wahlman walked inside. There was a man with gray hair and gray skin sitting on a stool behind the counter. He was drinking coffee and smoking a cigarette and reading a tattered paperback copy of a book called *Neighbots* by an author named Jesse Lecat. Some kind of science fiction thing, Wahlman guessed.

"Can I help you?" the man said.

"I was wondering if you had any job openings," Wahlman said.

"You want to work *here*?"

There were seven places of business located in the strip mall on Maple Drive. Rock Wahlman had entered five of them already, and he'd spoken to five different managers already. Four of the managers had said no flat-out, and the other one had said to try back in a few weeks. The next place in line had a *FOR LEASE* sign taped to the inside of the window, and then there was the bookstore, which smelled like decades of dust and tobacco and wasted opportunities.

"I could clean the place up for you," Wahlman said. "Straighten the books, put them in alphabetical order or whatever."

"Then what?"

"I'm just looking for something temporary."

"You know anything about books?" the man said.

"What's there to know?"

"You're joking, right? Get out of my store."

"I need money," Wahlman said. "I haven't eaten in three days."

Which was a lie. It had only been two.

The man behind the counter stood and twisted his cigarette into the grungy steel ashtray by the cash register. He opened the register and pulled out a one dollar bill and handed it to Wahlman.

"Here you go," he said. "Now take a hike."

"I'm not looking for a handout," Wahlman said.

"Suit yourself."

The man slid the bill back into the slot he'd taken it from and closed the cash drawer.

"I can unload those for you," Wahlman said, pointing toward a stack of cardboard boxes at the end of the counter. "I can do whatever you want me to do. Heavy stuff, dirty stuff, it doesn't matter."

The door swung open and two men walked in. One of them was wearing a tan jacket, the other a red sweatshirt. They were not big guys, but they weren't small either. Just average. They appeared to be in their mid-to-late twenties, and they appeared to be physically fit. They walked over to a wire rack on the wall opposite the counter and started looking at some magazines.

"Can I help you guys?" the man behind the counter said.

The man wearing the tan jacket turned and looked toward the counter, giving Wahlman the once-over, the way people do sometimes when you're six feet four inches tall and weigh two hundred and thirty pounds.

"Just looking," the man wearing the tan jacket said. He turned back toward the magazine rack, pulled a candy bar out of his pocket, peeled back the wrapper and took a bite.

"You want to make some money?" the man behind the counter whispered to Wahlman. "Get those guys out of here for me. They come in here and mess up my magazines, and they never buy anything. This is the fourth day in a row."

"There's no law against browsing," Wahlman said.

"They make me nervous. They might be planning to rob me or something. Who knows? I'll give you twenty dollars to escort them out of here."

Ordinarily Wahlman would have left it alone, but he needed the cash. He needed it desperately. Some of the money he'd saved from working in Washington and California had gone toward new identities for Kasey and himself, and the rest had gone toward the ragged-out SUV they'd been traveling and sleeping in. Right now Kasey was one block over, doing the same thing Wahlman was doing. Looking for work. Something that paid cash on a daily basis. Something that wouldn't leave any sort of paper trail.

Increasingly difficult to find these days.

Twenty dollars would buy some hamburgers and some gas, and maybe something better would come along tomorrow.

Wahlman walked over to the magazine rack.

"Maybe you didn't see the sign," he said. "No food or beverages inside the store."

"Maybe you didn't see the other sign," Tan Jacket said. "The one that says mind your own business."

"I'm going to have to ask you guys to leave."

"We'll leave when we're ready to leave," Red Sweatshirt said.

"I'm asking nicely," Wahlman said. "For now."

"And I'm saying *kiss my ass* nicely," Red Sweatshirt said. "What are you going to do? Pick us up and throw us out the door?"

"Only if I have to."

Red Sweatshirt slid his hand into his pocket. Maybe he had a knife in there. Or some brass knuckles. Or a pistol. Wahlman was about to reach over and rearrange the bones in his wrist when Tan Jacket tossed the magazine he'd been looking at back into the rack and motioned toward the door.

"Let's get out of here," he said.

"I'm not done looking," Red Sweatshirt said.

"Let's go."

Red Sweatshirt shrugged. He followed Tan Jacket toward the door, turned and looked back at Wahlman before crossing over the threshold.

"Next time," he said.

"Yeah," Wahlman said. "Next time."

Tan Jacket and Red Sweatshirt sauntered across the sidewalk and out to the parking lot. They climbed into a red pickup truck, Tan Jacket on the driver side.

The guy behind the counter opened the cash drawer, pulled out a ten dollar bill and handed it to Wahlman.

"Here you go," he said. "Nice job."

"You said twenty," Wahlman said.

"What?"

"You said you would give me twenty dollars to escort those guys out of your store. I did what you asked me to do. Now pay up."

"I said ten."

"You said twenty."

"I might have some more work for you."

"What kind of work?"

"A guy owes me some money. Two thousand dollars. I'll give you ten percent."

"You some kind of loan shark?" Wahlman asked.

"I sold him a boat. Two grand up front, two more in two weeks. That was the deal. He still hasn't paid me. It's been four months."

"Give me the rest of the money you owe me," Wahlman said. "Then maybe I'll think about it."

"I said ten."

"You said twenty."

The man behind the counter sighed. He opened the cash drawer again, pulled out another ten dollar bill. Handed it to Wahlman.

"There," he said. "Happy now?"

"Relatively," Wahlman said.

The man behind the counter tore off a strip of cash register tape and scribbled something on it with a ballpoint pen.

"This is the name and address of the man who owes me money," he said, handing the strip of paper to Wahlman. "Can you go talk to him today?"

"I never said I would take the job," Wahlman said.

"You said if I paid you twenty—"

"I said I would think about it."

"Well?"

"I'm still thinking."

"You don't want to make two hundred bucks?"

"What if this guy doesn't have any money to give me? Then it's going to be a waste of my time. And gasoline."

"He has money," the man behind the counter said. "He has plenty of money."

Wahlman looked at the strip of paper.

"What part of town is this?" he said.

"It's only a few blocks away. You could walk there if you wanted to. You could be back here in less than an hour."

Wahlman nodded. "All right," he said. "I'll see what I can do."

"You need to leave something here," the man behind the counter said. "Your wallet, or the keys to your car or something."

"Why?"

"So I know you won't run off with my money."

"You think I'm a thief?"

"If the situation were reversed, would you trust me?"

Good point, Wahlman thought. He pulled the keys to the SUV out of his pocket and tossed them on the counter.

"I don't even know your name," Wahlman said.

"Myers," the man behind the counter said. "My name is Myers."

3

Colonel Dorland walked into the downtown barroom and sat in the booth furthest from the door. The room was dark and it smelled like stale beer and cigarette smoke and something Dorland couldn't quite put his finger on. There were about a hundred coats of varnish on the floor. It was almost black. Dorland was wearing civilian clothes. Khaki pants, loafers, flannel shirt with a button-down collar. He looked like a regular guy. He was a little early. Mr. Waverly wasn't there yet. A waitress came and asked him what he wanted to drink.

"Bourbon on the rocks," he said.

The waitress nodded, walked away without saying anything. She was in her mid-thirties and had broken dreams written all over her. Maybe she was a songwriter. Or a singer. Or both. Nashville was full of them. Most of them didn't make it. They came to town with a suitcase and a guitar, and they left with a suitcase and a pawn ticket. Or they stuck around and drove cabs or washed dishes or waited tables. Hoping to be discovered. Hoping for their big break.

Dorland had grown up in the area. He knew all about it. One in a million. Like playing the lottery. A total waste of time and resources, in his opinion.

A man wearing a dark blue suit slid into the seat across from him.

"Colonel Dorland?" the man said.

"Yes."

"We spoke on the phone earlier. My name's Waverly."

"Pleased to meet you," Colonel Dorland said.

The waitress brought a shot glass with whiskey in it, along with some ice cubes and a red plastic cocktail straw in a separate glass. Do-it-yourself bartending, Dorland thought. He guessed it was so you could see you were getting a full shot.

Mr. Waverly ordered a soda water with lime. The waitress nodded again. Walked away without saying anything again.

"Pleased to meet you as well," Mr. Waverly said. "Tell me about this problem you need help with."

Dorland dumped the shot of bourbon over the ice, and then he slid a nine-by-twelve envelope across the table.

"Pictures," he said. "And some background. The man's name is Rock Wahlman. We think he's been traveling with a woman named Kasey Stielson. There are some pictures of her in the envelope as well."

"And you have reason to believe they're in this area?"

"No. But the woman's parents live nearby."

"And?"

"Do I have to spell it out for you?"

"That kind of thing hardly ever works out," Mr. Waverly

said. "More people, more complications."

"My understanding was that you specialize in cases like this," Colonel Dorland said. "If you don't think you can handle it—"

"I can handle it. But it's going to take some money up front."

"How much?"

Mr. Waverly reached over and grabbed a cocktail napkin from the caddy against the wall. He pulled a pen out of his pocket and wrote something on the napkin and folded it in half.

"This much," he said, sliding the folded napkin across the table.

Colonel Dorland reached into his shirt pocket and pulled out his reading glasses. He unfolded the napkin and stared down at the figures Mr. Waverly had written on it—the amount of cash he would need up front, and the amount he would need on delivery.

"That's a lot of money," Colonel Dorland said.

"People don't come to me looking for a bargain. They come to me because I get the job done. Every time."

"This guy is smart," Dorland said, nodding toward the nine-by-twelve envelope. "And resourceful. I've been through two other—"

"I'm not interested in what you've been through," Mr. Waverly said. "I'm only interested in what's happening right now. Today. Apparently it might be necessary to deal with secondary individuals at some point. The risks—*my* risks—increase exponentially when multiple people are involved.

The price is non-negotiable. Take it or leave it."

Dorland lifted the glass of whiskey and knocked it back in a single gulp. He set the glass back down on the table and rattled the ice around with the cocktail straw.

"I'll take it," he said.

"Great. Now tell me a little bit about the primary target. Why exactly is it that you want me to eliminate him for you?"

"I can't talk to you about that," Colonel Dorland said. "It's classified. Top secret."

"I need to know."

"Why?"

"Because I do. I never take a job unless there's some sort of solid reasoning behind the eventual outcome."

"What's your definition of solid reasoning?" Colonel Dorland asked.

"Something other than monetary gain. Or a personal vendetta. Or any number of other selfish or sociopathic reasons potential clients might think are good enough. So tell me, Colonel Dorland. Why do you want me to do this for you? Why this man? Why now?"

The waitress brought the soda water and lime. Colonel Dorland ordered another bourbon on the rocks, and then he took a deep breath and told Mr. Waverly everything.

4

Wahlman walked over to Oak Street, saw Kasey coming out of a seafood place called Portly Joe's Seafood Place. There were two park benches near the front entrance, out on the sidewalk beside some newspaper machines. Kasey sat on one of the benches. She looked exhausted. And sad. Wahlman walked over there and sat down beside her.

"Not hiring," she said.

"Let's go inside and eat," Wahlman said.

"You have money?"

"I have twenty dollars. I'll have more in a little while."

"How did you get twenty dollars?"

"I kicked some guys out of a bookstore over on Maple."

"The owner actually hired you to do that?"

"He did. Now he wants me to go collect on a boat he sold four months ago."

"I thought we said nothing illegal," Kasey said.

"How is that illegal?"

"You're supposed to beat the guy up if he doesn't pay you, right? I'm pretty sure that's against the law."

"I'm not going to beat the guy up. Unless he tries to start something. Last time I checked, it was still perfectly legal to defend yourself."

"You can't go around intimidating people. He could call the police and—"

"Okay," Wahlman said. "I won't do it."

"How much money are we talking about?"

"Two hundred dollars."

"Do it. But I'm coming with you."

"Want to get something to eat first?"

"No. Let's do the job first."

"I had to leave the car keys for collateral," Wahlman said. "It's a long walk."

"You gave someone our car keys? What if—"

"Don't worry. I'll get the keys back."

"And what if you don't?"

"You have the other set, right?"

"They're in the glove compartment."

A red pickup truck pulled into the parking lot in front of the seafood place. Wahlman could see the driver and the passenger through the windshield. Tan Jacket and Red Sweatshirt. They climbed out of the truck and started walking toward the benches. Tan Jacket was carrying a hammer.

"Still have the gun in your purse?" Wahlman said.

"Also in the glove compartment. Why?"

"Go inside and get us a table. We're going to eat first."

"Why is that man carrying a hammer?" Kasey said.

"Maybe he's going to fix that loose piece of trim on the window over there."

"Are those the guys you kicked out of the bookstore?"

"Yes."

"They followed you here?"

"Apparently. Go inside and get us a table."

Kasey didn't move.

Tan Jacket and Red Sweatshirt stepped up onto the sidewalk.

"This your wife?" Tan Jacket said, nodding toward Kasey.

"You guys should turn around and walk back to your truck," Wahlman said.

"Why should we do that?" Tan Jacket said.

"To save money on your next dry cleaning bill," Wahlman said. "Bloodstains are a bitch."

Red Sweatshirt laughed.

"Maybe we just stopped here to try the shrimp platter," he said.

"Not your scene," Wahlman said. "They have napkins and silverware and stuff."

Tan Jacket took a step forward. Lips snarling, neck muscles bulging, fingers wrapped tightly around the handle of the hammer. Wahlman figured he was fixing to rear back and take a swing, and he figured the best defense against such a maneuver was to stop it before it happened. Using the back of the bench for leverage, he buried the heel of his right boot in Tan Jacket's solar plexus, driving his diaphragm up toward his throat, knocking the air out of his lungs and dropping him on the sidewalk in a gasping, quivering heap.

Red Sweatshirt slid his hand into the same pocket he'd

slid it into at the bookstore, but before he had a chance to pull out whatever kind of weapon he had in there, a young man and a young woman walked out of the restaurant together.

Early twenties. Maybe still in college. Polo shirts and khaki pants and deck shoes that had probably never been anywhere near a deck.

"What happened to him?" the young man said, gesturing toward Tan Jacket, who was still doubled over on the sidewalk.

"I did that thing you're supposed to do when someone's choking," Wahlman said. "But I think I did it wrong."

"He was choking?"

"He might have been. I didn't want to take any chances."

"Want me to call an ambulance?" the young man said.

Wahlman glanced over at Red Sweatshirt.

"How about it?" Wahlman said. "Want him to call an ambulance? You're going to need one for sure if you don't get that hand out of your pocket."

Red Sweatshirt took his hand out of his pocket.

"We'll be okay," he said, helping Tan Jacket to a standing position and guiding him back toward the red pickup truck.

The young man looked at Wahlman and shrugged.

Wahlman shrugged back at him.

The young man pushed some coins into one of the newspaper machines, opened the door and pulled out a newspaper, and then he and the young woman walked to their car in the parking lot.

Wahlman reached over and picked up the hammer. He

walked over to the window and tapped the loose piece of trim back into place. It had been bugging him since he got there.

"Let's go make some money," he said.

5

Johnny Cappulista lived on a quiet street in a quiet subdivision. There was a newspaper on the porch and mail in the mailbox and no car in the driveway. Wahlman walked to the side of the house and peeked over the wooden privacy fence. The boat was in the backyard. It was an aluminum fishing boat. No motor, and one of the tires on the trailer was flat.

"I want to see," Kasey said.

"Okay."

Wahlman laced his hands together, creating a stirrup. Kasey stepped into it and lifted herself up to the top of the fence.

"He paid four thousand dollars for that?" she said.

"Maybe it was in better shape when he bought it," Wahlman said. "And there's probably a motor somewhere. Maybe it's a nice one."

Kasey climbed down.

"Think anyone's home?" she said.

"Doesn't look like it."

"Might as well check and see."

Wahlman nodded.

They walked back around to the front of the house and mounted the porch.

Wahlman knocked on the door.

A woman wearing a white terrycloth bathrobe answered. Her eyes were bloodshot and her skin was pale. She'd been drinking. Wahlman could smell it. Rum, he thought, along with some kind of citrus juice. Grapefruit, maybe. She was holding a cordless hairdryer, an expensive solar-powered model Wahlman had seen advertised on television.

"Mrs. Cappulista?" he said.

"Yes."

"I was wondering if I might have a word with your husband."

"He's at work. Is there something I can help you with?"

"It's about the boat," Wahlman said.

"What about it?"

"Are you familiar with Mr. Myers, over at the bookstore on Maple?"

"Never heard of him."

"He sold the boat to your husband four months ago. Your husband paid half up front. I was commissioned to collect the balance due."

"And how much is the balance due?" Mrs. Cappulista said.

"Two thousand," Wahlman said.

Mrs. Cappulista laughed. "He paid four thousand dollars for that piece of shit? You can go ahead and tow it away for all I care. The motor's in the garage."

"Mr. Myers isn't interested in—"

"You're going to have to talk to Johnny," Mrs. Cappulista said.

She slammed the door shut.

"Nice," Kasey said. "Now what?"

"Now we sit here and wait for Johnny to come home," Wahlman said.

"I'm hungry."

"Me too."

"Let's go get something to eat. Then we can come back and wait."

"Okay."

They walked back out to the main road and crossed over to a cluster of chain restaurants and fast food joints.

"Over there," Kasey said. "Beef ribs every Tuesday. All you can eat. Today's Tuesday, right?"

"It is," Wahlman said.

"What do you think?"

"Sounds good to me."

They walked into the budget steakhouse and followed the hostess to a booth near the back of the dining area. Wahlman sat on the side facing the door. Always on the lookout. Always acutely aware of his surroundings. The hostess brought menus and glasses of ice water, and a few minutes later a waitress came and asked if they were ready to order.

"We both want the special," Wahlman said.

"Comes with two sides," the waitress said. "Most people

get the baked potato and the coleslaw."

Wahlman looked across the table at Kasey. She nodded.

"That's fine," Wahlman said.

"Great. I'll have that out for you in just a few minutes."

The waitress walked away.

"There's a public library across the street," Kasey said. "Did you see it?"

"I did."

"Maybe we can stop there after we finish with Johnny Cappulista."

"I don't see the point," Wahlman said.

"We can't just give up. We can't keep living like this forever."

It already felt like forever, Wahlman thought. He'd been on the run for seven months. A New Orleans homicide detective named Collins was trying to track him down and have him arrested, and an army colonel named Dorland was trying to track him down and have him killed. At least the army colonel was supposedly named Dorland. Wahlman still hadn't found any evidence that an officer going by that name actually existed.

It had all started in New Orleans. Last year, in October.

Wahlman had discovered some remarkable things about himself since then. He'd discovered that he was a clone, an exact genetic duplicate of a former army officer named Jack Reacher. He'd discovered that he and a man named Darrel Renfro had been created in a laboratory from cells extracted over a hundred years ago, and that somewhere along the line someone had decided to erase every speck of evidence that the experiment had ever taken place, including the two human beings who had resulted from the experiment. Renfro was dead now—stabbed inside the diesel rig he'd been driving—and Wahlman was next on the list. His entire existence had been a lie, and now his entire existence depended on finding out why all this was happening and exposing the people responsible.

Kasey had been traveling with him for the past few weeks. He loved her, and he enjoyed having her with him, but he wasn't sure how much more she could take. She had a teenage daughter to think about, for one thing.

Natalie.

She was currently staying with Kasey's parents, at their lake house, which was probably the safest place for her to be, but Wahlman could tell that Kasey missed her fiercely, every moment of every day.

Which was totally understandable, of course, and totally exacerbated by the fact that any sort of contact could potentially put everyone involved in great danger.

"I don't think the library is going to be of much help to us anymore," Wahlman said. "We've researched every military database that's available to the public. There aren't any officers currently on active duty with the last name of Dorland."

"It's probably a codename. Like you said before."

"Right."

"Or maybe Mr. Tyler was lying."

"Right again."

"I know all that," Kasey said. "But maybe if we keep looking—"

"We're not going to find anything on the internet," Wahlman said. "We're going to have to break into the army's restricted databases, somehow. We're going to have to find someone on the inside willing to help us get to the bottom of all this."

"And how do you suggest we do that?"

"I'm not sure yet."

The waitress brought the food. Ribs, potatoes, coleslaw. The ribs were huge prehistoric-looking things. Wahlman picked one up and took a bite. The meat was tender and flavorful. Just the right amount of smoke, just the right amount of sauce. He stripped the bone clean in about thirty seconds.

"Good?" Kasey asked.

"Good," Wahlman said.

"I guess you can't really worry about table manners with something like this."

"No. You just have to dig right in."

Kasey dug right in.

There wasn't a lot of conversation over the next twenty minutes or so. They sat there slurping and gnawing, feasting like a couple of ravenous cave dwellers, chewing and swallowing in a continuous rhythmic gluttonous glow, looking up and smiling at each other occasionally, bonded by the hunger, the experience more than just the sharing of a meal, more like some kind of blissful existential fusion. They finished the first order of ribs, and then asked for seconds. And thirds. And fourths. By the time they finished, there was a pile of bones about a foot high on the center of the table.

The waitress came by and filled their water glasses.

"Anyone ready for dessert?" she said.

Kasey laughed. "Not unless you want to push me out of here in a wheelbarrow," she said.

Wahlman paid and they exited the restaurant and headed back toward Johnny Cappulista's house. When they got there, Wahlman noticed right away that the mailbox was empty. Someone had gotten the mail out of the box, but there was still no car in the driveway.

"Want to sit on the porch and wait?" Wahlman said.

"I'm not sure that's such a good idea," Kasey said.

Wahlman glanced toward the door. Mrs. Cappulista was standing there. She was still in her bathrobe, but there was no fancy hairdryer in her hand this time.

This time, she was holding a double-barrel shotgun.

6

Wahlman took a step toward the porch, positioning himself between where Mrs. Cappulista was standing and where Kasey was standing. He didn't think that Mrs. Cappulista would have walked out to the mailbox in her bathrobe. He figured Johnny was in the house now. Or maybe he'd been there all along. Maybe his car was in the garage, along with the boat motor.

"I need to talk to Johnny," Wahlman said.

"Go away," Mrs. Cappulista said.

Wahlman wondered if she'd finished the bottle of rum she'd been working on. Her eyes had moved a notch closer to the batshit zone on the crazy meter since last time she answered the door.

"Give me two thousand in cash," Wahlman said. "Then I'll go away."

"I could shoot you."

"But you won't."

"Johnny's at work."

"I don't think so," Wahlman said. "I think he's there in the house with you."

"You need to leave us alone," Mrs. Cappulista said.

She and the shotgun disappeared into the shadows, and then the door slammed shut again.

"Maybe he just doesn't have any money to give you," Kasey said.

"Myers said he has plenty."

"Maybe Myers was lying."

"Why would he have done that?" Wahlman said. "Why would he have sent me over here on a wild goose chase?"

"I don't know."

Wahlman stood there and stared at the house for a few seconds, considering their options.

"Mrs. Cappulista said we could take the boat and the motor if we want to," he said.

"But we don't want to."

"But we might have to."

"What are we going to do with a boat?" Kasey said.

"Sell it," Wahlman said. "We could probably get three grand for it, assuming the motor is okay. We could take Myers his two, and keep one for ourselves. Plus the commission."

"The trailer has a flat tire."

"There's a can of Fix-A-Flat in the car."

"Which we don't have the keys to," Kasey said.

"I was a master-at-arms in the navy," Wahlman said. "I dealt with criminals on a daily basis."

"So?"

"So there are ways to get into a car without the keys."

They walked back up to the main road, headed toward the discount superstore where they'd parked the SUV.

"Who are we going to sell it to?" Kasey asked.

"Huh?"

"The boat. We need to sell it quick, right? As in *immediately*. Today. Right now. How are we going to do that?"

"Myers didn't give me any sort of time limit. We don't necessarily have to sell it today."

"But we need money today. We're broke."

"True."

"So who are we going to sell it to?"

"I don't know," Wahlman said. "Want to just forget about it?"

Kasey stopped in her tracks.

"I'm tired of this shit," she said. "Sleeping in the car. Not knowing where our next meal is coming from. It's been almost two months, and we're not any closer to finding the people responsible for all this than when we started."

"I don't know what to tell you," Wahlman said.

"That's your answer? You don't know what to tell me?"

"Let's just get the car. Then we'll get the boat, and then we'll figure out what to do next."

Tears welled in Kasey's eyes. Wahlman put his arm around her, pulled her in close. She started sobbing against his chest.

"I need to see my daughter," she said.

"I know you do. We'll figure out a way for that to happen after we sell the boat."

"Promise?"

"Promise."

Kasey wiped the tears from her eyes. They walked on.

Past Oak Street, where Kasey had checked for work at the seafood place. Past Maple Drive, where Wahlman had checked for work at the bookstore. They crossed the thoroughfare at the next intersection, walked across the grassy area that bordered the superstore's parking lot.

"Didn't we park right over there?" Kasey said.

"We did," Wahlman said.

The SUV was gone.

7

The sign out front said *USED BOOKS.*

The sign on the door said *CLOSED.*

"It's only four o'clock," Kasey said. "Who closes a bookstore at four o'clock?"

"Maybe he stepped out for something to eat," Wahlman said.

"He stole our car."

"We don't know that for sure."

"The car's gone. He's gone. What other explanation—"

"He didn't even know where it was parked," Wahlman said.

"He knew it was around here somewhere. He could have walked around pressing the button on the fob until he found it."

"I guess that's possible."

"Everything we own is in that car," Kasey said. "We have to get it back."

"We will."

Kasey had a cell phone in her purse, a cheap throwaway

she'd bought out in California. She pulled it out and flipped it open and punched in a number. Wahlman stood there and listened to her end of the conversation. She was talking to her dad. She was telling him she'd decided to come and visit for a few days. Yes, she needed money. Yes, there was a money transfer service nearby. Right down at the other end of the sidewalk she was standing on.

"I'll call you back in a little while," she said. "I love you too, Dad."

She clicked off and dropped the phone back into her purse.

"You're leaving me?" Wahlman said.

"I have to see Natalie. She's out on a houseboat with some of my parents' friends right now, but she'll be back day after tomorrow. You can come with me if you want to. Dad's going to drive up to the house in Nashville to get an air mattress for me to sleep on. It's a queen, so—"

"I thought you told your parents to stay away from that house."

"It'll just be for a few minutes."

"We still need to find the car," Wahlman said.

"Dad said he would pay for plane tickets."

"We can't fly. You know that."

"I guess I wasn't thinking," Kasey said. "Bus tickets then."

"I thought you didn't want me to—"

"The army doesn't know about the lake house. I think it'll be all right."

Wahlman didn't like the idea. He had a target on his

back. Maybe he could spend some time with Kasey's family when this was all over. But not now. It just wasn't safe.

"You go," he said. "Take a cab to the bus station. I'll stay and deal with the situation here."

"Are you sure?"

"I'm sure."

They walked to the pharmacy at the end of the strip mall. There was a sign advertising the money transfer service in the window, behind the security bars. Wahlman had been in there earlier, asking about temporary employment. The manager hadn't been very polite about telling him no. Maybe she'd thought he was casing the place. Pharmacies had become prime targets for thieves in recent years.

"Aren't you coming in?" Kasey said.

"I'll wait out here."

"Okay. I'll be back in a few minutes."

Wahlman sat on the curb and waited. Traffic was starting to get heavy out on the main road. People coming home from work. Stopping for groceries or beer or whatever. Just everyday people doing everyday things. Surviving the day-to-day grind. Working and talking, eating and drinking, laughing and crying. Doing the same things people did in every town, large and small, all across the country, all around the world. They had mortgages and car payments and kids who needed braces. Their bosses were assholes and their parents were getting old and the dogs next door barked in the middle of the night sometimes.

Wahlman wondered how many of them took a little time every day to think about how good they had it.

Kasey exited the pharmacy. She sat on the curb next to Wahlman and handed him an envelope.

"What's this?" he said.

"I want you to get a room. And something to eat. That should be enough for a few days."

"Tell your dad I'll pay him back."

Kasey nodded. She called a cab, and then she gave Wahlman the cell phone. She told him she would get another one when she got to Tennessee.

"Try not to accidentally drop it in the toilet, like you did that one time," she said.

"Who said it was an accident?" Wahlman said.

Kasey laughed. She knew how much Wahlman disliked cell phones.

"If something does happen, use Message Moi," she said. "You still remember the password, right?"

"Of course."

Message Moi was a free voicemail service you could access through the company's website or through any touchtone phone. It came in handy for people who didn't want to own a cell phone and for people who didn't want to give out their phone numbers for one reason or another.

Wahlman didn't want Kasey to leave, but he knew that she had to. The car came and she kissed him and told him that she loved him and left him standing there alone on the sidewalk.

8

Wahlman waited outside the bookstore until it was almost dark. Myers never came. Kasey was probably right. He probably walked around with the fob until he found the car, and then he probably took it. Maybe he'd thought that Wahlman was taking too long on the little assignment he'd sent him on. Maybe he'd given up on ever getting his two thousand dollars.

Wahlman wasn't sure what he should do now. He couldn't call the police and report the car stolen. They might scan his ID and run it through the National Facial Recognition Database and discover the warrant for his arrest down in Louisiana. And the name on the vehicle registration and the name on his current driver's license didn't even match. Calling the police was out of the question. He could walk back down to Johnny Cappulista's house and try to be a little more persuasive with his collection efforts, but his gut instincts and Johnny's rum-swilling shotgun-toting wife were telling him that any further discourse along those lines would be counterproductive, at least for the immediate future. He supposed the best course of action would be to forget about the boat for now and come back to the bookstore in the morning. Then he could explain the situation to Myers and try to work something out.

He walked out to the main road and took a left. There were some hotels down by the interstate. A two mile walk, but it was a nice evening. Clear skies, low sixties.

Wahlman didn't have anything with him except the clothes on his back and his wallet and the phone Kasey had given him. He didn't even have a toothbrush. He thought about stopping to buy one, but then he remembered that most hotels will give you those kinds of things for free. No point in spending money when you don't have to. His belly was still full from the ribs, so food wouldn't be an issue until tomorrow. Maybe a snack later tonight from a vending machine. Maybe a candy bar or something.

The cell phone trilled. Wahlman pulled it out of his pocket and looked at it. The caller ID said *BLOCKED*. Probably Kasey's dad, Wahlman thought. Or her mom. They probably weren't aware that Kasey didn't have the phone anymore.

Wahlman flipped the phone open and answered the call.

"Mr. Wahlman?" a male voice said.

"Who's this?"

"I'm trying to reach a Mr. Rock Wahlman."

"May I ask who's calling?"

"Are you Rock Wahlman?"

"That depends. What do you want?"

"It's a simple yes or no question," the caller said. "Are you Rock Wahlman?"

Wahlman wasn't sure how to respond. Kasey wouldn't have told anyone his real name. Not even her parents. Which meant that the caller had gotten his name from someone else. But then how had the caller gotten the number to this phone? As far as Wahlman knew, Kasey hadn't given the number to anyone except her parents. Her mother, and her father. Which meant that one of them must have given the number to the caller. Which meant that the caller must have forced that to happen, somehow.

Which meant that the caller was up to no good.

"What do you want?" Wahlman said.

"I want to know that I'm speaking to Rock Wahlman."

"Yes. This is Rock Wahlman. What do you want?"

"I'll be in touch," the caller said. "Make sure to leave the phone on. You wouldn't want to miss my call."

Click.

Wahlman slid the phone back into his pocket. Someone must have gotten to Kasey's parents. Probably not the private investigator working with Detective Collins down in New Orleans. A PI wouldn't have handled it this way. Probably someone working for the army colonel. The colonel using the codename *Dorland*. Probably an assassin. Which meant that Kasey's parents were in grave danger. And since Kasey was headed that way, it meant that she was in grave danger as well.

Wahlman needed to get to the bus station. Fast. He needed to get there before Kasey got on a bus and left town.

He jogged down to the next intersection and waited for the light to change, and then he crossed over and started walking backwards with his thumb out. The light cycled and the traffic on the main road started moving again, slowly at first, then faster, the cars and trucks and motorcycles eventually whizzing by at fifty and sixty miles per hour, some of the vehicles powered by grid-generated or solar-generated electricity, some of them by magnetic turbines, and an increasingly-smaller number by fossil fuels. Lone occupants, couples, entire families. Babies in car seats, teens eating French fries, nurses heading in for another twelve-hour nightshift.

The technology behind moving people from one place to another had changed at an alarming pace since, say, the middle of the nineteenth century. But when you got down to it, the people being moved hadn't changed much at all. They were basically the same as they'd been for hundreds of thousands of years. Cautious. Self-preserving. Fearful of the unknown. Wahlman was a big man, tall and muscular and bearded and scarred. And he was walking alone. Hitchhiking at dusk on a busy highway. A frightening sight in frightening times. None of the drivers even glanced his way. It was almost as if he was invisible. As if the act of turning their heads and acknowledging his existence would somehow put them in danger. He didn't want to call a cab. He didn't want to wait that long. The bus station was only three or four miles away. A five minute drive. Ten at the most, even with the current traffic conditions.

If someone would just pull over to the shoulder and offer him a ride.

And then someone did.

Someone driving a red pickup truck.

9

Kasey Stielson's parents owned a house in a subdivision on the outskirts of Nashville. Mr. Waverly had gotten their address and the code to disarm their alarm system from Colonel Dorland, and he'd driven there from the downtown tavern where he and Colonel Dorland had met. Nobody had been home when Mr. Waverly had arrived at the house, so he'd walked around to the back door and had picked the lock and had gone inside and waited.

And waited.

Why weren't they home? Colonel Dorland had said that they were retired. What do retired people do all day? Mr. Waverly had always thought that they stayed home most of the time, but maybe he was wrong about that. Maybe they were out playing tennis or bridge or taking a long walk in a park somewhere. Or maybe they'd gone on a trip. A cruise or something. It was possible that they weren't even in the country.

Mr. Waverly had been sitting at the kitchen table for several hours, and he'd been close to calling it a day when a car had finally pulled into the driveway. The deadbolt on the front door had clicked open and a man in his mid-to-late fifties had walked in and had headed straight down the hall to one of the bedrooms.

Mr. Waverly had followed the man, and had pointed a sound-suppressed semi-automatic pistol at his face, and had told him to get down on the floor and put his hands behind his back, and to be very quiet if he wanted to live.

Mr. Waverly had asked the man his name as he wrapped his wrists with duct tape.

"Dean," the man had said.

"Where's your wife, Dean?"

"She's out of town."

"So I don't have to worry about her walking into the house anytime soon?"

"No."

"I need to speak with your daughter, Dean. I need to speak with Kasey."

"She doesn't live here anymore."

"Where does she live?"

"I don't know."

"I find that hard to believe, Dean. I have a pair of pliers in my pocket. I don't want to use them, but I will if I have to."

"She's been traveling around the country with some guy. He's in some kind of trouble. She won't tell us where she is."

Dean's fingers were trembling, and his voice was quivering. He wasn't used to this kind of thing. He would crack easily. Like a raw egg. Which, of course, was exactly what Mr. Waverly had been depending on.

"I want you to give me her phone number," Mr. Waverly had said.

"She doesn't have a phone."

"Am I going to have to get the pliers out, Dean?"

"Please. I have money. You can have anything you want."

"I don't want your money. And I don't want to hurt your daughter. I have business with the man she's traveling with. I need to speak to him, and the only way I know how to do that is through her."

"What kind of business?"

"That's not your concern. All you have to do is give me the phone number."

"You're not going to hurt Kasey?"

"No."

"I don't remember the number," Dean said. "It's on my cell phone. On my list of contacts."

"And where's your cell phone?"

"Outside. In my car."

Mr. Waverly had walked out to Dean's car and had picked up the phone from the center console, and then he had moved the car into the garage and had walked back into the house and had called Kasey's number, using an expensive and illegal mobile application that automatically pinpointed the location of any cell phone in any part of the country.

As it happened, Kasey hadn't answered the call.

Rock Wahlman had answered the call.

Which was nice, because that was who Mr. Waverly had wanted to locate anyway. Now all he had to do was contact the nearest Sun River satellite office, which he was in the process of doing now.

In a few short hours, he would call Colonel Dorland and tell him the good news.

Everybody happy.

Except Rock Wahlman, of course.

10

Tan Jacket climbed out of the driver side.

He was holding a tire iron this time.

Red sweatshirt climbed out of the passenger side.

He was holding a baseball bat.

The two men started walking toward Wahlman. They stopped when they were about five feet from where he was standing.

"Need a ride?" Tan Jacket said.

"I do," Wahlman said.

"Unfortunately, my truck only has two seats. I guess you could climb in the back, as long as you don't mind the smell of the cow shit I was hauling earlier."

"I thought that was your breath," Wahlman said.

"You're a smartass, aren't you?"

"So I've been told."

"You hurt me a while ago. I almost puked."

"I'm going to hurt you again if you don't drop the weapon."

"What makes you think this is a weapon?" Tan Jacket

said. "Maybe I just stopped to tighten my lug nuts."

Red sweatshirt took a step forward.

"And maybe I'm heading over to the ball field for a little batting practice," he said.

"I need to get to the bus station," Wahlman said. "I'll give you a hundred dollars to take me there."

Tan Jacket didn't say anything.

Red Sweatshirt didn't say anything either.

They were thinking it over. A hundred dollars for ten minutes of their time. Fifty dollars each. It was a good deal. They should have taken it. But they didn't. Red Sweatshirt cocked the bat and took a swing at Wahlman's head. Wahlman ducked and barreled forward and rammed Red Sweatshirt in the gut, knocking him backward, into Tan Jacket, both of the men severely off balance now as Wahlman wrestled the bat away and drove the fat end of it into Tan Jacket's face, crushing his nose, flattening it out like a wad of bubblegum on the bottom of a shoe. Blood started gushing from Tan Jacket's nostrils and dripping from his chin. The tire iron clanged metallically to the pavement as he staggered sideways and collapsed onto a patch of scrub grass, coughing and retching and then lying there quietly with his hands cupped over the part of his face that used to be a nose.

Red Sweatshirt was still on his feet. He reached into his pocket, the same pocket Wahlman had seen him reach into twice before, only this time he actually produced the object he'd only thought about producing the other two times, a small semi-automatic handgun, probably a .22, a weapon that some knucklehead in some barroom in some part of the world might have referred to as a peashooter, but a weapon that was deadly nonetheless, especially at close range, especially if it had been loaded with hollow point rounds, which it probably had.

Wahlman was still holding the baseball bat.

"Put the gun away," he said.

Red Sweatshirt didn't say anything. And he didn't put the gun away. He aimed the barrel at Wahlman's chest. There was a bright flash and a loud crack as the bullet exited the pistol. But Red Sweatshirt's aim was off. Way off. Because at the very same instant he pulled the trigger, Wahlman unleashed a world class swing, the kind of swing that sends baseballs out of stadiums, the kind that gets you a standing ovation and an eight-figure contract and the girl of your dreams.

The pistol went flying into the darkness as the shattered fingers that had been holding it started to swell, as the intricate webs of severely damaged neurons expedited a series of throbbing wailing flashing messages that traveled up through the affected extremity to an area of the brain called the thalamus, an unequivocal memorandum stressing that this was going to be the worst pain that Red Sweatshirt would ever experience, that it would last a long, long time, and that it would never subside completely, no matter how many medications were administered, no matter how many surgeries were performed.

Having received and processed this urgent bulletin in less than a second, Red Sweatshirt started pacing around in circles, shouting and grunting and cradling his ruined hand close to his chest in a futile attempt to dial the agony down to a level that was merely unbearable. He turned toward Wahlman and said something incomprehensible, and then he staggered over to the grassy area where Tan Jacket was lying and collapsed there in the shadows beside him.

Wahlman walked past the two men and climbed into the truck. He pulled the cell phone out of his pocket to make sure there weren't any messages on it. There weren't. He released the emergency brake and slid the shifter into gear and eased onto the highway. It took him seven minutes to get to the bus station. Seven minutes of weaving through traffic and tailgating and flashing the headlights from low-beam to high-beam. Seven minutes of accelerating through traffic signals when they were yellow, and honking through them when they were red.

Seven minutes.

Not bad, considering the vehicle he was driving and the time of day it was. He parked the truck and ran inside and started looking around. He looked in the waiting area and the ticket lines and the gift shop, and he stood outside the ladies' restroom for a few minutes and he checked the snack bar. He walked out to where the buses were parked and looked inside every one of them.

Kasey was not there.

He'd missed her, and he didn't know where she was going. Not exactly. He knew she was going to a lake house that belonged to her parents, and he knew that it was somewhere in Tennessee. Somewhere around Nashville, but

Kasey had wanted to keep her daughter's precise location a secret, even from Wahlman.

Supposedly, the army didn't know about the lake house. Which meant that Colonel Dorland didn't know about it. Which meant that the man who'd called the cell phone didn't know about it.

Yet the man who'd called the cell phone had gotten to Kasey's parents somehow. He must have, because he'd gotten the number from somewhere, and Kasey's parents were the only people on the planet—other than Kasey herself, of course, and Rock Wahlman—who knew what the number was.

Dad's going to drive up to the house in Nashville to get an air mattress for me to sleep on.

Maybe that was it. Maybe the guy who'd called the cell phone had been waiting at the house in Nashville when Kasey's dad had arrived there. Wahlman didn't know Kasey's dad, but he knew that he loved Kasey, and he knew that he wouldn't have given up the number voluntarily, that he must have been coerced, threatened, maybe told that great harm would come to him and his family if he didn't cooperate.

Wahlman walked over to the waiting area and sat on one of the plastic chairs and pulled the cell phone out again. The ringer was on, with the volume turned all the way up, and the vibrate function was on as well, but he wanted to be absolutely certain that the man who'd called earlier hadn't tried to call again.

It appeared that he hadn't.

And then it occurred to Wahlman that maybe he never would.

Make sure to leave the phone on. You wouldn't want to miss my call.

Which made it sound as though further instructions would be coming at some point. A ransom demand, maybe. Not for cash, but for an exchange. The caller probably intended to use Kasey's dad as a bargaining chip, hoping to force Wahlman to be at a certain place at a certain time.

That was the implication.

But maybe that wasn't really the plan.

Maybe the caller wasn't really interested in forcing Wahlman to go anywhere.

Maybe the caller already had what he wanted.

Wahlman's location.

There was a reason Wahlman didn't ordinarily carry a cell phone. Too easy to hack, too easy to track. Even the burners, like the one Kasey had bought, if you had the number.

And the caller had the number.

Wahlman had been thinking about it earlier, about the caller being able to track his location, but he hadn't been worrying about it much, because he'd assumed that the caller was somewhere far away. If you're in Des Moines, for example, how useful is it going to be to know that the person you're looking for is in Houston? Especially if the person you're looking for is constantly on the move. By the time you get to Houston, the person you're looking for will be somewhere else. It's not likely that you'll ever catch up.

Unless you're more than one person.

Maybe Detective Collins and his private investigator had orchestrated this whole thing after all. Maybe local, state, and federal police agencies were involved. Maybe those agencies now had the number to the cell phone in Wahlman's hand.

If that was the case, he needed to ditch the phone immediately.

But what if that wasn't the case? What if the man who'd called earlier really was going to call back with some kind of ransom demand?

If Collins, or someone hired by Collins, had managed to get the number to the phone, Wahlman would probably be arrested soon. If Dorland, or someone hired by Dorland, had managed to get the number to the phone, further instructions would probably come soon.

Or a bullet.

It didn't seem likely that Dorland had tapped into some sort of independent coast-to-coast network of hired killers, but Wahlman supposed it was possible.

He stood and headed toward the exit. As he passed through the doorway that led to the parking area, he thought about dropping the phone into the trash can. But he didn't. He decided it would be best to hang onto it for now. If he suddenly found himself surrounded by police, then so be it. Maybe that would be the least perilous thing that could happen at this point. Wahlman would be taken into custody, but at least he would know that Kasey and her family weren't going to be dealing with some sort of abduction situation.

He walked out to the truck and opened the driver side door and slid in behind the wheel. Sat there and debated with himself over what to do next. If anything. You don't spend twenty years as a master-at-arms in the United States Navy without learning to be patient in a wide variety of situations. Wahlman wanted to head for Tennessee, but he was afraid that his current batch of trouble might follow him there. He was afraid that his presence might make things worse. Kasey didn't need that. And her parents didn't need that. And her daughter definitely didn't need that.

So maybe it was best to just check into a hotel and wait. Eventually the caller would call back, or the police would show up, or a hired killer would make a move.

Wahlman slid the key into the ignition and started the engine.

And then the cell phone trilled.

Wahlman answered.

It wasn't the man who'd called earlier.

And it wasn't Kasey, or either of her parents.

It was someone Wahlman had never talked to before. Someone he'd never expected to talk to—ever.

It was his mother.

11

While everyone else had left the office hours ago, Craig Pullimon was still sitting at his desk, working on the payroll for the week. He wanted to get it out of the way so he could take off early tomorrow and play some golf with his boss.

Work hard, play hard.

That was Craig Pullimon's philosophy, and he'd done well with it at Sun River Disposal, going from material handler to assistant office manager in a little less than three years. He drove a fairly nice car and he lived in a fairly nice house in a fairly nice suburb. He was still single and he did okay with the ladies, and he'd managed to save quite a bit of money toward his next big purchase—a set of jet skis and trailer to haul them with.

Craig had managed to save quite a bit, but he was still about a year away from making it happen. That was one of the reasons he wanted to hit the links with his boss tomorrow. He wanted to ask for a raise, to speed the process along a little. It's always easier to talk someone into something like that after a few holes of golf and a few cans of beer. And of course it didn't hurt that his boss was a fellow Marine Corps veteran.

Craig was transferring some funds from one Sun River checking account to another when the cell phone in his left front pocket started vibrating—the special encrypted device he'd been issued after a series of private meetings with a man named Waverly.

Which meant that a man named Waverly was calling now.

Which was a good thing, especially if you needed some extra cash for one reason or another. Mr. Waverly managed the office in Nashville, and he coordinated the secret afterhours assignments that he often referred to as *side jobs*. The last time Mr. Waverly had called, Craig had been able to put a nice down payment on the house he was living in now.

"Hello?" Craig said.

"Can you take a job for me?" Mr. Waverly said.

"How soon?"

"Tonight."

"You mean you want the initial assessment performed tonight, right?"

"No," Mr. Waverly said. "I mean I need for the entire job to be completed tonight. I can call someone else if you don't think you can handle it."

"I can handle it," Craig said. "No problem. Got a number for me?"

Mr. Waverly gave Craig the target's cell phone number, which would allow Craig to track the target's exact location in real time.

"His name's Rock Wahlman," Mr. Waverly said. "He's six feet four inches tall, and he weighs two hundred and thirty pounds. It's still pretty chilly there where you are, so he's probably wearing a jacket. Light brown, all-weather material, and maybe a navy watch cap. I'll email some photographs to you."

"Where is he right now?" Craig asked.

"At the bus station."

"He's leaving town?"

"Maybe. That's why I need you to hurry."

"I'm on it," Craig said.

Mr. Waverly disconnected.

Craig set the security alarm and turned all the lights off on his way out of the office. There was a suitcase in the trunk of his car that contained everything he would need for the job.

Easy money.

Now he would definitely be able to get those jet skis he'd been wanting.

12

Wahlman switched off the ignition.

"How do I know it's really you?" he asked the woman claiming to be his mother.

"I guess there's no way for me to prove it," the woman said. "It's not like we even share the same DNA or anything. I was just a surrogate. Actually, I guess *incubator* would be a more accurate term. They implanted the fetus after—"

"I know about all that," Wahlman said. "What's your name?"

"Joanne."

"How old are you?"

"Sixty-four."

"How did you get this number?"

"A man called me and told me you didn't have long to live. He gave me the number, said it was up to me if I wanted to contact you or not."

"Someone from the army?" Wahlman asked.

"He wouldn't identify himself. But it must have been someone from the army, now that you mention it. Who else would have even known about me?"

"And he said I didn't have long to live?"

"That's what he said. I was very sorry to hear that. Are you ill?"

"Why did you decide to call?" Wahlman asked, ignoring the question about his health.

"I don't know. It seemed like the right thing to do."

"Why now? Why did you wait until you thought I was dying?"

"Well, I never knew—"

"I was raised in an orphanage," Wahlman said. "You're nothing to me. An incubator, like you said. But I'm glad you called, because now I know what I need to do."

"Why are you being so rude to me?"

"I'm almost forty-one years old. I've gone this long without a mother, so—"

"You don't carry a baby for nine months and not form an attachment," Joanne said. "Even when it's not really your baby. I wanted to keep you, but the army wouldn't let me. I'd signed a bunch of papers before the—"

"They cancelled the experiment," Wahlman said. "You could have worked something out. Instead, I was given a fake history and sent to that shithole in Memphis for eighteen years."

"I'm sorry."

"The cells used for the cloning procedure were taken from a man named Jack Reacher. Do you know anything about him?"

"No. They didn't even tell me the donor's name."

"Don't ever try to call me again," Wahlman said.

He hung up.

Started the engine.

It was time to return the pickup truck to its rightful owner.

He steered out of the parking area and started backtracking, minding the speed limit this time and stopping at all the red lights. He made a U-turn, and then he pulled over to the side of the road. Tan Jacket and Red Sweatshirt were still lying in the scrub grass beyond the shoulder. Wahlman climbed out of the truck and walked over there and watched them for a few seconds. Neither of them was conscious, but they were both still breathing. Red Sweatshirt's right hand looked like a catcher's mitt. Tan Jacket was lying on his side. Wahlman couldn't see his face. And he didn't want to. He started to feel sorry for the men, and then he remembered that they had intended to kill him. He figured they still would if they got the chance. He didn't despise either one of them more than the other, so the decision to slide the cell phone into Tan Jacket's pocket was purely random.

Wahlman's original theory had been correct. Someone had gotten the number to the cell phone, probably from Kasey's dad when he went to Nashville to get the air mattress, and now someone was tracking the phone. Someone hired by Colonel Dorland. An assassin.

A man called me and told me you didn't have long to live.

A kind and thoughtful gesture, Wahlman thought. Allowing him to talk to his mother before drilling a bullet into his brain. Good old Colonel Dorland. What a sport.

Wahlman tossed the truck keys onto the strip of grass between Tan Jacket and Red Sweatshirt, and then he started walking toward the strip of hotels down by the interstate. He saw a marquis advertising a price he liked, walked into the lobby and paid cash for one night. He asked the clerk for a toothbrush and some toothpaste. She cheerfully handed the items across the desk to him, along with a key card and a paper receipt. The room was on the second floor. Wahlman took the elevator. He was tired of walking. Tired in general. He opened the door and slid the *DO NOT DISTURB* sign onto the handle and peeled his clothes off and took a shower. He used the room phone to call Message Moi and leave a voicemail for Kasey, and then he climbed into bed naked and switched on the television and fell asleep.

13

The sniper's rifle in Craig's suitcase was equipped with laser sights and a sound suppressor and a penetrating infrared scope—an illegal military-grade device that sold for more money on the black market than Craig made in a year, a device you could literally see through walls with. Craig assembled the rifle, and then he accessed the locator software on his tablet computer and tapped in the cell phone number Colonel Dorland had given him. A street map appeared on the screen, along with a flashing green dot that indicated the location of the phone.

Craig zoomed in on the dot. The phone was on the east side of town, near a major thoroughfare, several miles from the bus station. Which meant that Wahlman hadn't left town. Which was a good thing.

But the dot wasn't moving. Not even a little bit. Which didn't make sense, really, based on the location, unless Wahlman had thrown the phone away, or unless he'd decided to camp there on the side of the highway. Or unless he was already dead, which didn't seem likely.

Craig set the auditory alarm on his tablet to beep loudly if the phone moved, even an inch, and then he started his car and headed toward the east side.

When Mr. Waverly contacted you for a side job, it was understood that the target was to disappear without a trace, and it was understood that a DNA specimen would be preserved for confirmation. And, most importantly, it was understood that there would be no eyewitnesses and that nothing would be caught on camera.

Which made it crucial for you to take your shot from a distance.

A hundred yards was a good rule of thumb, but the further the better, really, as long as you were confident in a positive outcome. Once the target was down, you could assess the witness situation and advance to the area Mr. Waverly referred to as the *exit zone*, and then you could draw a vial of blood or snip a lock of hair and start the removal and disposal process.

The best exit zones were private and contained. Abandoned buildings were ideal, but that hardly ever happened. Personal residences were good, as long as the target was alone, or as long as you didn't mind taking out whoever else was there. Same with hotel rooms. An open campsite near a busy highway? Not so great. Too many people and too many cameras. So Craig was relieved when the tablet started beeping. He pulled to the side of the road and saw that the green dot was moving now, and that it was moving very quickly. It made a left turn and then it circled around and came to a stop.

Craig zoomed in until he could see the name of the nearest building. *University Medical Center, Level One Trauma Center.* The phone had been taken to the hospital. Which meant that Wahlman had been taken to the hospital.

Which was not good.

Hospitals were extremely poor exit zones. Too much security, too many people milling around. Doctors, nurses, technicians, clerks. Not to mention the patients and their families. Lining up a shot wouldn't be a problem. But getting Wahlman out of there afterward would.

Then again, maybe not.

Craig eased back onto the highway and headed that way. He knew the area well. He knew that the trauma center was in a building that was separate from the main hospital, and he knew that there was a public parking garage directly across the street. Patients were treated and stabilized in the trauma center, and then they were transported by ambulance to the central emergency room half a block over.

It was true that hospitals were poor exit zones.

But Craig had a plan.

This was going to work out. He could feel it.

14

Wahlman had expected the phone in his hotel room to wake him at some point during the night. But it didn't. It never rang. At 5:27 he opened his eyes and switched on the bedside lamp and called Message Moi to see if Kasey had received his voicemail. A robot voice told him that the account had been accessed at 3:12 a.m. and that one message had been acknowledged by one recipient. Which was a little worrisome, because he'd told Kasey to give him a call at the hotel when she got the message. He'd wanted to tell her about the call he'd received on the cell phone she'd given him. He wanted to tell her his theory regarding that, and he wanted to tell her to stay away from her parents' house in Nashville. He'd wanted to warn her, but she hadn't called. Of course it was possible that she hadn't wanted to wake him at 3:12 in the morning, and it was also possible that the phones at the cheap hotel weren't working properly.

He took another shower and put the clothes he'd been wearing yesterday back on and walked down to the lobby. He stepped up to the desk and asked the clerk if there had been any calls to his room last night. The clerk told him that there had not. He asked the clerk if there was somewhere nearby where he could get a cup of coffee.

"You can get one here," the clerk said. "There's a breakfast area right around the corner, just past the restrooms."

"Thanks," Wahlman said.

He found the breakfast area and poured himself a cup of coffee, and then he pulled a pre-sliced bagel apart and slid the halves into a toaster. He stood there and waited until the bagel was hot and golden brown and he put it on a paper plate with some cream cheese and sat down at a table. He didn't like it that Kasey had received his message but hadn't called him back. The more he thought about it, the more he didn't like it. He needed to get the SUV. He needed to head toward Nashville. Nobody could track him now that he'd gotten rid of the cell phone. He was off the grid again. Invisible. The way he needed to be to survive.

He finished his breakfast and walked back to the lobby. There was a television behind the desk, tuned to one of the local network affiliates. The morning news was on. An attractive young lady with a microphone was standing in front of a sign that said *UMC LEVEL ONE TRAUMA*. According to the attractive young lady, someone had stolen an ambulance last night. Two emergency medical technicians were missing, along with the patient they'd been assigned to transport. Before the incident had occurred, the patient had been treated for a broken nose and severe dehydration.

The attractive young lady instructed someone named Ned to cut to a picture of the missing patient, a driver's license photograph taken two years ago. Wahlman recognized the man. It was Tan Jacket. In trouble with the law before. Considered armed and dangerous. Suspected of stealing the ambulance. There was a hotline number you could call if you spotted him.

Wahlman was pretty sure nobody was going to spot him. Ever again.

He was pretty sure that Tan Jacket was dead now, along with the emergency medical technicians, who just happened to be in the way.

Wahlman had planted the cell phone in Tan Jacket's pocket, which meant that he was somewhat responsible for whatever had happened to him. And he was okay with that. He hadn't intended for anything to happen to anyone else, and he was very sorry if something did, but there was nothing he could do about it. All he could do was continue trying to get to the bottom of why all this was happening and try to put a stop to it before more innocent lives were lost.

The hotel staff must have changed shifts at six. There was a different clerk working the desk. Wahlman asked her if anyone had tried to call his room while he was out. She clicked some keys on her keyboard and swiped at her monitor screen with her finger.

"There haven't been any calls to your room since you checked in," she said.

"Okay. Thank you."

"Would you like to go ahead and book the room for another night?"

"No thanks. I'll be checking out in a little while."

Wahlman took the stairs up to his room, used the phone to see if Kasey had left a voicemail via Message Moi. She had not.

But someone else had.

15

Mr. Waverly was furious.

Craig Pullimon had called him at five o'clock in the morning.

"We have a problem," Craig had said.

Mr. Waverly didn't like being called at five o'clock in the morning, and he didn't like problems.

Especially severe, irreparable ones.

Craig had followed the cell phone to a hospital trauma center. He'd maintained surveillance from across the street in a parking garage until the man he thought was Wahlman was discharged from the trauma center and loaded into an ambulance to be taken to the main hospital. He'd used the special scope on his rifle to see inside the ambulance, and he'd squeezed the trigger three times. Once for the woman in the driver seat, once for the man in the passenger seat, and once for the patient. Then he had trotted across the street to the turnaround where the ambulance was parked. He'd climbed in and had scooted the woman over to the space between the seats and he'd taken her place behind the wheel and had driven the ambulance to the special disposal facility where targets—and sometimes their vehicles—were processed, and he'd promptly discovered the huge mistake he'd made. The patient was not Rock Wahlman. The patient was a man named Speers. A career criminal. A smalltime hustler who'd experienced a variety of courtrooms and lockups in a variety of jurisdictions.

"How could you have messed this up so badly?" Mr. Waverly had asked.

"He had bandages on his face. They must have been soaked in a saline solution, which interfered with the infrared scope's ability to—"

"What part of *six feet four inches tall and two hundred thirty pounds* did you not understand? This guy's a pipsqueak compared to Wahlman."

"Sorry. He was on a stretcher in the back of an ambulance. The image on the scope was a little fuzzy, probably from all the electronic equipment back there. EKG machines and defibrillators and such. It was hard to tell how big or small he was."

"Now we have three bodies and a vehicle the size of a bread truck to get rid of, and the target's still out there."

"I'll find him," Craig had said.

"No you won't," Mr. Waverly had said. "As of now, you're off the job."

"But—"

Mr. Waverly had clicked off then. He was as angry as he'd ever been in his life, and he didn't want to hear another word from Craig Pullimon. He would deal with him later.

Right now he had his hands full. He was still at the house in Nashville, where he'd intended to keep Kasey Stielson's father hostage until he received confirmation from Craig Pullimon that Rock Wahlman was dead.

Now he had three hostages.

Dean's wife, Betsy, had shown up at a little after midnight, and his daughter, Kasey, had shown up at a little after three. Now Dean and his wife and his daughter were all in the back bedroom, all restrained with duct tape and gagged with washcloths.

It had taken some time and effort to persuade Kasey to reveal how she and Wahlman were keeping in touch, but she'd finally given in.

As they all do, eventually.

Human beings can only tolerate so much.

Mr. Waverly had accessed Kasey's Message Moi account, and had left a detailed voicemail for Wahlman.

Now all he had to do was wait.

16

Wahlman played the message.

"Kasey Stielson is fine," a male voice said. "As are her parents. If you would like for that to continue to be the case, you will do exactly as I say."

The man wanted Wahlman to be at a certain Nashville address by one o'clock in the afternoon. If he was late, someone would die. Maybe Kasey. Maybe one of her parents. The choice would be made randomly. If Wahlman still wasn't there by two, someone else would die. And so forth.

Wahlman rushed downstairs, exited the hotel and headed toward the bookstore. He needed to get the SUV back, and he needed to get it back now.

And he was willing to do whatever it took to make that happen.

Myers was sitting behind the counter again. Reading and smoking and drinking coffee again. He was reading the same book. He was almost finished with it.

"Where's my car?" Wahlman said.

"Where's my two thousand dollars?" Myers said.

"I couldn't get it. Mrs. Cappulista said you can have the boat back."

"Did you talk to Johnny?"

"No."

"You need to talk to Johnny. I don't want the boat back. I want my money."

Wahlman reached over and grabbed Myers by the shirt and dragged him across the countertop. Ashes and coffee went everywhere. The mug that Myers had been drinking from hit the floor and shattered into a million pieces.

"Where's my car?" Wahlman said again.

"I'll give you the car back when—"

Wahlman shoved Myers into the stack of boxes he'd offered to unpack for him yesterday. The boxes toppled and Myers stumbled sideways and slid to the carpet, instinctively trying to break his fall by extending his hand on that side, landing with a pained expression as his wrist folded back much further than it should have. He sat up and stared at the joint and massaged it with his other hand.

"Where's my car?" Wahlman said for the third time.

"I'm calling the police," Myers said, reaching into his pocket and pulling out a cell phone.

Wahlman walked over to where Myers was sitting and kicked the phone out of his hand. It hit the ceiling with a crunch and landed on top of one of the bookshelves.

"The next thing you pull out of your pocket better be my keys," Wahlman said.

Myers started massaging his wrist again.

"I think it's broken," he said.

"Want me to break the other one for you?"

"You're not going to get away with this," Myers said.

"If I break the other one, you won't be able to feed yourself or bathe yourself or wipe your own ass for a few weeks. If you would like for that to happen, just keep not handing over my keys for the next five seconds."

Myers clenched his teeth. His wrist had started to swell.

"They're in the cabinet under the register," he said.

Wahlman walked behind the counter, opened the cabinet door and grabbed the set of keys he'd given to Myers yesterday. They felt greasy, as if someone had eaten some bacon or something before handling them.

"Where's it parked?" Wahlman said.

"I drove it to work today," Myers said. "It's in the alley around back."

Wahlman exited the store and walked around to the other side of the building and climbed into the SUV.

Four hours later, he passed a sign that said *NASHVILLE CITY LIMITS*.

He pulled to the shoulder and checked to make sure the pistol in the glove compartment had a fully-loaded magazine, and then he continued toward the address the man on the Message Moi voicemail had instructed him to go to.

17

Wahlman just happened to glance down at the digital clock on the dashboard as it changed from 12:44 to 12:45. Which meant that he had exactly fifteen minutes to get to where he needed to be.

Which, according to the onboard navigation system, was physically impossible.

Which meant that someone was going to die.

Maybe Kasey.

Maybe one of her parents.

Which was unacceptable.

Wahlman took the next exit and steered into the parking lot of the first convenience store he came to. He screeched to a stop in front of the payphone and climbed out and punched in the number for Message Moi.

He entered the password and the code to initiate a new voicemail.

"I'm almost there," he said. "But I need more time. Just a few minutes. Please don't harm the people you have there with you. I will be there shortly."

He hung up and climbed back into the SUV and got back onto the highway.

12:51.

He floored the accelerator and started weaving through traffic, ignoring the increasingly stern warnings from the navigation system to reduce speed. At 12:54 he exited the interstate and took a right at the fourth light and a left at the next intersection and he drove for a couple of miles on a road with a lot of curves and hills and finally came to the turnoff that led to the address he was looking for.

12:58.

It was a nice neighborhood. The houses were fine big structures, most of them brick or stone, most of them on extremely large lots. Three or four acres, Wahlman guessed. Four-car garages. Trees and hedges and flowers and mulch. Every blade of grass trimmed to an exact height, every picket fence gleaming in the early afternoon sun.

It appeared that Kasey's parents had plenty of money, but Wahlman doubted that it would do them any good at this point. The only thing that would do them—and Kasey—any good was for him to crash through the wrought iron gate at the end of the driveway and speed to the concrete fountain at the center of the turnaround and skid to a stop and grab the pistol and tumble out of the SUV and scramble up to the porch and bang on the door.

Which he did.

At exactly one o'clock.

He'd slid the pistol into the back of his waistband, thinking there might be a brief window of opportunity to use it at some point, but when the deadbolt clicked past the strike plate and the intricately-carved wooden door swung open, he immediately knew that wouldn't be the case. A man wearing a dark blue suit and a ball cap and sunglasses stood on the other side of the threshold. A black bandana covered his nose and mouth and chin, and he was aiming a sound-suppressed semi-automatic pistol directly at Wahlman's face.

"You're late," the man said.

"Right on time by my watch," Wahlman said.

"The barrel of this pistol I'm holding was pressed against your girlfriend's forehead when you knocked. Another five seconds and her brains would have been splattered all over the wall."

"I'm very glad that didn't happen."

"You're going to die today. You realize that, right?"

"Maybe we can work something out."

"Are you carrying a weapon?"

"No."

"I'm going to ask you to step inside and lie face down on the floor, and then I'm going to search you. If you're lying—"

"It's in the back of my waistband," Wahlman said.

"Lace your hands behind your head. Then turn around. Slowly."

Wahlman laced his hands behind his head, and then he turned around slowly. If he was going to have any chance of making it out of this alive, now was probably the best time to make a move. He could have grabbed the man's wrist while simultaneously planting the heel of his boot into the man's instep, and then he could have used his weight to back the man further into the foyer and he could have taken the man to the floor and he could have beaten the man to death with his bare fists.

But he didn't. Because it wasn't just his life on the line. Kasey and her parents were somewhere in the house. If Wahlman tried something and didn't succeed, the man would probably kill all of them.

Of course it was possible that he would kill all of them anyway, but Wahlman didn't think so. That was what the black bandana was all about. And the ball cap. And the sunglasses. The man was making sure Kasey and her parents didn't see his face. That way, he could let them go when this was all over. The man had been hired to kill Rock Wahlman. He didn't care about the others. He was just using them for leverage until he could do what he'd been hired to do.

The man reached under Wahlman's jacket and pulled the pistol out of his waistband.

"Give Colonel Dorland my regards," Wahlman said.

"Pardon me?"

"I know that's not his real name. It's a codename. I was a master-at-arms in the navy for twenty years. I worked closely with intelligence officers sometimes. I know how they operate, and I know—"

"Walk backwards into the foyer," the man said. "Close the door on your way in."

"Then what?" Wahlman said.

"Then I'm going to shoot you."

"Do you even know what this is all about?"

"Actually, I do," the man said. "Colonel Dorland told me everything."

"What did he tell you?"

The man ignored Wahlman's question.

"Walk backward into the foyer," he said. "Do it now, or I'll make you watch Kasey die."

Wahlman walked backward into the foyer, pulling the door closed as he stepped past the threshold. This was it. He was going to die now, and there was nothing he could do about it. He didn't say anything. Thirty or forty seconds ticked by. Maybe a minute. Then he felt the cold barrel of the pistol on the back of his head.

Then someone knocked on the door.

"Anyone home?" a female voice said.

"Answer the door," the man wearing the black bandana said. "Tell her to come inside."

"It's probably just one of the neighbors," Wahlman said. "She probably doesn't know anything about anything."

"But she's here now. I can't just let her go."

"Why not?"

"Because your car's ten years old and it's sideways in the driveway and there are skid marks leading up to it. She's going to wonder about that. Then she's going to start thinking that maybe something's wrong. Then she's going to—"

"All right," Wahlman said.

He figured the man wearing the black bandana would put the woman with the others until the job was done. She would be unnecessarily traumatized, but maybe she would get over it in time.

Wahlman took a few steps forward and twisted the knob and pulled the door open. A middle-aged woman with a big smile on her face and an armful of brochures asked him if he was happy with his current swimming pool service.

"I'm pretty sure I can save you some money," the woman said.

"Come on in," Wahlman said.

The woman came on in.

Wahlman closed the door.

"This is such a nice neighborhood," the woman said. "How long have you—"

The woman screamed and dropped the brochures when she saw the man wearing the black bandana. She went from bubbly and cheerful to frantic and frenzied in a heartbeat. She started losing it. Totally. Tears were flowing down her cheeks and she was waving her arms and shrieking at the top of her lungs.

And then there was silence.

The woman slumped to the floor.

One bullet hole in the center of her forehead and one in the center of her chest.

"Why did you do that?" Wahlman said.

"You didn't really think I was going to let anyone leave here alive, did you?"

"We had a deal. I kept my end of it. Why would you want to kill anyone else but me?"

"Because of the voicemail I left you," the man said. "It's a loose end, evidence that could be used against me. Kasey—or her parents, if they have the password—could access the account and foreword the message to the police. Then every law enforcement agency in the country would have my voiceprint on file. Sorry, but that's just not going to happen."

Wahlman hadn't thought about that. The man was right. It was a loose end. Voiceprints were every bit as incriminating as fingerprints. Wahlman had made a huge mistake. He should have known that the man wearing the black bandana wasn't going to let Kasey and her parents go. He should have made a move earlier, when he had the chance.

Now it was too late.

Wahlman turned and faced the man wearing the black bandana.

Looked him directly in the eyes.

The man gripped the pistol with both hands and aimed it at Wahlman's heart.

The man didn't say anything.

Wahlman didn't say anything.

And then something very strange happened to the man wearing the black bandana.

His head exploded.

18

A bright ray of sunshine beamed in through a hole the size of a quarter, a hole located several inches to the left of the front door. Wahlman had heard the bullet whistle past his right ear. Either the shooter had been aiming at Wahlman and had missed by a fraction of an inch, or the shooter had actually intended to kill the man wearing the black bandana. There was no way for Wahlman to know for sure which of those possibilities was correct, so he continued to treat the situation as active and extremely hostile. He hit the deck and crawled away from the door, toward the living room, through the blood and the skull fragments and the chunks of brain tissue, grabbing the pistol that the man wearing the black bandana had taken from him earlier and the pistol that the man wearing the black bandana had been planning to shoot him with. As he crawled through the living room, toward a hallway that probably led to the first floor bedrooms, he considered a third possibility, that the bullet had been a stray round from a hunter, or from someone shooting cans off of tree stumps or something. The neighborhood was surrounded by hills, and Wahlman had noticed several paths winding away from the curvy road he'd driven in on, several single-lane dirt trails that could have led to hunting camps. So it was possible that a stray round had killed the man wearing the black bandana, but not likely. The odds of something like that actually happening were probably about the same as the odds of strolling down the sidewalk and being struck by debris from outer space. It was one of those things that could happen, but didn't. At least not often enough to worry about.

Wahlman made it to the end of the living room, looked back and saw the slimy red trail he'd left on the oak floor. He figured the damage to the house would be the least of Kasey's parents' worries at this point, but still. He didn't like seeing something so pristine turned to something so ugly.

When he rounded the corner, he heard moans coming from the end of the hallway. He stood with a pistol in each hand and carefully edged his way toward the muffled and distressed sounds. He turned the knob and pushed the door open and saw Kasey lying on the floor and a man and a woman he supposed were her parents lying on the bed, all three of them bound and gagged and shouting *hurry up and get us out of here* with their eyes.

Wahlman pulled the washcloths out of their mouths and unwound the duct tape binding their wrists and ankles. Kasey's mom sat on the edge of the bed and started sobbing uncontrollably. Kasey's dad put his arm around her and held her tight.

Kasey stood and pressed herself against the front of

Wahlman's body and dug her fingertips into the muscles on his back.

"I thought he was going to kill us," she said.

"He was," Wahlman said.

"What happened?"

"I'm not sure. He's dead. That's all I know."

"But—"

"I'll explain later. Right now I need to make sure it's safe for us to go outside and drive away from here."

"What are you talking about? Why wouldn't it be safe?"

Wahlman handed Kasey the pistol that had been in the glove compartment, the one she was familiar with.

"Stay here in the bedroom," he said. "I'll be back in a few minutes."

19

Craig Pullimon picked up the single brass casing from the ground and slid it into his pocket. He disassembled the sniper's rifle, pushed the individual pieces into their cushioned cutouts, snapped the suitcase shut and loaded it into the trunk of his car. He climbed in and started the engine and headed for home.

As far as he was concerned, nobody else needed to die today. He didn't have anything against Rock Wahlman. He didn't even know why Wahlman had been targeted in the first place. He didn't know, and he didn't need to know. These side jobs were nothing more than business transactions to him, and since it had been made perfectly clear that his services on this particular job were no longer required, there was no reason for him to care if it was ever completed or not. He didn't do this shit for free.

Of course nobody was going to pay him in dollars and cents for the excellent work he'd done just a few minutes ago—perhaps the most challenging kill shot of his civilian career, because of the distance—but he would be well compensated for it nonetheless.

The way he saw it, every day would be payday from now on. Sunshine and roses and root beer floats. Because the way he saw it, getting to breathe another day, and another day after that, was the best paycheck anyone could ask for.

How could you have messed this up so badly?

Several years ago, Craig had heard about another job that had been messed up badly. Another case of mistaken identity, where someone other than the intended target had been eliminated.

The operative responsible for the mistake had disappeared a few days later.

Nobody knew for sure, but the general assumption was that Mr. Waverly had personally taken care of him. And the general assumption from that point forward was that if you made a similar mistake Mr. Waverly would personally take care of you too.

Which was why Craig had been forced to personally take care of Mr. Waverly.

Craig had used the same technology he'd used to track Wahlman, the same software he'd been using to track targets for a while now. He'd pinpointed the location of Mr. Waverly's cell phone in a matter of seconds. According to the computer, the phone was inside a private residence in an exclusive neighborhood on the outskirts of Nashville. Which probably meant that Mr. Waverly was inside a private residence in an exclusive neighborhood on the outskirts of Nashville. Craig had driven down there and had found a nice flat ridge overlooking the neighborhood where the house was located, and he'd used the penetrating infrared scope to peer into the foyer. There had been no doubt in his mind that the man wearing sunglasses and a ball cap and a black bandana was Mr. Waverly. There had been no doubt in his mind, because a slight adjustment to the scope had allowed him to zero in and see through the disguise, almost as if it wasn't even there. No fuzzy static from stray currents this time, no bandages soaked in saline. The man who'd been standing on the far side of the foyer with a pistol in his hand was definitely Mr. Waverly, and he was definitely dead now.

And Craig didn't feel the least bit sorry for killing him.

20

Wahlman's idea of a lake house was a one-room cabin or an A-frame with a loft.

Dean and Betsy's place was something else entirely.

It was more like some kind of resort. Five bedrooms, a dining table that seated twenty, a multi-level deck and a pool and a boat dock, a finished basement with a game room and a gym and a sauna, everything impeccably maintained, not a single neighbor in sight. It was the kind of place you might like to stay for a good long time.

Unless you were Rock Wahlman.

He was sitting on the far end of the dock, alone, drinking a beer and watching a bobber, occasionally reeling his line in and checking the bait, mostly just thinking about what he was going to do next, where he was going to go.

And wondering if Kasey was going to come with him.

Natalie had returned from her houseboat adventure. She'd been there at the lake house by herself most of the day yesterday, wondering where her grandparents were, wondering why they weren't answering their phones. She'd been sitting on the front porch listening to some music when Wahlman's SUV, Kasey's rental car, Dean's pickup and Betsy's hatchback pulled into the driveway. Of course she'd been very happy to see Kasey, and of course Kasey had been very happy to see her. Everyone got cleaned up and Dean grilled some steaks, and after a very pleasant dinner and some nice conversation, Kasey took Natalie upstairs and talked to her privately for about an hour. She probably talked to her about some of the things she'd talked to Dean and Betsy about earlier, although probably not in as much detail. For instance, she probably didn't tell her about the dead bodies in the foyer at the Nashville house and about tripping the security alarm on the way out so the police would think that a burglar had been surprised by a door-to-door salesperson. She probably didn't tell her any of that, but she probably did tell her that Grandma and Grandpa could never go back to that house again—no matter what—until she told them that it was okay.

Scary stuff for a fourteen-year-old, for sure—or for anyone, for that matter—but Natalie seemed to be taking it all in stride. Kasey was a good mom. Wahlman was certain that she'd assured Natalie that her safety was of utmost importance and had never been in question.

Wahlman sipped his beer and watched his bobber. He heard footsteps. He turned and saw Kasey walking toward him. She was carrying a small cooler. She sat beside him and pulled two beers out of the cooler and dangled her legs over the side of the dock and tested the water with her toes.

"Still way too cold to swim in," she said.

"That must be what all the fish think too," Wahlman said.

"You haven't caught anything?"

"Not even a nibble."

Kasey stood and put her hands on his shoulders and leaned over and bit down gently on his right earlobe.

"There," she said. "Now you've had a nibble."

"Best kind," Wahlman said.

Kasey sat back down.

"Mom and Dad said you can stay as long as you want," she said. "And they said we can sleep in the same room from now on if we want to."

Last night Wahlman had slept on a couch in a bedroom that had been converted into an office, and Kasey had slept on an air mattress in one of the bedrooms that hadn't been furnished yet.

Separate quarters, which seemed like the proper thing to do under the circumstances.

"What about Natalie?" Wahlman said.

"What about her?"

"You're not going to feel weird about sharing a bed with me while she's in the same house?"

"She's fourteen. She knows I've been traveling with you. She's not stupid."

"Have the two of you talked about that kind of stuff?"

"Yes. It was one of the things I discussed with her last night. So don't worry about it."

"Okay," Wahlman said. "I won't worry about it."

Kasey took a sip of beer.

"We could live here indefinitely," she said. "You could do the work you need to do from here."

"What am I supposed to do about money?"

"Mom and Dad have plenty. They want to help you get your life back."

"They said that?"

"Yes."

Wahlman gazed out at the hills in the distance.

"What's up there?" he said.

"I don't know. Just woods, I guess. Maybe some hunting camps or whatever. I can't imagine that anyone would want to live up there on a permanent basis."

Plumes of gray smoke rose from one of the ridges. From a campfire, Wahlman thought, or maybe a chimney. Southeast of where he was sitting. Five miles away, or maybe a little further.

"I should probably leave tomorrow," he said. "Or maybe day after tomorrow."

"Why?"

"This is a safe place for you and your family. I don't want that to change because of me."

"Nobody knows about this place," Kasey said. "Really. We can be comfortable here. We can live like normal people."

The bobber disappeared and the line went taut. Wahlman gave the rod a quick jerk to set the hook, and then he started reeling in the fish. It was a fighter. Maybe a largemouth bass. Maybe four or five pounds. It was going to be difficult to get it up on the dock without a net, and

Wahlman hadn't thought to bring one with him. He hadn't anticipated catching anything bigger than a bluegill or a sun perch. With a bass that size, the rod would break or the line would snap and the fish would swim away with the hook in its mouth and die. Which would be a shame. Wahlman figured he could make a nice contribution to the dinner table tonight with a fish that big, even if he didn't catch anything else all day.

"How deep is the water right here?" he said.

"I don't know," Kasey said. "This is my first time here too, remember?"

"Can you run up to the house and get me a net?"

"Okay."

Kasey stood and bolted toward the other end of the dock, toward the shore and the boardwalk and the steps that led up to the back of the house, toward the storage shed where Dean and Betsy kept their fishing gear.

Wahlman adjusted the drag on the reel and gave the fish some line, just enough to ease the tension a little, hoping the fish wouldn't be able to swim deep enough to get the line snagged on something at the bottom of the lake. He kept playing with the drag and reeling the fish in a little at a time until Kasey made it back with the net.

"You're going to see the fish soon," Wahlman said. "I want you to dip the net under it and lift it out of the water."

"There it is!" Kasey shouted.

It was indeed a largemouth bass. It was beautiful. Seven or eight pounds, Wahlman guessed, bigger than any freshwater fish he'd ever caught in his life. It broke through the surface of the water, jumping at least two feet in the air, thrashing and whipping and opening its mouth as wide as it would go, frantically attempting to free itself, attempting to get back to its ordinary existence, back to the business of just being a fish in a lake in Tennessee. Wahlman tightened the drag and reeled it in closer, the rod severely bowed and probably near its breaking point as Kasey reached out with the net and scooped the enormous fish out of the water and pulled it up onto the dock.

"I've never seen a bass this big," Wahlman said. "Not even down in Florida."

"It's gorgeous. Daddy probably knows someone who could mount it for you, if you want to do that. Or we could just eat it."

Wahlman crouched down and wrestled the hook out of its jaw, careful to do as little damage as possible to the surrounding tissue. The mouth was opening and closing and the gills were fanning out and the slick muscular body was flopping rhythmically against the wooden planks as Wahlman brushed back the spiny dorsal fin and gently lifted the fish from the dock and slid it back into the water. It swam away immediately and disappeared into the murky depths.

Kasey seemed baffled. Astonished.

"It was too beautiful to kill," Wahlman said.

"But you worked so hard to get it up here."

"It takes a long time for a bass to get that big. It should be allowed to die of old age."

Kasey moved in closer, wrapped her arms around

Wahlman's waist and rested her head against his chest.

"I never knew you were so sensitive about things like that," she said.

"Don't let it get around," Wahlman said.

They stood there and held each other for a long time and Wahlman thought about staying but he knew that he couldn't. He knew that his troubles would follow him eventually. And as much as he enjoyed having Kasey on the road with him, and as much as he needed her help, he knew that her place was here with her daughter.

Maybe he could leave for a while and do what he needed to do and then come back and start over.

Maybe.

If Kasey still wanted him.

At any rate, he could leave the lake house knowing that Kasey and Natalie and Betsy and Dean would be all right, safe and secure in this isolated wonderland somewhere between Mont Eagle and the middle of nowhere.

.357 SUNSET

THE REACHER EXPERIMENT BOOK 5

1

What kind of idiot tries to steal a piano?

A baby grand.

Wide as a car.

Rock Wahlman stood there in the ankle-deep water, trying to wrap his head around the absurdity of such a thing. He'd been walking along the alley that ran parallel to Sunset Road, minding his own business, heading two blocks west toward the main thoroughfare, taking a shortcut to a place he'd been told was a good place to get something to eat, when he'd heard a trickling sound and had turned his head enough to notice that a set of French doors on the back of one of the houses was standing wide open.

When he'd walked up to the doors and peeked in, it was immediately obvious that water was leaking into the house from somewhere, and when he'd stepped inside and started looking around, it was immediately obvious that a wall had been partially demolished with a sledgehammer, and that a copper pipe had been severely damaged in the process.

No furniture in the house, other than the piano. The

thief—or team of thieves, probably, the more Wahlman thought about it—had been trying to push the bulky instrument from one room to another, moving it closer to the French doors, closer to the alley, where a truck was probably waiting. They'd busted the wall apart in an attempt to widen the interior doorway.

Not a bad plan, Wahlman supposed, as far as dumbass plans devised by dumbass people went, but apparently the dumbass people had given up when the water had started gushing out of the broken pipe.

"Hands on your head," a male voice from behind Wahlman shouted. "Turn around and face me. Slowly."

"I was just trying to—"

"Hands on your head, asshole. Now!"

Wahlman didn't like being told what to do, and he didn't like being called an asshole. But the man had him at a disadvantage. From the sound of the man's voice, Wahlman figured he was standing approximately ten feet away from where Wahlman was standing. Wahlman was a very large man, and he had a very long reach. But not that long. The man standing behind him spoke authoritatively. Unwaveringly. Probably a cop, Wahlman thought. Probably aiming his service weapon in the general direction of Wahlman's heart.

Wahlman laced his fingers together behind his head, turned around slowly and faced the man, who was indeed a cop, and who was indeed standing approximately ten feet from where Wahlman was standing, and who was indeed aiming the fat barrel of a semi-automatic pistol in the general direction of Wahlman's heart.

The man wore a dark blue uniform. There was a silver badge pinned over his left breast pocket, and a black microphone attached to his right epaulet. Black patent leather holster. Wahlman figured he had matching shoes, but it was impossible to tell for sure at the moment, because they were covered with four or five inches of smelly gray water.

The engraved banner at the top of the officer's badge said RPD. Reality Police Department. The plastic nameplate above the banner said Hurt.

"I can explain," Wahlman said.

"Shut up," Officer Hurt said.

He keyed his mic, identified himself to the dispatcher, and requested backup. Breaking and entering, he said. Three fifty-seven Sunset Road. One suspect, currently being detained at gunpoint.

A few minutes later, three more officers showed up.

A few minutes after that, Wahlman was sitting in the back of Officer Hurt's police car with his hands cuffed behind his back. The door Wahlman had been forced into, the door on the rear passenger side, had been left open, and the four officers were standing a few feet away, talking about something in hushed tones.

Wahlman had spent twenty years as a Master-At-Arms in the United States Navy. So he had a pretty good idea of what Hurt and the other guys were talking about. They were probably discussing whether or not they had enough evidence against Wahlman to actually arrest him. If they thought they did, Officer Hurt, who had been first on the scene, would probably read Wahlman his rights and then drive him to the station for processing. If they thought they didn't, Officer Hurt would probably remove the handcuffs and send Wahlman on his merry way.

Officer Hurt turned and stepped closer to the car.

"What were you doing inside the house?" he said.

"I was trying to find the main water valve," Wahlman said. "I was going to shut it off."

"Why?"

"Seemed like the neighborly thing to do."

"You live around here? Is that what you're saying?"

"I'm saying it seemed like the neighborly thing to do. You can do something neighborly without actually being a neighbor."

"Why don't you have any identification with you?" Hurt said.

"I already answered that question. Right after your friend over there patted me down."

"Answer it again."

"I left my wallet in my car," Wahlman said.

Which was a lie. Wahlman had actually left the wallet in his hotel room, but he didn't want the police to know that he had such easy access to it. Once your phony driver's license got scanned and put into the system, you pretty much had to get a new one right away. And the good ones were expensive.

"Where's your car?" Officer Hurt said.

"Reality Auto Repair. Sunset and Fifth. They were

closing up just as I left. I took one of their business cards from a stack on the counter. It was in my front pocket. Your friend over there took it. I need it back."

Wahlman had been traveling west on the interstate when his SUV broke down. He'd been planning on making it through Missouri and into Kansas before dark, but the engine had started making a strange rattling sound, and then it had quit running altogether. Back in the day when most people still used cell phones on a regular basis, most people would have stayed with the vehicle and called for a tow truck. But those days were long gone. Cell phones were still around. Some people still carried them. Most didn't. Wary of the growing number of hackers out to steal their lives, most people had reverted to landlines in their homes, and most people had started using payphones if they needed to make calls while they were out. Wahlman hadn't owned a cell phone in a long time, and he certainly wouldn't have been carrying one now that he was on the run. Too easy to hack, too easy to track, as the old saying went. So when his car had broken down, Wahlman had pulled to the shoulder and had climbed out of the vehicle and had walked to the nearest exit.

There had been a sign at the bottom of the ramp, with two arrows painted on it. One of the arrows pointed east, and the other pointed west.

The arrow that pointed east said *FANTASY 1.4 MILES.*

The one that pointed west said *REALITY 1.3 MILES.*

Wahlman had chosen Reality. It was a tenth of a mile closer, for one thing, and it was west of where he'd broken down, which would put him that much closer to Kansas once his SUV was towed in and repaired.

The people over at Reality Auto Repair had seemed very nice, and the people at the hotel across the street had seemed very nice, but now Wahlman was starting to wish that he'd walked in the opposite direction.

Reality was getting a little hard to deal with at the moment.

"What's wrong with your car?" Officer Hurt said.

"I don't know," Wahlman said. "I'm not a mechanic."

"What are you?"

"Just a guy."

"What's that supposed to mean?"

"It's not supposed to mean anything."

"What's your name?"

"I already answered that question too."

"Answer it again."

Wahlman gave Officer Hurt the same fake name he'd given the officer who'd searched him earlier. The officer who'd searched him earlier was named Tingly. Short and round and balding. Sergeant's stripes. Thick brown mustache, littered with some powdery remnants of the doughnut he'd been eating when he'd gotten the call to come for backup.

Tingly was still standing a few feet away from Officer Hurt's cruiser, standing there with the other two guys, the three of them laughing about something now.

Wahlman didn't know the names of the other two guys. He'd never gotten close enough to them to read their nameplates.

"Must be a slow crime day in Reality," Wahlman said, nodding toward the jolly trio.

"Where do you live?" Hurt said.

"The Reality Hotel. Sunset and Fifth. Right across the street from—"

"I know where it is," Hurt said. "I need a home address."

"I'm currently between residences," Wahlman said.

"You mean you're moving somewhere?"

"You could say that."

"Where?"

"I was on my way to Kansas when I broke down."

"Why were you walking down this particular alley, at this particular time of the evening?"

"Because this is the United States of America, and I'm allowed to do that."

Officer Hurt nodded. He turned and stepped over to where the other three officers were standing. Tingly and the other two guys. A couple of minutes later, Officer Hurt walked back over to the cruiser and helped Wahlman out and removed the cuffs.

"We're going to let you off with a warning this time," he said, handing over the folded wad of cash that Tingly had taken from Wahlman's front pocket, along with the business card from Reality Auto Repair.

"What are you warning me not to do?" Wahlman said.

"I'm warning you not to be a smartass, for one thing. And I'm warning you not to walk into houses that aren't yours."

"What if I'm invited into a house that isn't mine?"

"What did I just say about not being a smartass?"

Wahlman shrugged. He massaged some circulation back into his wrists, and then he proceeded toward the place he'd been told was a good place to get something to eat.

2

Wahlman sat at the counter. Not on the stool closest to the door, but the one next to that. He didn't like being on the very end. There never seemed to be enough elbow room. A waitress gave him a menu and a glass of ice water and she walked away and came back a couple of minutes later and he ordered a double bacon cheeseburger. Well-done, fully dressed, mayonnaise on the side. He ordered the platter, which came with fries and coleslaw and a drink.

Any drink you wanted, any size.

Wahlman wanted coffee.

"What size?" the waitress said.

She was holding a ballpoint pen and a pad of guest checks. Old school. Like something you might see in a classic film.

"This is not a to-go order," Wahlman said. "I'm going to eat here."

He looked to see if the waitress was wearing a nametag. She wasn't. She was young. Twenty-one, maybe twenty-two. She had blue eyes and light brown hair and perfect teeth.

She was working the counter by herself. It was dinnertime, and the place was busy, but everyone except Wahlman was sitting at a table or a booth. Which meant that he pretty much had her to himself for the moment. A nice relaxed situation, ordinarily. But it didn't seem that way. There was a tenseness about the waitress. A sense of urgency. As if there were ten customers sitting at the counter instead of just one.

"I still need to know what size coffee you want," she said, thumbing the clicker on her ballpoint pen.

Nervously.

Repeatedly.

Annoyingly.

"I want a ceramic mug," Wahlman said. "Whatever size that is. And I want you to come and fill it for me every time it gets close to being empty."

"That's not how it works here," the waitress said.

"How does it work here?"

"We have paper cups. You can get any size you want with the platter you ordered, but if you want more after that, it costs extra."

Wahlman thought about that. He figured The Reality Diner served hundreds of drinks every day. Which meant that hundreds of paper cups were being tossed into the trashcan every day. It seemed very wasteful. Not to mention that a number of the cups probably ended up on the side of the highway.

"This is the first diner I've ever been to that doesn't serve coffee in real cups," Wahlman said.

"They're real cups," the waitress said. "They're just made out of paper."

"Is there another restaurant around here?"

"You want to cancel your order?"

"No. Just wondering."

"There's a place over in Fantasy."

"Do they serve coffee in paper cups?"

"I don't know. I've never been there."

"I guess I'll take a large," Wahlman said. "What's your name?"

"We're not allowed to tell customers our names," the waitress said. "Sorry. You want cream and sugar with that?"

"No thanks. Is there a payphone here somewhere?"

"Outside. By the newspaper machines."

Wahlman got up and walked outside. He pulled the business card out of his pocket, slid some coins into the phone, and punched in the number. A man picked up after four rings.

"Reality Auto," the man said.

"I was calling to check on my car," Wahlman said.

"Which one is yours?"

"The white SUV."

"You need a fuel pump."

"Okay. What time do you think you'll have it done?"

The man laughed. "We closed an hour ago," he said. "Technically, I'm not even supposed to be answering the phone this late."

"Are you the guy I talked to a while ago?"

"That's me."

"So what happened?"

Earlier, Wahlman had offered to pay the man extra

money to perform the repair right away. A hundred dollars. Sort of a bonus. Straight from Wahlman's pocket to the man's pocket. The man had agreed to those terms. He'd wanted the money up front, and Wahlman had given it to him. The man had promised to get the job done, even if it took until midnight.

"Couldn't get the part," the man said. "I put in a special order. Should be here sometime in the morning. At least by lunchtime. But we're kind of backed up right now, so—"

"I need to be in Junction City by two o'clock tomorrow afternoon," Wahlman said.

"Don't know what to tell you," the man said.

Wahlman had been searching for information pertaining to an army colonel who went by the name of Dorland. It was a codename. Wahlman knew that much. It had to be, because Wahlman had searched every military database available to the public, and there weren't any officers currently on active duty with that last name.

Which meant that Wahlman needed to gain access to the army's restricted databases.

Which meant that he needed passwords.

He'd set up a meeting with a professional hacker, a civilian who worked part time in one of the offices at Fort Riley. The guy hadn't made any promises, and he hadn't given Wahlman any details about how the exchange of information was going to work. That was what the meeting was supposed to be about. The guy refused to discuss the matter over the phone or online.

Which was understandable.

The guy would be taking a huge risk if he ended up actually doing what Wahlman wanted him to do.

Now it was starting to look like the meeting wasn't even going to happen, because it was starting to look like a fuel pump wasn't going to happen. Not tonight, anyway. Special order, the man had said.

"What about my hundred dollars?" Wahlman said.

"What hundred dollars?" the man said.

Wahlman thought about ripping the receiver away from the steel-coated cable it was attached to and carrying it over to Reality Auto Repair and shoving it up the man's ass. But he didn't. He calmly told the man that he would stop by in the morning to discuss the matter further, and then he hung up the phone.

Now the man would have all night to think about it. Maybe he would decide to give Wahlman the money back on his own. Or maybe he would need a certain amount of persuasion. Either way, Wahlman wasn't leaving Reality until the cash he'd given the man was back in his pocket.

He walked back into the diner and sat on the same stool he'd been sitting on earlier. He'd been hoping that the food he'd ordered would be waiting for him, but it wasn't. The Waitress With No Name hadn't even poured him any coffee yet. She was talking to a pair of guys at the other end of the counter. Both of the guys were wearing jeans and flannel shirts and ball caps, and neither of them had shaved in a while. They were older than the waitress, but younger than Wahlman. Late twenties, early thirties. Wahlman figured they'd walked in while he was on the phone.

The waitress glanced over at Wahlman, and then she turned back around and held up an index finger to let the guys she'd been talking to know that she would be right back. She walked to Wahlman's end of the counter and asked him if he still wanted coffee.

"Why wouldn't I?" Wahlman said.

"Just checking," the waitress said. "I didn't know if you were coming back or not."

She rattled off another staccato series of clicks with the ballpoint pen. Wahlman tried not to look as aggravated as he felt. The waitress poured some coffee into a gigantic insulated paper cup and set it on the counter in front of him.

"I still want the double cheeseburger platter too," he said.

The waitress nodded. She jotted the order down on her pad, and then she turned around and tapped her finger on a computer screen a few times. Relaying the order to a monitor screen back in the kitchen, Wahlman supposed. Or a printer. Or whatever. When she finished tapping on the screen, she walked back over to where the flannel shirt guys were sitting. The guys had paper cups in front of them, identical to Wahlman's, except theirs had lids. The waitress leaned over the counter toward the guy on the left, and he leaned over the counter toward her, and they kissed on the lips. Then both of the guys got up and headed toward the door.

Wahlman watched them as they exited the restaurant.

The man who hadn't kissed the waitress was wearing black leather work boots. Well worn, but not worn out.

The man who had kissed the waitress was wearing work

boots too. But his weren't black. They were tan. Khaki. The shade of sand in the desert.

Similar to the ones Wahlman was wearing.

And, similar to the ones Wahlman was wearing, they were wet up to the ankles.

3

It was the kind of place people sometimes referred to as a hole in the wall. Depending on the time of day you pushed your way through the heavily-tinted steel and glass door, you might see a wrinkled old drunk slumping over a shot glass or a middle-aged couple meeting for an extramarital highball or a cluster of restaurant workers drinking beer and complaining about how busy or how slow their shifts had been.

Jackson P. Feldman didn't see any of that. He was the only customer at the moment. He limped up to the bar, his left knee still bothering him from an injury he'd sustained in Bakersfield, California. He usually told people that he'd been playing tennis out there in the desert, trying to get back in shape, but that wasn't the truth. Jackson P. Feldman hadn't played tennis in years, and getting back in shape was the furthest thing from his mind these days. The truth was, he'd gotten his ass kicked by a man named Rock Wahlman, a fugitive from justice he'd been hired to locate.

"What can I get for you?" the bartender said.

"Bourbon on the rocks," Feldman said. "Make it a double."

Feldman figured the bartender was probably in his early twenties. He wore black pants and a black polo shirt and a tooled leather belt with a fancy silver buckle on it. Light brown hair, buzzed short on the back and sides. Like a military cut. You could tell he spent some time at the gym. Not too much, just enough. He was toned, but not musclebound. Clean. Quick. Balanced. He grabbed a short heavy glass from a shelf behind the bar, dropped a couple of ice cubes in it with a pair of tongs, picked up a bottle of inexpensive but fairly respectable Kentucky bourbon whiskey from the stainless steel well rack at his knees, poured a generous amount of the amber liquid into the glass. Counting off the seconds in his head with the red plastic speed pourer attached to the neck of the bottle, Feldman supposed, rather than using any sort of precise measuring device. Bar owners weren't especially fond of that sort of technique, but customers were, because they tended to get a little more liquor than they were paying for. Which frequently resulted in a bigger tip for the man or woman doing the pouring.

The man doing the pouring at this particular establishment slapped a cocktail napkin on the bar in front of Feldman, and then he gently set the drink on the napkin.

"You want to start a tab?" he said.

"Sure," Feldman said, handing the young man his credit card.

Feldman had been wearing a brace on the knee, but it still hurt. Really bad sometimes. Alcohol was the only thing that seemed to keep the pain at bay. Feldman knew that he should have seen a doctor the day he'd sustained the injury, knew that he should have gone to the emergency room and had x-rays and all that, but he hadn't wanted to take the time. And he didn't like doctors. The ER physician probably would have referred him to a surgeon, and the surgeon probably would have wanted to operate. And that just wasn't going to happen. Feldman didn't have the time, and he didn't have the money. He figured the joint would eventually heal on its own. In the meantime, there was whiskey.

He took a long pull from the glass in front of him.

There was a television mounted on the wall behind the bar. The bartender picked up a remote control and started clicking through channels.

"Let me know if you see anything you want to watch," he said.

Feldman rarely watched television, because there was rarely anything on it that he wanted to see. It was a waste of time, as far as he was concerned. But he didn't tell the bartender that.

"Someone's supposed to meet me here at six," he said. "We'll probably move to a booth. So watch whatever you want."

The bartender shrugged, set the remote back beside the plastic napkin caddy at the edge of the bar, where it had been before he picked it up. He'd stopped on an old situation comedy from the middle of the twentieth century. Which, in Feldman's opinion, was the only time in history that television had been very entertaining. He glanced up at the screen for a few seconds, but the volume was too low for him to hear any of the dialogue.

"You a cop?" the bartender said.

"What makes you think that?" Feldman said, caught off guard by the question.

"I don't know. You just have the look. Not that I have anything against cops. They come in here all the time."

"I'm not a cop," Feldman said. "But I used to be one."

"Retired?"

"Yeah."

Feldman didn't see any point in telling the bartender any more than that. The fact that he was one of the most respected private investigators in the country was none of the bartender's business.

Feldman drained the last of the bourbon from his glass, nodded for the bartender to give him a refill.

"You want some pretzels or anything?" the bartender said, pouring another double over the same ice cubes.

"No thanks," Feldman said.

A sudden wedge of temporary brightness flooded the room as a tall and thin man entered and made his way over to where Feldman was sitting. The tall and thin man was wearing jeans and a western-style shirt and cowboy boots. He looked like he was going to a rodeo. All he needed was a hat. He had a fresh haircut and a clean shave and he smelled like some kind of cologne you might pick up at a grocery store.

"You Feldman?" he said.

"Yes," Feldman said.

"I'm Decker. Let's talk over here."

Feldman picked up his drink and climbed off of the stool he'd been sitting on and followed Decker to the far right corner of the room, to the booth furthest from the bar. Decker sat with his back to the wall, facing the door. Feldman slid into the seat across from him, trying not to grimace as an electric spear of agony traveled from his knee to the top of his scalp.

"You don't want anything to drink?" Feldman said.

"I don't drink," Decker said, unsnapping one of his shirt pockets and pulling out a pen and a notepad. "What did you want to talk to me about?"

"I wanted to talk to you about tracking a guy."

"I figured that. It's what I do. Tell me the particulars, and I'll let you know if I might be able to help you."

"The guy I'm looking for is a suspect in a murder case," Feldman said. "His name is Rock Wahlman. He's six feet four inches tall, and he weighs—"

"Who hired you to find him?"

"A detective named Collins. Down in New Orleans."

"So you're being paid by the NOPD?"

"Correct."

"And who's going to be paying me?"

"I am," Feldman said. "Out of my own pocket."

"I told you my rate over the phone. You're good with that?"

"I'm good with it."

"Why don't you just find this Wahlman guy yourself?" Decker said.

"I was a police officer for twenty years," Feldman said. "I've been a private investigator for a little over seven. If there's one thing I've learned, it's that there's no shame in asking for help when you need it. Wahlman's smart, and he's deadly, and he doesn't want to be caught. He's getting money from somewhere, substantial amounts of cash for travel expenses and fake driver's licenses and whatnot. No paper trail. At least I haven't been able to find one."

"Any idea where he's getting the money?"

"He was traveling with a woman named Kasey Stielson. Her family's pretty well-off. I think they might be funding his current lifestyle."

Decker wrote something on the notepad. Feldman took a swallow of whiskey.

"When you say family, you mean her parents?" Decker said.

"Yes," Feldman said. "Her parents."

"Got an address for them?"

"I do. I have their home address, but they're not living there right now. It's like they abandoned the place. That's one of the problems. I have no idea where they went."

"Tell me the address," Decker said.

Feldman told him the street number and zip code. Decker wrote it all down.

"The house is only a few miles from here," Feldman said. "But they might have left the country for all I know."

"I doubt it. You said they're rich. They probably have another house somewhere. I'm assuming you checked the county real estate records for a second address."

"I did," Feldman said. "If they have another house, it's not in Davidson County. I ran a national search on one of the databases I subscribe to, came up with nothing."

"How current is the database?"

"They update it twice a year. I guess it's possible that—"

"Right. I have access to a national real estate site that gets updated weekly. It's expensive, but it's worth it. Especially for someone in my line of work. I use it all the time."

Feldman knew about the database Decker was referring to. He'd tried it for a while, found it to be unreliable about half the time. But maybe it had gotten better. He decided not to say anything negative about it for the moment.

"If you can find Kasey's parents, that would be a good start," he said.

"I'll find them," Decker said. "Their name's Stielson?"

"No. Kasey was married to a guy named Stielson. He was shot in his car out in the Mojave Desert, but we don't think—"

"What's the name of the people I'm looking for?" Decker said.

"Lennik," Feldman said. "Dean and Betsy."

"Dean and Betsy Lennik. Got it. Does Kasey have any other relatives I should know about?"

"She has a daughter."

"Name?"

"Natalie. She's a minor. Fourteen. Same last name as her mom. Stielson."

"Great. Now tell me all about the murder suspect you're trying to track down."

Feldman took another drink of whiskey, and then he told Decker everything he knew about Rock Wahlman.

4

There were a million different ways the man who'd kissed the waitress could have gotten his boots wet. Perhaps he'd stepped in a puddle of rainwater. Or maybe he'd been fishing from a leaky boat. Maybe he installed sprinkler systems for a living.

There were a million different ways.

It seemed highly unlikely that he'd been involved in the situation over at 357 Sunset.

Highly unlikely, but possible.

Wahlman tried to shrug it off. It was none of his business. He had things to do. Pressing matters to take care of.

The Waitress With No Name brought the double bacon cheeseburger and the fries and the coleslaw.

"Is there a bus station around here anywhere?" Wahlman said.

"I don't know if you'd really call it a station, but there's a little shack where a guy sells tickets. Two blocks west, right on the corner."

"Okay. Thanks."

"Where you heading?"

"Junction City. I have an appointment tomorrow afternoon. My car's in the shop, and it doesn't look like it's going to be finished in time."

"So you're going to Junction City, and then you're coming back here?"

"Looks that way."

The Waitress with No Name nodded.

"Junction City isn't that far," she said. "My boyfriend could probably give you a ride in his truck. It wouldn't be free, but it would be cheaper than taking a bus."

"What makes you think your boyfriend would want to do that?" Wahlman said.

"He's out of work right now. He could use the money."

Wahlman thought about it. A ride in a personal vehicle would be more convenient than a ride on a bus. And more comfortable. And less expensive. But Wahlman didn't want to get involved with any of the locals in Reality, Missouri. He didn't want to get involved with any of the locals anywhere. He needed to be as anonymous as possible, talk to as few people as possible.

"Thanks anyway, but I think I'll take the bus," he said.

"Okay. Suit yourself."

The Waitress With No Name turned and walked away. There was a phone on the wall, a couple of feet to the right of the coffeemakers. She picked up the receiver and punched in a number and started talking to someone.

Whispering.

Wahlman couldn't hear what she was saying, and he didn't care what she was saying. He squirted some ketchup on his plate, dragged a French fry through it, and took a bite.

5

The bus station was exactly as The Waitress With No Name had described it. A shack on the corner. More like a miniature hut. There wasn't enough room for two regular-sized people to fit in there, and there wasn't enough room for one Wahlman-sized person to fit in there. It reminded Wahlman of a structure he'd seen in a history book one time, where people dropped photographic film off to be processed. You put your name and address on an envelope and sealed your roll of film in there and the attendant told you how many days it would be until your pictures were ready. Hard to imagine. Like traveling across the country in a covered wagon or something. Just unfathomably slow.

A woman with long blonde hair and a nice smile slid the window open when she saw Wahlman approaching.

"Can I help you?" she said.

"I need to get to Junction City, Kansas," Wahlman said. "Tonight, if possible."

The woman tapped the monitor screen in front of her with a nicely manicured fingernail a few times, and then she consulted a three-ring binder that was bulging with printouts.

"There's a coach coming in from New York City, headed toward Topeka. It'll be here tomorrow afternoon, a little after one if it's running on time. From Topeka you can connect to—"

"That's too late," Wahlman said. "I need to be in Junction City by one or one-thirty. Two at the latest."

"Oh. Then I don't know what to tell you."

"Where's the nearest airport?"

"There's an airstrip over in Fantasy. But they don't land any passenger planes over there or anything. Just those little ones people buzz around in for fun."

"Where's the nearest real airport?" Wahlman said.

"Jefferson City."

"How soon can a bus get me there?"

The woman tapped the screen some more and paged through the binder some more.

"That coach should be coming through here around noon tomorrow," she said. "But even if you were able to get a flight out of Jefferson City right away—"

"So you're telling me that there's no way you can get me to Junction City by two o'clock tomorrow afternoon?"

"Sorry. A bus left here for Topeka about fifteen minutes ago. Too bad you didn't stop by a little sooner."

"Yeah," Wahlman said. "Too bad."

He walked back down to the diner, sat on the same stool. The Waitress With No Name was standing over by the coffee machine, sorting silverware and rolling it into paper napkins. When she turned to carry a handful of the wrapped utensils over to the bin where they were being stored, she saw Wahlman sitting there.

"You're back," she said.

"Could I get another large coffee, please?"

"Sure."

The waitress lowered the silverware into the bin, walked back over to the coffee setup and filled one of the gigantic paper cups. She set it on the counter in front of Wahlman. It was hot and it smelled fresh.

"Thanks," Wahlman said.

"How did it go at the bus station?"

"Not so good."

"Sorry to hear that."

"I was wondering if your boyfriend might still be interested in giving me a ride," Wahlman said.

"I can give him a call and ask, if you want me to."

"Yes. I would appreciate that."

The Waitress With No Name stepped over to the telephone and punched in a number. Started whispering again. A few seconds later, she hung up and walked back over to where Wahlman was sitting.

"He's on his way over here," she said.

"Great," Wahlman said.

He sipped his coffee and waited. The coffee was fresh, but it had a faint aftertaste he hadn't noticed earlier. Like the glue on the flap of an envelope when you lick it.

Wahlman had thought about walking up to the highway and hitchhiking, but that was always hit or miss. Especially with a man Wahlman's size. He was six feet four inches tall, and he weighed two hundred and thirty pounds. Chest muscles as big as frying pans, abs like a six-pack of sledgehammer heads. He looked like the kind of guy who could break you in half if he wanted to. And he was that kind of guy. Not that he ever went looking for trouble. He didn't. But motorists tended to shy away when he walked along the shoulder with his thumb out, sometimes to the point of changing lanes to maximize the distance, as if he might reach out and yank them from their seats as they whizzed by at eighty miles an hour.

Hitchhiking was always an option, but it was one that Wahlman avoided for the most part. The meeting with the hacker in Junction City tomorrow was too important to risk missing. It was probably Wahlman's best chance at identifying and locating the army colonel who'd been trying to kill him, at getting to the bottom of why all this was happening. Wahlman needed to be there on time, and he needed a mode of transportation that would be more dependable than hitchhiking.

The Boyfriend of The Waitress With No Name walked into the restaurant. He'd changed clothes. He wasn't wearing the tan boots anymore. Different shirt, different jeans. He walked up to the counter and sat down, leaving one stool between him and Wahlman.

"You the guy who needs a ride?" he said.

"Yes," Wahlman said.

"What's your name?"

"Is it important?"

"I guess not. We can just remain anonymous as far as I'm

concerned. You ready to go now?"

"My meeting's at two o'clock tomorrow afternoon," Wahlman said. "After the meeting, I'm going to need a ride back to Reality."

"We can leave at ten tomorrow morning if you want to," The Boyfriend Of The Waitress With No Name said. "That should give you plenty of time."

"And you'll wait around for me, and then bring me back?"

"Sure."

"How much?"

Boyfriend gave Wahlman a price. It was a little steep, but Wahlman wasn't in a position to haggle.

"I'll meet you here at the diner at ten in the morning," Boyfriend said.

"Okay," Wahlman said. "Is there a place around here where I can buy a phone?"

"Yeah. About a mile from here. It's on my way home. I can drop you off if you want me to."

"I would appreciate that."

Wahlman requested a lid for his cup, and then he followed Boyfriend out to the parking lot.

6

Wahlman bought a cheap little disposable flip-top cell phone—the kind you use for a few days and then crush with the heel of your boot. He activated the device, and then he walked to the hotel and called Kasey from his room. She was still staying at her parents' lake house in Tennessee. It had been a couple of days since Wahlman had talked to her.

"Where are you?" she said.

"Missouri," Wahlman said, always careful not to be very specific about his location, in case someone was listening in. Unlikely, but there was no point in taking any chances.

Kasey knew the drill.

"I thought you would be further west by now," she said.

"The SUV broke down. I had to have it towed."

"You need money?"

"No. I have enough for now."

"Are you sure?"

"I'm sure."

"Are you still planning to meet with that guy tomorrow afternoon?"

"My car's not going to be ready in time. I'm paying someone to drive me."

"You think you're going to be able to get the information you need?" Kasey said.

"I hope so."

"I hope so too. I'm not sure how much more of this I can take."

Kasey's tone had changed abruptly. She sounded anxious. Distraught.

"How much more of what?" Wahlman said.

"Being separated like this. I don't know. Just the uncertainty of it all."

Wahlman had left his home in Florida and had been out on the road for months. Literally running for his life. He loved Kasey, and he wanted to be with her, but he couldn't just hide out there at her parents' lake house forever, as she had previously suggested. He was afraid that his troubles might follow him there, for one thing, putting Kasey and her family in great danger. He needed to find out why he had been targeted, and he needed to figure out a way to put a stop to it.

And he needed to do it alone.

Then he could deal with the charges that had been brought against him in New Orleans. Then maybe he and Kasey could have a chance at some kind of life together.

"I'm doing the best I can," he said.

"I know you are. It's just that—"

"Everything's going to work out. I just need a little more time."

There was a long pause.

"There's someone at the door," Kasey said. "Call me tomorrow and let me know how it goes, okay?"

"Okay," Wahlman said.

He clicked off. Sat there on the bed and stared into the mirror behind the dresser. He hadn't weighed himself lately, but his face looked thinner than usual, and there were dark circles under his eyes. His hair had started graying at the temples. He was only forty years old, but some of the teenage cashiers at some of the fast food joints he went to sometimes were already starting to ask him if he qualified for the senior discount. He still felt good. Strong. But the nightmare that his life had become had taken its toll on his physical appearance.

He stripped down and took a shower, and then he pulled a clean pair of underwear out of his backpack and put them on and climbed into bed. It was early, not even nine o'clock yet, but he'd only been sleeping four or five hours a night lately, and it was starting to catch up to him.

He turned onto his side and closed his eyes. He didn't need to set the alarm clock or arrange for a courtesy call. He knew that he would wake up at the usual time, at 5:27 in the morning.

7

Kasey walked to the door and looked through the peephole. Her parents had gone into town to do some shopping—a twenty-mile trip, each way—and Natalie had gone with them, hoping to find a new bathing suit for the summer. Before leaving, Kasey's dad had called a service technician to perform some routine maintenance on the central heating and air conditioning system, and the guy had said that he was extremely busy this time of year and that it might be late into the evening hours before he could make it over.

So Kasey hadn't immediately felt uneasy about someone knocking on the door, but the guy standing on the porch didn't really look like a service technician. He was wearing a white shirt and a tan sports jacket, jeans and boots and a white cowboy hat. Dark brown hair. Mustache.

Kasey was certain that she'd never seen him before.

She was thinking about walking over to the bureau at the end of the foyer and opening the drawer and grabbing the pistol that was in there when she noticed the white van in the driveway. *JOE'S HEATING AND AIR*, the side panel said, in big brown letters. So maybe the guy on the porch was going to put some coveralls or something on before starting the work he'd come to do.

Kasey opened the door.

"Hi," she said. "My dad's not here right now, but I guess you can—"

"Are you Kasey Stielson?"

"Yes."

"I need to talk to you."

Kasey glanced over at the van. A guy wearing a gray shirt and a red ball cap climbed out and started walking toward the east side of the house, where the outside air conditioning unit was located. Then Kasey remembered what her dad had said, that the previous owners had used the same heating and air conditioning company for years and had highly recommended their services, that the guys were familiar with the setup, and that it really wasn't necessary for anyone to be home when they came and performed the annual cleaning and refrigerant check.

"What do you want?" Kasey said to the man on the porch.

"May I come in?"

"I don't think so. Are you trying to sell something, or what?"

"I'm looking for a man named Rock Wahlman."

"Never heard of him," Kasey said.

She glanced up the hill, saw a long black sedan parked along the side of the road. She took a step backward and started to close the door.

The man slid his foot between the door and the jamb.

"I'm pretty sure you have heard of him," the man said. "This is going to be a lot easier for both of us if you cooperate."

"And what if I don't cooperate?"

"I know your parents live here, and your daughter. Don't make this any more difficult than it needs to be."

"Are you threatening to do physical harm to me and my family?" Kasey said.

"Of course not," the man said. "But Rock Wahlman is wanted for murder. Anyone who helps him stay hidden from the authorities could be charged with a number of serious crimes. You, your parents, and your daughter—even though she's still a minor. Is that what you want? Do you want Natalie to spend the rest of her teenage years in a juvenile detention center?"

"Who are you?" Kasey said.

"My name's Decker. I'm a professional tracker and bounty hunter. I'm working with a private investigator from New Orleans. Guy named Feldman. He was hired by the New Orleans Police Department as a special consultant in the case against Mr. Wahlman."

"You're wasting your time," Kasey said. "I don't know where he is."

"May I come in?"

Kasey took a deep breath, and then she opened the door wide enough for Decker to cross the threshold. He took his hat off as he entered the house. He was wearing some kind of cologne or aftershave, a scent that reminded Kasey of a certain brand of floor cleaner that she'd used recently.

She led him into the living room and motioned for him to have a seat on the leather couch, and then she rolled the chair from the computer desk over to the coffee table and sat across from him. She didn't offer him a cup of coffee or even a glass of water. She wanted to get him out of there as soon as possible so she could contact Rock and warn him.

"I'm telling you, I don't know where he is," she said.

"When was the last time you talked to him?"

"He called just a little while ago. But he never tells me his exact location."

"Concerned that someone might be listening in?"

"Of course. And concerned that someone like you might show up and start asking questions."

"Does Mr. Wahlman ever tell you his approximate location?" Decker said.

"No."

"I find that hard to believe."

"I don't really give a shit what you find hard to—"

"You need to give a shit," Decker said. "If I'm not satisfied with the information gained from our little interview session here, the next person who knocks on your door will be from the state police. You and your daughter and your parents will be charged with aiding and abetting a fugitive from justice. The four of you will be taken into custody and extradited to Louisiana, where you will be given a court date. You might be released on bail, if you can afford it, but your lives will be disrupted for a long time. Months. Years maybe. Then, if you're convicted, you might be facing—"

"Natalie wasn't involved in any of this," Kasey said.

"Okay. Let's say she wasn't. She's only fourteen years old. The court's not going to let her just walk away and live independently. I understand that her father is deceased, so there's a very good chance that she would become a ward of the state. It's a heartbreaking situation. I've seen it happen more times than I care to remember. So yes, you need to give a shit about what I believe and what I don't believe. As of now, you and your family haven't been charged with anything, but that could change very quickly. All I want is Wahlman. Tell me what you know, and I'll leave you alone forever."

Tears welled in Kasey's eyes. She didn't want to see anything bad happen to Rock. She loved him. She wanted to be with him forever.

But the welfare of her daughter came first.

"He's in Missouri," she said. "He has an SUV with a fake registration. It broke down, and it's going to be a while before he can drive it again. He's staying somewhere while it's being worked on, but I don't know exactly where."

"Would you happen to know the tag number on that vehicle?" Decker said. "And the phone number he called you from a while ago?"

Kasey told him the tag number, and the phone number, and then she lost control of her emotions. She started sobbing uncontrollably, knowing in her heart that she would never see Rock Wahlman again.

8

It had been years since Wahlman's internal alarm clock had failed him, so it came as a complete shock when he opened his eyes and glanced over at the nightstand and saw that it was 8:57 in the morning.

He'd slept for about twelve hours.

He climbed out of bed and took a quick shower and headed over to the diner.

The breakfast crowd had come and gone, and he had the counter to himself again. The Waitress With No Name wasn't there. Another young lady stepped over and asked him if he would like a cup of coffee. She was petite and perky with short blonde hair and eyes the shade of robins' eggs.

The Waitress With No Name 2.

"Yes on the coffee," Wahlman said, studying the laminated menu he'd picked up on the way in. "And let me get the number four breakfast platter, with a side of hash browns."

"How do you want your eggs?"

"Fast. I'm meeting someone here in a little while, and—"

"I mean how do you want them cooked?" The Waitress With No Name 2 said, never cracking a smile.

"Scrambled will be fine," Wahlman said. "And make the coffee a large, please."

The Waitress With No Name 2 poured some coffee into a large paper cup and set it on the counter in front of Wahlman, and then she punched his breakfast order into the computer.

"Should be out in a few minutes," she said.

"Thanks. I'm going to step outside and get a newspaper. I'll be right back."

Wahlman stepped outside and fed some coins into the machine and grabbed a paper from the top of the stack. As he was turning to head back into the diner, he saw the man he'd hired to give him a ride to Junction City.

The Boyfriend Of The Waitress with No Name stepped up onto the sidewalk. He was wearing the tan leather work boots again. They appeared to be dry now, but they were discolored up to the ankles.

Like Wahlman's.

From sloshing around in the flooded house over on Sunset.

"You ready to go?" Boyfriend said.

"You're early," Wahlman said. "I was going to eat some breakfast."

"We better get going. You wouldn't want to miss your appointment."

"Why would I miss it? Junction City's only three hours from here."

"You never know what traffic's going to be like."

Wahlman shrugged. "All right," he said. "You mind if I eat in your truck?"

"Not at all."

Wahlman walked inside and asked The Waitress With No Name 2 to change his order to a carryout, and a few minutes later he climbed into the truck with Boyfriend and munched on a strip of bacon as they made their way toward the interstate.

But Boyfriend didn't take a left where he should have. He didn't turn onto the road that led to the on-ramps. Instead, he kept going straight. Toward Fantasy.

"I think you should have turned back there," Wahlman said.

Left-handed, and with lightning speed, like some kind of ambidextrous gunslinger from the old west, Boyfriend pulled a handgun out from the other side of the driver seat and aimed the barrel at Wahlman's face.

"Shut up and eat your breakfast," he said. "We're going to take a little detour."

9

The red and white sign mounted over the service bays said
REALITY AUTO REPAIR. Decker steered into the parking
lot, climbed out of his car, entered the building through a
steel and glass swinging door that led to an enclosure with a
counter and a waiting area.

A guy wearing a blue shirt with an embroidered blue and
white patch that said *GERRY* over the left breast pocket was
sitting behind the counter staring at a computer screen. He
had oily hair that didn't appear to be quite natural in color,
and a thick and gaudy pair of rhinestone-studded eyeglasses
that didn't appear to be quite from this planet. Blackened
fingernails, scabbed knuckles. He glanced up from his
monitor and asked Decker if he could help him.

"You working on this car?" Decker said, sliding a piece
of paper across the counter with the tag number Kasey
Stielson had given him written on it.

Gerry picked up the piece of paper, tapped some keys on
his keyboard.

"It's not ready yet," he said.

"But it's here?"

"Yeah. It's here. It's parked around back."

"I'm looking for the man who brought it in," Decker said. "Any idea where he might be staying?"

Gerry raked his greasy fingers through his greasy hair.

"Is he a friend of yours or something?" he said.

"Or something," Decker said.

"I don't know where he's staying. Not for sure. But he's probably over at The Reality Hotel."

"Where's that?"

"Right down the road. You could walk there if you wanted to."

Decker folded the piece of paper and slid it back into his pocket. He handed the mechanic a blank business card with a phone number written on it.

"Give me a call if you hear from the owner of that vehicle," he said.

"Is he in some kind of trouble or something?"

"More than you can imagine. Just give me a call if you see him or if he calls the shop."

"Okay."

Decker left the repair shop and drove to the hotel. The wormy little clerk at the check-in desk cited some sort of privacy policy, but he suddenly became much more cooperative when Decker told him that Wahlman was wanted for murder and that anyone hindering the investigation could be charged with a serious crime.

Wahlman wasn't in his room, but he hadn't checked out of the hotel, so Decker figured he would be back.

Feldman had agreed to pay Decker his normal fee for this kind of thing, but that was peanuts compared to the bounty that was out on Wahlman. Big bucks, and Decker wanted all of it. Which meant that he would have to deliver Wahlman to the NOPD himself. Which could be quite a problem with a guy that big, a guy with a history of violent confrontations, a guy determined to evade capture at all costs.

But that was okay.

Because, as of late last night, Wahlman's wanted status had been changed. He was now wanted dead or alive, and Decker had a nice big car with a nice big trunk.

He sat in the parking lot and waited.

10

The gun must have been strapped between the seat and the door. Completely out of sight from the passenger side. No way for Wahlman to have seen it when he'd climbed into the pickup. It was a .357 revolver. Wahlman had owned one similar to it when he was in the Navy. Bright stainless steel finish, rubber grips. Wahlman could see the fat tips of the magnum rounds through the holes in the cylinder.

"Where are you taking me?" Wahlman said.

"You'll see," Boyfriend said.

He took a left onto a gravel road that gradually turned to dirt after a quarter mile or so, and then he made a series of disorienting turns through the woods, finally stopping at the edge of a clearing, about fifty yards from a large wooden barn. Wahlman had been waiting for a chance to lunge over and twist the gun out of his hand, but the chance had never come. Boyfriend had kept the pistol aimed at Wahlman's core the entire time. One little hiccup, and a hole the size of a quarter would be bored through Wahlman's left bicep and into his chest. Deep into his left lung, for sure, and maybe all the way into his pericardial cavity. It was highly unlikely that he would survive such a wound, much less be able to fend off a second shot. So he hadn't made a move. Not yet. He was waiting for a mistake, or some kind of diversion. Anything that might give him an opening.

"Now what?" Wahlman said, staring straight ahead through the windshield, toward the barn.

"You'll see," Boyfriend said.

"You and your buddy tried to steal that piano, didn't you?"

"Shut up."

"Your boots gave you away. They were wet, up to the ankles, just like mine. I figured it was probably a coincidence. But I figured wrong, didn't I?"

"I guess you think you're pretty smart," Boyfriend said. "But that kind of reasoning can work both ways. My girlfriend told me that you were staring at my boots when I left the restaurant yesterday. Then she told me that your boots looked the same as mine. Wet up to the ankles. Two plus two equals four. You know? I talked to a friend later on. Brad Tingly. He's a cop. He confirmed my suspicions. You should have minded your own business. Then you wouldn't be—"

"I was a cop too," Wahlman said. "United States Navy, Master-At-Arms. It's not my nature to mind my own business, especially when I see something that's obviously wrong. Like a vacant house with the back door standing open."

"You should have kept walking."

Wahlman couldn't argue with that. He'd gotten himself into something that was going to be very difficult to get out of, all for what appeared to be some sort of theft ring.

"What's in the barn?" he said. "You and your buddy have a nice little business going here, don't you?"

"Open the door and climb out of the truck and get on the ground," Boyfriend said. "Facedown, hands behind your head. Slow and easy, if you want to keep breathing."

Wahlman didn't move.

"Why a piano?" he said. "And why right there in Reality, where you live? Seems pretty stupid to me. Almost like you were trying to get caught."

"I don't want to get blood all over my interior, but I'll shoot you where you're sitting if I have to. Out of the truck. Now."

"Was it your idea, or your buddy's idea? A Baby grand piano. I've run across some dumbass criminals in my day, but that pretty much takes the cake. I've been trying to figure out why in the world anyone would—"

"Now!" Boyfriend shouted.

He leaned over and jammed the barrel of the pistol into Wahlman's ribcage.

Which presented a potential window of opportunity.

Boyfriend was off balance now. Mentally, and physically. Which, from Wahlman's perspective, could have ended up being a very good thing, or a very bad thing. Wahlman figured he had about a fifty percent chance of successfully leaning forward and avoiding the brunt of the initial blast, perhaps only being grazed by the bullet as it whizzed by or scorched by the muzzle flash as the powder exploded out of the barrel. Then he could quickly grab the gun and break Boyfriend's arm in three or four places—and maybe crush a few facial bones while he was at it—and leave him there in the clearing writhing on the ground, hoping someone would show up to take him to the hospital.

But that wasn't what happened. Not exactly.

Just as Wahlman was about to make his move, a second pickup truck sped into the clearing, whipping around 180 degrees on the soft earth, stopping nose-to-nose with Boyfriend's truck, just a few feet away, a few feet closer to the barn.

A man climbed out of the truck. It was the guy Boyfriend had been hanging out with at the diner yesterday. Boyfriend's partner in crime, the way Wahlman had it figured. He was wearing shorts and sneakers and a muscle shirt and a ball cap backwards. He took a few steps toward Boyfriend's truck, opened the passenger side door and grabbed Wahlman by the arm.

Which was a stupid thing to do, considering that the barrel of Boyfriend's revolver was still jammed against Wahlman's ribcage.

"Get out," Partner In Crime said.

Wahlman didn't say anything.

And he didn't get out of the truck.

In a single swift and precise motion, he swung his elbow like a pendulum, knocking the barrel of the gun toward the backrest of the bucket seat, managing to lean forward, toward the dashboard, a split second before Boyfriend pulled the trigger.

There was an earsplitting blast and a simultaneous shower of blood and bone and brain tissue as the top of Partner In Crime's head exploded against the blueness of the late-spring Missouri sky.

Wahlman yanked the hot revolver from Boyfriend's hand and clouted him in the forehead with it and Boyfriend's eyes rolled back in his head and he collapsed sideways against the driver side door. His face immediately went pale, as if someone had swiped it with a brush dipped in grayish-white paint.

Wahlman leaned over and checked his pulse. It was weak and rapid and there was a rattle in his throat every time he tried to take a breath and it was doubtful that he would live much longer, with or without medical attention.

He probably wasn't going to make it, no matter what, but it wasn't in Wahlman's nature to just sit there and do nothing. He used the cell phone in Boyfriend's pocket to call 911. He made the call, but he didn't say anything. He didn't want his voice to be on the recording. He left the line open and set the phone on the center console. It would only take a couple of minutes for the operator to pinpoint the signal, and then she could send help. Under the circumstances, Wahlman felt that it was the best he could do.

Mr. Conscientious. He just hoped it wouldn't come back to bite him on the ass.

He grabbed the revolver and maneuvered his way out of the truck, careful not to step in the puddle of goo that had been a living breathing human being just a few seconds previously.

Partner In Crime's truck was still running.

And it had a full tank of gas.

Wahlman climbed in and put it in gear and headed back through the woods, toward the highway. He figured he still might be able to make his appointment in Junction City, if he hurried.

11

The hacker had wanted to meet at a certain park, at a certain time, on a certain bench. Old school. Like spies in classic movies did it sometimes. Which was fine with Wahlman. Whatever worked. Whatever would lead him to getting the information he needed.

He abandoned the pickup truck a few blocks from the park and walked the rest of the way and found the bench. It was 1:43 in the afternoon. It was a beautiful day. Warm, but not too humid. Birds were chirping and squirrels were scurrying and little kids were swinging on the swings and sliding on the slides and climbing on the jungle gyms.

Wahlman waited.

He took a deep breath. His stomach was churning, because he was getting ready to do something that could potentially get him into deeper trouble than he was already in. He was getting ready to commission an act of espionage. Which, in essence, would make him a conspirator to an act of espionage. Which would make him eligible for the death penalty, if anything went wrong.

But apparently someone in the army had already sentenced him to die anyway. Just because of who he was. Just because he was an exact genetic duplicate of a man named Jack Reacher. A military policeman whose DNA had been extracted from blood samples taken over a hundred years ago.

There had been two clones produced from those samples. Rock Wahlman, and a man named Darrell Renfro. The army had been conducting some sort of experiment, but for some reason the experiment had come to a screeching halt while Wahlman and Renfro were still toddlers. They'd been sent to different orphanages in different states. Now, almost forty years later, the army was trying to eliminate any shred of evidence that the experiment had ever taken place. Renfro had been murdered already, and Wahlman knew that he was next.

He just didn't know why.

And he needed to know why. He needed to expose the forces behind what was happening. It was the only way that he was going to be able to survive. If it meant committing what would technically amount to a capital offense, then so be it. If it meant committing a hundred such crimes, then so be it. He was all in. He was ready to go the distance. The only other real choice was to lie down and die. And that just wasn't going to happen. There was something in his DNA that would never allow that to happen. Not as long as he still had the strength to put up a fight.

At exactly two o'clock, a man carrying a brown leather briefcase walked up and sat on the wooden park bench, leaving a distance of approximately two feet between himself and Wahlman.

"Do you have a cigarette?" the man said.

The preselected code question.

Wahlman was still rattled from the ordeal with Boyfriend and Partner In Crime, and he couldn't remember if he was supposed to say yes or no. A sense of panic washed over him. He was going to blow the whole deal right off the bat. He could feel the sweat beading on his forehead. He looked at the man and shrugged.

Then it came to him.

"I don't smoke," he said. "It's bad for your health."

The man breathed a sigh of relief. "You had me worried there for a second," he said.

"Sorry," Wahlman said. "I had kind of a rough time getting here. So how is this going to work?"

"The information you asked for is in the briefcase."

"The information on Colonel Dorland? You have it already?"

"Yes. I have his real name, a copy of his service record, and an outline of his current assignment. And a map that shows the exact location of his current personal quarters and the exact location of the unit he's currently commanding."

Wahlman unzipped his jacket and pulled an envelope out of the inner pocket. The envelope contained exactly ten thousand dollars in cash, given to Wahlman by Kasey's parents. Which, in essence, made them conspirators too. Not that anyone would ever find out about their involvement. The only way anyone would ever find out was if Wahlman turned, and that wasn't going to happen.

He set the envelope on the bench, approximately halfway between where he was sitting and where the hacker was sitting.

"Take it and walk away," Wahlman said. "Leave the briefcase here."

The hacker didn't move.

"I'm going to need more than that," he said. "I'm going to need twenty."

"You said ten."

"I'm going to need twenty."

Wahlman clenched his teeth. He felt like reaching over and grabbing the hacker by the throat.

"What's stopping me from caving your skull in with my bare hands and taking the briefcase and keeping the money?" he said.

"This," the hacker said, pulling his right hand out of his pocket and revealing a stainless steel box about the size of a deck of cards. "There's a button on the box. I'm pressing it with my thumb right now. If I choose to take my thumb off the button, or if something happens that causes my thumb to be taken off the button, the briefcase will explode."

Wahlman squinted toward the little box. He figured the hacker was bluffing. Why risk your own life for a measly twenty grand? Or for any amount of money, for that matter. Wahlman figured he was bluffing, but there was no way to know for sure. Which meant that he was going to have to play ball with this guy.

"How do I know the briefcase really contains the

information you said it contains?" Wahlman said.

"Are you calling me a liar?"

"You lied about the amount of money it was going to cost me. How do I know you're not lying about everything else? You're going to have to give me something. Some kind of proof that you really—"

"Earlier this year, Dorland's unit abruptly abandoned a secret complex that had been set up in the Mojave Desert," the hacker said.

Which was true.

Wahlman knew it was true, because he'd gone into the secret complex and had looked around, after Dorland and his intelligence unit had bugged out. So maybe the hacker was legit after all. And maybe the briefcase really was rigged with explosives. It seemed odd that the hacker would be willing to blow himself up over something like this, but maybe he really needed the cash. Maybe it was for a gambling debt, or a medical procedure, or to keep his house from going into foreclosure. Wahlman supposed there were all kinds of events that might have caused the hacker to become desperate enough to risk being blown to smithereens.

"That's all the money I have," Wahlman said, gesturing toward the envelope. "I'll have to owe you the rest."

The hacker laughed. "This isn't the kind of thing you can pay for with an installment plan," he said. "Give me the money today, or the deal's off."

"How can I give you what I don't have?"

"I'm sure you'll figure it out. There's a coffee shop at the corner of First and Main. It's only a few blocks from here.

There's one of those payday loan places on the way. Maybe they can help you out. Meet me at the coffee shop in one hour. If you're not there with the money, you'll never see me again."

The hacker put his hand back in his pocket, and then he got up and walked away.

12

Wahlman put the envelope back in his pocket and zipped his jacket. He stayed there on the bench, gazing out toward the playground and wondering how he was going to come up with another ten thousand dollars in less than an hour. He thought about trying to sell the pickup truck he'd driven to Junction City. It was a nice truck. It was probably worth forty or fifty grand. Wahlman had noticed a pool hall not far from the park. He could go in there and ask around, maybe find a dirty pawnbroker who would look the other way on the paperwork.

But all that would take time, something Wahlman was extremely short of at the moment. So there was really only one way to get the money.

Wahlman got up and started walking west, toward First Street. It was uphill from the park and the day had gotten warmer and there wasn't much of a breeze and he could feel the sweat trickling down his back. He stopped in front of the payday loan place the hacker had mentioned. There was a sign taped to the window that said they had a money wiring service there as well.

Wahlman thought about it for a few more seconds, and then he pulled out his cell phone and punched in Kasey's number. She answered on the third ring.

"I need ten thousand dollars," Wahlman said.

"Unbelievable," Kasey said. "You call me on the phone, and those are the first words out of your mouth?"

"Sorry. I need it in a hurry. The man I met with a while ago has the information I need. This whole ordeal could be over in a matter of days. But I have to have the money."

"I thought Daddy already gave you what you needed for that."

"The guy I met with wants more. He wants twice the amount we originally agreed on. What can I do? I have to pay him, or he's going to disappear on me. Then I'll be back to square one."

"How do you know this guy really has the—"

"I talked to him. He knows things. I'm pretty sure he has the information I need to get to the bottom of all this. He knows about Dorland. He has a copy of his service record, and he knows where he is. And he knows his real name."

There was a long pause. Wahlman could hear whispers in the background and paper shuffling.

"Do you have a place in mind where we can wire you the money?" Kasey said.

"Yes. I'm standing outside a place right now."

"Daddy says he will do it, but that this is the last time. Okay?"

"Okay."

Another long pause.

"There are some things I need to talk to you about," Kasey said.

"What things?" Wahlman said.

"You said you're in a hurry. Go ahead and do what you need to do. We can talk later."

She hung up.

Somewhat perplexed by Kasey's attitude, but having no time to dwell on it right now, Wahlman walked into the payday loan place. A few minutes later, he added another ten thousand dollars to the envelope in his pocket, and then he headed toward the coffee shop.

13

As it turned out, Wahlman was almost twenty minutes early. The hacker wasn't there yet.

The coffee shop was not busy. Wahlman and the barista were the only people in there at the moment, and the barista behaved as though she would rather be almost anywhere else. No smile, no friendly chitchat. Just going through the motions. Maybe she wasn't always like that, Wahlman thought. Maybe she was just having a bad day. Maybe her boyfriend had broken up with her five minutes ago. No telling. Wahlman ordered a cup of coffee and sat at a table by the front window.

There was a horse-drawn carriage parked at the curb. For twenty-five bucks, the driver would take you on a fifteen-minute tour of the historic district. It was the kind of thing normal people did. People who weren't running for their lives.

Wahlman looked forward to the day when he could do things like that again. Ordinary things. Joyful things. He wanted to go to the movies. He wanted to walk into a restaurant without having to watch his back every second.

He wanted to be able to use his real name again. He wanted to own things. A house. A car. He wanted to settle down with Kasey. Maybe start a family. All of that was starting to seem within reach now. He knew there was still a lot of work to do, but acquiring the information on Dorland would go a long way toward achieving his ultimate goal, toward getting his life back.

He looked at the clock on the wall over the service counter. Ten more minutes, and the briefcase would be his.

Ten more minutes.

He watched the seconds tick by, one at a time.

Nine more minutes.

Eight.

A uniformed police officer walked into the coffee shop. He sauntered up to the counter and said something to the barista. She seemed as bored and uninspired as she had when she'd waited on Wahlman. The officer seemed chipper and energetic, but he didn't appear to be in any sort of hurry. Probably working the middle shift, Wahlman thought. Probably just getting started. This was probably morning coffee for him. Maybe his first cup of the day. Maybe his only cup, depending on how many calls came in during his shift.

The barista brought the officer a paper cup with a lid on it. The officer handed her some cash, turned around and exited the shop, nodding at Wahlman on his way out. He was young. Early twenties. Two or three years on the job, at the most. Probably not a rookie, but probably not very experienced either. He waved at the driver as he walked past the carriage, and then he treaded up the hill to where his cruiser was parked.

Wahlman looked at the clock again. Three more minutes. The hacker had been punctual for the first meeting, and there was no reason to think that he wouldn't be for this one.

No reason until those three minutes ticked by and the hacker still wasn't there.

Wahlman went to the counter and bought another cup of coffee. Carried it to the table by the window and sat back down. The hacker was four minutes late now, and Wahlman was starting to get concerned. Maybe the hacker had gotten cold feet. Maybe he'd thought about it some more, and had decided against passing the information along to Wahlman after all, regardless of how much money would change hands. Maybe he'd disabled the little detonator and had thrown the briefcase off a bridge. Those were the thoughts going through Wahlman's head when the percussive wave from an enormous blast somewhere west of the coffee shop knocked him out of his chair and caused the plate glass window he had been staring out of to shatter into a million pieces.

The horse out at the curb started rearing and thrashing and the people out on the sidewalk started running and screaming.

Wahlman reached up and gripped the seat of the chair he'd been sitting on and pushed himself to a standing position. He brushed the tiny pieces of glass off his clothes and dizzily made his way to the counter to make sure the barista was okay. She was on the floor, hunkered into a corner, hugging her knees and staring blankly at a stack of paper cups that had toppled over into the sink.

"You all right?" Wahlman said.

She nodded.

Wahlman turned and staggered to the door and jerked it open and stepped out onto the sidewalk. Something was on fire, just over the hill, just beyond where the police car was parked. The cop was nowhere in sight, but the cup of coffee he'd bought was on the top of the cruiser, behind the light bar, somehow undisturbed by whatever had taken place on the other side of the hill.

There was no way for Wahlman to know exactly what had happened, but his best guess was that the hacker had done something to draw the attention of the police officer, and that the subsequent encounter had somehow led to one nervous thumb being lifted from one detonator button. Which of course had led to the explosion.

Maybe the hacker had left his car in a no parking zone or something. Maybe he'd jaywalked. Maybe the officer had recognized him from some sort of previous encounter. Wahlman had no idea, and he would never have any idea, because he didn't plan on sticking around long enough to find out.

He stared at the black plumes of a smoke rising in the air, and then he turned and started walking in the opposite direction, back down the hill, back toward the park.

14

Wahlman had been planning on taking a bus back to Reality and hiding out until the repair shop closed for the day. He'd been planning on leaving some money and finding his keys and skipping out unnoticed sometime after dark. He certainly didn't want anyone from that area to see him driving the truck he'd taken. It was possible that Boyfriend had survived the blow to the head, possible that he would wake up at some point, possible that he would eventually be coherent enough to talk to the police. Not likely, but possible. And if Boyfriend did wake up, and if he did talk to the police, there was no telling what kind of story he might tell them about his friend being shot.

So Wahlman had been planning on taking a bus, and he'd been planning on getting into and out of Reality as quickly as possible.

But things had changed.

A police officer had been killed, and Wahlman had walked away from the scene, and the melancholy barista at the coffee shop could identify Wahlman if she needed to, and that was all he needed, more trouble with the law.

So he didn't really want to hang around in Junction City long enough to take a bus, but he didn't really want to drive the pickup truck back to Reality either.

He was starting to wonder if he should just forget about the SUV. Chalk it up as a loss. Forget about it and never go anywhere near Reality, Missouri again.

He strolled into the park and sat on the same bench he'd been sitting on earlier. It had been a rough day. First the incident with Boyfriend and Partner In Crime. Then the hacker had wanted twice as much money as Wahlman had in his pocket. Then the hacker and a police officer and no telling how many innocent bystanders had been blown to bits. Not to mention the briefcase, which had supposedly contained the information Wahlman needed to start getting his life back.

At least he knew now that the information he needed was attainable. It was just a matter of time until he could find someone else to help him get it. A matter of time, and a matter of money. It had been one of the worst days of his life, but at least he knew now that the situation was not impossible.

And at least he still had Kasey.

He pulled out his cell phone and punched in her number.

"How did it go?" she said.

"It didn't," Wahlman said. "I better not elaborate over the phone, but I'm pretty much back to where I was when I started. Back when I left Tennessee."

"Do you still have the money?"

"Yes."

"Maybe you can get someone else to help you."

"That's what I was thinking," Wahlman said.

Silence for a few beats.

"I need to go," Kasey said.

"A while ago you said there was something you needed to talk to me about."

"There is, but—"

"What is it?" Wahlman said.

He could tell by Kasey's voice that she was upset about something. She sounded as though she might be on the verge of tears.

"A man was here looking for you," she said.

"What man?"

"His name is Decker. He's a professional tracker. And a bounty hunter. He's working for a private investigator. The one you got into a fight with in Bakersfield, I guess."

"Did he mention the private investigator's name?" Wahlman said.

"Feldman. I think that's what he said. Something like that."

Wahlman couldn't believe what he was hearing.

"This is all very significant," he said. "Why didn't you tell me earlier?"

"I was afraid. He started talking about aiding and abetting and the state taking Natalie away from me and—"

"You need to be afraid," Wahlman said. "Since Decker was able to find you at the lake house, it means that

Dorland's people will eventually be able to find you there as well. And Dorland's people won't be interested in charging you with any sort of crime. Dorland's people will do whatever it takes to pinpoint my location. You're not safe there anymore."

"I know," Kasey said. "We packed some things and left last night."

"You left the lake house?"

"Yes. And don't ask me where we are, because I can't tell you."

"I wouldn't want you to. You know how it is with these cellular phones. You never know who might be—"

"It's not because of that," Kasey said. "This just isn't going to work out. I can't talk to you anymore. I can't see you anymore."

"What are you talking about?"

"Daddy said not to worry about the money. Keep it. Use it for whatever you need it for."

"Kasey. Listen to me. I'm getting close to resolving this thing. I can feel it. I just need a little more time. I need for you to—"

"I'm sorry. I'm really, really sorry."

"What did you say to Decker? You didn't tell him anything, did you?"

For a brief moment, Wahlman heard Kasey sobbing in the background.

Then she clicked off.

15

Wahlman sat there on the park bench for a few minutes and considered his options. He was totally alone in the world now, and—as if he didn't have enough problems to deal with already—a professional tracker named Decker was on his tail.

A tracker, and a bounty hunter.

The last time Wahlman had checked, the bounty put out on him by the New Orleans Police Department had increased to an amount that was practically unheard of. It probably wasn't quite enough for a man like Decker to retire on, but it was probably close. The online wanted posters that Wahlman had seen had specified that he was to be delivered alive and in good health, but that had been a while back. The conditions of the reward might have changed by now.

Decker was sort of a celebrity, one of those guys you see on the national news channels sometimes. *Special Investigative Consultant*, or something like that. He was known for his dogged persistence. If he was looking for you, it was only a matter of time until you were found. A fugitive had stowed away on a rocket ship to Mars one time. It didn't matter. Decker eventually caught up to him and brought him back to Earth. Decker was expensive, but he was the best. He was the guy you called when you wanted your chance of success to be one hundred percent.

Wahlman had no idea how much information Kasey had provided to Decker, but it was a pretty safe bet that Decker had squeezed her for everything he could get. Threatened her with prosecution and all that. If she'd told him everything she knew, he was probably in Reality right now. He'd probably gone to the repair shop. Maybe the hotel. Maybe the diner. Everywhere that Wahlman had been. And he was probably hanging out at one of those places and waiting for Wahlman to return.

Which ordinarily would have sent Wahlman hightailing it in the opposite direction.

But this was Decker.

He only worked for one client at a time, and he never gave up. The day he was hired, it became his sole mission in life to find Rock Wahlman and deliver him to the authorities. And that was exactly what he would do. And if the requirements for the bounty had changed, he would proceed accordingly. He wouldn't pull any punches. He would find Wahlman and ambush him and send him to Louisiana in a box.

Which meant that Wahlman needed to find him first.

Wahlman got up and slid his phone back into his pocket and started walking to where he'd parked the pickup truck. He still had the .357 revolver he'd taken from Boyfriend. It was in the glove compartment. He started the truck and eased away from the curb and made a U-turn at the first intersection he came to and headed back toward the interstate.

Back toward Reality.

16

Decker was accustomed to sitting and waiting for long periods of time. It was basically what he did for a living. Hours and hours of extreme boredom, followed by short bursts of intense excitement. The excitement part was kind of like a drug. An addiction. It was what Decker lived for.

It was almost five o'clock in the afternoon, and he hadn't eaten anything all day. And he didn't plan on eating anything until the job was done. Hunger was part of the experience. It added to the tension. The anticipation. There would be no eating—or sleeping—until Rock Wahlman was taken care of.

Decker's cell phone started vibrating. He pulled it out of his pocket and checked the caller ID. It was Feldman.

Decker didn't like to take calls while he was on a stakeout. It was a distraction. It diverted your attention from where it needed to be. It took your mind off the job at hand, and when you were the best in the world at what you did, you needed to stay focused. Every second. Because things could go very wrong in a heartbeat.

Decker usually turned the phone off, but he'd forgotten to this time.

Feldman.

Shit.

What could he possibly want?

Decker decided to go ahead and answer the call, but he was determined to keep it short.

"I'm working," he said. "What do you want?"

"Where are you?" Feldman said.

"Where I am is not important. What is important is that I'm very close to completing the job you hired me to do. Now if you'll excuse me, I would like to get back to—"

"We have a lead on a man who fits Wahlman's description."

"What kind of lead?" Decker said.

"Detective Collins called me a while ago. He and every other law enforcement officer in the country received an encrypted message from the National Terrorist Alert System. A briefcase bomb exploded in Junction City, Kansas earlier this afternoon. The paper documents that had been inside the briefcase were destroyed, but the man who had been holding the case had an interesting note tucked in his wallet."

Decker sighed. "I'm listening," he said.

"The note described a man who was very tall and very muscular, with dark brown hair and blue eyes and chiseled features. Wahlman doesn't have dark brown hair, of course, but it's very likely that he's been dying it since he's been on the run."

"What else did the note say?"

"It said that this tall and muscular man was working to obtain government secrets. He'd contacted the man with the briefcase through a mutual acquaintance, and—"

"Did the man with the briefcase have a name?" Decker said.

"His name hasn't been released yet. The note said that if anything happened to him, the tall and muscular man was to be held responsible. Then there was an apology, from whoever wrote the note—presumably the man who'd been carrying the briefcase—an apology to his family and to his colleagues and to the United States of America. It said that he was very sorry for the role he'd played in this affair, and that he hoped the people in his life could remember him for the good things he'd done."

"Sounds like the man with the briefcase was getting ready to sell some kind of classified information to the tall and muscular man," Decker said.

"Exactly," Feldman said. "But the most important part of that note, as far as we're concerned, is that it places the tall and muscular man in Junction City. That's something we can use."

"The tall and muscular man could have been anyone," Decker said.

"True. But I have a strong hunch that it was Wahlman. We're working to secure the footage from several nearby security cameras. We should know for sure by the end of the day if it was him or not."

Decker thought about that for a few seconds. It didn't

really matter where Wahlman had gone that morning, or what he had done that afternoon. His primary mode of transportation was still in Reality, Missouri, and it didn't seem likely that he would just abandon it. Decker was betting that Wahlman would return to the hotel, and that it wouldn't take him much longer to get there.

"Okay," Decker said.

"That's it?" Feldman said. "Seems like you would want to—"

"Like I said, I'm working. I'll call you if I need anything, but you probably won't hear from me until the job is done."

There was a long pause.

"And when might that be?" Feldman said.

"Soon," Decker said. "Very soon."

17

Wahlman pulled over to the shoulder and switched off the ignition at approximately the same spot his SUV had stopped running yesterday. He climbed out of the pickup truck, slid the revolver into the back of his waistband. Walked to the bottom of the exit ramp again and saw the sign again and headed west toward Reality again. But he didn't walk along the side of the highway this time. He trotted across the grassy runoff that ran parallel to the road and made his way to the edge the forest.

He didn't go very deep into the woods. Just a few feet past the tree line. Just far enough from the highway to be invisible to traffic. Not that there was much, but he didn't want to take any chances. He didn't want to be seen by the police or The Waitress With No Name or the mechanic at the repair shop or the clerk at the hotel. He didn't want to be seen by the ordinary folks traveling from Reality to Fantasy, or from Fantasy to Reality, and he didn't want to be seen by anyone who had taken the wrong exit and was now lost somewhere between the two. He didn't want to be seen by anyone. He wanted to sneak into town and take Decker by surprise.

If Decker was indeed there waiting for him.

Which was a good possibility, but not a certainty.

If Decker wasn't there, Wahlman would go back to his original plan. He would wait until it was dark outside and break into the repair shop and get his keys and haul ass. But if Decker was there, he needed to take care of that situation first.

Walking as quickly as he could through the tangles of wild vegetation, it took him about thirty minutes to make it to the town limit sign. He kicked away some of the underbrush and sat down and leaned against the trunk of a pine tree and waited for the sun to go down. It took a while. Over an hour. When the first stars started showing over the horizon, he got up and put his Navy watch cap on and followed the highway into town. It wasn't nearly cold enough to be wearing the wool toboggan, but Wahlman figured it would keep the streetlights from reflecting off his forehead. He needed to keep a low profile, and he figured every little bit would help.

He crept around in the shadows and made his way to the auto repair shop. There was a light on in the office. A guy was sitting there at the counter with a stack of receipts. Finishing his paperwork for the day. Wahlman could see him through the big plate glass window in front. It was the guy with the weird glasses, the same guy Wahlman had handed a hundred dollars in cash to yesterday, to expedite the repair on his SUV. With everything that had happened since then, Wahlman had forgotten about that little detail. But now he remembered. Maybe Mr. Conscientious wouldn't leave any money on the counter after all.

The doors to the service bays had been secured for the night, and Wahlman's SUV was parked in a fenced-off area adjacent to the office. Which probably meant that the work on it had been completed.

Probably, but Wahlman needed to know for sure. He ducked behind a bush at the far end of the parking lot, pulled out his cell phone and punched in the number on the business card he'd been given yesterday. The man sitting at the counter answered the call.

"Reality Auto Repair," the man said.

"Just checking to see if my car is ready yet," Wahlman said.

"Which one is yours?"

"The white SUV."

"Yeah, it's ready. You're going to need a new battery soon. We can go ahead and take care of that for you first thing in the morning if you want us to."

"Okay," Wahlman said.

"I'll add it to the work order. You should be good to go by nine, if not sooner."

"I'll give you a call in the morning before I come, just to make sure," Wahlman said, knowing that he wouldn't really give the man a call in the morning, or ever again, knowing that he and his vehicle would be hundreds of miles away by the time the shop opened for another day of business, whether Decker was in town or not.

"You're staying at The Reality Hotel, right?" the man sitting at the counter said, his voice taking on a tone of congeniality Wahlman hadn't noticed before. Like an old friend who wanted to meet for a cocktail or something.

Wahlman didn't answer the question. He wondered why the man was suddenly interested in where he was going to sleep tonight. It was an odd thing for a mechanic to ask a customer.

Extremely odd.

Wahlman clicked off and slid the phone into his pocket and walked across the parking lot and entered the office. The man sitting at the counter still had the landline receiver he'd been talking into in one hand and he was punching a number into the keypad on the base of the phone with the other. Wahlman grabbed him by his greasy shirt and pulled him across the countertop and slammed him on the floor and pressed the barrel of Boyfriend's revolver against his forehead.

"Did someone come here looking for me?" Wahlman said.

The man's eyes got big and his lips curled into an extreme frown.

"Please don't kill me," he said. "I don't know anything about anything."

"Did someone come here looking for me?" Wahlman repeated.

"He gave me a number to call. It's on the counter. I don't know anything about anything. I was just trying to—"

"What did he want?"

"He asked me where you were staying. I told him I didn't know for sure, but that most likely you would be at the—"

"What kind of car was he driving?"

"It was a sedan. Black, with tinted windows. I'm not sure of the make and model. Seems like I would know, being a mechanic and all, but cars look so much alike these days it's hard to—"

"Shut up."

Wahlman grabbed the telephone the man had been using and ripped the cord out of the wall and used it to tie the man's wrists and ankles.

There was a patch sewn to the man's shirt, just above the breast pocket. It said *GERRY*. Wahlman hadn't noticed it before. If he remembered correctly, Gerry had been wearing a plain white t-shirt yesterday. Maybe all of his shirts with nametags had been at the cleaners or something.

"You can't just leave me here like this," Gerry said. "There won't be anyone here until seven o'clock in the morning."

"Would you prefer I leave you here unconscious?" Wahlman said. "Because that can definitely be arranged."

Silence.

Wahlman ferreted through the papers on the counter until he found a blank business card with a phone number written on it.

Then he exited the office and walked back out into the night.

18

It only took Wahlman a few minutes to walk to the hotel. He saw the black sedan in the parking lot right away, but he didn't know if Decker was inside the car or not. The car was too far away, and the windows were too heavily tinted.

Wahlman crouched behind the sculpted row of hedges growing along the edge of the sidewalk and considered his options. He had a hunch that his status had changed from *Wanted: Alive and Healthy* to *Wanted: Dead or Alive.* As a general rule, Decker didn't take cases that required suspects to be breathing when they were brought into custody. As a general rule, he would petition for your status to be downgraded if need be, and then he would stalk you until he found you.

And then he would gun you down with no warning.

That kind of aggressive—and in Wahlman's opinion, barbaric—method of law enforcement had been made possible by the Capital Crime Control Act of 2087. Wahlman had been a Master-At-Arms in the United States Navy at the time, and had been bound by the Uniform Code of Military Justice, so he'd never been in a position to deal with the controversial legislation firsthand, but he'd voiced his opposition to it in letters to elected officials, and it was one of the reasons he'd never signed on to work for a state or city law enforcement agency after leaving the Navy.

It was a bad law. It allowed people like Decker to cash in on people like Wahlman for the price of a bullet. All it took was a judge's signature on the bounty decree. Then it was open season on your ass. It was a terrifying direction the country had gone in, and Wahlman hoped someone would put a stop to it soon.

But nobody was going to put a stop to it tonight.

Which didn't give Wahlman much of a choice about what he needed to do next.

He pulled Boyfriend's .357 from the back of his waistband, stood and stepped over the hedge and started walking across the parking lot, toward the black sedan. He stopped when he was about thirty feet away from it.

The driver side door opened and Decker climbed out.

He had a pistol in his hand.

He pointed it in Wahlman's direction.

"On the ground," he shouted. "I'm not going to tell you twice."

Wahlman pointed the revolver in Decker's direction.

"You get on the ground," Wahlman said. "I'm not going to tell you twice either."

"You're coming with me," Decker said. "I can cuff you and put you in the back seat, or I can kill you and put you in the trunk. Either way is fine with me."

Before Wahlman could respond, a pair of RPD cruisers squealed around the corner, screeching to a stop in the area between where Wahlman was standing and where Decker was standing.

Two uniformed officers climbed out of the car closest to Wahlman, and two more climbed out of the car closest to Decker.

The two officers closest to Wahlman aimed shotguns at him and told him to drop his weapon and get on the ground.

He dropped his weapon and got on the ground.

He didn't have a choice.

The two officers closest to Decker did likewise on that side. They told Decker to drop his weapon and get on the ground.

"I'm a professional tracker," Decker said. "My credentials are in the—"

"Drop it," one of the officers shouted. "Now!"

Wahlman heard Decker's pistol hit the pavement. Two minutes later, Wahlman and Decker had been cuffed and shackled and were now standing next to each other against one of the police cars.

The other cruiser was parked directly in front of them. Someone was sitting in the back, on the passenger side. One of the officers opened the door, and a man climbed out.

A man with tan leather work boots and a bloodstained shirt and a big bruise on his forehead.

19

A third cruiser steered into the parking lot, and then a fourth. Now there were eight cops on the scene.

Boyfriend's hands were cuffed behind his back. Wahlman guessed that he'd been taken to the hospital, and that the police had found the barn full of stolen property while investigating the shooting death of Partner In Crime.

A shooting death that would now be blamed on Wahlman.

He would be taken into custody, and it would only be a matter of time until the Reality Police Department found out that his driver's license and vehicle registration were fake, and it would only be a matter of time until they learned his true identity and the troublesome baggage that went along with it.

If the RPD did a good job with their investigation—with interrogation and forensics and ballistics and so forth—it might eventually be proven that Boyfriend actually fired the shot that killed his friend. It was possible that Wahlman would be exonerated for that particular crime, but whether he was or wasn't, he would eventually be extradited to Louisiana, where he would be forced to face the charges that had been brought against him there.

Big case, lots of publicity.

Wahlman was an obvious flight risk, so there would be no chance for him to get out on bail. His general location would be known to the public, and Colonel Dorland would find a way to get to him. Make it look like an accident, or maybe a gang-related hit. A shank to the gut while he was sleeping or standing in the chow line. Dorland had the resources to make something like that happen.

Which basically meant that Wahlman's life was over.

One of the officers took a couple of steps closer to where Boyfriend was standing.

"Well?" the officer said.

"That's him," Boyfriend said. "That's the man who shot Vernon."

"Which one?"

The officer was now standing about an arm's length from where Boyfriend was standing. The officer looked familiar. Short and round and balding. Wahlman squinted, focused in on his nametag. It was Sergeant Tingly, from yesterday. He'd shaved his mustache. Maybe he'd gotten tired of combing the doughnut crumbs out of it.

Wahlman stared down at the pavement for a few seconds, trying to think of a way to get out of this. But there was no way. This was it. The end of the line.

"I don't have time for this shit," Decker said. "Take these chains off of me right now, or I'm going to—"

"Shut up," Tingly said.

"Do you even know who I am? You're going to be in deep shit when I get through with you. Heads are going to roll. I can tell you that right now."

Tingly shrugged. He sidestepped a little closer to Boyfriend. Now they were almost shoulder to shoulder.

"Which one?" Tingly repeated.

Wahlman looked up and gazed directly into Boyfriend's eyes. He saw anger. Fear. A need for revenge.

And maybe just a little bit of gratitude.

If Wahlman hadn't called 911, it was very likely that Boyfriend would have died. A lot of things had gone wrong for Boyfriend over the past ten hours or so. His career as a thief was over now, and his life was in shambles, and he would be dealing with some very serious problems for a long time to come.

But at least he was alive.

And the fact that Wahlman had played a part in that was the only possible explanation for what happened next.

"That one," Boyfriend said, gesturing toward Decker. "He was the one who killed my friend. Shot him right in the head. I saw it with my own two eyes."

An expression of astonishment washed over Decker's face.

"Bullshit," he shouted. "I don't even know what he's talking about."

Two of the officers grabbed Decker and forced him into the back of the fourth cruiser that had shown up.

Tingly pulled a set of keys out of his utility belt and

walked over to where Wahlman was standing.

"I could still take you in if I wanted to," Tingly said, unlocking the handcuffs and the ankle cuffs and the chain connecting the two. "You realize that, right?"

Wahlman nodded. He'd been holding the .357 revolver when the police showed up. That was a crime in itself. And he'd been pointing it at Decker's chest. Which was an even bigger crime.

But Sergeant Tingly and his crew had apprehended a suspect in a murder case. A suspect that had been unequivocally identified by an eyewitness. Decker would get off. There was no doubt about that. But right now Tingly was probably thinking that he and his guys had solved the case, and that they'd done it in a matter of hours. It was the kind of thing that led to big pats on the back from the chief. It was the kind of thing that led to promotions.

So right now, in Tingly's mind, Wahlman had helped the Reality Police Department capture a killer. Tingly wasn't going to arrest Wahlman. He was more likely to recommend him for a medal or something. Those notions would undoubtedly change by morning, but Wahlman would be long gone by then.

"So I'm free to go now?" Wahlman said.

"We're going to need a written statement. Are you still staying here at the hotel?"

"Yes."

"We can do it here, or we can do it at the station."

"Here would be good," Wahlman said.

"All right. A couple of our guys will come by your room

in an hour or so. We have your driver's license on file now, so—"

"Don't worry," Wahlman said. "I'm not going anywhere."

But of course that was a lie.

Wahlman didn't know exactly where he was going, or what he was going to do when he got there, but he planned on being as far away from Reality as possible by the time the officers knocked on his door.

20

Wahlman got his things out of his room and left the hotel without checking out. He walked over to the repair shop and entered the office. Gerry was still on the floor where Wahlman had left him.

"I want to pay you for the work you did on my car," Wahlman said.

"Untie me and we'll call it even," Gerry said.

"Not going to happen. What was the total on the fuel pump replacement?"

"A million dollars."

Wahlman walked over and rested his right foot on Gerry's right kneecap. Lightly. Just to send a message. Gerry told him the real total. Parts and labor and sales tax. Wahlman counted out some cash and slapped it on the counter.

"I subtracted the hundred dollars you tried to scam me out of," Wahlman said. "Where are my keys?"

"Behind the counter. Top drawer."

Wahlman walked behind the counter and found his keys.

He went outside and climbed into the SUV and started it and took a right out of the parking lot, toward the interstate. When he got to the turnoffs for the on-ramps, he decided to go east, for no particular reason. It was a random choice. He had nowhere to go. Nobody to see. He'd been through the wringer on multiple occasions, and he was no closer to achieving his goal that when this whole thing had started.

And apparently the woman he loved was out of the picture now. He wanted to hear the sound of her voice. Touch her. Kiss her. Hold her in his arms. He longed for her, and it broke his heart to know that he might never see her again.

He realized—from a logical standpoint—that it was probably for the best. It was totally understandable that Kasey had chosen the safety of her family and herself over trying to maintain a romantic relationship with a man in Wahlman's situation.

But it still hurt.

It was almost more than he could bear.

He traveled fifty miles or so, and then he exited the interstate and took some side roads and some two-lane highways, continuing east for the most part, ending up at a truck stop somewhere between Bowling Green, Kentucky, and Nashville, Tennessee. He bought some gas, and then he walked inside, past the souvenir stand and into the restaurant area, which smelled like greasy meat and mop water.

He sat at the counter. A waitress came and asked him if he wanted coffee and he said yes. The waitress had a nametag. Her name was Sally. She brought the coffee in a ceramic mug.

"You want something to eat?" she said.

"No thanks," Wahlman said.

"You're going to need something. You can't drive all night on an empty stomach."

"How did you know I'm going to be driving all night?"

"Almost everyone who comes in here is going to be driving all night."

Wahlman shrugged.

"I guess I'll take a cheeseburger," he said.

"Fries?"

"Okay."

Sally walked to the other side of the counter and punched the order into a computerized cash register.

Wahlman sat there and stared into the oily blackness of the coffee in front of him. He was tired. Beat. He didn't know what he was going to do next. He thought about how close he was to the lake house, where Kasey and her parents and her daughter had been staying. Less than a hundred miles, probably. He thought about driving down there. Maybe Kasey and Natalie and Dean and Betsy hadn't really left yet. Maybe he and Kasey could work things out, somehow.

No.

He needed to leave her alone. He needed to honor her wishes. Trying to force the issue would only make matters worse. He needed to accept the fact that he would never see or talk to Kasey Stielson again for the rest of his life. He needed to move on.

Sally brought the food.

"There you go," she said. "Let me know if you need anything else."

"Thanks," Wahlman said.

He took a bite of the burger. It was good. Everything tasted fresh. The meat, the bun, the lettuce leaves, the tomato slices. Even the pickle wedge on the side of the plate was top-notch. The fries were crispy and seasoned just right, and Sally was there with a steaming decanter every time the coffee in his cup started getting low. Rock Wahlman had traveled all over the world during his career in the Navy, and he could honestly say that the food on the plate in front of him was some of the best he'd ever eaten—anywhere.

He finished his meal and paid Sally and left her a nice tip and got a cup of coffee to go. Walked out to the SUV and climbed inside and started the engine. He needed a new driver's license and a different automobile. He couldn't continue being the same man he'd been in Reality, Missouri, and he couldn't continue driving the same vehicle. Within forty-eight hours, every law enforcement agency in the country would have a copy of his current license and all the details on the SUV. It was only a matter of time until a cop spotted him and pulled him over.

New credentials would cost some money.

But he had some money.

He had twenty thousand dollars in his pocket.

He would eventually find a way to pay Kasey's parents back, even though they had said not to worry about it. He would pay them back, but right now he needed the cash to continue doing what he was doing. He would basically be starting from scratch, and he would be totally on his own now. But that was okay. He would dig deep and find a way to carry on.

It was what he did.

It was who he was.

It was in his blood.

REDLINE

THE REACHER EXPERIMENT BOOK 6

1

Way back in the middle part of the twenty-first century, around the time Rock Wahlman was born, practically every filling station in the country had been fitted with charging ports for electric vehicles. The batteries that provided the power to propel those cars and trucks from one place to another had gotten more and more sophisticated over the decades—even more so in recent years—and now, in the summer of 2098, in the United States of America and in many other nations around the world, you could drive up and plug in and be fully charged in about five minutes.

But you needed a credit card.

And Rock Wahlman didn't have a credit card.

He paid cash for everything, and in the summer of 2098 you could still find places that would accept cash for gasoline purchases, and that was why he had traded his SUV for another vehicle with an internal combustion engine, a compact sedan this time. He couldn't sleep in the sedan, as he had in the SUV on occasion, and he sometimes banged his right knee on the steering wheel climbing in and out, but the little car was pretty fast and it was cheap to drive and you could back it into one of the narrowest spots in a parking garage if you needed to disappear for a few days.

Those were the thoughts going through Wahlman's mind as he cruised past the exit for Greensboro, North Carolina, at four o'clock in the afternoon on the eighth of July. Those were his thoughts, but he didn't actually say any of those things to the man sitting in the passenger seat.

"I just like the sound of a real motor," Wahlman said, trying to explain why he'd purchased a car that ran on gasoline, trying to keep the conversation to a minimum.

"Electric motors are real," the man said. "And they're better for the environment."

The man sitting in the passenger seat seemed to know a lot about the environment. He seemed to know a lot about everything. He was getting along in years. Probably in his eighties, Wahlman guessed. The skin on his face was an odd shade of yellow, what you might come up with if you mixed some mustard into a cup of tea, and his eyes looked as though someone might have dribbled broken egg yolks into them. He had been walking backward along the edge of the highway, facing traffic, holding a cardboard sign that said *MYRTLE BEACH*. Wahlman wasn't planning on going anywhere near that area, but he figured he could get the guy a hundred miles or so closer to the coast, and he figured every little bit helped.

Wahlman was on his way to visit an old friend, a fellow Master-At-Arms who'd settled down in Virginia after retiring from the Navy. The guy had been pretty good with computers, and he knew other guys who were pretty good with computers, and Wahlman was hoping that he might be able to assist him in gaining access to some classified information. Maybe the old friend could help. Maybe he couldn't. It was worth a try.

Wahlman had stopped and picked up the hitchhiker about an hour ago. Now he was starting to wish he hadn't. The guy talked too much, and he smelled like cigarettes and rotgut whiskey.

"I'll be getting off the interstate and heading north in a few minutes," Wahlman said. "Want me to drop you off at the next exit?"

"I wouldn't mind going all the way to Norfolk with you, if that's okay."

"Norfolk is north of here. Since you're trying to get to Myrtle Beach—"

"I can catch a bus for next to nothing in Norfolk," the man said. "It's a straight shot, right down the coast."

"Okay," Wahlman said.

He reached over to turn on the radio, hoping it would keep the old man from talking so much.

It didn't.

"I've been sitting here beside you for over an hour, and I don't even know your name," the man said.

"Wendell."

It was the name on Wahlman's latest fake driver's license. Wendell P. Callahan. Wahlman didn't know what the *P* stood for. He figured he would just make something up if anyone ever asked.

"I'm Rusty," the man said. "That's what my friends always called me, anyway. Back when I had friends who were still alive. Back when I had hair that was still red."

Rusty chuckled, his laughter quickly turning to a cough, the kind of gurgling hack that sounds like there might be something seriously wrong, the kind that you try to hold your breath for when you're passing by the person doing the hacking in a grocery store aisle.

"You okay?" Wahlman said.

"I'm okay. You got a tissue or something?"

"Glovebox."

Rusty opened the glove compartment, reached in and pulled out a couple of paper napkins that Wahlman had saved from couple of different fast food joints. Rusty coughed into the napkins, and then he wadded them up and tossed them on the floorboard.

"Bet you can't guess why I'm going to Myrtle Beach," he said.

"Why would I want to guess?" Wahlman said. "It's none of my business."

"Just thought you might be curious."

Rusty coughed again. A narrow thread of bright red blood tricked down from the corner of his lips. He wiped it off with his shirt sleeve.

Wahlman had seen a lot of things as a law enforcement officer in the Navy. He had a strong stomach. There wasn't much that bothered him. A guy sitting inches away and coughing up blood was one of the things that did. He switched off the radio. He thought about pulling over and handing Rusty a twenty and making him get out of the car right there. But he didn't. He felt sorry for the old guy. It was obvious that he didn't have a lot of time left.

"All right," Wahlman said. "Tell me why you're going to Myrtle Beach."

"Maybe I shouldn't tell you, come to think of it."

"Okay."

"It's kind of a secret, if you want to know the truth."

"Okay."

"I guess I could tell you. But you have to promise not to tell anyone else. I signed some papers, and I could get into big trouble if anyone ever—"

"Tell me or don't tell me," Wahlman said. "It doesn't matter to me."

"You promise not to say anything to anyone about it?"

"I promise."

Rusty reached into one of his pockets and pulled out a piece of peppermint candy, the kind you see in bowls on cashiers' counters at diners sometimes. He peeled off the cellophane and slid the sugary red and white disk into his mouth. He didn't offer Wahlman a piece. Maybe it was his last one. He contemplatively twisted the sticky little wrapper with his thumbs and forefingers for a few seconds, and then he flicked it on the floor next to the soggy napkins.

"Let me just start by saying that I'm a veteran," he said. "Army. They're the ones responsible for the shape I'm in right now, and they're the ones who'll be footing the bill to fix me up."

Wahlman wondered what kind of medical procedure

could possibly benefit a man of Rusty's advanced age, a man with such glaringly obvious health issues. Doctors could do some pretty spectacular things with some pretty spectacular equipment these days, but their knowledge and skills and technological expertise could still only go so far. They still hadn't developed a remedy for the human condition commonly known as TMB—*Too Many Birthdays.* They still hadn't found a cure for that. Not that Wahlman had ever heard about.

But then maybe he hadn't heard about everything.

He sat there with his eyes on the road and his hands on the wheel and listened while Rusty talked.

2

Rusty said that he'd recently celebrated his ninetieth birthday. Which meant that he'd been born in 2008. Which meant that he was almost fifty years older than Wahlman. He'd experienced things that Wahlman had only read about in history books. He'd seen driverless cars and thought-enhancing brain implants and flying robots that could do everything from changing a flat tire to delivering a baby. He'd seen all of that come and go. He'd seen technological advances that surely must have seemed like a good idea at the time but that had ultimately done more harm than good.

"Teleportation," Wahlman said. "That was the last straw, right? That was when the leaders of the world got together and decided that everything needed to be dialed back a notch."

"Ten notches was more like it," Rusty said. "But yeah. When they figured out how to disassemble and reassemble inanimate objects at a molecular level, and when they figured out how to use specially-designed satellites and lasers to move those objects from one part of the planet to another, that was a big game changer. It revolutionized the shipping industry, for one thing. You could go online and order a couch or whatever and have it delivered to your living room in a matter of seconds."

"Sounds great."

"Sure. It was great. But it was all done with computers. Ninety-nine percent of it, anyway. Unemployment skyrocketed. Most of the positions that had been crucial to that particular industry were suddenly obsolete. Then other industries were affected. Just about everything you can think of. It all started toppling, like a row of dominoes. It all came too fast. The human race just wasn't ready for it."

"The schematics for those types of satellites and lasers are probably locked in an underground vault somewhere," Wahlman said. "It's only a matter of time until—"

"I don't think so," Rusty said. "And I'll tell you why. If you can move a couch through space and plop it down in the middle of a living room, then you can move a bomb through space and plop it down in the middle of a city. That was where we were heading. They hadn't figured out how to do it with nukes, but they probably would have eventually."

"Not possible, from what I've read."

"A lot of things are not possible, until suddenly they are. Anyway, the technology of the day only worked with inorganic material, so biological weapons were out, but certain enemy factions had started experimenting with a variety of chemicals. That's why I'm coughing right now. I was exposed to KAP-Blue on the battlefield one time."

"KAP-Blue?"

"Look it up. You'll find it on some of the conspiracy theory sites. Nasty shit. It'll take your ass out in a heartbeat. The Army hasn't officially admitted that it exists, but I can tell you that it does."

"If you were exposed to it, then how—"

"I was wearing full protective gear, but the respirators they were issuing to non-coms at the time turned out to be defective. I know for a fact that I didn't breathe in much of that shit. If I had, I would have been dead. But I inhaled enough of it to make me sick."

"That must have been decades ago," Wahlman said. "How do you know that being exposed to KAP-Blue was responsible for your current condition?"

"They found traces of the compound in my liver," Rusty said. "It was right there in black and white on the lab report. There was no way the Army could deny it. That's why I'm on my way to Myrtle Beach right now. The Army's performing some clinical trials down there. Experimental shit. I volunteered for it. I probably won't live through the procedure, but maybe what they learn from me will be beneficial to some other soldiers in the future. That's the way it works with science sometimes, right? Trial and error."

Experimental shit. That got Wahlman's attention. Now he was genuinely interested in what Rusty had to say.

Last year, in October, Wahlman discovered that he was an exact genetic duplicate of a former Army officer named Jack Reacher. The cells used to produce Wahlman had been taken from Reacher in 1983, over a hundred years ago. Reacher had been in Beirut, Lebanon at the time. In a hospital. Wounded. A phlebotomist had drawn some blood from him and some other officers one morning and had sent the specimens to a lab back in the States. Cells were extracted and cryogenically preserved, and then they were used for cloning experiments decades later.

Now someone was trying to hide the fact that any of that had ever taken place.

A secret experiment carried out by the Army was the reason Wahlman existed, and it was the reason that a current Army officer going by the name of Dorland was trying to make sure that he stopped existing. There had been another clone. A man named Darrell Renfro. He was dead now. Murdered. Wahlman knew that he would be next. There had been several attempts on his life already. He'd been forced to abandon his home, and his best friend had been killed, and the woman he loved had brought their relationship to a screeching halt, concerned for the welfare of her family. He needed to get to the bottom of why all this was happening, and he needed to try to put a stop to it.

"What kind of experimental shit?" he said.

"They're going to give me a new heart, and a new liver, and a new pair of lungs."

"What's so unusual about that?"

"Plenty," Rusty said.

But he refused to elaborate any further.

Because of the papers he'd signed.

"How do I know you're not just making all this up?" Wahlman said.

"Why would I do that?" Rusty said.

"I don't know. That's what I've been trying to figure out. Maybe you think I'll be curious enough to drive you all the way down to Myrtle Beach. Then maybe you'll climb out of my car and have a good laugh on the way to the nearest liquor store."

"Well?"

"Well what?"

"Are you curious enough to drive me all the way down to Myrtle Beach?"

"Maybe," Wahlman said. "I'm still thinking about it."

But Wahlman wasn't really still thinking about it.

He'd made up his mind already.

He was going to Myrtle Beach.

3

Since April, when the elite military intelligence unit he was in charge of bugged out of their secret complex in the Mojave Desert and relocated to Tennessee, Colonel Dorland had been living alone in a one-room cabin on the edge of a cliff. He liked it up there, for the most part. It was extremely private, and on a clear day you could walk out onto the deck and see for miles.

July 8 was a clear day.

But Colonel Dorland wasn't seeing what he wanted to see.

"Too much foliage this time of year," Lieutenant Talfin said, stepping up to the railing and gesturing out toward the landscape. "But I can assure you that it's down there. You can probably see the roof, right here from your deck, in the late fall and winter, after the trees lose their leaves. No telling what you might be able to see with a telescope that time of year, or even a good pair of binoculars."

Talfin had broken the news to Colonel Dorland over the phone a couple of hours ago. There was a fairly large lake at the bottom of the mountain, down in the valley, and according to Talfin, a very nice house had been built on a thirty-acre parcel of land that skirted the shore. Kasey Stielson's parents owned the property, and Kasey and her daughter had been staying there with them until recently. Apparently Rock Wahlman had been staying there too, at least for a while. His fingerprints were all over the place.

Colonel Dorland could see part of the lake from his deck, but he couldn't see the house.

"Why are we just now finding out about this?" he said.

"The deed was registered under a corporate name. Kasey's father owns several—"

"Where's Kasey's father now?"

"We don't know, sir. The whole family's gone. They must have found another—"

"We're supposed to be an intelligence unit," Colonel Dorland said. "We're supposed to be the best in the world at this kind of shit. You're telling me that Wahlman was right under my nose. He was right down there in that valley, less than five miles away, and I didn't even know it. This phase of our operation could have been completed months ago. Yet here we stand with our clueless collective thumbs up our clueless collective asses. Do you know what kind of shit storm I'm likely to be facing because of this, Lieutenant Talfin? Do you have any idea?"

"We'll find them, sir. It's just going to take a little more time."

This wasn't the first time that Talfin had dropped the ball, or even the second time. He was the kind of officer who was really smart when it came to books. Second in his class at WestPoint, first in his class at MCO—the Army's two-year program for newly-commissioned officers interested in careers that involved covert operations. He was extremely knowledgeable, but he didn't seem to be able to put much of that knowledge to use when it came to practical applications. He'd been in charge of cyber security at the facility in California. After the breach that prompted the Code Charlie Foxtrot and the subsequent emergency location change, Dorland had allowed him to continue working with the unit as Second Research Officer. So far, he'd managed to maintain the rank of lieutenant, but he'd been skating on thin ice for quite some time now.

And the ice just kept getting thinner.

"Just remember that shit rolls downhill," Colonel Dorland said. "Get off my porch. I want a written report on my desk by zero seven hundred tomorrow morning. Think you can handle that?"

"Yes, sir."

Talfin saluted, and then he walked back through the cabin and exited through the front door.

Dorland pulled his cell phone out of his pocket and pressed the *SEND* button on a text message he'd composed earlier. He heard Lieutenant Talfin start his car, and he heard the sound of rubber on gravel as he backed out of the driveway. And that was all he heard. He didn't hear Talfin skidding to a stop when he got to the roadblock a mile or so down the mountain, and he didn't hear Talfin shout and scream as he was being dragged out of his vehicle and forced to walk into the woods. He didn't hear any of that, and he certainly didn't hear the gunshot that drove a bullet into Talfin's brain, because the staff sergeant he'd sent the message to always used a sound suppressor on these types of occasions.

4

The alleged facility where the alleged experiments were taking place wasn't actually located within the Myrtle Beach city limits. It was on a small island, a couple of miles off the coast. Only accessible by boat or helicopter.

Wahlman steered away from the ticket booth and joined a line of cars and trucks waiting to board the ferry. The flow of traffic was being regulated by a signal at the edge of the boarding ramp. It changed from red to green when the crew was ready for another car to make its way up onto the parking deck. The boat had probably been around for a century or so, but it appeared to be in pretty good shape. In fact, there were parts of it that appeared to be brand new. The original diesel inboards had been replaced with solar-tidal hybrids from a company called Motion-Prop, and the decks had been coated with a gritty heat-absorbing compound that had only been around for a few years. Wahlman was impressed. Too many vessels from that era were sold for scrap or intentionally sunk and left to rust away at the bottom of the ocean. It was nice to see one that had been properly refurbished.

Wahlman lifted his foot from the brake, allowing his car

to inch forward as one of the vehicles ahead of him boarded the ferry. He looked over at Rusty, who was screwing the cap back onto a half-pint bottle that was a little less than half full.

"I'm curious as to why the Army didn't provide transportation for you," Wahlman said.

"They sent me some money," Rusty said. "I used it for other things. Necessities."

"Food and shelter are necessities. Whiskey and cigarettes are not."

Rusty shrugged. "Are you going to lecture me now?" he said.

"No," Wahlman said. "But weren't you concerned that you wouldn't be able to get here in time?"

"I'm not scheduled to report until tomorrow morning. So I'm actually going to be early."

"That's not what I meant," Wahlman said.

Rusty seemed puzzled for a few seconds. Then it sunk in.

"Oh," he said. "You meant that I could have died while I was out there on the road, trying to hitch a ride. To tell you the truth, the thought never really crossed my mind."

Wahlman inched forward some more. He was next up to board the ferry. The light turned green and he eased the sedan up the ramp and onto the parking deck. One of the crew members directed him toward the last available slot, a cramped sliver of space between a black pickup truck and a gray SUV.

"What do you think?" Wahlman said.

"Looks pretty tight," Rusty said. "We might have to wait for the next ferry."

Wahlman didn't feel like waiting. He had to back up and pull forward a couple of times, but he finally managed to squeeze into the spot. He switched off the engine, glanced into the rearview mirror and saw another one of the crew members dragging a heavy steel chain across the boarding lane. The crew member secured the chain, and then he distributed three orange traffic cones along the length of it. A few minutes later, the ferry pulled away from the ramp and started moving out into the bay.

"I'm going to get out and walk around for a while," Wahlman said.

"Mind if I join you?"

"It's a free country."

"That's right. And some of us fought to keep it that way."

Wahlman thought about telling Rusty that he too was a veteran, that he too had engaged in multiple fierce battles in multiple faraway places, that he'd taken the oath and had served honorably and had experienced more horrific action in twenty years than anyone should experience in twenty lifetimes. He thought about telling Rusty those things, but he didn't. He reminded himself that he was on the run, living under an alias. The more you say about yourself in a situation like that, the more likely you are to be caught in a lie. So you say as little as possible. You talk to as few people as possible. And when you do talk to someone, you say things that can't easily be verified.

Wahlman climbed out of the car. There was a walkway along the starboard side of the ferry, a platform about as wide as a diving board, and there were two signs bolted to the railing, a rectangular one that said *TO OBSERVATION DECK,* and an arrow-shaped one that said *ONE WAY PEDESTRIAN TRAFFIC.* There was an identical platform on the port side, but there was only one sign on the railing over there. It said *DO NOT ENTER.* Which made it obvious to Wahlman that the platform on the port side was for getting back to the parking deck. Sort of like walking around the block, everyone moving counterclockwise, keeping people from having to squeeze past each other on the narrow pathways.

The observation deck was a flat rectangular area about half the size of a tennis court. It overlooked the lane on the bow where all of the vehicles would eventually disembark. There was a ladder on the starboard side to get up there, and one on the port side to get down. One-way traffic. Just like the platforms. Wahlman stepped up to the railing and gazed out over the choppy water. The sun was behind him, low in the sky, and there was a warm breeze blowing up from the south.

"It's nice out here," Wahlman said, turning and noticing that Rusty had stopped a few feet short of the railing. He was standing there with his arms folded, staring down at the textured deck.

"I don't like the water," he said. "Never have."

"The railing is solid steel," Wahlman said. "It's bolted to the deck. There's nothing to worry about."

"I'd rather keep my distance."

"You can swim, right?"

"No. And I have no desire to learn how. You can put me

on an airplane and hand me a parachute and tell me to jump out over enemy territory, and I'll have no problem with that. Just don't tell me to jump into the deep end of a pool. Or even the shallow end. Not going to happen."

Wahlman was just the opposite. He was okay with water. Not that he was any sort of great swimmer, but he could tread water for hours if he needed to, and he could get from one end of a pool to another easily enough with his own clumsy version of the backstroke. But he didn't care for heights. Especially the kind Rusty was talking about. Jumping out of a perfectly good airplane didn't make a lot of sense to him. You find a proper landing strip, and then you find a car and go wherever it is you need to go. That was how that worked.

"What else are you afraid of?" Wahlman said.

"Doctors. That's why I've been trying to stay drunk for the past few days. I gave up alcohol and tobacco years ago. But this shit is making me nervous. You know what I mean?"

"Yeah. I guess it would make me nervous too."

A tone sounded through the loudspeakers, and a pleasant-but-obviously-mechanical male voice announced that the ferry would be docking in approximately ten minutes.

"Please return to your vehicles now," the robot said, its programmed sing-song inflections dripping with faux enthusiasm. "And don't forget your safety belts!"

Wahlman turned and started walking toward the portside ladder.

Rusty didn't move.

"Let's go," Wahlman said.

"I'm not feeling very well," Rusty said.

"Because of the water?"

"I guess so."

Wahlman looked around. The other passengers who'd been enjoying the observation deck were gone now. He and Rusty were the only ones left.

"You can't just stand out there in the middle of the deck while the boat mates up with the ramp," Wahlman said. "It's not safe."

"Nothing is safe," Rusty said.

"Take a deep breath. You'll be fine."

Rusty nodded. He took a deep breath, and then he followed Wahlman around to the ladder and down to the pathway. He shuffled along slowly, gripping the railing with one hand and Wahlman's shirttails with the other.

The breeze had picked up, and Wahlman had to hold onto the baseball cap he was wearing to prevent it from ending up in the water. As they made their way back to the parking area, Rusty started coughing again, and when Wahlman stepped up to his car to open the doors, Rusty started walking around in circles and mumbling incomprehensibly out on the open end of the deck.

"Arno snow la bertiga," he said. "Arno snow la bertiga!"

"Get in the car," Wahlman said.

But Rusty didn't get into the car. A pained expression washed over his face, and a fat stream of bright red blood shot out of his mouth, and he spit and coughed and staggered toward the stern and twirled past the orange traffic cones and stumbled into the heavy steel chain and did a little backflip and splashed headfirst into the churning froth.

5

Colonel Dorland hadn't felt particularly good about sending out the order to eliminate Lieutenant Talfin, but he hadn't felt particularly bad about it either. The truth was, he hadn't had much of a choice in the matter. Talfin had proven himself to be a bungling bonehead on multiple occasions, and you can't just reassign a guy like that to a supply outfit or something. Once you make it to a certain level in the intelligence community—once you know practically every government secret there is to know—you can't expect to just walk away and pretend to be a regular old officer doing a regular old job. Talfin had been perfectly aware of what he was signing up for from the beginning. And with the recent severe errors he'd committed, he had probably known what was coming. When you make the choice to inhabit the extremely specialized covert world of military intelligence and then follow that choice with gross incompetence, you might as well stick your head between your legs and kiss your ass goodbye. That was the way it worked. Every time. No exceptions.

At any rate, Colonel Dorland didn't have time to dwell on it. He was packing some uniforms and some civilian clothes into a suitcase and a garment bag, getting ready to go on a little trip. Not a vacation, exactly, although he planned on getting in a few rounds of golf while he was away. He was stuffing some socks and underwear into the top left corner of the suitcase when his cell phone trilled.

It was Foss.

Colonel Dorland picked up.

"Hello, General," he said.

"Just wanted to follow up on our previous conversation," General Foss said. "I assume you're on your way."

"There was a pressing matter I needed to take care of earlier this afternoon, so I'm getting sort of a late start. I'm packing some things right now. I'll be on the road in less than an hour."

"What kind of pressing matter? Is it something I need to know about?"

"No, sir. It was just a personnel issue. It's all taken care of now."

General Foss sneezed, not bothering to cover his phone's mouthpiece with his hand as he did so. The abrupt cacophonous blast did a number on Colonel Dorland's left ear.

"It's getting kind of late," General Foss said. "Our first patient is scheduled to report first thing in the morning. I was hoping you could be there with the others to greet him."

"I'll be there," Dorland said. "Looking forward to it."

"Good. It's quite the momentous occasion. It's what

we've been working toward for a long time, and now it's finally going to happen. And of course this is only the beginning."

"It's an amazing time. That's for sure."

Colonel Dorland was trying to sound as excited about the project as General Foss undoubtedly expected him to sound. Dorland truly was excited about it, and it truly was an amazing time, and it truly was only the beginning.

But there was still one problem.

One loose thread.

General Foss didn't know that Rock Wahlman was still out there. He was under the impression that the matter had been taken care of months ago.

General Foss had given Colonel Dorland a strict deadline, and Colonel Dorland had managed to confirm the kill with DNA specimens, but the specimens had not actually been taken from Wahlman. They'd been taken from the other clone. From Darrell Renfro. Since both of the men had been produced with cells that had originated from the same unsuspecting donor, both of the men had ended up sharing the exact same DNA. Which had made the deception relatively easy. The technician working the graveyard shift at the city morgue in New Orleans didn't make a lot of money, so it wasn't very difficult to persuade him to give up a couple of vials of blood and a couple of tissue samples. Not very difficult at all.

At the time, with the deadline looming, Dorland had been certain that Wahlman would be eliminated in a matter of days. He'd paid a lot of money to make sure of it. When it didn't happen, he couldn't just admit to General Foss that he'd tampered with the DNA samples. If he ever admitted to that—to purposefully falsifying a Priority-1 intelligence report that had been funneled directly to a superior officer— he might as well stick his own head between his own legs and kiss his own ass goodbye.

So the deception continued, but it couldn't continue indefinitely. The risks kept getting greater, and the stakes kept getting higher, and Dorland was more determined than ever to find Wahlman and take him out of the picture. Wahlman's existence threatened to disrupt the flow of cash being pumped into the current project, and it threatened to disrupt the flow of blood being pumped into Colonel Dorland's arteries. Wahlman had to go, and it had to be soon.

"Are you still there?" General Foss said.

"Yes, sir. Sorry. I was just thinking about how exciting this project is. I can't wait to get down there and see everything for myself."

"You're going to love it," General Foss said. "What we're going to accomplish at that facility is going to go down as one of the most marvelous achievements in human history. It's an honor to be a part of something like this. It's a great time to be alive."

"It certainly is," Colonel Dorland said. "It certainly is."

6

Wahlman ran to the chain. He got down on his hands and knees and leaned over the edge of the deck and stared down into the bubbling wake. After several seconds of foamy gray nothingness, he got up and grabbed one of the life preservers from the railing and was about to jump in when a pale blood-streaked hand floated by and stopped him in his tracks. The hand was attached to a wrist and the wrist was attached to a forearm and the forearm was attached to nothing. The swirling tide gripped the severed limb and rocked it back and forth, making it appear as though it was waving goodbye.

Which, in a sense, it was.

The rest of Rusty's lifeless form surfaced and tumbled around in the forceful stream of the engines before following the arm into the murky depths of the bay. It was a gruesome sight. The old man's head had been twisted around so that his face and his ass were pointing in the same direction. It was the kind of image that you can never fully forget, the kind that's likely to show up in nightmares from time to time, the kind that makes your heart feel like it's going to beat its way right out of your chest.

Wahlman thought about calling for help.

There were two reasons he decided not to.

Rusty was gone, and there was nothing anyone could do to bring him back. That was one reason. The other was somewhat selfish. If Wahlman called for help, the captain of the boat would have to report the incident to the police. The detectives assigned to the case would want to talk to Wahlman, and eventually they would want to scan his driver's license. The guy Wahlman had bought the license from had guaranteed that it was clean, but Wahlman didn't want to bet his life on it. If Wendell P. Callahan had one unpaid parking ticket, the detectives would then have probable cause to dig deeper, and there was no telling what kinds of problems might follow from there.

Extradition to Louisiana on a first-degree murder charge came to mind.

So Wahlman didn't call for help. He slid the life preserver back onto its hook and walked to his car and climbed in and stared at the rear bumper on the cargo van parked in front of him. He was relieved that all of the vehicles on the ferry were facing the bow, making it unlikely that anyone had witnessed what had happened to Rusty. The corpse would eventually float to the surface, but Wahlman doubted that there would be much of an investigation. Not for a ninety-year-old man with a whiskey bottle in his pocket. There would be an obligatory report written up and a halfhearted effort to locate any next-of-kin, and there would be a three-inch column in the metro section of the local newspaper, and that would be that.

Only that wouldn't be that.

Not in this case.

Not if Rusty had been telling the truth.

Because if Rusty had been telling the truth, some people were expecting him to show up first thing in the morning. Military people. On the island. At some sort of secret research facility. Out in the middle of nowhere. Doctors, nurses, technicians, everyone eager to get started on whatever it was they were going to do.

A new heart, and a new liver, and a new pair of lungs.

But not an ordinary series of transplants.

Something special.

Something experimental.

The procedure had been explained and the forms had been signed and the money for transportation had been sent. It was a done deal. Rusty was supposed to be there, and the United States Army was going to be mighty interested in knowing why he wasn't.

Which meant that Wahlman didn't have much time.

He needed to find the facility, and he needed to find out exactly what was going on there, and he needed to do it before the staff started showing up for the day.

7

It was dark by the time Wahlman made it off the boat. He wanted to get an idea of the layout of the island. He didn't have a cell phone or any other device that might have helped with navigation, so he stopped at a filling station and walked inside and asked if they had any maps.

They didn't.

"You can check at the place across the street," the clerk said. "They used to have maps."

Wahlman checked at the place across the street. They didn't have any maps either. The young man standing behind the counter didn't even seem to know what Wahlman was talking about.

"A roadmap," Wahlman said. "It's a big piece of paper with squiggly lines all over it. You open it and look at it for a while, and then you try to fold it back the way it was, but you never can so—"

"Why can't you fold it back the way it was?" the young man said.

"Because you can't. It's just one of those things. Like

perpetual motion. It's scientifically impossible."

The young man shrugged.

Wahlman filled his tank and bought a hotdog and a bag of chips and drove around for a while and got lost for a while and ended up back at the ferry dock, where he'd started.

He drove up to the ticket booth.

The attendant slid the window open. He was enormously fat and his head was shaved completely bald. He was eating a sandwich. A giant sub. Lots of meat and fresh vegetables and the bread looked fresh. Wahlman was still hungry. He'd taken one bite of the hotdog and had thrown the rest away.

The attendant wiped his mouth with a paper napkin.

"Can I help you?" he said.

"When's the next ferry?" Wahlman said.

"Ten minutes or so. You want a ticket?"

"If I buy a ticket now, can I use it later?"

"It's good for twenty-four hours."

"Okay. I'll take one."

Wahlman handed the attendant some cash. The attendant printed a ticket and handed it to Wahlman.

"Have a nice night," the attendant said.

"Do you know of a place around here that sells roadmaps?" Wahlman said.

"Not right offhand. Where you trying to go?"

Wahlman hesitated for a few seconds. He couldn't exactly tell the guy the truth. He couldn't tell him that he was looking for a secret research facility being run by the United States Army. He couldn't tell him that he was planning to nose around and try to find out what the Army was up to. He couldn't tell him that all he knew about the place was that it was somewhere on the island, somewhere out in the middle of nowhere.

Wahlman couldn't tell the attendant any of that. But he figured that the facility would be guarded, and he figured that the guards would be military guys, and he figured that some of those guys would be young and single, and he knew from experience that a certain percentage of those young and single guys tended to gravitate toward certain types of establishments when they were off duty.

"Nowhere in particular," Wahlman said. "I'm just looking to have a good time tonight. If you know what I mean."

"I'm not sure that I do," the attendant said.

"You know. Have a few drinks. Maybe talk to some women."

"Third Avenue," the attendant said.

"How do I get there?"

The attendant gave Wahlman directions.

"Just watch yourself," the attendant said. "Some of those places over there are kind of rough."

"Okay. Thanks."

"No problem. Have a nice night."

"I have one more question," Wahlman said.

"Yeah?"

"Where did you get that sandwich?"

8

It was like Bourbon Street on steroids.

Drums thumping, guitars wailing, vocalists screaming emphatically about everything from eating their favorite breakfast cereal to having their nipples twisted off with pliers. The music coming from one of the clubs was so loud it seemed to make the sidewalks vibrate. There were massage parlors and tattoo parlors and pool halls and smoke shops. There were hotels where you could rent a room for the night, and there were others where you could rent a room for an hour. Neon everywhere, street vendors on every corner.

Wahlman bought a can of beer and sat on a bench outside a t-shirt shop. He had known that none of the Army guys would be in uniform, but it didn't matter. He'd been a Master-At-Arms in the Navy for twenty years, and he could spot active duty military personnel a mile away. He could see it in the way they walked. The way they carried themselves. And if he got close enough, he could see it in their eyes. He could usually tell the lifers from the short-timers, and he could usually tell A.J. Squared Away from Joe Shit The Rag Man.

The guy who walked out of the t-shirt shop probably fell somewhere in the middle. Wahlman figured that he did what he was supposed to do, but that he rarely went above and beyond. He wore fashionably-tattered jeans and a sleeveless gray hoodie with black lightning bolts printed on the sides. He had an earring in each ear and a tattoo on each arm and he could have used a haircut. He wasn't a perfect soldier, but he wasn't a dirt bag either. Just an average guy.

As he was stepping toward the curb, Wahlman stood and turned, intentionally bumping into him, intentionally spilling some beer on his nice gray shirt.

"Sorry," Wahlman said.

"I just bought this shirt, asshole."

The guy stared down at the stain. He was carrying a crumpled paper bag with the shop's logo printed on it. Wahlman figured that he'd bought the gray hoodie there and had stuffed the shirt he'd been wearing into the bag.

"Sorry," Wahlman said again.

"You're going to be really sorry when I shove that beer can up your—"

Wahlman reached out and grabbed the guy's wrist and dug his thumb into a pressure point. The guy dropped the bag and his knees buckled and he curled into a fetal position there on the sidewalk. All in about two seconds.

"You're not going to shove anything anywhere," Wahlman said. "Who's your commanding officer?"

"What?"

"Did I stutter? Who's your CO? Where do you work?"

"You an MP or something?"

"Who's your CO?"

"Look, man, let's just forget about it, okay? You go your way and I'll go mine and—"

"Answer my questions or I'm going to break the wrist. Then, after I drive you to the emergency room, I'm going to drive you to Beaufort and lock your sorry ass up."

"What do you want from me?"

"Where do you work?"

The guy's ears were turning purple. He looked like he might be getting ready to puke. The people passing by didn't seem to be paying any attention. Business as usual. Just another Army guy squirming on the sidewalk, being busted for whatever.

Wahlman dug his thumb in deeper.

"All right," the guy said. "I'm working here on the island. Guard duty."

"Where?"

"It's a concrete building, over off Highway Thirty. It doesn't really have a name. Not that I know of. Everyone just calls it The Box."

"Who's your CO?"

"Major Combs. She's in charge of the guard detail."

"Combs. Like the kind you comb your hair with?"

"Right."

"What are you guarding? What's going on inside the concrete building?"

"I'm on TDY. They don't tell me things like that."

TDY. Temporary duty. It didn't sound right. Not for an installation where secret experiments were taking place.

Special clearances would be required. Not worth it for someone who was only going to be there for a short time. It sounded like something the guy had been coached to say.

Wahlman could have tried to coax the truth out of him, but he didn't want to take the time. He needed to get away from there before a city cop or an MP showed up.

He eased off the pressure point.

"What's your name?" he said.

"Bridges."

"Like the kind you drive a car over?"

"Yeah. Or the kind you jump off of, if you're me right now."

Bridges looked genuinely concerned about what might happen next. And of course he would have had good reason to be apprehensive if Wahlman had still been an active duty Master-At-Arms. If Wahlman had still been on active duty, Bridges would have been in handcuffs by now.

"I'm going to let you off with a warning this time," Wahlman said.

"A warning?"

"Just try to maintain some military bearing from now on, whether you're in uniform or not. You never know who you might be dealing with."

"Yes, sir."

"I'm not a sir. You can call me Senior Chief."

"Yes, Senior Chief."

Bridges stood and brushed himself off. He cupped his wrist in his hand, trying to massage some of the pain away. Wahlman leaned over and picked up the crumpled paper bag and handed it to him.

"Beat it," Wahlman said.

Bridges nodded. He stepped off the curb and headed toward the nightclub where the extremely loud music was playing.

9

Colonel Dorland had only been driving for a couple of hours, but he was already starting to get sleepy. He was accustomed to going to bed early and getting up early. It had been a long time since he'd pulled an all-nighter, and that was exactly what this was going to be. Nine and a half hours from his cabin in Tennessee to the research facility off the coast of South Carolina. Nine and a half hours, if everything went perfectly. Which it rarely did, on a trip that long. There was usually at least one major traffic snag along the way. Which meant that nine and a half hours was an optimistic estimate. Ten hours was more likely, maybe even eleven.

General Foss had denied Colonel Dorland's request for a helicopter. The general had reminded him that The Box was a Top Secret facility, and that any movement to and from The Box should be considered Top Secret as well. Dorland hadn't pressed the issue, but it seemed to him that a helicopter ride to Myrtle Beach and a rental car from there would have been secret enough. Now he was going to have to stay awake all night, and he was going to have to be all smiles and handshakes and exaggerated enthusiasm for the dog and pony show that was supposed to start at seven o'clock in the morning.

Not that the research being conducted at the facility wasn't a big deal. It was. But not quite as big as Foss made it out to be. Not in Dorland's opinion. There's really only one first time for everything, no matter how much you pretend otherwise. You can never really erase the truth. You can bury it and hope that it's never revealed, but you can never eliminate it completely. Not as long as one person still knows every little detail behind what really happened, along with every little detail behind the conspiracy to conceal what really happened. Not as long as one person still has every little detail recorded on a flash drive.

Dorland stopped at a filling station and hooked his car up to one of the chargers. He walked inside and used the restroom, and then he purchased a large coffee and two chocolate donuts and a six pack of energy drinks and some chewing gum and walked back out to his car. As he was sliding the coffee cup into the cup holder on the center console and tossing the brown paper bag that contained the other items onto the passenger seat, his phone started vibrating in his pocket. He was expecting it to be Foss again. Checking up on him again. It wasn't Foss. The caller ID said *UNKNOWN.*

Which was strange.

In fact, it was unprecedented.

Colonel Dorland's cell phone, the one he used for official communications with select members of the intelligence community, had been engineered in a secret underground laboratory in Colorado. It operated on secure frequencies. There were only a handful of people on the planet who knew the number, which was updated weekly, along with the voice and text encryption codes. The odds of that particular device receiving a call from anyone other than General Foss or one of the senior members of Colonel Dorland's staff were a trillion to one.

Yet there it was.

UNKNOWN.

Dorland decided that it must be some kind of glitch. The caller ID must have malfunctioned. There was no other explanation.

It was probably Foss again. Checking up on Dorland again.

Dorland decided to answer the call.

It wasn't Foss.

It was a woman.

She only said one word.

"Run," she said.

And then she hung up.

10

Wahlman had parked his car on Main Street, two and a half blocks east of Third Avenue. As he turned the corner and started heading away from the hubbub, he heard footsteps coming up from behind him. Three guys. He knew that there were three of them without having to turn around. He could tell by the sound of their shoes on the pavement. Three military guys. He knew that they were military because they had fallen in step with each other. Force of habit. From marching drills.

Wahlman didn't speed up, but he didn't slow down either. He kept a steady pace. The guys got closer. Maybe they were expecting Wahlman move to the side, step off onto the street so they could pass by.

Wahlman didn't move to the side.

He stayed in the middle of the sidewalk. It was just as much his as it was theirs. If they wanted to pass by as a group, they were the ones who were going to have to step off onto the street.

"Hey," one of the guys said.

Wahlman didn't turn around.

"Hey you," another one of the guys said.

Wahlman still didn't turn around.

"Hey Senior Chief," the third guy said.

Wahlman recognized the voice. It was Bridges, the guy he'd muscled the information out of a few minutes ago.

Wahlman stopped walking. He stood there with his back to the guys. Which was a gamble. They could have clubbed him in the head. Or knifed him in the back. They could have jumped on him and taken him to the pavement and beat him to a pulp. But they didn't. They knew that he could handle himself. Bridges had told them all about it. They were under the impression that they were dealing with a Senior Chief Petty Officer, a Master-At-Arms in the United States Navy. They were under the impression that they could get in a lot of trouble if things didn't go their way.

"What do you want?" Wahlman said, still not bothering to turn around.

"I was just wondering if I could see your military ID," Bridges said.

"What for?"

"We have strict orders not to tell anyone where we work," one of the other guys said. "We just need to know that you really are who you say you are."

"I didn't say I was anybody."

"You said you were a Senior Chief," Bridges said.

"I said you can call me that," Wahlman said. "It's not my fault you jumped to conclusions."

"So you're not a Senior Chief?"

"You guys should march on back to the club. While you're still able."

"Impersonating an officer," Bridges said. "That's a pretty serious—"

Before Bridges could finish his sentence, before the neurological network connecting his brain to his lips and vocal chords could fire off the nearly-instantaneous impulses it was going to take for him to form and articulate the word *offense*, Wahlman turned around and came down hard on the bridge of his nose with a closed fist. There was a sickening wet crunch, like the sound of a raw egg being smashed with a mallet.

Bridges staggered backward. Bright red blood gushed from both of his nostrils and his eyes rolled back in his head and he crumpled to the sidewalk in a heap.

Bridges had been standing between the other two guys.

Bonehead One and Bonehead Two.

Wahlman could tell that Bonehead One had consumed quite a bit of alcohol. His eyes were bloodshot and fearless. He was probably around six feet tall, and he probably weighed around two hundred pounds. He had a slim waist and broad shoulders and biceps the size of grapefruits. Bonehead Two was much smaller. Five-eight, one sixty. He didn't look to be much of a threat, but Wahlman knew that looks could be deceiving. One of the lessons he'd learned as a Master-At-Arms was to never underestimate an opponent, not even one who is eight inches shorter and seventy pounds lighter than you are. Guys like that can surprise you sometimes, compensating for their disadvantage in size with speed and technique. If you're not careful, guys like that can kill you with their bare hands in a split second.

Both of the off-duty soldiers stood there with looks of astonishment on their faces. Then Bonehead One pulled something out of his pocket. It could have been a small pistol or a canister of pepper spray or a set of brass knuckles, but it wasn't any of those things. It was a knife. A switchblade. Cheap and disposable and deadly. Similar to the weapon Wahlman had been on the wrong end of in Barstow, California a few months ago. So similar that it gave him a momentary sense of *deja-vu*.

Bonehead One thumbed the little button on the side of the mother-of-pearl handle, allowing the shiny silver blade to spring free and lock into place. He didn't say anything, but there was something in his eyes that made his intentions obvious. He wasn't planning to hurt Wahlman. He was planning to kill him. He gripped the handle and started slicing the air in front of him, moving forward with slow and heavy steps, his motions sloppy and stupid, like some kind of angry and disoriented wild predator, like a hibernating bear that had been jabbed with a stick.

In Barstow, Wahlman had defended himself with a park bench. This time, there was nothing like that within reach.

But there was something better.

Bonehead Two.

As Bonehead One advanced with the knife, Wahlman took a quick step to the left and planted the heel of a size fourteen leather work boot into Bonehead Two's solar plexus. Stunned and suddenly unable to breathe very well,

Bonehead Two stumbled backward and tripped over his own feet and landed on his ass at the edge of the curb. Wahlman reached down and grabbed his ankles and swung him like a baseball bat, slamming the top of his skull into Bonehead One's jaw. The results of the impact were impressive, even to Wahlman, who had seen practically every kind of horror that human beings are capable of inflicting on each other. The knife skittered into the gutter and Bonehead One spun around and wobbled over to a grassy area and started spitting out teeth. He stood there for a while, and then he sat down and crossed his legs and stared blankly into the distance.

Bonehead Two appeared to be unconscious. His eyelids kept fluttering and his fingers kept making little jerky movements and he was probably unaware that he was being held upside down and that blood from the gash in his forehead was dripping onto the sidewalk like a leaky faucet. Wahlman carried him over to the grassy area and lowered the back of his head onto Bonehead One's lap, and then he dropped the rest of him onto the ground.

Bridges was starting to wake up. He rolled onto his side and coughed and wiped some of the blood off of his face with the sleeveless gray hoodie.

Wahlman walked over to where he was lying.

"Still want to see my military ID?" Wahlman said.

"I'm going to let you off with a warning this time," Bridges said.

Then he passed out again.

Wahlman picked up the knife and folded the blade into

552

the handle. He slid the weapon into his pocket and walked to his car and climbed in and started the engine. He eased away from the curb and headed west, back toward the dock, back toward the turnoff he'd seen for Highway 30.

11

Colonel Dorland sat there and stared down at his phone for a few seconds, wondering exactly how such a call could have gotten through. Wondering exactly what the caller had been expecting to accomplish.

Run.

What was Dorland supposed to run from? His duty as the commanding officer of an elite intelligence unit in the United States Army? That wasn't going to happen. Only cowards shirked their sworn duties, and Colonel Dorland was no coward. He realized that he had problems, and that he was going to have bigger problems if General Foss ever found out about the Wahlman situation, but he was determined to see this thing through, determined to make everything right, determined to come out smelling like a rose in the end.

The successful completion of this assignment would undoubtedly result in a promotion, and the next step up was a big one.

Brigadier General.

Dorland liked the sound of it. He could see himself wearing the uniform. He wanted that star more than he'd ever wanted anything. It was what he'd spent his entire career working toward. It was where he wanted to be.

And it was where he was going to be.

He wanted the promotion more than anything, which basically meant that he wanted Wahlman dead more than anything. Wahlman was the only roadblock at this point. Once that situation was taken care of, all kinds of good things were bound to happen.

Dorland had decided that he was going to have to take care of the matter himself. He was going to have to get his hands dirty. He had a plan, and he was going to put that plan into action as soon as he was finished with his obligations down at The Box. Day after tomorrow, if everything went well.

Right now he needed to talk to the officer in charge of the night watch, back at the headquarters in Tennessee. Lieutenant Driessman, if he remembered correctly. Driessman was new. Colonel Dorland hadn't had a chance to go through his file yet, so he didn't know a lot about him, but like everyone else assigned to the unit, he'd been checked out thoroughly by the personnel division. Which meant that he was a top-notch officer and one hundred percent loyal to the United States of America. Dorland tapped in the number for the duty phone, got an answer on the first ring.

"Hello, Colonel Dorland. How are you tonight, sir?"

"Driessman?"

"Yes, sir."

"Someone called my cell phone a few minutes ago," Dorland said. "I need to find out who it was."

"Someone called your secure line?"

"Right."

"Someone who's not on your list of contacts?"

"Right."

"I can check into that for you, sir. It might take a few hours. Of course I'll need the access codes for your phone."

Dorland gave him the codes, knowing that everything stored on the processor for more than a week was protected by several extra layers of encryption.

"Call me as soon as you know something," Dorland said.

"Yes, sir."

Dorland clicked off.

He stared at his phone some more, and then he peeled the lid off of his coffee cup and took a sip. The coffee was bitter, and it wasn't very hot, but Dorland didn't really need it anymore anyway. He wasn't sleepy anymore. He was wide awake now. He grabbed a napkin and one of the chocolate doughnuts from the bag on the passenger seat, and then he started his car and headed back out to the interstate.

12

Highway 30 was still under construction. One of the signs planted along the shoulder said that it was eventually going to be an Official United States of America Toll Road. Right now it was free. Which was good. Official United States of America Toll Roads required electronic passes, and electronic passes required proper identification, and the Department of Transportation guys who did the checking were experts at spotting fakes. Rock Wahlman avoided driving on Official United States Toll Roads like he avoided eating spoiled fish. For a man in his situation, purchasing one of those passes would have been tantamount to turning himself in, and turning himself in would have been tantamount to signing his own execution warrant. Not going to happen. So he was happy to know that the road was still free for now, happy to continue moving forward.

The highway sliced through the heart of a pine forest for about twenty miles inland, and then it turned to dirt. Several A-frame barricades with blinking yellow lights on top of them separated the paved part from the dirt part. Beyond the barricades, off to the side, there were some dump trucks and bulldozers and concrete mixers that had been parked for the night, along with a singlewide trailer that probably served as an office for the foremen and engineers. Wahlman figured that the crew would be back at it bright and early.

He turned his car around and headed back the other way. He'd driven the entire twenty miles, and he hadn't seen anything that even remotely resembled what Bridges had described. Which meant that Bridges had been lying, or that there was a turnoff somewhere that Wahlman had missed. He drove back to where the highway started, and then he drove all the way to the barricades again. Nothing. No turnoff. He turned around again and headed back the other way again. He thought about finding Bridges and breaking his nose again.

Then he saw it.

There was a slight opening in the tree line, a semicircle that had been carved into the thick tangle of vines and underbrush. Like a tunnel, with dense foliage serving as the walls and ceiling. The opening was only wide enough for one vehicle, and it was nearly invisible from the highway. If Wahlman hadn't been driving close to thirty miles an hour under the posted speed limit, and if he hadn't been intensely focused on finding anything out of the ordinary, he never would have seen it. Like one of those pictures where you're supposed to find a hidden object. If nobody tells you there's a basketball somewhere in the wagonload of pumpkins, you're probably not going to notice it.

Wahlman drove about half a mile past the opening, and

then he veered off into the grass and parked at the edge of the woods. He broke some branches and ripped out some vines and draped everything over the side of the little sedan in an effort to camouflage it. There hadn't been any streetlights installed on the highway yet, so he figured he was good to go until daybreak, which was still several hours away.

He crept along the tree line until he made it back to the opening, and then he got down on his belly and turned the corner and crawled through. A few feet past the mouth of the tunnel there was an enormous steel sign bolted to two steel posts.

AUTHORIZED PERSONNEL ONLY.

Huge red letters. Reflective paint. The sign said some other things directly beneath the red letters, in smaller print that was black. Something about this being an official United States government facility. Something about trespassers being shot on sight.

Wahlman ignored the warnings and continued using his knees and elbows to propel himself deeper into the tunnel. It doglegged to the left, and then it led to a clearing with a guard shack and a heavy-duty chain-link gate connected to a heavy-duty chain-link fence.

Barbed wire. Razor ribbon.

A lone sentry stood outside the shack. He was wearing combat gear. Vest, helmet, the works. There was a pistol strapped to his right hip, and an assault rifle slung over his right shoulder. Night vision scope, thirty-round magazine. The guy was holding a tablet computer, swiping and tapping, probably documenting that all was secure. He probably did it every thirty minutes. Maybe more often than that at a place like this. Maybe every fifteen. He seemed focused and alert and ready to do whatever it took to defend his post.

The building that Bridges had described was about thirty yards beyond the gate. It was immediately obvious to Wahlman why they called it The Box. It was a concrete cube about as wide as an average convenience store and about twice as tall. No windows, no doors. Not that Wahlman could see. There had to be a way in and out, of course. Maybe on the other side. Or maybe the Army had brought back the technology for teleportation, and maybe they had figured out how to use it on living beings this time. Maybe they had figured out how to do it without turning a person into a quivering pile of gelatinous goo. Wahlman was lying there on his belly pondering the possibility when he saw the silhouette of a man walking along the edge of the roof.

Another guard. Another vest and helmet and pistol and rifle.

On top of the building.

So maybe that was it. Maybe there was some kind of hatch up there. It made sense. A single portal on the roof would make the facility virtually impenetrable to outsiders. One way in, one way out. Great for security. Not so great if you needed to evacuate everyone in a hurry.

Wahlman took a few seconds to consider what such a blatant disregard for safety might or might not mean, and then he shifted his gaze to the left and stared into the forest.

He wanted to do some scouting before he decided on how to proceed. He wanted to walk into the woods and recon the perimeter of the property. He wanted to see the sides of the building, and he wanted to see what was in back. He wanted to see if there were more guards. More than the one standing outside the shack and the one on the roof. He wanted to know if there was a ladder bolted somewhere along the concrete façade. And if there was a ladder, he wanted to know exactly where it was, in case he needed to get to it in a hurry.

He wanted to do some scouting, but he couldn't. The underbrush was too thick. It would have taken him hours to make it all the way around the building. Even with a machete, which he didn't have. All he had was Bonehead One's cheap little switchblade. Not much help against vines as thick as ropes.

Another guard appeared outside the shack. Now there were two of them. They were talking, but Wahlman couldn't hear what they were saying. The guy who'd been there first gave the other guy the rifle and the pistol and the tablet computer.

Apparently they were changing shifts.

The guy who'd been there first walked into the shack. Wahlman figured he was going in there to get his things, his lunchbox and his keys and whatnot, and that he would be back out momentarily. But he wasn't. Not after five minutes. Not after ten. Wahlman wondered what the guy was doing, and then it occurred to him that maybe the guy wasn't even in there anymore. Maybe he was on his way home. Back to the barracks, or wherever he stayed when he wasn't on duty.

Wahlman hadn't seen the second guy walk up to the shack. His appearance had been sort of sudden. He'd shown up at some point while Wahlman was staring into the woods. Wahlman had only taken his eyes off the shack for a brief period. Thirty seconds, maybe less.

Interesting.

Maybe there was an underground tunnel, a passageway that connected the guard shack to the main building. Maybe the tunnel went all the way to the back of the building, and maybe there was a parking area back there and an alternate route out to the highway.

Maybe there was indeed a hatch on the roof, but maybe that wasn't the only one. Maybe there were two guard shacks, one on each end of the property, and maybe there was a portal inside each of the shacks, and maybe there were tunnels connecting everything to everything.

Wahlman mapped it all out in his head. He was only guessing, of course, but it seemed like a feasible layout. It seemed like overkill, but maybe whatever was inside the big concrete building warranted such extravagant security measures. Maybe whatever was inside the big concrete building was the biggest and best-kept secret in the history of the world.

Wahlman tried to shake off the hyperbolic thoughts. The truth was, a certain amount of money had been allocated to build the facility. When you're in charge of something like that and you're given a certain budget to work with, you tend to make sure that there's nothing left by the time you're finished. You tend to spend every penny. You don't want to give any of it back. It's the way it works in the military, and in the private sector—all the way down to average guys with average jobs asking their wives for permission to take a little out of savings to build a game room in the basement. You spend what you have, because you're not likely to get more anytime soon.

So it was possible that the absurdly tight security measures were a product of over budgeting. Then again, it was possible that the government was hiding something truly remarkable and unprecedented. Something that might be of great interest to Rock Wahlman. Something that might shed some light on his current predicament.

He needed to know.

He was trying to figure out a way to get inside the guard shack without having to kill the guard when a bright orange flash of light reflected sharply off a strip of razor ribbon and a searing bolt of pain drilled its way into the right side of his neck.

Wahlman immediately knew what had happened. He knew that he'd been shot. The guy on the roof must have spotted him with the night vision scope.

The guy had fired one shot.

The guy had nailed it.

Wahlman could feel the blood trickling down his throat. He figured the bullet had clipped his right jugular vein. He figured it wasn't the kind of wound that he was likely to recover from. He figured it was the kind that was likely to kill him.

Then he knew. He knew that this was it. The world got narrow, and then it was just a little white dot, and then it disappeared completely.

13

Colonel Dorland never heard back from Lieutenant Driessman. He decided to let it go for now. He had too many other things to think about. He made it to the research facility at 06:04. There was a sentry posted at the front transport module, just outside the fence line. The young soldier popped to attention and saluted and pressed the button to open the gate. Dorland returned the salute and drove through and steered around to the back of the building and parked his car. There were plenty of spaces. The doctors and nurses and technicians hadn't shown up for work yet. Dorland figured the parking lot would start filling up in another thirty minutes or so. He switched off the engine and climbed out of the car and walked up to the rear transport module, as General Foss had instructed him to do.

The exterior facades of the front and rear modules were identical. They were designed to look like ordinary guard shacks. Wood-frame construction, metal roofing panels, lapboard siding. A PFC wearing a dress blue uniform stepped out onto the concrete apron and saluted.

"Good morning, sir," he said.

"Good morning. Are you my escort?"

"Yes, sir."

"Do you have a name, soldier?"

"Yes, sir. Sorry, sir. My name is Watley, sir."

Watley was about six feet tall, and he appeared to be in excellent physical condition. He wore eyeglasses with thick black plastic frames, the kind they issue in basic training. Which indicated to Dorland that he probably hadn't been in the military very long. Hardly anyone kept those frames for longer than a paycheck or two. There was an Expert Marksman badge pinned above his left breast pocket. Impressive for someone just out of boot camp.

"I was told that a guy named Bridges was going to be my escort," Colonel Dorland said. "What happened to him?"

"Private Bridges didn't show up for duty this morning, sir."

"Why not?"

"We're not sure yet, sir."

"Is someone looking for him?"

"Yes, sir. A detail was sent out about an hour ago."

Dorland nodded. "All right," he said. "Where to first?"

"I need to get you checked in at the security office. They'll give you a temporary ID badge and a list of codes for the electronic locks."

"Then what?"

"I'll give you a complete tour of the facility. Our first patient is due to report no later than zero seven hundred, and—"

"We'll welcome him aboard with a special breakfast in the chow hall at eight," Dorland said. "I already know about that."

"Yes, sir."

Watley pushed his eyeglasses up on the bridge of his nose, and then he just stood there and stared out at nothing. He'd been alert and attentive up to that point, but now he seemed to be off in another world.

"Well?" Dorland said.

"Sir?"

"Let's get on with it, Private. We don't have all day."

"Yes, sir."

Dorland followed Watley into the transport module. The interior of the space was unfinished. Bare studs, plywood flooring. It looked like a good place to store your rakes and shovels and hedge trimmers. But Dorland knew better. He'd been briefed on these types of modules. He'd read the manuals and watched the videos. He knew what to expect. He knew what was coming next.

There was a fingerprint scanner and a keypad mounted to one of the studs. Watley punched some numbers into the keypad, and then he pressed his right forefinger against the scanner. A section of the floor opened up and a transparent capsule appeared, a sealed chamber about as wide as a porch swing and about as tall as a kitchen countertop. There were two bucket seats inside the oblong bubble, each equipped with a hinged shoulder harness and a head and neck stabilizer cushion. Kind of like the seats you see on some of the more elaborate rollercoasters at some of the more elaborate amusement parks. The seat to Dorland's right was marked *OPERATOR,* and the seat to his left was marked *PASSENGER.* Above the headrests there was a sign that said *WEIGHT LIMIT 500 POUNDS.*

"This is my first time in one of these things," Dorland said. "I understand it can get kind of rough."

"It's not too bad, once you get used to it," Watley said. "Have you eaten anything this morning?"

"I had a couple of energy drinks in the car."

"Do you ever experience motion sickness?"

"Not usually."

"Are you claustrophobic?"

Dorland hesitated for a second.

"No," he said.

"Great. You should be fine."

Watley opened the capsule and motioned for Colonel Dorland to climb in.

"Has anyone ever died doing this?" Dorland said.

"No. It's actually much safer than the old setups they used in installations like this. Catwalks and ladders and whatnot. The capsule is unbreakable. You could drop it from an airplane and it wouldn't crack."

"What if it did crack?"

"You mean while we're riding in it?"

"Yes."

"Our heads would explode," Watley said. "That's what I've heard, anyway. From the sudden change in pressure. I don't know if it's true or not."

Colonel Dorland took a deep breath, and then he climbed down into the passenger seat.

14

Wahlman woke up strapped to a gurney. A blue towel had been draped over his groin area. Otherwise, he was naked. There was a big round reflective light shining down on him, the kind they use in operating rooms. To his right there was a wall of shelves, the syringes and cotton balls and tongue depressors and other medical supplies visible through a series of heavy glass doors. To his left there was rolling bedside table with a plastic pitcher and a plastic drinking cup on it. Next to the table there was a guard with a machinegun.

Wahlman tested the leather cuffs and tethers securing his wrists and ankles, decided right away that there was no way for him to break free.

"Where am I?" he said.

The guard didn't say anything. He just stood there gazing expressionlessly into the glass cabinets, the barrel of his rifle pointed directly at Wahlman's core.

Wahlman was having trouble remembering what had happened to him. Then it all came flooding back.

He'd been shot.

In the neck.

A double set of doors swung inward and a woman walked into the room. A military woman. Army. Late thirties or early forties. Dress blues, hair pinned back tightly. She was slender and prim and the expression on her face was one of fierce determination, like a thoroughbred running a close second heading into the stretch. There was a semi-automatic pistol holstered above her right hip. The soles and heels of her patent leather shoes clicked pertly on the hard rubber floor tiles as she stepped up to the gurney.

"I'm Major Combs," she said. "I have some questions for you."

"I have some questions for you, too," Wahlman said.

Major Combs laced her fingers together and rested them at the front of her midsection.

"Okay," she said. "You go first."

"It's cold in here," Wahlman said. "Could I have a blanket or something?"

"Maybe. In a little while. If you cooperate."

"Where am I?"

"The infirmary."

"Could you be a little more specific?"

"No."

Wahlman glanced over at the guard. He hadn't moved. He was still staring across the room. Toward the shelves. Toward a stack of plastic wash basins.

"Why am I still alive?" Wahlman said.

"What do you mean?"

"The sign in the woods said—"

"It says that trespassers will be shot on sight," Major Combs said. "It doesn't say that they will be killed on sight."

"So what are we talking about? Rubber bullets?"

"Micro-darts. Loaded with a certain type of medication."

"Like a tranquilizer? Like the kind of shit they—"

"More sophisticated than an ordinary tranquilizer. But yes, the effects are similar."

"I tasted blood," Wahlman said.

"You tasted the medication as it entered your bloodstream. Like an IV bolus from a syringe."

"So I didn't need surgery?"

"No. You needed a square of gauze and a strip of tape. Which you got. Now it's my turn to ask some questions, and your turn to provide some answers. Why were you trying to infiltrate our facility?"

"I don't know what you're talking about," Wahlman said.

"Don't lie to me. Who are you working for?"

"I'm not working for anyone."

"Why were you trying to infiltrate our facility?"

"You already asked me that."

Major Combs was only a foot or so away from the table. Wahlman could smell the soap she'd used to wash herself with that morning. There was a very plain wristwatch on her left wrist. Black leather band, stainless steel housing. There were no rings on her fingers.

"Our infrared surveillance cameras recorded everything you did," she said. "You covered your car with vines and branches, and then you walked along the edge of the woods until you came to our entryway, and then you—"

"The most you can charge me with is trespassing," Wahlman said. "And I really don't see that going anywhere. In fact, I think I could make a pretty good case that my rights were violated."

"You ignored our sign."

"I was traveling alone on a dark and unfamiliar highway. I had car trouble. I hid my vehicle because it's all I have and I was worried that someone might try to steal it. I started walking toward town, but it was a long way back. Ten miles or more. I was tired and thirsty and I didn't think I was going to make it. I desperately needed some help, and when I ran across a place where I thought there might be some people, I naturally gravitated toward that place. I could barely stand up, so I got down on my belly and crawled. I was too weak to look up and read a sign. I didn't even see it. I crawled right past it. I got a little scared when I saw the guys with guns, so I decided to stop and wait and think it over for a while. Next thing I know, someone has taken all my clothes and strapped me to a—"

"You need to answer my questions," Major Combs said. "I'm trying to be reasonable, but my patience is wearing thin. If I can't get any answers from you, I'll send someone in who can."

"I'm not in the military," Wahlman said. "You don't have any authority over me. If you want to bring one of the local police agencies in, you can tell them your version of what happened, and I'll tell them mine. I'll be sure to tell them that I was injected with some kind of drug that knocked me out for a few hours."

Major Combs didn't say anything. She turned and exited the room. She didn't order the armed guard to follow her, but he did anyway. As if it was expected. Prearranged. As if something very discreet was about to happen. Something the guard wasn't supposed to see.

Wahlman tested the leather restraints again. There was a little bit of play in the ones binding his wrists. He could lift his arms a few inches off the table, but he couldn't pull his hands through the cuffs, no matter how hard he tried. They were buckled too tightly.

Wahlman tried to relax. Tried to think. The bright overhead light and the aftereffects of the drug he'd been injected with made it difficult to concentrate. Not to mention the monotonous electrical hum coming from one of the glass cabinets. The one in the corner. The one furthest from the door. Wahlman wondered if that section of the unit was refrigerated. He figured it was. Dozens of plastic containers were stacked up in there. The containers were not marked. Wahlman had no idea what was inside them. Some sort of medication, he guessed. His mind kept wandering. He couldn't seem to stay focused on one thing for more than a few seconds at a time. He thought about Highway 30. About how dark it was. About how he'd traveled back and forth and hadn't seen any businesses or any other vehicles. He thought about Kasey, about how much he still missed her.

A guy wearing white scrubs and a white lab coat walked in. Early twenties, average height. Broad shoulders and a thick middle and a double chin. He had dark hair and an immature mustache, everything trimmed to military specs, but just barely. He could have used a trip to the barber shop and about a hundred trips to the gym. He covered Wahlman's legs and torso with a wool blanket, and then he wheeled the bedside table closer to the gurney.

"I'm going to be your nurse today," the guy said. "I need to insert an INT, and I need to change your dressing, and I need to draw some blood."

"What's an INT?" Wahlman said.

"An IV site. Peripheral. You know, in one of your arms."

"I don't want that," Wahlman said. "You need to let me go."

"Sorry. Doctor's orders."

The guy started pulling some things out of his pockets. He had a packet of gauze and a roll of surgical tape and a pair of bandage scissors. He had a rubber tourniquet and some individual alcohol wipes that were sealed in little foil packets. He had a pair of surgical gloves and some glass vials for the blood specimens and a plastic and cardboard blister pack with a sterile eighteen-gauge IV needle in it and a syringe that had been filled with some sort of clear liquid. He grabbed the gloves and stretched one over each hand and started lining everything up in neat little rows on the bedside table. It took him a couple of minutes to get everything just right. Just the way he wanted it.

"You're making a big mistake," Wahlman said.

"Don't worry," the guy said. "Everything's going to be fine."

He picked up the roll of surgical tape and tore off a piece that was about four inches long. He ripped the piece in half, lengthwise, creating two narrower strips that were identical in length. He stuck the ends of the two narrow strips to the edge of the table, allowing them to dangle there like a couple of translucent streamers. He tied the tourniquet around the upper part of Wahlman's right arm, and then he tore open one of the foil packets and pulled out the alcohol wipe that was inside it and leaned in to find a vein.

He leaned in a little too far.

In one swift and violent motion, Wahlman arched his back and neck and head-butted the guy just above his left ear. It was a brutal bone-to-bone blow. It sounded like a bat hitting a ball. The impact gave Wahlman an immediate headache. It gave the guy in white scrubs an immediate skull fracture. The guy slumped over Wahlman's abdomen, and then he slid to the floor like a sack of potatoes.

Wahlman reached for the bedside table, but the tether that connected the cuff on his right wrist to the frame of the gurney wasn't quite long enough. He could brush the edge of the table with the tip of his middle finger, but that was as close as he could get. He strained and pulled and jerked and stretched, but it was no use. He wanted the bandage scissors. He wanted them as much as he'd ever wanted anything. They were as crucial to him as the air he was breathing. They were his ticket to freedom. They were his only chance.

He wasn't cold anymore. Sweat was dripping down his face. His head was throbbing and he was starting to feel some numbness in his right arm. Pins and needles. Because of the tourniquet. He thought he might be able to stretch down and untie it with his teeth, but his range of motion was limited by the restraints, and by the bulk of the muscles in his chest and shoulders. He took a deep breath. He was trying not to panic. Trying to think of a way out of this. He wasn't ready to give up. He would never do that. But he wasn't delusional either. The odds were against him. A million to one, maybe. If he could get to the scissors. Which he couldn't. He stretched again. Strained again. Brushed the tip of his finger against the edge of the bedside table again.

Then something wonderful happened.

The guy on the floor grunted, and then he must have rolled over or shifted his position in some other manner. Wahlman couldn't see the guy, but he could hear him. There was a rattle in his throat every time he took a breath. Maybe he was dying. Maybe his damaged brain had sent out some emergency signals to the muscles in his arms and legs in a last ditch effort to survive. To run away. Like the jerky spasms you have sometimes when you're dreaming. Whatever the case, the movement he'd made had caused the table to roll a little closer to the gurney. Now Wahlman could reach it. Easily. He gripped the edge with his thumb and forefinger and pulled it in closer.

There were three rows of supplies. The items the guy had planned to use to start the INT were in the front row, and the items he'd planned to use for the blood draw were in the middle.

The scissors were in back.

Way in back.

They must have slid when the table moved. They weren't in line with the packet of gauze anymore. They were closer to the edge.

Wahlman grabbed the blister pack and used it to extend his reach. He thought it was going to work. He thought he had this now. But he didn't. He couldn't pull the scissors closer to his fingers. The blades were pointed toward him, and he couldn't get any traction against the slick stainless steel. He set the blister pack down and grabbed one of the strips of tape dangling from the front of the table. His fingers were numb. He could barely feel what he was doing. He managed to crumple the strip of tape into a sticky little ball, and then he managed to press the sticky little ball onto the edge of the blister pack.

He reached for the scissors again, using the contraption he'd assembled. It worked. The sticky little ball stuck to the shiny steel blades, allowing him to guide the cutting tool toward the gurney. A sense of elation washed over him. He felt like celebrating. He felt like whooping and hollering. He fumbled around for a few seconds and finally managed to get his fingers through the handles of the scissors and he curled his right wrist as far as it would curl and he snipped the tether and proceeded to snip the others until all four of his limbs were free. He untied the tourniquet and sat up, fighting off a wave of vertigo as he pivoted and planted his bare feet on the cold rubber tiles.

Then he heard footsteps in the distance, clicking pertly.

15

The chow hall was packed, but nobody was saying much.

Colonel Dorland stared down at his breakfast plate. Scrambled eggs, bacon, biscuits, hash browns. There were several doctors and scientists sitting at the table with him, including the geneticist who'd developed the formula for the growth medium and the surgeon who'd perfected the actual procedure. There were colorful plastic balloons taped to the walls and colorful paper streamers tacked to the ceiling. Over in the far right corner of the room, there was a guy sitting at a grand piano, but he wasn't playing anything.

Because the party hadn't officially started yet.

Because the guest of honor hadn't arrived yet.

Dorland took a sip of coffee from the ceramic mug next to his plate. He looked at his watch, and then he turned and locked eyes with PFC Watley, who was sitting at the next table over.

"It's eight-thirty already," Dorland said. "How long are we supposed to wait?"

"I'll call the security office again," Watley said. "Maybe

he's down there checking in right now."

"Why wasn't someone assigned to escort him from his home to the facility? That's what I don't understand. Seems like a no-brainer, for something this important."

"Sir, I don't—"

"What was the name of the officer I met with earlier? The one in charge of security?"

"That was Major Combs, sir."

"Get her on the phone. Tell her I want to talk to her. ASAP."

"Yes, sir."

Watley pulled out a cell phone and punched in some numbers. He had a brief conversation with someone on the other end, and then he clicked off.

"Well?" Colonel Dorland said.

"She's not in the office right now," Watley said. "She's on her way to the infirmary."

"What's wrong with her?"

"She's okay. There's a—"

"How do I get to the infirmary?"

"I can go with you if you want me to, sir. Or I can try to reach Major Combs on her cell phone."

Colonel Dorland considered those options, decided against them. Major Combs needed to be counselled, but there was no point in making a public display of it. There was no point in embarrassing her in front of her subordinates.

"The things I need to say to her need to be said in person," Dorland said. "And in private. I can manage on my own. Just tell me how to get there."

16

Wahlman needed a weapon.

Fast.

He tied the blanket around his waist and stepped over to the glassed-in storage area, to the unit in the corner that seemed to be refrigerated. He was hoping that the plastic bins stacked up in there were full of micro-darts and that the micro-darts had been loaded with the same medication that had been used to knock him out. He pulled on the door, but it didn't open. It was locked. There was a keypad and a card scanner mounted to the side of the unit. Wahlman figured you had to scan your ID and punch in a code to get the door to open. Alternatively, you could walk back over to the gurney and grab the blue towel and wrap it around your fist and break the glass. Probably not the recommended method, but effective nonetheless.

Wahlman reached in and grabbed one of the containers. It wasn't filled with medication. It was filled with plastic IV bags, and the plastic IV bags were filled with blood. For transfusions. Fat paper labels had been glued onto the bags, indicating the blood type and the Rh factor. Below the stack of plastic bins there was a drawer marked *PATIENT BELONGINGS.* Wahlman opened the drawer and reached in and ferreted through the pile, found his wallet and his keys. He figured the drawer was located in that particular cabinet in case patients brought medications from home that needed to be refrigerated. He set his things on the bedside table and grabbed the scissors. Someone had taken the time and energy to donate the unit of blood he was holding. Someone had endured the pain of the needle. Someone had risked the potential side effects. It was a generous thing to do. A caring thing. It was a dirty rotten shame to waste even one drop, but Wahlman didn't feel as though he had any choice. He cut one of the corners off the bag and walked over to the double set of doors and squirted the entire unit on the floor. He retreated back to the bedside table and quickly fashioned a shank using some gauze and some tape and a shard of glass from the broken cabinet. A few seconds later the doors swung open and Major Combs and a short skinny guy carrying a red toolbox walked in and promptly proceeded to slip and fall on their asses. Wahlman darted over there and crouched down and held the shank to Major Combs's throat and unsnapped her holster and pulled out the pistol.

"Be careful with that," Major Combs said. "It's loaded with real bullets."

"You're going to do exactly what I tell you to do," Wahlman said. "Or two of those real bullets are going to come out real fast."

Wahlman held the gun on Major Combs and the guy who'd walked in with her and tossed them the scissors and the blue towel and the roll of surgical tape and gave them specific instructions on how to gag each other and tie each other up. Once most of the work was done, Wahlman finished it off by taping Major Combs's wrists together behind her back.

The nurse was still on the floor, over by the gurney. His breathing sounded a little better than it had earlier. Still pretty ragged, but better. Wahlman pulled the guy's shoes off and his scrub pants and his lab coat and slid into everything as quickly as he could. There was a phone and an ID card in the left front pants pocket. The guy's name was Sebley. He was a second lieutenant. The shoes were a little tight and the sleeves on the lab coat were a little short, but Wahlman wasn't complaining. It could have been worse. They could have sent a female nurse, and the female nurse could have been wearing a dress. Then Wahlman would have been forced to try to escape naked. So he wasn't complaining, and he wasn't nearly as curious about what was going on at the facility as he had been last night. Getting out of there in one piece was the only thing on his mind at the moment. Then maybe he could investigate from a distance. Maybe get some interest from the media. There was definitely a story here. Wahlman still had no idea what it was, but he knew it was something big. Something that the Army was devoting a great amount of time and effort and money to conceal.

The lab coat had some fairly large patch pockets sewn

onto the front, just below the waistline, one on each side of the snaps. Sebley had been carrying his supplies in them. They were empty now. Wahlman dropped his wallet and his keys into the pocket on the left side. He kept a grip on the pistol and slid his right hand into the pocket on the right side and stepped over the slippery puddle of blood he'd created and exited the room.

The hallway appeared to be about fifty feet long. It was covered with some sort of industrial-grade vinyl. Green. Pale and dull. The kind of stuff that would probably last a thousand years. There were wooden doors on both sides of it, marked with numbers. Wahlman could see the end of it. He could see that it doglegged to the right. He strolled along at a steady pace. Not too fast, not too slow. He didn't want to draw attention to himself. He was just a nurse, a staff member, heading from one area to another. No big deal. Eyes forward, one foot in front of the other. He was hoping that there was an exit right around the corner. Or an elevator. Or a stairway. He was hoping that he wouldn't run into anyone on the way out.

But he did run into someone.

Literally.

As soon as he turned the corner.

17

The guy Wahlman bumped into was less than six feet tall. Five-eight, five-nine maybe. He was a colonel. Full-bird. Blue eyes, bald on top, gray around the temples. Dress blues, lots of ribbons. There was a lanyard around his neck. Attached to the lanyard there was a transparent plastic sleeve, and inside the sleeve there was an identification card.

VIP

TEMPORARY

DORLAND, J.L.

UNITED STATES ARMY

Wahlman's heart did a flip flop. He stared down at the card and read it again, just to make sure.

It was him.

It was Colonel Dorland.

"Watch where you're going," he said.

He made an attempt to step to the side and continue down the hallway, toward the infirmary. Wahlman pulled out the pistol and pointed it at his face.

"I already know where I'm going," Wahlman said. "Same

place you're going."

Dorland stared into the barrel of the gun.

"Are you insane?" he said. "You see this bird on my collar? You better put that weapon away before I stick it up your—"

"Look at me," Wahlman said.

Dorland snarled. The muscles in his jaw were as tight as banjo strings. He looked up and stared into Wahlman's eyes. It took him a few seconds, but then he knew.

His expression relaxed into one of stunned resignation.

"We can work this out," he said.

"I don't think so," Wahlman said.

"What are you going to do? Shoot me? Here?"

"Maybe."

"What do you want?"

"You're going to lead me out of here," Wahlman said. "Then we're going to talk."

"There's too much security. There's no way I can—"

"You have that bird on your collar. And a VIP designation on your ID. You can go anywhere you want to."

"And where exactly is it that I want to go?"

"To your car."

"What makes you think I have a car?"

Wahlman shrugged. "Helicopters flying in and out of here would attract too much attention," he said. "I'm guessing you took the ferry from Myrtle Beach and then drove in on Highway Thirty, just like I did. I'm guessing Highway Thirty is the only way in and out of here by land vehicle. And I'm guessing it's not even a real highway. It's open to the public, but nobody uses it. Because it doesn't go anywhere. It's a dead end. Future toll road. Currently under construction. Right. The dozers and dump trucks are parked out there for looks. Just in case someone—"

"You're pretty smart," Dorland said.

"I'm going to put this pistol back into my pocket, and then I'm going to follow you to the exit. I'll have my hand on the gun the entire time, so don't do anything stupid."

"What if someone tries to stop us?"

"Nobody's going to try to stop us. You're a colonel. I'm a nurse. It's all good."

"We'll have to take one of the capsules," Dorland said.

"What are you talking about?"

"The pneumatic transport system. It's the only way out of the building. I should make it clear right now that I've never actually operated one of those things. I've read the manuals, but I haven't been signed off on—"

"We'll figure it out," Wahlman said. "Move."

Dorland turned around and headed back in the direction he'd come from. Wahlman followed, staying three or four steps behind.

Twenty feet or so from the corner where Wahlman and Dorland had bumped into each other, there was a set of stainless steel doors. Like elevator doors, but wider. Dorland pushed a button and the doors parted, revealing a clear plastic carriage with two bucket seats in it.

"Have you ever ridden in one of these?" Dorland said.

"I'm here, so I must have," Wahlman said. "I guess I was unconscious at the time."

"Climb in, and I'll secure your harness for you."

Wahlman laughed. "You think I'm stupid?" he said. "You climb in first. You're going to be the passenger, and I'm going to be the operator."

"This is not a pony ride at the state fair. These things can be dangerous if you don't know what you're doing."

"Get in. You can tell me what to do. If you touch any of the controls, I will shoot you."

Dorland climbed into the carriage. Wahlman secured the padded harness on that side, instructed him to keep his hands in his pockets.

"Be careful with that gun," Dorland said. "Once we get going, there's going to be an enormous difference in pressure between the inside of the capsule and the outside of the capsule. If you accidentally discharge the weapon—"

"I'm not going to accidentally do anything," Wahlman said. "If I pull the trigger, it's going to be deliberate."

He climbed into the operator's seat and closed the hatch.

"My car's parked in the lot at the rear of the facility," Dorland said. "See the dial that says exterior rear module?"

"Yes."

"Set the dial to seven. Then you'll need to scan my ID and punch today's code into the keypad."

"What if I set the dial to eight? Or nine? Or ten?"

"The higher the number, the faster we'll get there. Seven is standard. The higher numbers are generally only used for extreme emergencies. Believe me, seven is fast enough."

An alarm sounded in the distance. An angry pulsating buzz.

Someone must have alerted the security office. Wahlman figured the hallway outside the carriage would be flooded with soldiers in a matter of seconds. He set the dial to twenty. The max. He reached over and pulled Dorland's ID card out of the plastic sleeve.

"What's the code?" Wahlman said.

Dorland told him the numbers.

Wahlman punched in the code and pressed *ENTER* and off they went, whistling through the darkness. The gravitational pull pinned Wahlman to his seat. He couldn't move. He couldn't have fired the weapon he was holding, even if he'd wanted to. He could barely breathe. It was as if he'd suddenly gained a thousand pounds.

Then it was over. The carriage slowed down for a very brief period, and then it came to an abrupt stop. Wahlman figured the ride had lasted about ten seconds from start to finish. He released his harness and opened the hatch and climbed out.

He stepped over to the passenger side and reached down to help Dorland.

"I thought I was going to pass out," Dorland said.

"Let's go."

"Give me a minute. I don't think I can—"

Wahlman yanked Dorland out of the seat, forced him to stay in front as they exited the wooden shack and stepped out onto a concrete apron.

"Where's your car?" Wahlman said.

"Over there. The blue one."

"Give me the keys."

Dorland reached into his pocket and pulled out a set of keys. He handed them to Wahlman.

"They probably have the exit blocked by now," Dorland said. "They're not going to let you leave the facility alive. You know that, right?"

Wahlman pressed the barrel of the pistol against the back of Dorland's neck and pulled the hammer back. If he wasn't going to be able to leave the facility alive, then Dorland wasn't going to be able to either.

"Walk," Wahlman said.

Dorland stepped down onto the asphalt and started walking toward his car. Wahlman kept the barrel of the pistol pressed against the back of his neck, hyper-focused on moving forward one step at a time. He didn't look to see, but he figured that there were guards up on the roof by now, and he doubted that their rifles were loaded with micro-darts. He figured that their rifles were loaded with high-velocity full-metal-jacket rounds, the kind that would bore a hole the size of a quarter all the way through you faster than you could blink. He figured the back of his skull was in the crosshairs, but he figured he had some leverage. This was a hostage situation now. Nobody was going to take a shot from the roof. Not when it meant risking a senior officer's life. Dorland was a colonel in the United States Army. He was an asset. Heads would roll if anything happened to him. Nobody was going to take a shot. Wahlman was counting on it.

And nobody did.

Wahlman used the transmitter on the key ring to unlock

the car doors and start the engine. He opened the driver side door and forced Dorland to climb over the center console to the front passenger seat, and then he slid into the driver seat and jerked the shifter into gear and pulled out of the parking space. He steered around to the outer edge of the lot, out to the front of the building, out to the front guard shack, which he now realized housed another portal for the pneumatic transport system. There were eight soldiers dressed in full combat gear blocking the traffic lanes on both sides of the shack, four on the entrance side and four on the exit side, all of them facing the little blue electric car Wahlman was driving, all of them aiming their rifles directly at the driver side of the windshield.

Wahlman stepped on the accelerator. He continued forward, toward the right side of the shack. He was relatively certain that the guys standing there wouldn't take any shots, for the same reasons he'd been relatively certain that the supposed rooftop guys wouldn't take any.

But this time he was wrong.

The guards opened up like a firing squad.

18

It was like driving through a sudden hailstorm. Alarming, noisy, damaging to the car's paint and glass.

But ultimately not life-threatening.

"Your car's bulletproof?" Wahlman said.

"Of course," Dorland said, almost cheerfully. "Standard issue for senior officers in the intelligence community. Windows, tires, everything. They would need a tank to stop this vehicle."

Dozens of rounds pinged off the windshield as Wahlman sped forward. The guards on the exit side of the shack jumped out of the way a split second before they became human bowling pins. Wahlman barreled toward the rat-hole-shaped opening at the edge of the woods, navigated the narrow tunnel of foliage, and fishtailed out onto the highway. He headed west, toward town. He'd noticed a couple of good hiding places last night while he was driving around lost. He kept his right hand on the wheel, and he kept his left hand wrapped around the grips of the semi-automatic pistol he'd taken from Major Combs. Finger on the trigger, barrel aimed at Colonel Dorland's core.

"Is there any way to make this thing go faster?" Wahlman said, glancing down at the speedometer, which seemed to be maxing out at eighty miles per hour.

"This thing, as you so eloquently referred to it, is equipped with all sorts of surprises," Dorland said. "One of them is an onboard voice-activated computer that will pretty much do whatever I tell it to do."

"Tell me how to activate it."

"I'm afraid I can't do that."

"Tell me, or I'm going to shoot your ass right now."

"You don't understand. I mean that I literally cannot tell you how to activate the computer. It's programmed to respond to my voice and my voice only."

"Tell it to make the car go faster."

"Eighty is fast enough."

Wahlman raised the pistol and pointed it at Dorland's head.

"Tell it to make the car go faster."

Dorland's jaw muscles tightened again. Wahlman wasn't sure if he was going to comply, or if he was bracing himself to take a bullet in the brain. He was silent for thirty seconds or so, and then he took a deep breath and spoke to the computer.

"Gertrude, please change the maximum cruising speed from eighty miles per hour to one hundred and fifty miles per hour," he said.

"*Changing the maximum cruising speed now,*" a pleasant female voice said.

The increased acceleration was immediate and impressive. Speedometer pegged, tachometer jittering nervously along the border where caution met redline.

"What else can your computer do?" Wahlman said. "Is it possible to—"

"Gertrude, please lock all of the doors and windows."

"*Locking all doors and windows now.*"

"Gertrude, please disable the braking system while maintaining the current cruising speed."

"*Cruise control set at one hundred and fifty miles per hour. Braking system disabled.*"

"What are you doing?" Wahlman said.

"Gertrude, please cause this vehicle to self-destruct in exactly five minutes, and remind me how much time is left every minute."

"*Self-destruct timer set for five minutes.*"

Dorland stretched his legs and crossed his ankles and relaxed against the back of his seat.

"Okay, Mr. Wahlman," he said. "If there's something you want to talk to me about, now would be the time."

19

Wahlman shifted his right foot from the accelerator to the brake. Nothing happened. The car continued moving forward at exactly one hundred and fifty miles per hour.

"You have four minutes left on the timer."

Wahlman kept the pistol trained on the left side of Colonel Dorland's head.

"You need to cancel that shit," Wahlman said. "You need to cancel it right now, or I'm going to blow your brains all over the interior of this car."

"Go ahead and shoot me," Dorland said, maintaining his relaxed posture. "Go ahead and throw away your only chance of making it out of this alive."

Dorland was right. He was holding all the cards now.

Wahlman lowered the weapon.

"What's your real name?" he said.

"I don't see how that's relevant, now that you've found me."

"It's going to be relevant when I take the story to the media."

"You have less than four minutes to live. You're not taking the story anywhere."

"If I die, you die," Wahlman said.

"That seems to be the case. At any rate, I'm not telling you my real name. As a member of the intelligence community, it's imperative that I maintain a certain degree of—"

"*You have three minutes left on the timer.*"

Wahlman decided to move on to the next question.

"You've been trying to have me killed for months," he said. "Why?"

"Because I was ordered to have you killed," Colonel Dorland said.

"Okay. But there must have been a reason. You targeted me, and you targeted a man named Darrell Renfro."

"How much do you already know about that?"

"I know you got Renfro. I saw the tractor-trailer he was driving go off a bridge and crash into a canal a few miles east of New Orleans. I tried to save him, but I couldn't. I know that Renfro and I were products of a human cloning experiment, exact genetic duplicates of a former Army officer named Jack Reacher."

"Did you know that you and Mr. Renfro were the first human clones ever produced?"

"No."

"And did you know that no others have been produced since then?"

"No. Get to the point. Why did the Army decide to—"

"That is the point," Colonel Dorland said. "A certain

four-star general decided that history needed to be altered a little bit. He made this decision for the reason that a lot of decisions are made, because of money. Our current project is not being funded by the United States government. It's being funded by a group of ordinary citizens—ordinary except for the fact that they're all billionaires. This group has been assured that the human clone soon to be produced in our laboratory is going to be the first in history."

"Why is that so important?" Wahlman said.

"Think about it. Do you remember the name of the second man who walked on the moon?"

Wahlman shrugged. "I guess that's a good point," he said. "But I didn't even know I was a clone when this first started. You could have said whatever you wanted to say about your new project. Nobody would have ever known the difference. There was no reason to kill anyone."

"We couldn't take a chance on you or Mr. Renfro ever finding out about the facts behind your true heritage, couldn't take a chance that those facts might eventually become publicized. It would have exposed us as frauds, and it would have cost us billions of dollars."

"*You have two minutes left on the timer.*"

"I picked up a hitchhiker named Rusty," Wahlman said. "He was coming here for some kind of procedure. What was that all about?"

Dorland was silent for a couple of beats.

"So that's how you found out about the facility," he said. "What did this Rusty fellow tell you?"

"Nothing. He just needed a ride."

"He was supposed to report this morning, no later than zero seven hundred. What happened to him?"

"Answer my question first," Wahlman said. "Then I'll answer yours."

"Rusty is going to provide the donor cells for our first clone," Dorland said.

"Why him?"

"Because he volunteered. And because his condition is terminal. If something goes wrong during the procedure—"

"Why would anything go wrong?" Wahlman said. "It's a simple blood draw. That was how they harvested the cells from Jack Reacher, right?"

Dorland nodded. "I suppose I should explain that what we're doing now is much different than what they were doing when you and Renfro were born. There was a codename for that project, but it was long and alphanumeric and everyone eventually just started referring to it as The Reacher Experiment. The goal back then was to manufacture super-soldiers. Entire battalions of them. Huge, strong, intelligent. Like Jack Reacher. Like you. It was ambitious, and revolutionary. But it was illegal, and it was costing a fortune, and the administration at the time decided to ditch it in favor of a new line of fighter jets."

"All this stuff is written down somewhere?"

"It was. The files have been destroyed. You and Renfro were the only loose ends. Now it's just you."

"Human cloning is still illegal," Wahlman said.

"Not for long. There's a bill right now in the—"

"I've heard about the bill. It's not going anywhere. The sponsors don't have the votes."

Dorland laughed. "Don't believe everything you read in the newspapers," he said. "The bill will pass, and it will be signed into law. Guaranteed."

"You said that the experiments you're doing now are different from the ones they were doing back when Renfro and I were born. How so?"

"Our project has nothing to do with national defense. It's more of a business venture than anything else. A couple of years ago, one of the principal scientists approached the four-star general I mentioned earlier, and soon after that the four-star general approached me. It's going to make us very wealthy men, and it's going to assure our places in history."

"You have one minute left on the timer."

"I don't know about the general, but in sixty seconds your place in history is going to be a greasy spot on the highway," Wahlman said. "Cancel the timer."

"Give me the gun, and I will."

"I'm not giving you the gun."

"Then I'm not cancelling the timer."

"You're willing to die for this shit?"

"I am."

"You're bluffing."

Dorland laughed. "Do you really think so?" he said.

"Yes," Wahlman said.

"Gertrude, please make the self-destruct timer irreversible, starting now."

"Your last command requires a positive confirmation. You want the self-destruct timer to be irreversible, starting now. Is this correct?"

"Yes," Dorland said. "And please start an audible countdown immediately after executing the next verbal command."

"*Audible countdown ready to start following the next verbal command.*"

Dorland sat up straight, checked his seatbelt.

"You were right," he said. "I was bluffing."

"What are you talking about?"

"Gertrude, please eject the passenger seat now."

The roof receded and Dorland shot out of the top of the car like a rocket. Wahlman glanced into the rearview mirror, saw a parachute open, saw the lines become tangled, saw Dorland dropping like a rock into the forest. It was doubtful that he made it to the ground. He was probably up in the trees somewhere, skewered on some splintered branches, bleeding out slowly and painfully. Wahlman cringed at the thought of it. He couldn't think of a worse way to die.

The roof closed as quickly as it had opened. It mated into the slot at the top of the windshield with a definitive click.

"*Twenty-five…twenty-four…twenty-three…*"

"This is insane," Wahlman said. "It can't end like this. It just can't."

"*Eighteen…seventeen…sixteen…*"

"Shut up, Gertrude."

There was a brief pause.

"*Discontinuing audible countdown,*" the computer said.

"Gertrude?"

"*Awaiting next verbal command.*"

Dorland must have been lying about the computer being

programmed to recognize his voice and his voice only. Wahlman felt like an idiot now for taking him at his word.

"Gertrude, discontinue the self-destruct timer."

"*Negative. The command to self-destruct was made irreversible.*"

Shit.

"How much time is left?" Wahlman said.

"*You have eight seconds left on the timer.*"

Shit.

Wahlman considered his options. He had command of the vehicle now. He could use the brakes to come to a complete stop, and he could unlock the doors, and he could unbuckle his seatbelt and climb out and take off running.

But there just wasn't time.

So he did the only thing he could do.

He gave the command, even though he'd seen what had happened to Colonel Dorland.

"Gertrude, eject the driver seat," he said.

And she did.

20

Phoning from a second story hotel room on the outskirts of Myrtle Beach, Wahlman had spoken to ten different investigative reporters at ten different major metropolitan newspapers. Every one of them had told him the same thing. You can't go after a story like that without some kind of proof. Photographs. Documents. Video recordings. Voice recordings. Witnesses willing to come forward and corroborate.

Wahlman had nothing.

He knew for a fact that the Army was planning to conduct secret human cloning experiments out on that island, and he knew that there was more to it than that, but he didn't know any of the details. *It's going to make us very wealthy men, and it's going to assure our places in history.* Dorland had seemed ready to spill it all, but then time had run out.

Wahlman couldn't prove that he'd been captured and held against his will, and there was no physical evidence that any harm had been done to him. He'd watched the fancy little spy car explode from fifty feet in the air, and then he'd floated safely to the grassy area that ran parallel to the shoulder along Highway 30. He'd hiked through the woods and had waited until dark and had paid a rather inebriated fishing boat captain to take him back across the bay. He was fortunate that he'd made it off the island alive, but now all he could think about was going back. He needed more details about what the Army was doing out there, and he needed documentation. Then maybe the media would listen. Maybe they would believe that someone was trying to kill him.

Wahlman knew what he needed to do, but he was getting low on cash and he didn't have a car anymore and the security at the research facility was going to be even more insane now than it had been to start with. So maybe it would be best to just disappear for a while. Maybe hang out in Norfolk for a month or so. Find some sort of work, save some money, take some time to think about how to proceed. Take some time to regroup, keeping in mind that none of this was over yet, that even if Dorland was out of the picture now, someone would be assigned to take his place.

21

General Foss steered into the gravel driveway that ran alongside the cabin, veered off onto the pine needles and parked beside the boxy little hatchback that Colonel Dorland had been issued for his drive back to Tennessee, a no-frills temporary replacement for the ultra-high-tech multimillion-dollar vehicle he had destroyed. Foss climbed out of his SUV, walked around to the back of the cabin and joined Dorland on the deck. Dorland was sitting in a folding chair, staring out at the valley below. There was an orthopedic brace strapped to his left leg and a pair of aluminum crutches leaning against the railing.

"There's a fresh pot of coffee in the kitchen," Dorland said.

"I can't stay. I just wanted to stop by and talk to you for a few minutes. In person. I figured I owed you that."

"Sir?"

"There's a helicopter waiting for me in Nashville. I have some business to take care of in Washington."

"There's a meat and cheese tray in the refrigerator. Case of beer. I thought—"

"I'm relieving you of your command," Foss said. "You are to vacate the premises immediately, and you are to report to the Senior Officer Processing Station in Memphis no later than midnight tonight."

"You're sending me to SOPS?"

"You're off my team. I need people I can trust. You're no longer one of those people."

"General, please. Things just got out of hand for a while. There's no reason we can't—"

"I have nothing else to say to you."

Dorland took a deep breath.

"I'll need some time to pack my things," he said.

"Your uniforms and other personal items will be boxed and shipped to Memphis first thing in the morning. The only thing you need to do right now is to get in your car and drive."

"What about our business venture? I have a lot of time and money invested in—"

"You'll be reimbursed. We're going to need for you to sign some non-disclosure agreements. I'm sending a man to SOPS to talk to you about all that. He should be there tomorrow."

Dorland reached up and grabbed the deck railing, pulled himself to a standing position.

"All I can say is that I'm sorry," he said.

"Get out of my sight," Foss said.

Colonel Dorland grabbed the crutches and positioned them under his arms and crossed the deck. He turned and saluted, and then he walked through the cabin and exited through the front door.

General Foss pulled his cell phone out of his pocket and pressed the *SEND* button on a text message he'd composed earlier. He heard Dorland start the boxy little hatchback, and he heard the sound of rubber on gravel as he backed out of the driveway. And that was all he heard. He didn't hear Dorland skidding to a stop when he got to the roadblock a mile or so down the mountain, and he didn't hear Dorland shout and scream as he was being dragged out of his vehicle and forced to walk into the woods. He didn't hear any of that, and he certainly didn't hear the gunshot that drove a bullet into Dorland's brain, because the lieutenant he'd sent the message to—a promising young deep encryption expert named Driessman—always used a sound suppressor on these types of occasions.

END GAME

THE REACHER EXPERIMENT BOOK 7

1

"My name is Rock Wahlman. In exactly thirty-seven minutes and twenty-nine seconds, I'm going to die."

37:28…

37:27…

37.26…

Wahlman was talking out loud, hoping that the security cameras in the room were still functioning, hoping that the audio would end up on a remote mainframe somewhere, hoping that someone would eventually hear the story he was about to tell.

For reasons that weren't quite clear, the two-star general in charge of an ultra-clandestine intelligence command had decided to destroy the research facility run by the same command—the building that some of the military staffers casually referred to as The Box—where human genetic engineering trials and other medical experiments had been taking place for several years. The doctors and nurses and technicians had been cleared out and the demolition crew had arrived and the stainless steel table Wahlman was tied to had been moved from the medical supply room to a room closer to the center of the basement.

Now, in a matter of minutes, the carefully-placed charges would explode and gravity would bring tons of concrete and glass and wood and metal directly down to where Wahlman was lying. He would be reduced to molecules, and the molecules would be buried in the rubble.

No more Wahlman.

The scumbags who'd rigged the explosives had set a timer for one hour—enough of a window to haul ass and distance themselves from the lung-popping percussive wave sure to be generated by the blast. They'd placed a laptop computer on a wooden chair and had positioned the chair a few feet to the left of Wahlman's table, the digital countdown displayed prominently on an otherwise blank screen, presumably to make Wahlman's final moments on the planet as anxiety-ridden as possible.

"We hope you've enjoyed your stay," one of the sweaty little punks had said, laughing maniacally as he'd exited the room.

Wahlman had not enjoyed his stay. Not even a little bit. He wished that he'd never come back to the facility. He wished that he'd given it more thought. Maybe there could have been another way to accomplish what he'd wanted to accomplish, another way to find out exactly what was going on and gather enough evidence to put a stop to it.

After he'd escaped from the facility the first time, Wahlman had spent a couple of nights in a hotel on the outskirts of Myrtle Beach, and then he'd hitched a ride to

Norfolk and had shown up on the doorstep of an old friend, a guy named Joe Balinger who'd been a fellow Master-At-Arms in the Navy.

"Where's your car?" Joe said. "Did you walk here?"

"I hitchhiked most of the way," Wahlman said.

Joe lived in a nice house in a nice subdivision. Wahlman knew from corresponding with him over the years that he'd started his own security firm after retiring from the Navy, and that he had twenty or so guys working for him now.

Joe was doing okay. More than okay. He was doing great.

He motioned for Wahlman to come on in. Wahlman stepped over the threshold, into the foyer, which was decorated with framed artwork—paintings that looked like they belonged in a museum that specialized in the macabre. The largest of the bunch, a nightmarish scene of a man with a whip and a whistle being torn to shreds by the lion he was supposed to be taming, actually sent a chill down Wahlman's spine, even after all of the real-life horrors he'd experienced recently.

"Kind of takes your breath away, doesn't it?" Joe said.

"Kind of," Wahlman said.

He stared at the painting some more. It was horrible to look at, yet hard to turn away from.

"Chalk one up for the animals," Joe said.

"Where did you get these things?" Wahlman said.

"I got that one in Brazil. You want a beer or something?"

"I was hoping I might be able to stay here for a few days," Wahlman said.

"Okay. You want a beer or something?"

"Sounds good. Mind if I take a quick shower first?"

Wahlman took a shower, and then he joined Joe on the brick patio at the back of the house. A white vinyl privacy fence surrounded the yard, which was probably about a quarter of an acre and needed to be mowed. There was a cooler full of ice and beer out there on the patio and a barbecue grill and some potted plants and a glass-top table with an umbrella and four chairs.

Wahlman pulled a bottle of beer out of the cooler and sat at the table across from Joe.

"Been a while since I've heard from you," Joe said. "What brings you to Norfolk?"

"There has to be a reason?" Wahlman said.

"You know you're welcome any time. But honestly, you don't look so great. How many pounds have you dropped since last time I saw you? Ten? Twenty?"

"More like thirty," Wahlman said.

"So what's going on?"

"Do you really want to know?"

Joe took a long pull from his bottle.

"I don't know," he said. "Do I?"

Wahlman shrugged. "Actually, I'd originally planned to see if you could help me gather some information on a certain colonel in the United States Army," he said. "Some information that I hadn't been able to gather myself."

Joe gazed out at his weedy lawn for a few seconds, and then he reached into the cooler and pulled out two more bottles of beer.

"Maybe you should start from the beginning," he said.

Wahlman told him about the letter that had lured him to New Orleans last October, about witnessing a semi-truck crashing into a canal, about trying to rescue the driver—a man named Darrell Renfro who, as it turned out, looked exactly like Wahlman. He told him about the subsequent events that led to the confirmation that he and Renfro had been cloned from cells taken from a former Army officer named Jack Reacher over a hundred years ago. He told him about the attempts on his life and about the New Orleans homicide detective named Collins and about the warrant for his arrest that was still active and about the online wanted posters and the reward money for capturing him dead or alive. He told him about the private investigator named Feldman, and about the bounty hunter named Decker. He told him about falling in love with Kasey Stielson and about ultimately losing her, and he told him about the elderly hitchhiker named Rusty and about infiltrating the secret research facility off the coast of South Carolina.

"I ended up running into the officer I'd been looking for," Wahlman said. "I forced him to help me escape from the facility."

"Where is he now?" Joe asked.

"I'm pretty sure he's dead," Wahlman said.

"Care to elaborate?"

Wahlman told him about the little joyride he'd taken with Colonel Dorland.

"Not that it's going to make any difference," Wahlman said. "They'll just assign someone else to my case. I need to go back."

"To the research facility?"

"I need details. Documentation."

"What do you know so far?"

"Only what Dorland told me. According to him, the Army's current project is being funded by a group of billionaires, investors who are under the impression that the first human clone in the history of the world is going to be produced there at that facility. But that's not the truth. Darrell Renfro and I were the first human clones in the history of the world. We were the first, and that's why we were targeted. That's why our files were erased, and that's why hits were put out on us—because the senior military officers in charge of the current project were afraid that the billionaires would take a hike if they found out about us."

"That's a pretty remarkable story," Joe said. "Seems like the media would be all over it."

"Like stink on shit," Wahlman said. "Except I don't have any proof. Right now it's going to be my word against the military's. Retired Senior Chief Petty Officer Rock Wahlman against the United States Army. Guess who's going to come out on top."

"The Army."

"Correct. And guess whose ass is going to be left flapping in the breeze."

"Yours."

"Exactly. Once I go public, I won't last a day without some kind of protective custody."

"So what's the plan?" Joe said.

"I'm not sure yet," Wahlman said. "I need to find out

exactly what's going on there at the facility. They want to be known for producing the first human clone, but there's more to it than that. Rusty was dying, and he was going there for some kind of treatment. He said that the Army was going to give him a new heart and a new liver and a new pair of lungs. But not with ordinary transplants. Something different. Something new. He wouldn't go into it, but I'm wondering if the Army is planning to produce clones for the purpose of harvesting their organs."

"I doubt it," Joe said. "Ethical concerns aside, I just don't see how it would work. If you need a new heart, you need it now. Not ten years from now. Or twenty. Or however long it would take."

"Yeah. So I don't know."

Joe pulled two more beers out of the cooler.

"Is there anything I can do to help?" he said.

"Maybe," Wahlman said. "Do you still have that admiral's uniform you confiscated in Okinawa that time?"

2

Joe still had the uniform. It was in a closet in one of his spare bedrooms, covered in plastic. If Wahlman had been at his normal weight, he never would have been able to get into it.

But Wahlman was not at his normal weight. He'd lost thirty pounds.

The admiral that the uniform had belonged to was a tall and lanky Academy man named Swanson. He'd developed a serious gambling problem while stationed overseas, and he'd started taking kickbacks from a company that exported canned tuna from Japan to the United States. In exchange for a certain number of dollars, the admiral allowed the company to load a certain number of crates onto a certain number of military transport planes headed for San Francisco. The company saved a bundle on shipping charges, and the admiral collected a tidy sum to help feed his blackjack habit. Everybody happy, until a surprise inspection revealed that a number of the crates contained handguns instead of tuna. A major investigation followed, and one of the company executives flipped, and Admiral

Swanson was arrested and flown to San Diego to be court martialed. Two Master-At-Arms petty officers—Rock Wahlman and Joe Balinger—had been assigned to sort and catalog the admiral's personal belongings and move them from the house he'd been renting in town to a storage unit on the base, where in all likelihood they would remain for decades. Knowing that—and knowing that the admiral probably wouldn't be an admiral much longer anyway—Joe had tossed one of the dress uniforms onto the discard pile and had kept it for a souvenir.

A souvenir that just happened to fit a somewhat-emaciated Rock Wahlman perfectly.

"Looks good on you," Joe said. "You're not really thinking about—"

"Why not?" Wahlman said. "It's not like I have a lot to lose at this point."

"I just don't see how you could get away with it."

"Got any better ideas?"

"Yeah. Let's go drink some more beer."

Joe exited the room. Wahlman took the uniform off, draped the plastic over it and hung it in the closet. He slipped back into his grungy road clothes, knowing that Joe would have offered him something clean to wear if they had been anywhere near the same size. Joe was about a foot shorter than Wahlman, and he'd always been fond of things like beer and fried chicken and apple cobbler. He'd been a frequent member of what some of the sailors joking called the Fat Boy Club—the early-morning workout sessions you had to attend if you flunked a routine physical fitness test—

and he was probably a little chubbier now than he'd been back then.

On his way out of the bedroom, Wahlman noticed a picture of a woman on Joe's dresser. She was very beautiful. Dark hair, eyes as warm as cinnamon toast. He picked up the photograph and looked at it, and then he walked back out to the patio.

There was a fresh beer waiting for him on the table. He took a sip, slid into the same chair he'd been sitting in earlier.

"I could go out there on Saturday," he said.

"Out where?" Joe said.

"To the research facility. You know how it is at places like that on the weekends. Quiet. Laidback. Duty staff only, everyone wishing they were out fishing or playing tennis or doing whatever it is they like to do."

"Duty staff or not, they're not going to let you just waltz on in and take over," Joe said. "I don't care what kind of uniform you're wearing."

"We'll need to draft a fake set of orders," Wahlman said.

"We?"

"And of course I'll need a driver."

Joe picked at the label on his beer bottle.

"I don't think I can afford to get involved," he said. "I recently got engaged to be married, and—"

"I saw her picture on the dresser," Wahlman said. "She's very pretty."

"She's also very pregnant. We were planning on getting married anyway, but the baby puts a whole new spin on things."

"Congratulations," Wahlman said.

"Thanks."

"Is it still okay if I stay here for a few days?"

Joe didn't say anything. He picked at his label and chewed on his lower lip. He'd obviously given it some thought, and he'd obviously decided to withdraw his offer to help Wahlman with his problems. Which was understandable. Wahlman's problems were big problems. Life and death problems. Joe had always been a good friend, but every good friend has his or her limits. Apparently the notion of aiding and abetting a fugitive from justice in his quest to infiltrate a secret government research facility by impersonating a senior Naval officer had set off some sort of alarm in Joe's soon-to-be-a-family-man consciousness.

And that was okay. Wahlman had become accustomed to doing everything alone. He would get through this, somehow.

Those had been his thoughts as he drained the last few ounces of beer from a sweaty green bottle out there on Joe's patio.

But now, as he watched the seconds tick off the timer, he wasn't so sure.

3

Joe had given Wahlman the admiral's uniform, along with a set of summer whites with E-6 patches sewn onto the sleeves, and he'd loaned him some money, enough to rent a car and a hotel room for a few days.

Wahlman had chosen a generic-looking four-door sedan, a black one that closely resembled some of the official government vehicles he'd seen at the research facility, and he'd driven it back down to the Myrtle Beach area and had checked into the same place he'd stayed at previously. He used one of the desktop computers in the lobby to create a fake set of orders for the fake flag officer he was planning to become, knowing that the paperwork wouldn't pass any sort of rigorous inspection process and pretty much betting his life that it wouldn't have to. He bought some dark brown hair dye at a nearby pharmacy and a dark brown mustache at a nearby costume shop, and he bought an audio recording device about the size of a quarter at a nearby electronics store.

Now all he needed was a driver.

It was a crucial part of the plan, because generals and admirals never drove themselves anywhere. They always had a personal assistant assigned to them, an E-4 or an E-5 or an E-6 who served as a chauffeur and a secretary and a baggage handler and an errand runner. Skate duty, as long as the officer you were assigned to wasn't an asshole.

Wahlman got up early Saturday morning and drove to an employment agency that specialized in daily work for daily pay. The place wasn't scheduled to open for another hour, but there were already a hundred or so men and women standing in line. Wahlman parked his car and climbed out and walked forward from the back of the queue, searching for male candidates between the ages of twenty-five and thirty-five who could fit into Joe Balinger's old petty officer first class uniform and who weren't exhibiting any major withdrawal symptoms from whatever substance they were trying to earn enough money to purchase after work.

A tweaker who could have posed for one of the ghastly paintings in Joe's foyer shouted for Wahlman to get his ass to the back of the line.

"I'm not here to work," Wahlman said. "I'm here to hire."

"What kind of job?" the tweaker said.

"The kind you're not qualified for."

Wahlman kept walking. A few seconds later, he felt a tap on his right shoulder.

It was the tweaker.

"How do you know what I'm not qualified for?" the guy said.

His breath smelled horrible. Like a rat that had drowned in a urinal. A week ago.

"Get lost," Wahlman said.

"Give me five bucks and I'll leave you alone."

"I'm not giving you shit."

"Then I'm not leaving you alone."

Wahlman kept walking. The tweaker followed.

"You should get back in line," Wahlman said.

"I already lost my place now," the tweaker said.

"Not my problem."

"It's going to be your problem when I slap you upside your head."

Wahlman laughed. He reached into his pocket and pulled out a five dollar bill.

"Here you go," he said. "Take the day off."

The tweaker grabbed the money and scurried away like a squirrel with a peanut.

A guy with a three-day beard and a belly the size of a watermelon stepped over and took his place.

"I heard you're hiring," the guy said.

Wahlman looked him over. He was the right size, but that was about all he had going for him. Long stringy hair, flip-flops, crimson roadmaps for eyes.

"You got a driver's license?" Wahlman said.

"Yes."

"I'm only going to need you for one day."

"That's fine."

"Hundred bucks."

"That's fine."

"It's going to be a long day."

The guy clawed at the stubble on his chin.

"Most of the outfits that hire through the agency do half days on Saturdays," he said.

"If that's what you're looking for, then you need to keep looking," Wahlman said.

"How long you plan on working?"

"As long as it takes."

The guy shrugged.

"Okay," he said.

"I'll need you to get a haircut," Wahlman said. "And a shave."

"I don't have any money," the guy said.

"I'll take it out of your pay," Wahlman said.

The guy shrugged again. Said okay again.

Wahlman checked the guy's driver's license. His name was Donald Puhler. The address on the license was a rooming house not far from the employment agency. Puhler admitted that he didn't live there anymore. He said that he didn't live anywhere anymore.

Wahlman took him to a barbershop, waited in the parking lot until the place was supposed to open for business, and then waited twenty more minutes until the place actually did open for business. There were two barber's chairs, but there was only one barber on duty, a guy in his late twenties or early thirties who'd spent a great amount of time in gymnasiums and tattoo parlors. His nametag said Nate. He smiled and told Wahlman and Puhler good morning and said that he would be right with them.

"Just need to get everything set up real quick," he said.

Wahlman nodded, leaned against the doorjamb and folded his arms across his chest.

Puhler walked over to one the wooden benches against the wall and grabbed a magazine. He thumbed through the slick pages for a couple of minutes, and then he stood and gazed through the barbershop's plate glass window. There was a bakery across the street and a television repair shop and a furniture store. Wahlman figured Puhler was looking at the bakery.

"We'll get some breakfast when we leave here," Wahlman said.

"Sounds good," Puhler said.

Nate opened the safe behind the counter, pulled out a cash drawer and slid it into the computerized register. He pushed some buttons and the drawer popped back open and he counted the money and pushed some more buttons and ran a report tape and jammed the drawer back into its slot. The entire process took about ten minutes.

In a perfect world, the guy responsible for opening a place up for the day would arrive thirty minutes prior to the posted opening time and would promptly take care of everything that needed to be taken care of. It was the way Wahlman would have handled it if he had been a barber. Or a baker. Or a TV repairman. It was the Navy way. It was Wahlman's way. No other way made sense. Maybe there weren't usually any customers in the shop that early. Maybe that was the reason Nate had become such a lazy shitbird slacker. Or maybe it was just the opposite. Maybe Nate had been a lazy shitbird slacker all along and there weren't any customers in the shop that early because everyone knew what a lazy shitbird slacker he was. He finally finished with the register and grabbed a white cape with little blue sailboats on it from an overhead cabinet and stepped over to the barber's chair closest to the entrance.

"All set," he said.

Puhler climbed into the chair. Nate draped the cape around him, tilted him back to the sink and gave him a quick shampoo and rinse. He patted him dry with a towel and asked him what kind of cut he wanted.

"It needs to be short enough to pass a military inspection," Wahlman said. "And give him a shave, too."

"I don't do that," Nate said.

"You don't do what?" Wahlman said.

"Shaves."

Wahlman glanced up at the painted wooden sign mounted to the wall behind the register. The sign listed the services provided by the shop, the different types of haircuts and beard trims you could get, along with the prices the shop charged for each service.

The word *SHAVE* was at the bottom of the list.

Wahlman pointed toward the sign.

"It says right there that you—"

"Some of the guys who work here do shaves," Nate said. "I'm not one of them."

"What time will the guys who'll do what the sign says they'll do be here?" Wahlman said.

"About an hour from now. You want to wait?"

"No. You can either give the man in your chair a shave, or we're going to walk out of here and never come back."

"Are you his dad or something?" Nate said. "Why can't he—"

"I'm his boss," Wahlman said. "And right now I'm your boss too. Give him a shave."

Nate laughed. He tapped Puhler on the shoulder.

"What kind of haircut do you want?" he said.

Wahlman walked over and grabbed the cape and pulled it off of Puhler.

"Let's go," Wahlman said.

Puhler climbed out of the chair.

"You still owe me for a haircut," Nate said.

"How do you figure that?" Wahlman said.

"I already shampooed him. I could have been halfway through with the cut by now if you hadn't started—"

"Let's go," Wahlman said again.

He turned and headed toward the door. Puhler followed.

Nate stepped over and grabbed Puhler by the arm.

"Somebody needs to pay me," Nate said.

Wahlman wrapped his hand around Nate's wrist.

Twisted it counterclockwise.

Heard it snap.

Nate screamed. It was a high-pitched wail, incongruent with the manly physique and body art. He started stomping around the shop, whimpering, cupping the wounded joint with the hand that still functioned, the expression on his face a combination of disbelief and agony.

There was a phone by the register. Nate staggered over

there and reached for the receiver, but Wahlman beat him to it.

"I don't have time for this shit," Wahlman said.

He clocked Nate with the cordless handset, just above the right ear. Nate collapsed to the floor, banging his chin on the counter on the way down.

Puhler was still standing by the door.

"Now what?" he said.

"Get back in the chair," Wahlman said. "I'll cut your hair myself."

4

Wahlman gave Puhler a crewcut with a set of clippers, and he gave him a shave with a straight razor. He only cut him twice. Used an alum block from one of the drawers behind the chair to help stop the bleeding.

A customer walked into the shop, turned around and walked back out.

Probably unimpressed with Wahlman's skills.

Nate was still unconscious behind the counter when Wahlman and Puhler left the shop.

It was almost ten by the time they made it to the hotel.

"Take a shower, and then put those on," Wahlman said, pointing toward the set of summer whites on the bed.

"You want me to dress up like a Navy guy?" Puhler said.

"Right."

"Isn't that illegal?"

"Yes."

Puhler clawed at his chin. It was smooth now. No more stubble. One of the little cuts started bleeding again.

"I don't want to do anything that might get me in

trouble," Puhler said. "Not for a hundred bucks."

"How about two hundred?" Wahlman said.

"How about two-fifty?"

"Okay."

Puhler walked to the bathroom and closed the door. A few seconds later, the shower started running.

Wahlman stripped naked and secured the little disc-shaped audio recorder between his butt cheeks with a piece of tape, and then he put the admiral's uniform on. Once the recorder was switched on, it would only run for about an hour before the battery went dead, so Wahlman left it off for now. It would be there when he needed it.

Puhler was in the shower for a long time. He actually started singing at one point. Wahlman recognized the tune. It was an old country and western line dance song. Puhler was really belting it out. Wahlman hoped he was better at driving than he was at singing.

Wahlman had been thinking about Kasey Stielson. He'd been thinking about her a lot. He'd never stopped loving her. He had no idea where she was now, but he still had the password to their old *Message Moi* account. *Message Moi* was a free voicemail service for people who didn't have phones or who didn't want to give out their numbers for one reason or another. The password to the account was in Wahlman's wallet. He'd written it down on a strip of paper. He wanted to tell Kasey how he felt about everything before leaving for the research facility, knowing that it might be his last chance. Knowing that he might not make it out of the facility alive this time.

He sat on the bed by the nightstand and punched the toll-free number into the room phone and entered the password and spent the next few minutes pouring his heart out.

Of course it was possible that Kasey would never receive the message. It was possible that she would never log into the *Message Moi* account again for as long as she lived. Wahlman hoped that she would, but there was nothing he could do to make it happen.

Puhler finally came out of the shower and put the E-6 uniform on.

"The shoes don't fit," he said. "They're way too small."

"Wear your flip-flops," Wahlman said. "Nobody's going to see your feet anyway."

"What exactly is it that we're going to be doing?"

"All you have to do is drive. I'll be getting out of the car for a while, and you'll be waiting for me in a parking lot."

"That's it?"

"Basically. If I think of anything else, I'll tell you on the way."

They took the ferry over to the island, stayed in the car the whole time. Wahlman didn't want to walk around on the observation deck where people could see him. The uniform he was wearing was a major head turner. Uniforms tended to attract attention anyway, but an admiral's uniform tended to attract it exponentially. The gold stars, the power they represented. It was something most people just didn't see every day. Puhler stayed in the driver seat, alone in front like a chauffeur, and Wahlman stayed directly behind him, shielded from casual view by Puhler himself and by the car's tinted windows.

When they disembarked from the ferry, Wahlman gave Puhler directions to Highway 30, and then he showed him the discreet turnoff that led to the research facility.

Puhler pulled to the side of the highway and braked to a stop before steering into the tunnel of dense foliage.

"You think they'll just wave us on in?" he said.

Wahlman handed him the fake set of orders he'd printed.

"Give these to the guy at the gate," he said. "Most sentries aren't going to give an admiral a hard time. Most sentries are going to be nervous, fearful that their lives will be ruined if they don't salute crisply enough and say *sir* enthusiastically enough."

"What if this particular sentry starts asking a bunch of questions?" Puhler said.

"I'll climb out of the car and make him wish he hadn't," Wahlman said.

Puhler nodded. He slid the shifter into gear and headed into the tunnel.

5

Kasey Stielson slid the glass door open and walked outside. She sat in one of the cushioned deck chairs and stared out at the vast Virginia wilderness that had become her back yard. The family would be safe here, her father had told her. Only a handful of people knew about this place, he'd said. Totally off the grid.

So far, so good. Nobody had shown up looking for Rock Wahlman. No private investigators or bounty hunters or professional assassins. This had been a safe place, just as her father had said it would be, and Kasey wanted to make sure it continued to be a safe place. For her, and for her parents, and especially for her fifteen-year-old daughter, Natalie, who'd originally considered the situation a grand adventure, but whose attitude toward it had been steadily deteriorating over the past few weeks.

Understandable for a girl that age, but still a bit trying at times.

The conversations had become somewhat typical.

"When can we go home?" Natalie had said, yesterday afternoon.

"I don't know," Kasey had said.

"I miss my friends."

"I know you do."

"It's not fair."

"You're right. It's not."

"Can't I at least have my phone back?"

"Maybe in a few days."

"You always say that!"

And so on and so forth. Round and round, on a daily basis.

There was one functional cell phone in the house, to be used for emergencies only. Kasey had been following that particular rule for the most part, although lately she'd been checking the *Message Moi* account she and Rock had set up, knowing that she shouldn't be using the phone on a regular basis but doing it anyway.

Doing it once a day, every day, out there on the deck where she was sitting now.

Because while Natalie was the most important person in her life, and while nothing would ever change that, she had to admit that she missed Rock.

Severely.

She'd been thinking about him lately.

She'd been thinking about him a lot.

And the reasons weren't altogether personal. If he had somehow managed to resolve his problems with the Army, it was something she needed to know about. And if the New Orleans Police Department had caught up to him and had taken him into custody, she needed to know about that too.

She needed to know what was going on so that she and Natalie and Dean and Betsy really could go home and resume some sort of normal existence.

Kasey's parents had occasionally mentioned the possibility that Rock had been killed, but Kasey refused to give that sort of talk any credence. She somehow knew that he was still alive, still out there somewhere.

She picked up the phone and punched in the number and entered the password and waited for the robotic attendant to tell her what it always told her, that she didn't have any new messages.

Only this time it didn't tell her that.

This time, it told her that she did have a new message.

Her heart skipped a beat, and a few seconds later she heard the voice she'd been longing to hear.

6

The guard at the gate stepped up to the car and motioned for Puhler to roll the window down.

"Show him the papers," Wahlman said. "Try to look confident. Try to say as little as possible."

Puhler rolled down the window.

"This is a restricted area," the guard said. "Authorized personnel only."

Puhler didn't say anything. He handed the guy the orders. The guy glanced down at the first page, and then he leaned in and glanced into the back seat. His eyes got big and he popped to attention and saluted, as if some sort of switch had been thrown.

Wahlman returned the salute from inside the car.

The guard opened the gate, and Puhler drove through and steered around to the back of the building.

"Told you he'd be nervous," Wahlman said.

"I'm nervous too," Puhler said.

"There's a portal to the PTS inside that shack over there," Wahlman said. "I'm going to get out of the car and use it to get inside the building. I might be a while."

"PTS?"

"Pneumatic transport system."

"How long will you be gone?"

"I don't know."

"What if they find out you're not really an admiral?"

"They'll take me into custody."

"Right. And I'm just supposed to sit here and—"

"They won't find out," Wahlman said.

Puhler dabbed at the sweat on his forehead with a paper napkin he'd saved from breakfast.

"If they take you into custody, they'll probably take me into custody too," he said.

"Probably," Wahlman said.

"I don't remember that being part of the deal."

"Give me two hours," Wahlman said. "If I'm not back by then—"

"What about my pay?"

"It's in a drawer, back at the hotel. There's a room key in the glove compartment."

"So what's stopping me from hauling ass as soon as you get out of the car?"

"You don't want to do that," Wahlman said.

"Why not?" Puhler said.

"Because, if you do, it means that you're betting against me making it in and out of the facility in a smooth and timely manner. Which, of course, is what I intend to do. If I come out here within the next two hours and see that you've left me stranded, I will hunt you down and rip your throat out with my bare hands."

Puhler dabbed at the sweat on his forehead some more.

"All right," he said. "Two hours."

Wahlman figured that if he wasn't back in two hours that he would probably be dead. But there was no point in letting Puhler in on that particular tidbit. No point in making him more nervous than he already was.

Wahlman climbed out of the car and walked over to the shack. There was a United States Navy Master-At-Arms sitting at the desk, drinking coffee and reading a paperback novel. He nearly fell out of his chair when Wahlman opened the door and stepped over the threshold.

"Attention on deck!" the guard shouted.

It was an automatic reaction, drilled into him since his first day at boot camp. Kind of ridiculous under the circumstances, considering he was the only person attending the shack.

He stood erect and looked straight ahead. Thumbs lined up along the seams of his pants, shoes at a forty-five degree angle.

"At ease," Wahlman said.

The guard relaxed his stance. He was probably around twenty-five years old. Blond hair, blue eyes, freckles on his cheeks. His uniform was slightly faded, but the patches on his sleeves looked brand new. Which told Wahlman that he'd just recently gotten his crow—his promotion from seaman to petty officer third class. His nametag said Hurkley.

"How may I assist you, sir?" he said.

"The general's meeting me here later," Wahlman said. "In the meantime, he wants me to familiarize myself with the facility and get a breakdown on the research that's being conducted."

"General Foss is coming here? Today?"

"It's a surprise inspection," Wahlman said. "So don't tell anyone."

"I won't, sir."

"Do you know how to operate the PTS?"

"Yes, sir. But—"

"Take me inside. Then I'll need someone with the right kind of clearance to show me around and explain the procedures that are being performed here."

"Dr. Walker is here today," Hurkley said. "She would be the person for you to talk to."

"Great. Take me to her."

"I'm not supposed to leave my post, sir. We're a little short-staffed today, so I'll need to call the security office and—"

"Just get me inside and show me the way to Dr. Walker's office," Wahlman said. "It'll only take a few minutes."

Hurkley raked his hair back with his fingers. Tensely. Nervously. There was a senior military officer standing three feet in front of him, ordering him to abandon his post. Ordering him to do something he'd been taught never to do, no matter what. It was a true dilemma, and Wahlman knew that it could go either way. Hurkley could either disregard military protocol and potentially face severe consequences somewhere down the line, or he could disobey a direct order and assuredly face severe consequences right now.

He stood there thinking it over.

Wahlman figured he would obey the order. He was counting on it. Because once you really thought it through, obeying the order was the only logical course of action. It was the only way to maybe not get in trouble at all. It wasn't likely that any sort of security issue would come up while Hurkley was gone. It wasn't likely that anyone would ever know. Especially on a Saturday.

"Sir, I'll be happy to escort you to the portal closest to Dr. Walker's office," Hurkley said. "Should I call and let her know that you're on your way."

"That won't be necessary," Wahlman said. "We want it to be a surprise. Remember?"

"Yes, sir. A surprise."

"And I'll need for you to come and get me when I'm finished."

"Yes, sir. I'll write down the number to the phone here in the shack, and you can call me as soon as you're ready to exit the facility."

Hurkley tore a strip of paper from a notepad he'd been doodling on, wrote down the number and handed it to Wahlman. He helped Wahlman into the transport capsule, and a few seconds later they were on their way.

7

The door to Dr. Walker's office was open. She was sitting at a desk, staring at a computer screen. She wore a white lab coat with her name embroidered over the pocket and a white blouse with tiny blue and red polka dots on it and a wristwatch with a black leather band. Dark brown hair, shoulder length, with a few strands of gray on top, just enough to let people know that she was forty-something and proud of it. Maybe she would start having it dyed in a few years. Maybe not. She certainly didn't need to. She was very attractive, and she was going to remain attractive, in Wahlman's opinion, no matter what happened with her hair.

She wasn't wearing a uniform under the lab coat, which meant that she was probably a civilian. Which meant that she wasn't going to be nearly as intimidated by the stars on Wahlman's sleeves as Hurkley and the guard at the gate had been.

Wahlman slid his hand into the back of his pants and switched on the audio recorder. Dr. Walker glanced up from her monitor screen as he stepped into the office.

"May I help you?" she said.

"Hello," Wahlman said. "I'm Admiral Callahan. Naval Intelligence. I know you weren't expecting me, but—"

"Please, come in. Have a seat."

Wahlman stepped forward, sat in the steel and vinyl chair at the side of the desk. He told Dr. Walker the same set of lies that he'd told Hurkley.

"I thought you might be able to show me around before General Foss gets here," he said.

"I'm just curious as to why he chose to do this on a Saturday."

"I'm sure he has his reasons."

"Right. Well, I was just finishing up with some research statistics, and I was planning on going home after that. My granddaughter has a soccer game this afternoon, and—"

"Granddaughter?" Wahlman said. "You're kidding. You don't look nearly old enough."

"Thank you. I have two already, a boy and a girl. Would you like to see some pictures?"

"I would love to," Wahlman said.

He scooted closer to where Dr. Walker was sitting, and she showed him some photographs on the computer. Wahlman went on about what lovely children they were, and how much the little girl looked like her grandmother.

"I suppose I could miss her game this one time," Dr. Walker said.

"All I need is a quick tour," Wahlman said. "Maybe you can show me around and still make it out to watch her play."

Dr. Walker nodded. She closed out the work she'd been doing on her computer, and then she led Wahlman out of the office and down the hall to an elevator. She pressed a button with a picture of an arrow pointing upward on it, and the stainless steel door slid open immediately. Wahlman followed her into the compartment. It was big enough for the two of them, but just barely. Their arms touched when they turned around and faced the door.

"How much do you already know about the work we're doing here?" Dr. Walker asked, pressing the button for the fourth floor.

"I know you're conducting experiments that involve genetic engineering," Wahlman said. "I know you're attempting to produce the world's first human clone."

"That's really just the tip of the iceberg," Dr. Walker said. "In fact, we already have several mature clones. That was the easy part."

The elevator reached its destination. The door opened, and Wahlman followed Dr. Walker out into the hallway. She led him through a confusing maze of corridors, and finally to a solid steel door guarded by a keypad and a fingerprint scanner.

"Where are we?" Wahlman said.

"This is the main laboratory. You're going to see some things in here that very few people have ever seen. If you're the least bit squeamish—"

"I'm not," Wahlman said.

"Have you ever witnessed a surgical procedure or an autopsy?"

"Yes."

"Okay. You should be fine."

She punched some numbers into the keypad, and then she pressed her right index finger against the scanner. The door opened automatically. Inside, there was an anteroom with a desk and a computer and some cabinets and a couch. Dr. Walker used a key to unlock the wooden door at the far end of the room.

Wahlman followed her into the lab.

She switched on some lights.

The room was enormous. You could have played basketball in there. It reminded Wahlman of his high school biology lab, only ten times bigger. There were tables and stools and sinks and gas outlets. Beakers and burners and tubes and clamps. Microscopes, equipment bins, portable lights that looked like they belonged on a construction site.

A huge glass tank with partitions positioned vertically every three or four feet had been built into the wall on the left side of the room. Like an aquarium, only there weren't any fish swimming around in it. Instead, each section housed what appeared to be a well-preserved human cadaver. Adult males in their early twenties, suspended in a substance that resembled lime-flavored gelatin.

"Looks more like something you might expect to see at a medical school," Wahlman said, gesturing toward the tank.

"What do you mean?" Dr. Walker said.

"The bodies. You're planning to dissect them, right?"

"Why would we do that?"

"I just assumed that a tank full of dead people would be for—"

"They're not cadavers," Dr. Walker said. "Those are the clones. And they're very much alive."

8

Kasey had listened to the message dozens of times. She'd gone inside for a notebook and had transcribed it word for word. Rock had told her how much he loved her, and how much he missed her, and how sorry he was that it hadn't worked out. He'd told her how close he was to finding the answers he needed to find. He'd been to a secret military research facility on an island off the coast of South Carolina, and he was going back there today in an effort to obtain more details. More evidence. Enough to take to the media. Enough to break the story on the world stage. If he was successful, his problems could potentially be resolved in a matter of days. If he was not successful, it wasn't likely that he would make it off the island alive.

Which was why he'd wanted Kasey to know the alias he'd been using and the name of the hotel he'd been staying at. So that if he died, she could make an anonymous phone call and point the authorities in the right direction.

Of course all of that had depended on Kasey retrieving the voicemail in the first place. Which, Rock admitted, was a long shot. He could only hope that she would, and that the facts pertaining to his predicament would eventually be told.

Kasey called the hotel, hoping that he hadn't left the room yet, or that he'd gone and returned already, but there was no answer.

The back door swung open and Natalie stepped out onto the deck.

"Hi, Mom," she said.

"Hi."

"What are you doing?"

Kasey closed the notebook.

"Nothing," she said.

"I saw you using the phone."

"Maybe you just imagined it."

"It's not fair, Mom. Why do you get to use the phone and I don't?"

"Because I'm a grownup and you're a kid?"

"I'm fifteen."

"Like I said."

Natalie pulled a chair over and sat next to Kasey.

"Please, Mom. Just one phone call."

"You want the bad guys to find us?"

"I want my life back."

Natalie climbed out of the chair and started to walk away.

"Wait," Kasey said. "There's something I need to talk to you about. Serious business. Come here and sit back down."

"Are you going to let me use the phone?"

"No."

"Then I'm not going to sit back down."

"Fine. Stay where you are. Just listen to me for a minute, okay?"

Natalie folded her arms across her chest and leaned against the back door.

"I'm listening," she said.

"I've been using the phone to check for messages on a voicemail service," Kasey said.

"Messages from who?"

"Rock."

"I thought you were done with him."

"I still love him," Kasey said.

Natalie returned to the chair.

"He's been leaving messages for you?" she said.

"He left one today. This is the first time I've heard from him since I broke it off. It sounds like he's really close to getting to the bottom of all this."

"That's good, right?"

"Yes. But he's going somewhere today that might be very dangerous."

"He's done dangerous things before," Natalie said. "He can take care of himself."

"I know. And I know there's no point in worrying. But I can't help it. I feel like I should be there for him. I feel like he needs me right now."

"Then go."

"But you need me too."

"I'll be fine, Mom. It's not like I'm alone here. And it's not like I'm a little kid, either. Even though you seem to think I am."

"I'm still not sure if I'm going to go or not," Kasey said. "I'm going to have to think about it some more. And of course I'll need to talk it over with Mom and Dad."

"If you love him, you should go."

"Do you really think so?"

"Yes. But you should leave the phone here."

"Ah. An ulterior motive. Now I see how it is."

"I'm just joking, Mom."

Kasey smiled.

"I know you are, sweetheart," she said. "I know you are."

9

Wahlman stood there and stared into the glass tank.

"What do you mean they're alive?" he said.

"They're being kept in a hypometabolic state," Dr. Walker said. "We provide their nutrition and oxygenation parenterally."

"Why?"

"So they'll be ready for us when we need them."

"Need them for what?"

Dr. Walker stepped closer to the tank. She reached out and touched the glass with her fingertips.

"We were supposed to perform the first transplant last week," she said. "But the donor never showed up. We're still not sure what happened to him."

"So you're harvesting organs?" Wahlman said. "That's what this is all about?"

"No. Not at all. Are you familiar with the part of the brain called the right temporal lobe?"

"I'm not a scientist," Wahlman said. "My background is in law enforcement."

"The right temporal lobe is the center of self-awareness and autobiographical memory," Dr. Walker said. "It's basically the core essence of a person. It's what you are, what you've become over the course of your lifetime. All of your thoughts and experiences, wrapped up in a section of tissue that would fit in the palm of your hand. What we're hoping to accomplish is to transplant that center of self-awareness and autobiographical memory from one person to another—from the donor to the donor's genetic duplicate—thereby extending the lifespan of that particular individual by as much as a hundred percent."

"So you're basically going to be doing brain transplants," Wahlman said.

"You could think of it like that if you want to. But it's not really the entire brain. Just a little part of it."

"So you could take an old sick person and transfer his or her consciousness into a young healthy person?"

"Yes. In fact, the donor who was supposed to show up last week was very ill. His name was Rusty. We're thinking he must have died while he was traveling to get here, although we don't know that for sure yet. This is his clone over here."

Dr. Walker stepped to the right and pointed toward one of the creepy human figures suspended in green gelatin.

"That guy has to be at least twenty years old," Wahlman said, pointing toward Rusty's clone. "So you've been working on this for decades?"

"Believe it or not, the man you're looking at now was produced from a single cell six months ago," Dr. Walker said.

"How is that possible?"

"The accelerated growth medium. The AGM. It allows us to produce a full-grown specimen in months instead of years."

"The green stuff?" Wahlman said.

"Yes. Quite revolutionary. It's really the only reason any of this is possible. The technology to produce human clones has been around for a long time, and the theory behind temporal lobe transplantation has been around for a long time, but the AGM is what has allowed us to combine the two in a practical way."

"So when I get old, you could transfer all of my thoughts and memories into a younger version of myself?" Wahlman said.

"That's it in a nutshell," Dr. Walker said.

"Let's say it works," Wahlman said. "Let's say you do all that and I'm good to go for another fifty years or whatever. What's going to stop me from doing it again and again?"

"You can't do it again and again," Dr. Walker said. "You can only do it once."

"Why?"

"Because of the AGM. I don't want to bore you with a bunch of technical details, so let me just say that it does funny things to the immune system. Immediately after being removed from the tank, the clones become severely allergic to that particular chain of molecules. Once the transplant is completed, the clones can never go anywhere near the AGM again. If they do, they die. It's sort of a built-in safeguard against abusing the technology. Although, to be honest, it was entirely unintentional."

"What about some of the other ethical implications?" Wahlman said. "You're growing genetic duplicates in a laboratory. These are living, breathing human beings, right? You grew a young Rusty, and you were essentially planning to murder him so that the old Rusty could live longer. Murder is murder, right? How can anyone with a conscience agree to be part of that?"

"The AGM causes the right temporal lobe to shut down very early in the cloning process," Dr. Walker said. "The clones are basically brain dead until we perform the transplant. So taking them out of the tank and using them for our purposes is not like murder at all. More like pulling the plug on a comatose patient when there's absolutely no hope for recovery."

Wahlman didn't like that answer. What the Army was doing was wrong, in his opinion.

Very wrong.

"I'm assuming you're planning on taking the whole thing mainstream at some point," he said. "So you can make a bunch of money off of it."

"The investors should do well," Dr. Walker said. "We're still in the trial phases, of course, but if the procedure works, it'll be like getting a second chance at life. Who wouldn't sign up for that?"

It was an interesting question. If you could suddenly inhabit a younger and physically-stronger version of yourself while retaining all of your current knowledge and memories, would you do it? Would you really want to live through your twenties again? Your thirties? And so on.

Wahlman figured that most people would say yes. But he wondered if most people would learn anything from all of the mistakes they'd made along the way. He wondered if they would muff things up just as much the second time around.

"So when are you planning to put all of these theories to the test?" he said.

"Another donor is scheduled to arrive a week from Monday," Dr. Walker said. "His clone is the one on the very end over there. We've provided an escort for the donor this time, so there shouldn't be any issues getting him here. We're planning to perform the surgery a week from Tuesday."

Wahlman figured he had enough to take to the media now. There would be no surgery a week from Tuesday. Or ever. Or at least for a long time. Because by Monday it would be revealed that the first human clones in the history of the world were not produced at this facility, but instead were produced over forty years ago. They were given identities and bogus family histories and placed in orphanages and recently targeted for elimination to conceal the fact that they ever existed in the first place. The funding for the current project would dry up immediately. The case would be in the courts for years. Decades maybe. General Foss, and everyone else who'd been involved in the cover-up, would be arrested, and there wasn't a judge on the planet who would grant any of them any sort of bail in a case like this.

Which meant that Wahlman could go home. He could

start living like a normal person again. No more watching his back every second of every day. No more wondering which direction the next bullet was going to come from. He could even try to get back with Kasey.

A sense of elation washed over him. It all seemed too good to be true.

And it was.

Because as he turned to let Dr. Walker know that he needed to go out to his car for a minute, a uniformed soldier walked into the lab.

Army.

Private First Class.

There was a strip of surgical tape on the bridge of his nose and a semi-automatic pistol on his right hip.

His nametag said Bridges.

10

It was the guy Wahlman had questioned out in town last week.

The guy he'd ended up clobbering out on the street on the way back to his car.

PFC Bridges. His face was heavily bruised. He looked angry. Stressed. Like he'd been having a rough time lately. He pulled his pistol out of its holster, walked over to where Wahlman was standing and stared into his eyes.

Dr. Walker took a step toward Bridges. Aggressively, as if she wasn't the least bit concerned about the gun in his hand.

"This is a restricted area," she said. "You're not allowed to be here."

"This man's an imposter," Bridges said. "He's not an admiral. He's not even in the Navy."

"Pardon me?" Dr. Walker said.

"Put the gun away," Wahlman said. "That's an order."

Bridges didn't put the gun away.

"Last week he was pretending to be a senior chief," he

said. "He asked me a bunch of questions. Then he broke my nose when I wanted to see his military ID."

"This is outrageous," Wahlman said. "I've never seen this man before. He's obviously delusional. I would suggest that he be taken into custody and—"

Bridges reached up and ripped the fake mustache off of Wahlman's lip, taking a layer or two of skin along with it.

Dr. Walker's jaw dropped. She backed away from Wahlman and leaned against the glass tank as four more soldiers entered the lab. Two of them stood by with machineguns as Bridges and the other two forced Wahlman to the floor. They patted him down, took his wallet and some loose change and the key to his hotel room. They secured his arms and legs with cuffs and shackles and steel chains and pulled him off of the floor and led him to the elevator. A few minutes later, he was back in the same room he'd been in the first time he'd infiltrated the facility.

"Put him on the table," Bridges said. "No leather restraints this time. Use the cables."

The four guys Bridges seemed to be in charge of led Wahlman to a stainless steel table and forced him onto his back. They tightened the chains that connected the cuffs on his wrists to the shackles on his ankles, and then they looped some plastic-coated steel cables through some of the links and under the table, finally securing everything with a heavy-duty combination lock, the kind you might find on a gate or a toolshed.

"He won't get loose this time," one of the soldiers said.

"Give us the room," Bridges said.

The soldier nodded.

"We'll be out in the hallway if you need us," he said.

The four soldiers exited the room in a single file, the last one closing the door on his way out.

"What are you going to do now?" Wahlman said. "Rough me up? Kill me?"

"General Foss is on his way to the facility," Bridges said. "He should be here sometime this afternoon. You're in big trouble."

"So are you," Wahlman said.

Bridges laughed.

"And just how do you figure that?" he said.

"I'm assuming Major Combs is off today," Wahlman said. "I'm assuming she left you in charge of the security office. Shit rolls downhill, soldier. You know that as well as I do. Someone's going to have to take the blame for the fact that I made it inside again. Someone's going to have to take a fall. You might as well say goodbye to those stripes on your sleeves, because you're not going to have them much longer."

Bridges reached into his pocket and pulled out a set of brass knuckles. He slid his fingers through the holes.

"I was the one who captured you," he said. "If anything, I should get a promotion out of this. At any rate, I feel that it's my obligation to interrogate you to the best of my ability before the general arrives."

"How much do you know about what's going on here?" Wahlman said.

"I'm going to ask the questions, and you're going to

answer them," Bridges said. "That's how this is going to work."

"Just trying to help."

"Help what?"

"Save your career."

"You're full of shit," Bridges said. "Who are you working for?"

"I'm working for me," Wahlman said. "And if you were smart, you'd be working for you, starting right now. Especially if you were telling the truth when I questioned you out in town last week. If you really don't know that much about what's going on here, you might be able to avoid prosecution. General Foss is going to be arrested, along with Dr. Walker and everyone else who's involved with—"

"Shut up," Bridges said. "The only person who's going to be arrested is you. Tell me who you're working for. Now."

"Where are you from?" Wahlman said. "Do you have family back home? Just think about how ashamed they're going to be when they have to tell people what happened to you. Just think about how—"

Bridges stepped forward and punched Wahlman in the ribs with the brass knuckles. It was like being hit with a hammer. Wahlman grunted and coughed and retched, the pain swirling through his core like an electrified tornado.

"That's just a sample," Bridges said. "I have authorization from General Foss to break whatever I need to break. Tell me who you're working for."

"I'm not working for anyone," Wahlman said.

Bridges punched him again, in the exact same spot. Flashbulbs exploded in front of his eyes. Blue and yellow and red. And then nothing. Total darkness. Like a cave. Cold and black and suffocating. He felt himself sliding deeper and deeper into it, and then he didn't feel anything at all.

11

Twenty-four hours after discussing the idea with her daughter out on the back deck, Kasey was on her way to South Carolina. Her parents had tried to talk her out of it. They'd initially refused to loan her any money for the trip, but had finally given in when she'd started backing out of the driveway with seven dollars in her pocket and half a tank of gas. They'd given her the money she needed and had waved goodbye from the porch as she left, trying but failing miserably to mask the heartache and disappointment and worry they were feeling.

Natalie was the only one who seemed to understand. She'd followed Kasey out to the driveway and had given her a kiss on the cheek and had told her to be careful.

"I love you, Mom," she'd said.

"I love you too, sweetheart. I'll be back in a couple of days."

"Promise?"

"Promise."

Kasey had called Rock's hotel room multiple times before

leaving the house, hoping that he might have gone back there after successfully completing his mission, hoping to hear that all was well and that this whole ordeal would be resolved soon.

Unfortunately, she'd never heard any of that, because he'd never picked up.

She knew he was still a guest there at the hotel, registered under the name Wendell P. Callahan. Which meant that he hadn't left the Myrtle Beach area. Which wasn't necessarily a bad thing. Maybe he was out celebrating. Out having a good time somewhere. Enjoying the sunshine. The ocean breeze. The freedom.

Or maybe he'd been captured and was being held against his will.

Or maybe something even worse than that had happened.

Kasey needed to know.

She'd left the family cell phone with her parents, and had picked up a disposable flip-top at a discount store. Which, as it turned out, had been a good idea. Because, as it turned out, the gas gauge on her car was not working properly, and the half a tank she'd thought she had starting out was really only about a quarter.

The car died less than a hundred miles into the trip. Kasey pulled to the side of the road and called the toll free number on the back of her insurance card and was promptly informed by the guy who answered that her coverage had lapsed and that she would need to go to the company website and renew her policy by credit card if she wanted them to help her.

"I don't have access to a computer right now," she said. "And I don't have a credit card right now either. Just send someone out with a couple of gallons of gasoline and—"

"We don't do that," the guy said.

"You don't do what?"

"Dispatch trucks to random people who call this number."

"I'm not a random person. I'm a client. I just forgot to pay the bill."

"Sorry."

"So you're just going to leave me stranded here on the side of the highway?"

"I can give you the number to the closest service station, if that would help."

He gave her the number, and she called it, and the woman who answered said that it was just her and the tow truck driver working today and that the tow truck driver was out on a run.

"He should be back in an hour or so," the woman said. "You want to wait?"

"I guess I don't have any choice," Kasey said.

"Will you be paying by cash or credit card?"

"Cash."

The woman told Kasey how much it was going to cost to deliver two gallons of gasoline out to the highway on a Sunday afternoon. It was a lot. Kasey thought about trying to negotiate the price, but she figured it would be a waste of time. She agreed to the terms and disconnected and sat there and watched the traffic whiz past and wondered how she was going to get by on the amount of money she had left. She'd planned on getting a hotel room down in Myrtle Beach. That was out now. She'd planned on eating. That was out now too. After paying for the roadside assistance, she would have enough cash to stop at the next exit and fill her gas tank, and that was about it.

She tried Rock's hotel room again. Still no answer.

She considered the possibility of fueling up and then turning around and heading back home to get some more money, but there was a gnawing feeling in her gut that Rock's situation had become urgent and that she needed to get down there as soon as possible.

So she sat there and waited, hoping that it wasn't already too late.

12

Wahlman struggled to regain consciousness. He forced himself awake with a musculoskeletal jerk, the way you do sometimes when you're trying to break out of a nightmare.

Someone had stripped him down to his boxers and had inserted a urinary catheter. The right side of his ribcage throbbed with every breath. Like a rusty old locomotive pulling carloads of agony down a rusty old track from his armpit to his hip. The injury looked as bad as it felt, the yellow and purple bruise extending all the way to the edge of his right nipple.

He looked around. Bridges was gone. There was a lone sentry standing beside the exit, a guy Wahlman had never seen before, a guy with pimples and a long skinny neck and a machinegun.

"What day is it?" Wahlman said, lifting his head up as far as he could, cringing miserably from the effort.

The guard ignored the question. He keyed a walkie-talkie and said, "Unit four to base. The detainee is awake. I repeat, the detainee is awake."

"Copy that," a voice on the other end said.

The guard clipped the walkie-talkie back onto his belt.

"What day is it?" Wahlman said again.

The guard ignored him again. A few minutes later, the doors swung open and two more guards walked in, followed by an officer in full dress uniform.

An officer with two gold stars on each shoulder.

He stepped over to the stainless steel table that Wahlman was cabled to.

"I'm General Foss," he said. "How are you feeling?"

"Terrible," Wahlman said.

"Good. That's the way you should feel. That's the way I want you to feel."

"I'm thirsty. I need water."

"I know who you are," Foss said.

"I know who you are, too," Wahlman said.

"Then you must realize that you're not going to live much longer."

"I realize a lot of things. I realize that you're a piece of shit. I realize that you put hits out on Darrell Renfro and me to ensure that the funding for your little research project would continue to flow."

"The project's not so little," General Foss said. "In fact, it's huge. It's going to be one of mankind's greatest achievements."

"It's some scary-ass shit if you ask me," Wahlman said.

"Nobody asked you. Anyway, I just wanted to let you know that the research will continue, but that we're preparing to destroy this particular facility for reasons that have nothing to do with you or your situation."

"Why should I care about your stupid building?"

"Because you're going to be inside it when it comes down."

"You should let me go," Wahlman said.

"Why should I do that?"

"People are going to be looking for me. The story's going to get out, one way or another. Why add another murder to your list of offenses?"

"Nobody's going to find you," Foss said. "Because there's not going to be anything left to find. Your friends can say whatever they want to say. It's not going to make any difference."

"They know you're producing human clones here."

"How do they know that? Because you told them? There's not going to be any proof that we did anything wrong. There's not going to be any evidence. It's all going to be destroyed. And maybe you didn't hear the news, but human cloning became legal as of last week. So once we move into our new facility, that part of our research won't need to be such a big secret anymore. We can make all the clones we want to make."

"You kill people for money," Wahlman said. "You're nothing but a common criminal."

"Who did I kill?"

"Darrell Renfro, for one. Not you personally, of course. You weren't the one who sunk the knife into his chest. But you arranged for it to happen. And you and your coconspirators will ultimately benefit financially from the fact that it did happen."

"It's true that the formula for the accelerated growth medium is going to make some of us very wealthy men," Foss said. "But it was never about the money for me. It was about securing my place in history. I must admit, I was concerned about the future of the project for a while, mainly because of you, but it looks like everything's going to work out fine now. I would say that my name will be known for many generations to come. Wouldn't you say so?"

"Sure. You'll be right up there with a guy named Frankenstein."

Foss laughed.

"You're a funny man," he said. "And clever too. The admiral's uniform was a nice touch. Would you mind telling me exactly how you acquired it?"

"I borrowed it from a friend," Wahlman said. "I'm going to need to give it back, so I hope you're having it cleaned and pressed."

"Actually, we were able to trace it to its original owner, using the microscopic serial numbers embedded in the buttons. Bet you didn't know about those, huh? Most people don't. Highly classified. Anyway, we know that the uniform belonged to a man named Swanson, and we know that he got into some trouble a few years ago, and we know that his belongings were temporarily placed into the custody of two sailors, a Master-At-Arms named Rock Wahlman and a Master-At-Arms named Joe Balinger. Would Balinger happen to be one of the friends you were talking about? One of the ones who are eventually going to be looking for you?"

Wahlman didn't say anything.

Foss turned and gave the pair of guards who'd escorted him into the room a nod. They exited through the swinging doors and returned a few seconds later with a rolling stainless steel table identical to the one Wahlman was lying on. There was a man on the table. Someone had stripped him down to his underwear and had inserted a urinary catheter. A rectangular sheet of blue surgical paper had been draped over his head. A slit in the paper exposed his nostrils, which were caked with dried blood.

The guards stepped away from the table. General Foss donned a pair of surgical gloves, walked over there and lifted the blue paper from the man's face.

A bolus of rage-infused adrenaline shot through Wahlman's core like a cannonball. The man on the table was Joe Balinger. Both of his ears had bandages on them, and both of the bandages were soaked with blood.

A shiny steel pole had been attached to the table, and a video monitor had been attached to the pole. The monitor showed Joe's heartrate, and his blood pressure, and his oxygen saturation level, all of which were dangerously out of whack. The EKG display resembled the teeth of a sawblade, the spiked waves clipping along at nearly two hundred beats a minute.

"How are you doing?" General Foss said.

"Please," Joe cried. "I can't take it anymore."

Foss shrugged. He walked over to one of the guards, reached down and pulled his pistol out of its holster, walked back to the table and pressed the barrel against Joe's forehead.

The guards retreated warily toward the other side of the room.

Wahlman bucked and thrashed and shouted and pleaded, but it didn't make any difference.

It didn't stop Foss from pulling the trigger.

13

Kasey made it into the Myrtle Beach area at around seven o'clock. She stopped for coffee at a convenience store near the hotel Rock had been staying at and tried calling his room again.

This time, someone answered.

"Hello?" a muffled male voice said.

"Rock?"

There was a long pause, and then a click, and then nothing.

Kasey punched in the number again.

No answer.

She called the front desk to make sure that Wendell P. Callahan hadn't checked out of the hotel. He hadn't. Which meant that Rock had answered the phone and had hung up when he'd heard Kasey's voice. Or that another person was in the room with Rock. Or that another person was in the room alone.

The only scenario that made sense to Kasey at that moment was that someone was in the room with Rock, and it seemed to be a safe bet that whoever it was didn't have Rock's best interest in mind.

Kasey decided to drive over there, knowing that it was probably going to be the most dangerous thing she'd ever done in her life, knowing that it would be smarter to just turn around and drive back home and forget about Rock Wahlman forever.

But knowing that she could never do that, no matter how hard she tried.

Rock had been on her mind the entire time they'd been apart. She longed for him the way she longed for her next breath. She needed him. She loved him. She wanted to be with him for the rest of her life, and she was willing to do whatever it took to make that happen.

On the way to the hotel, she tried to think of something that she might be able to use as a weapon. What she needed was a gun. But she didn't have one. She didn't even have a knife. Or a chain. Or a baseball bat.

She steered into the hotel parking lot and pulled around to the back of the building and found a spot between two pickup trucks. She dug through her purse, found a miniature can of pepper spray her dad had given her a while back and a fingernail file she'd borrowed from her mom. The fingernail file was pointy on the end. Good for extremely close range, but not much else. The pepper spray could be an effective weapon under certain circumstances, but it probably wasn't going to stop anyone who really wanted to get to you, especially in a hotel room, or in the hallway outside a hotel room, or in any other tightly contained area.

So the weapons weren't great, but they were better than nothing.

Kasey switched off the ignition and climbed out of the car. She slid the fingernail file into her back pocket and cupped the pepper spray in her hand and walked around to the front of the building. She stopped and took a couple of deep breaths, entered the lobby through a revolving glass door and made a beeline for the elevator bank, walking purposefully, eyes straight ahead, trying to behave as though she'd been there before and belonged there now.

Rock's room was on the fourth floor. Kasey stepped off the elevator and followed the arrows. She walked past the room nonchalantly, and then she stood in front of a vending machine at the end of the hallway and pretended to be deliberating over which snack to buy. She stood there for a long time. Nothing happened for a long time. Then the elevator dinged and a young lady pushed a stainless steel cart out into the corridor. There was a domed plate on the cart and some silverware rolled up into a cloth napkin and an unopened bottle of beer. The young lady walked to the room directly across the hall from Rock's room and knocked on the door. Waited. Knocked again. Waited some more. Knocked some more.

"Hey," Kasey said, stepping away from the vending machine and walking toward the young lady.

"Did you order a steak and a salad?" the young lady said.

"Yes. Thank you."

"Want me to open the beer for you?"

"No thanks. I have an opener in my room."

Kasey reached into her pocket and pulled out the last of her money and handed it to the young lady for a tip.

"Thanks," the young lady said. "Have a nice evening."

"You too," Kasey said.

The young lady walked back to the elevator bank. Pushed the button. Stepped into the carriage.

Kasey waited until the elevator doors closed completely, and then she unrolled the napkin and grabbed the steak knife and slid it into her back pocket, next to the fingernail file. She wheeled the cart across the hall and knocked on the door to Rock's room. The peephole darkened and the chain rattled and the door swung open slowly. A guy wearing an extremely wrinkled United States Navy uniform and smelling strongly of whiskey and tobacco stood there and stared down at the cart.

"What's that?" he said.

Kasey shot him in the face with pepper spray. As he staggered backward and tripped over his own feet and fell to the floor, Kasey rammed the cart forward and pushed her way into the room and slammed the door shut.

"Room service," she said, straddling the drunken sailor's fat belly and pressing the blade of the steak knife against his right jugular.

"Wait," the guy said. "I'm just—"

"Where is he?" Kasey said.

"Who?"

Kasey pressed down harder with the blade. A scabbed-over nick, probably from the last time the guy shaved, opened up and started bleeding, the bright red trail trickling down the guy's double chin and blooming like a miniature carnation on the inside of his collar.

"Where is he?" Kasey said again.

"You talking about Callahan?"

"Yes."

"He told me to go ahead and leave if he wasn't back in two hours," the guy said. "I didn't think it would do any harm to stay here in the room for a night or two."

"Wait," Kasey said. "Start over. I want to know exactly what happened."

The guy told Kasey exactly what had happened. He told her about the tall guy named Callahan who had approached him in line at the employment agency, about accepting the job offer, about the barbershop and the uniforms and getting through the gate at the research facility, about waiting in the parking lot for two hours and then an extra ten minutes just in case, about driving back to the hotel and taking the elevator up to the room to retrieve the monetary compensation that Callahan had left there for him.

"I figured the room was paid for already," he said. "No point in letting it go to waste."

"What's your name?" Kasey said.

"Puhler. Can you let me up now? I think I'm bleeding."

"I'm going to need your help finding Callahan."

"That's no problem," Puhler said. "The building he went into is called The Box. And that's what it looks like. A big concrete box. No windows, no doors. You have to use some kind of pneumatic transport system to get inside. I can tell you where the building is, but I'm not going back there, if that's what you had in mind."

"That's exactly what I had mind," Kasey said.

"Not going to happen."

"Is going to happen."

"You can't make me do something I don't want to do," Puhler said. "Anyway, Callahan must have gotten caught impersonating an officer. They're not going to let anyone through that gate now, not without a thorough identification check. And Callahan might not even be there anymore. They might have taken him somewhere else."

"I don't think they took him anywhere else," Kasey said. "If you're detaining someone, any sort of movement increases the risk of escape—which is something that Callahan is really good at, and something his captors know he's really good at. If Callahan's still alive, I'm pretty sure he's still in that building."

"What do you mean if he's still alive?"

"Long story."

"I don't think I want to know."

"I don't think you do either. Tell me how to get to the research facility."

Puhler gazed up at the ceiling. His eyes looked like he'd been rubbing them with pencil erasers. He told Kasey how to get to the research facility from the hotel.

"But it doesn't really matter if he's still in that building or not," he said. "Security's going to be tight as a toenail now."

"Tight as a toenail?"

"Or something. I need coffee."

Kasey eased the blade away from Puhler's throat. She could tell that he was pretty drunk. There was an empty whiskey bottle on the nightstand, and she doubted that he'd shared any with anyone.

"I'll get you some coffee," she said. "Then we're going to try to figure this out."

14

General Foss pushed his way through the swinging doors without saying another word. One of the guards who'd escorted him into the room followed him out to the hallway. The other one put some gloves on and walked over and switched off the video monitor and wiped the blood and bone fragments off the shiny steel pole with a paper towel. He covered Joe's lifeless body with a sheet and wheeled him out of the room, showing no more emotion that he might have shown pushing a wheelbarrow full of bricks. The guard who'd been there when Wahlman woke up went back to his spot beside the door.

Wahlman's ears were still ringing from the pistol report, and his heart was still trying to pound its way out of his chest, and the Pain Train was still roaring down the track, whistling and smoking and rattling its way through flesh and bone and internal organs. Wahlman wondered if the brass knuckles had been traded for a jackhammer at some point. The intensity of the pain just kept getting worse, and there was nothing he could do about it. He couldn't even reposition himself.

He stared up at the ceiling, felt a tear escape from the corner of his right eye. Joe Balinger had been a friend for many years. An all-around good guy. One of the best. Wahlman remembered that he'd been planning to get married, but he couldn't remember his fiancé's name. Maybe he'd never mentioned it. He would have been a good husband and a good dad.

Wahlman looked down at the urine that was pooled at the curve of the catheter tubing. It was dark amber in color, a sign of dehydration. Maybe they were going to make him lie there and die of thirst.

"I need water," he said.

The guard stared straight ahead. He didn't say anything.

Wahlman had no idea what time it was, or even what day it was. There were no clocks in the room, no windows. He looked over at the line of supply cabinets against the wall. The glass he'd shattered on his previous visit to the facility had been replaced. Everything looked as good as new. And now, according to General Foss, it was all going to be destroyed. Maybe Foss had been lying about that. Why would they have gone to all the trouble of repairing the supply cabinet just so they could blow it up? Didn't make sense.

Wahlman kept thinking about it until he couldn't think anymore. He closed his eyes and drifted into a dream-saturated semiconscious state that teetered on the precipice of true sleep, his brain probably sensing that going all the way would mean never coming back. In his dream, or his hallucination, or whatever it was, he was in Florida, and

678

Kasey Stielson was his wife, and he'd finally gotten his private investigator's license, and he was in an office, sitting behind a desk, talking to a potential client, a very beautiful woman with dark hair and eyes as warm as cinnamon toast.

Wahlman shuffled through some papers.

"What was your name again?" he said.

"Why do you need to know that?" the woman said.

"It's just one of my standard questions. We can come back to it. So tell me, what brings you to my office today?"

"He's dead, isn't he?"

"Ma'am?"

"The man I was going to marry. The man who was going to be the father of my children. He's dead, and it's your fault."

The woman opened her purse and pulled out a knife and stabbed Wahlman in the arm with it.

"Don't do that," Wahlman said.

He opened his eyes. A man wearing a white lab coat and a surgical mask was standing beside the table tapping air bubbles out of a syringe.

"I put an IV needle in your left arm," the man said. "I'm going to give you something for pain, and then I'm going to start some fluids."

"Why?" Wahlman said.

"To keep you hydrated."

"Why?"

"Because General Foss told me to."

"General Foss made it clear that I don't have long to live," Wahlman said. "So why is he trying to keep me alive?"

"You'll have to ask him about that."

The man injected the contents of the syringe into the tubing taped to Wahlman's left arm.

The effects were immediate.

As if someone had swept the pain away with a brush.

Wahlman felt like a million bucks. He might have done a cartwheel if he hadn't been tied down with steel cables.

The man spiked a liter of normal saline and bled the air out of a tubing set and adjusted the drip with a thumb clamp.

"Thank you," Wahlman said. "I feel much better now. I think I'll just go on home."

The man laughed. He gathered his things and threw away the plastic wrappers from the IV supplies and exited the room.

A few minutes later, PFC Bridges walked in.

"The pain medicine was the general's idea," Bridges said.

"Tell him I said thanks."

"I was against it."

"I'm not surprised," Wahlman said.

"The IV drip was my idea."

"Okay."

"We're going to keep you going until the demolition crew gets here tomorrow morning. Should be quite a show."

"If you consider cold-blooded murder to be a show," Wahlman said.

Bridges shrugged.

"The general has arranged for me to be his personal assistant," he said, proudly. "We're going to be looking at a live video feed. I might even make some popcorn to eat while I watch."

Wahlman wanted to grab Bridges by the shirt and make him eat his own front teeth.

"What about the rest of the staff?" he said.

"They've all been notified that we're bugging out. Almost everyone who was here for the weekend is gone. Now, if you'll shut up for a minute or two, I need to go ahead and explain exactly how everything's going to go down tomorrow."

"Why would you want to do that?" Wahlman said.

"Because the general told me to. And because I want to see the expression on your face when you find out how horrible the last few hours of your life are going to be."

"The expression on my face isn't going to change," Wahlman said. "Not for a piece of shit like you."

Bridges reached into his pocket and pulled out the brass knuckles.

"We'll see about that," he said.

15

Kasey called room service and ordered a pot of coffee. When it came, she politely asked Puhler to answer the door, hoping to avoid a second encounter with the young lady she'd talked to in the hallway earlier. Because of the fraudulent procurement of the stainless steel cart with the domed plate and the silverware rolled up into a cloth napkin and the unopened bottle of beer on it. As it turned out, a young man delivered the coffee. Puhler tipped him and sent him on his way.

Kasey sat across from Puhler at the little round wooden table in the corner and they shared the steak and the salad and an overcooked baked potato and some butter and a roll. Puhler kept eyeing the bottle of beer. Kasey kept shoving more coffee in front of him.

"I need you to sober up," she said. "So we can figure this out."

"You keep saying *we*," Puhler said. "I told you I'm not going back there."

"Yes you are."

"No I'm not."

"I need your help."

"Sorry," Puhler said. "But I almost had a heart attack the first time. Now you're telling me that there are killers behind those walls? That kind of shit's not for me. I'm going to hitch a ride back to the ferry, and I'm going to buy a ticket to cross the bay, and I'm going to be standing back in line at the employment agency tomorrow morning."

"How much did Callahan pay you?" Kasey said.

"I don't think that's any of your business."

"Tell me how much he paid you. I'll double it. All you have to do is—"

"You don't have any money," Puhler said. "You didn't even have enough to tip the guy for the coffee."

"My father's very wealthy," Kasey said. "I'll have the money wired here as soon as we're finished. How much did Callahan pay you?"

"Five hundred."

Kasey figured he was lying. She didn't care.

"I'll give you a thousand," she said.

Puhler picked a piece of meat from between his teeth with a fingernail.

He sipped his coffee.

"How can I be sure you're going to pay me?" he said.

"You can hold the keys to my car until we're finished. How about that?"

Puhler shrugged.

"I'll think about it," he said.

"Or how about this," Kasey said. "I'll call the shore patrol over in Myrtle Beach and tell them that an inebriated man wearing a United States Navy uniform with Master-At-Arms insignias on the rank patches is giving me a hard time. They'll take one look at you and arrest you on the spot, and when they find out that you're wearing the United States Navy uniform illegally, they'll—"

"All right," Puhler said. "A thousand bucks."

"Great. So let's talk about how we're going to get inside."

"I don't think it's really going to be much of a problem," Puhler said.

"Why do you say that?"

"I overheard some things while I was sitting out in the parking lot. Apparently they're going to be moving to a different location. Everyone's going to be gone by five o'clock in the morning. Everyone but Callahan."

"Why didn't you tell me that before?"

"Must have slipped my mind."

"Maybe because you sat here and drank a fifth of bourbon all by yourself."

"Maybe."

"Or maybe because you just didn't feel compelled to help me until I threatened to call the shore patrol."

"Maybe."

Kasey was starting to wonder if she could trust anything that was coming from Puhler's mouth, including the business about the operation moving to a different location.

"Why everyone but Callahan?" she said. "Why are they leaving him there by himself?"

"I don't know. I didn't catch that part. And they didn't

refer to Callahan by his name. They called him *the general's detainee.* I just figured that's who they were talking about. This was right before I started the car and drove away. If I'd stayed much longer, I probably would have been a detainee too."

"Probably. I want to get to the facility as soon as possible. Let's go ahead and—"

"The ferries don't start running until four-thirty," Puhler said. "So there's no point in thinking about doing anything before then. We can get some sleep, head out around four."

Kasey glanced over at the bed.

"I hope you don't think you're staying in this room tonight," she said.

"Where else am I supposed to stay?"

"You can sleep in the rental car."

"But I was here first," Puhler said.

"You're a squatter. You don't belong here."

"But—"

"Plus, I'm going to be paying you a lot of money. I get the room. You get the car. End of discussion."

Puhler grabbed the bottle of beer, rested the edge of the cap against the edge of the table, popped it off by slamming it with the butt of his hand.

"Fine," he said. "But don't complain about the way I smell after sweating my ass off out there in the car all night."

"Don't worry," Kasey said. "I'll wake you up in plenty of time to take a shower."

16

The pain medicine Wahlman had received was no match for the fresh set of bruises.

No match at all.

PFC Bridges had worked on the left side of his ribcage this time.

Now there were two locomotives, one on each side of Wahlman's body, two enormous greasy black engines cranking it out down two wobbly sets of tracks, almost like a competition, like some sort of sadistic race where the grand prize was a bucketful of misery.

Choo! Choo!

Right now the left side was winning, but the right side was starting to pick up speed again. Wahlman figured the two would be neck and neck in a little while. He clenched his teeth and flexed his muscles and grunted and shouted and writhed.

Before leaving the room, Bridges had explained how everything was supposed to go down tomorrow morning.

At 03:00, a pair of guards would come and wheel the

table Wahlman was lying on into a different room, a room closer to the center of the basement. At 03:30, the demolition experts would arrive and place a number of explosive charges at a number of load-bearing locations within the facility. A computerized timer would relay an electrical pulse to the charges at a prescribed time, resulting is a series of explosions that would cause the building to collapse in on itself.

And that would be that.

Wahlman was going to spend the next few hours in agonizing pain, and then he was going to die. Those were the facts, and there was nothing he could do to change them. He was too weak to put up any sort of fight, even if an opportunity presented itself. The cuffs and shackles and chains and cables were extreme overkill now. He wasn't sure that he could even stand up on his own at this point.

It had been a pretty good life, for the most part. The orphanage had been kind of tough sometimes, but at least they'd provided him with the basic necessities. He'd thrived as a law enforcement officer in the Navy, and there were times he wished he'd stayed in for another ten years. He'd laughed a lot and loved a lot and had been to places most people only dreamt about. It had been a pretty good life, but now it was over. And he was okay with that. He wasn't afraid to die. He only hoped that the gross injustices he and Darrell Renfro had been dealt would eventually come to light, and that all of the dealers would eventually get what they deserved.

He took some quick and shallow breaths, opened his eyes

and looked around. The guy with the machinegun was still standing at the door. Still staring straight ahead.

"Please," Wahlman said. "I need water. Just a sip."

"I'm not supposed to talk to you," the guard said.

His voice was deep and raspy. Like he'd recently swallowed a handful of sand or something.

"I'm dying," Wahlman said. "What harm could it possibly do to give me a drink of water?"

The guard leaned his gun against the fat strip of steel molding that surrounded the door frame, crossed the room and grabbed a little paper cup from a little plastic dispenser that was mounted to the wall over the sink. He filled the cup with tap water, walked over to the table and held it to Wahlman's lips.

The guard was a corporal. His nametag said McGaff.

"I could get in big trouble for doing this," he said.

Wahlman slurped the water into his mouth, absorbing it like a sponge.

"Thank you," he said.

"Let me know if you want some more. I'm here for the duration."

"What time is it now?"

"Almost midnight."

"Saturday?"

"Sunday," Corporal McGaff said.

He tossed the paper cup into the trashcan, walked back to the door and picked up his gun and stood there and stared straight ahead.

17

Kasey stared at the digital clock on the nightstand until the alarm went off. She climbed out of bed, took a quick shower, walked out to the parking lot.

Rock's rental car was gone.

Which meant that Puhler was gone.

Which meant that he was a total piece of shit. A total waste of oxygen.

Maybe he'd made another trip to the liquor store. Maybe he was sleeping it off on a park bench somewhere. Kasey felt stupid for trusting him to do what he said he was going to do, stupid for not taking the keys to the rental car and hiding them somewhere. She started walking toward her car to see how much gas she had left, and then she remembered that her gauge wasn't working.

Shit.

She hadn't thought to check the odometer when she filled up, but she knew she'd driven at least a couple of hundred miles since then. Maybe she still had around half a tank.

It seemed absurd that Rock's life might depend on such a trivial matter, but apparently that was the case. If there had been more time, Kasey would have called her dad and asked for more money, just to be on the safe side. But it was almost four already, and Rock was going to be left alone at the facility at five, and there was no telling what would happen after that. Nothing good, that was for sure.

So Kasey needed to get moving. Not in an hour or so, the time it would take to make the call to her dad and fill out the forms and wait at the front desk for the transfer approval codes. She needed to get moving now. She would steal some gasoline if she had to. She would do whatever it took to get to Rock in time and get him out of the facility safely.

She walked to her car, climbed in and started the engine, steered out of the hotel parking lot and headed toward the dock to catch the ferry.

The ferry.

Shit.

That was going to cost money too. Money that Kasey didn't have.

She made a U-turn. She was going to have to go back to the hotel and call her dad and wait for a money transfer to go through. No choice.

She pounded on the dashboard with her fist. She felt as frustrated as she'd ever felt in her life. She stopped at an intersection, thought about running the red light, but didn't. The way things had been going, she would probably end up getting pulled over, which would waste even more time.

While she was sitting there waiting for the light to change, she pressed the button to spray some fluid onto the windshield, hoping to wash away some of the grime and insect carcasses from the interstate. The wiper on the driver side scooted noisily about halfway into its arc, and then it stopped completely. Kasey ducked down and squinted and saw that a folded piece of paper had been stuffed under the blade. She switched off the wipers and rolled the window down and reached out and grabbed the paper and unfolded it.

Five twenty dollar bills fell in her lap.

She used the miniature flashlight that she kept on her keychain to read the note.

Dear Kasey,

Sorry about leaving, but I just couldn't go through with it. I hope you're able to do what you set out to do. I hope this helps.

Puhler

So maybe he wasn't a total waste of oxygen after all.

Kasey didn't really blame Puhler for bailing on her. He'd obviously decided that returning to the research facility was just too much of a risk, no matter how much money was involved. And he was right. A thousand dollars wasn't enough. A million wouldn't have been enough. Not for the potential danger he would have been facing. Not if his heart wasn't in it.

Kasey's heart was in it.

And a hundred dollars would definitely help.

A hundred dollars would make all the difference.

Kasey wadded the note into a ball and tossed it over onto the passenger side floorboard and waited for the light to turn green. As soon as it did, she made another U-turn and headed back toward the dock, determined more than ever to make it across the bay to the research facility by five, determined more than ever to do whatever needed to be done once she got there.

18

Most of the power to the facility had been shut down hours ago.

PFC Bridges was sitting in the security office with General Foss and Corporal McGaff, drinking coffee and watching live video feeds from the handful of cameras that were still in operation. Foss had made it clear that the three of them would be the last people to leave the facility—other than Wahlman, of course, who wasn't ever going to leave.

Bridges didn't care much for the arrangement, although he was quite aware of the tradition behind the general's decision to set it up that way.

The phone on the desk rang.

"That's going to be Kelsoe again," Foss said, staring into one of the monitors. "Looks like they're about finished."

Kelsoe was the foreman on the demolition crew. He'd been checking in every thirty minutes or so.

Bridges switched the call to speakerphone and picked up the receiver.

"Security," he said.

"It's me again," Kelsoe said. "We're about to wrap things up. Just need to activate the timer. You want it set for one hour, right?"

Bridges looked at Foss.

Foss nodded.

"Affirmative," Bridges said. "One hour."

There was a brief period of silence, followed by a series of electronic beeps.

"Okay," Kelsoe said. "The clock is ticking."

"General Foss wants you guys to use the ladders and the service walkways to get back outside," Bridges said.

"Right. We already talked about that."

"Just wanted to make sure you understood."

"Yeah. And it's kind of a long walk, so I better get going. Have a great day."

Kelsoe disconnected.

Bridges lowered the receiver back into its cradle.

"Sir, I think we should head on up to the PTS now," he said.

"We're going to wait until the demo crew makes it outside," General Foss said. "Then we're going to wait until they climb into their truck and drive away. Shouldn't take long. Ten minutes max. That'll leave us plenty of time to take the PTS up to the front portal."

"There are three of us, sir. Which means that—"

"Relax," Foss said. "We'll have plenty of time."

Bridges tried to relax, but he couldn't. He stared at the video monitors, hoping that he didn't look as anxious as he felt. It was quite an honor to be selected as the general's personal assistant, and he didn't want to get off to a bad start by questioning the general's judgement on this matter.

But he also didn't want to get blown to bits.

The demolition crew consisted of four men. Bridges watched as they made their way into the tunnels and up the ladders and finally through the heavy steel service hatch, emerging into the harsh glare of the exterior lights about fifty feet west of the front guard shack. They walked over to the gate and loaded their tools into the back of their van, which was parked beside the dark green luxury sedan that Bridges would eventually be using to transport General Foss and Corporal McGaff away from the facility.

"Grab some flashlights," Foss said.

He stood and walked over to the electrical panel and started switching off generators, killing power to everything except the elevators and the pneumatic transport system. The overhead lights in the security office went dark, as did the video monitors.

Bridges passed a flashlight to Corporal McGaff, and then he handed one to the general.

"Here you go, sir," he said. "We really should be going now."

"That's why I shut everything down," Foss said, gruffly. "Because we are going now."

"Yes, sir."

Bridges looked at his watch. In forty-seven minutes, the building would be reduced to rubble. Forty-seven minutes was plenty of time for the three of them to make it outside and drive far enough away to escape any effects from the blast. It was at least twice as much time as they actually needed. Bridges knew that. But he also knew that shit happened. If he had been running the show, he would have set the timer for two hours. Maybe even three.

He opened the door and exited the security office. General Foss was a couple of steps behind him, and Corporal McGaff was a couple of steps behind General Foss. They made it to the elevator and up one floor, and then they walked through the corridor that led to the PTS portal. Bridges set the pace, which was somewhere between a brisk walk and a trot. When they made it to within a few feet of the portal, General Foss stopped and turned and rested his hand on Corporal McGaff's shoulder.

"Private Bridges and I will go first," Foss said. "You'll see the green light for the capsule-return mode soon after we make it out to the shack."

"Yes, sir," McGaff said.

Bridges helped the general into the passenger seat, and a minute or so later they were whizzing through the system like an enormous bullet that had been shot from the barrel of an enormous rifle. They would make it to the shack in less than a minute. Then, two or three minutes after that, McGaff would join them and they would all climb into the dark green sedan and wave goodbye to The Box and everything inside it, including the man tied to the table in the basement.

Bridges felt kind of silly now for worrying so much. He smiled, knowing what a great assignment this was going to be, knowing that a series of quick promotions would be coming his way, figuring he would be wearing sergeant's stripes in less than two years. Everything was going to be great from this point forward. Everything was going to work out just fine.

"What's that noise?" General Foss said. "And why are we slowing down?"

Bridges didn't know what that noise was.

And he didn't know why they were slowing down.

"I don't know, sir," he said.

A few seconds later, they weren't slowing down anymore.

A few seconds later, they had come to a complete stop.

"What's going on?" Foss said.

Bridges frantically started pushing buttons and flipping switches, but nothing he did made any difference. The PTS capsule wouldn't move forward, toward the portal in the front guard shack, and it wouldn't move backward, toward the portal they'd just come from. It wouldn't move an inch in either direction.

"I think we're stuck, sir," Bridges said.

"What do you mean we're stuck? We can't be stuck. Get us out of here, private. That's an order."

"I'm trying, sir."

"Just open the door. We'll climb out and crawl the rest of the way."

"The door won't open, sir. It's designed to stay closed while the capsule is inside the transit tube."

"Isn't there some sort of emergency escape hatch?"

"No, sir."

"Why not?"

"It's a safety issue, sir. Regarding the extreme difference in pressure on the other side of the capsule."

Foss started pounding on the instrument console in front of him.

"What do people usually do when one of these things gets stuck?" he said.

"I've never heard of anything like this happening before," Bridges said. "But the manual they gave us when we were in training for these systems said that any sort of malfunction should be reported to the maintenance department immediately."

"The maintenance department left hours ago."

"Yes, sir."

"So what are we going to do?"

"I don't know, sir."

"McGaff. He's waiting for the capsule to come back to him. When it doesn't, he's going to know something is wrong. Would it be possible for him to shut the power off and crawl down here and push us through manually?"

Bridges thought about that.

"Yes, sir," he said. "I think that would work."

"How much time do we have?"

"Forty-one minutes, sir."

A dry growl came from somewhere deep in the back of the general's throat.

"That's not going to be enough, is it?" he said.

"No, sir," Bridges said. "I don't think it is."

19

"My name is Rock Wahlman. In exactly thirty-seven minutes and twenty-nine seconds, I'm going to die."

Before the guards had come to transport Wahlman to the room he was in now, the man wearing the white lab coat and the surgical mask had returned and had administered another dose of IV pain medicine, along with some sort of stimulant, a drug that had instantly jolted Wahlman into a state of extreme hyperawareness. Currently pain-free and super-duper energized, he felt like climbing off the table and running a marathon or two just for fun.

Of course he couldn't really climb off the table. He couldn't do anything except watch the screen on the laptop computer that had been placed in front of him. Which, as of several minutes ago, had become the only source of light in the room.

37:28…

37:27…

37.26…

"Rock," a distant female voice shouted. "Rock, are you here?"

Wahlman ignored the voice, which was obviously an auditory hallucination, the result of sleep deprivation and the intravenous chemical cocktail he'd received. He figured the medication had been ordered to ensure that he would be awake and alert right up to the last minute, right up to the point where the explosive charges went off and the building started crumbing down on top of him.

He continued talking out loud, telling his story, hoping that the security cameras were picking it up, hoping that someone would eventually hear what he was saying.

The female voice interrupted him again, calling out his name again.

The voice seemed closer this time.

It seemed to be getting closer by the second.

The door to the room creaked open. Wahlman tilted his head to the left and saw a pinpoint of light, a bright little blueish-white star that was slowly moving toward him.

"Go away," he said. "You're not real."

"Rock? It's me. Kasey."

A split second before he repeated the command for the hallucination to go away, Wahlman felt a soft cool hand grip his left forearm.

"Kasey?" he said.

"What have they done to you?"

"Kasey? Is that really you? How did you find this place? How did you—"

"I'll tell you all about it later. Right now I just want to get you out of here."

"No. You need to run as fast as you can. See the numbers

counting down on that monitor over there? When those numbers get to zero, some electronic relays are going to trigger some explosive charges and this whole building is going to come down like a sandcastle at high tide. You need to get out of here. Now."

"I'm not leaving without you," Kasey said.

"They tied me to the table with steel cables. The cables are secured with a padlock. There's just not enough time."

"I walked into some sort of maintenance room a few minutes ago. There were tools in there. Just tell me what I need."

"You need to go. You need to get as far away from here as possible."

"I'm not leaving without you," Kasey said again.

"Then you're going to die."

"Okay."

Wahlman felt like shouting, but he didn't. Because he knew it wouldn't do any good. Because he knew Kasey. Once she had her mind set on doing something, there was no talking her out of it.

"Why do you have to be so stubborn?" he said.

"Just tell me what kind of tool I need."

"Bolt cutters," Wahlman said. "Or a hacksaw. Or even a hatchet, if that's all you can find. Bolt cutters would be best."

"What do bolt cutters look like?"

"They have long handles. Maybe two feet long. Blades on the end that mate up flush with each other."

"I'll be right back," Kasey said.

She returned a couple of minutes later with a set of bolt

cutters and a hacksaw and a hatchet and a battery-powered lantern.

"Just snip the lock with the bolt cutters," Wahlman said.

Kasey snipped the lock with the bolt cutters. She unwound the steel cables, and then she cut the chains on the handcuffs and shackles.

Wahlman sat up, fought off a wave of vertigo, climbed off of the table and held Kasey in his arms and kissed her and told her how much he loved her.

"I love you too," she said. "Think we should be going now?"

"I think that would be a good idea."

"We need to find you some clothes. Or at least some shoes."

"There's no time for that. I'll be all right."

Kasey picked up the lantern.

"Follow me," she said.

Wahlman used the bolt cutters to free himself from the drainage bag that was attached to his catheter, and then he grabbed the hatchet and followed Kasey out of the room.

"How are we going to get out of the building?" Wahlman said. "The pneumatic transport system requires a fingerprint scan and an access code. And even if we were able to get past all that, someone cut the power a while ago. The system isn't even going to be—"

"Actually, the system is still up and running," Kasey said. "But we're not going to be using it. We're going to get out the same way I got in."

She led Wahlman through a disorienting series of

hallways and into an alcove that housed what appeared to be the central vacuum unit for the PTS. She turned the knob on an unmarked red door and exited into a walkway with a steel grate for a floor and a concrete ceiling that was only about six feet high. Wahlman had to stoop as he entered the space, and the grate was rough on his bare feet, and urine from the severed catheter was trickling down his right leg, but none of that mattered, none of it prevented him from breaking into a trot to keep up with Kasey as she hustled toward a steel ladder at the far end of the tunnel.

A situation that had seemed utterly hopeless only minutes ago now promised to be one of the best days of Rock Wahlman's life. He gripped the hatchet and used it as an extension of his right hand as he mounted the ladder, taking it one slippery rung at a time, guided by the light from Kasey's lantern, which was spilling over the edge of the platform above.

Wahlman was almost to the top, only a second or two from joining Kasey on the next level, when a deep and raspy male voice shouted, "Stop, or I'll shoot!"

20

Wahlman recognized the voice.

It was Corporal McGaff, the guard who'd been posted by the door in the medical supply room, the guard who'd stood there for hours, at least a double shift, maybe a triple.

Wahlman wondered why he was still in the building.

But he didn't wonder for long.

Because it didn't really matter.

The guard was in the way, which meant that the guard would have to be taken out of the way.

Amped on adrenaline and the super-therapeutic dose of drugs he'd been given, Wahlman climbed onto the platform and positioned himself between Kasey and Corporal McGaff, who was still holding the machinegun he'd been holding earlier.

McGaff aimed the barrel of the gun directly at Wahlman's core.

"Drop it," Wahlman said.

"I don't want to shoot you, man."

"I know you don't. So drop the rifle. We'll walk out of

here together. You can go your way, and I'll go mine."

Sweat beaded on McGaff's forehead. He was thinking it over. Considering his options.

He was obviously very nervous, unsteady, the tip of the gun barrel jittering like the needle on a pressure gauge, a needle that had crept into the red zone, a needle that was extremely close to being pegged.

He tightened his grip on the handguard, clicked off the safety.

"What happened to General Foss and Private Bridges?" he said.

"I don't know," Wahlman said.

"I'm going to have to take you into custody."

"No you're not."

"I can't just let you go."

"Sure you can."

Something clattered metallically against the wall to McGaff's left. Something with some weight. Probably a coin from one of Kasey's pockets. Probably a penny or a nickel or a dime or a quarter, discreetly tossed to the side of the walkway to create a momentary diversion. McGaff instinctively made a slight turn toward the disturbance, and the barrel of the gun made a slight turn with him, and with absolutely no hesitation, Wahlman reared back and threw the hatchet as hard as he could, the way he would have thrown a fastball in the bottom of the ninth with bases loaded and two outs and a full count on the guy at the plate. The steel head and the hardwood handle whizzed through the air end-over-end, came to an abrupt stop when the razor-sharp blade thudded deeply into the center of McGaff's chest. An earsplitting burst of machinegun fire echoed through the space as he collapsed forward onto the grate, the weight of his body pushing the heavy cutting tool even deeper into his sternum.

Wahlman took a few steps forward, leaned down and grabbed the automatic rifle.

"I didn't want to kill him," he said.

"You didn't have a choice," Kasey said.

"He was all right. He gave me water."

"He should have let you go. He chose not to."

Wahlman nodded.

"Foss and Bridges," he said. "Any idea what he was talking about?"

"Who are Foss and Bridges?"

"Foss is a two-star general. He's in charge of the entire operation. Bridges is his personal assistant."

"I have a feeling they might be stuck somewhere in the PTS," Kasey said.

"Because of something you did?" Wahlman said.

"Yes."

"This day just keeps getting better and better."

"We should go."

"Lead the way," Wahlman said. "I'll be right behind you."

21

After a two-hour visit to an urgent care center and a forty-eight hour visit to the bed in his hotel room, Wahlman had delivered a ten-page written statement and the disc-shaped audio recording device to one of the investigative reporters he'd spoken to previously. The story broke a day and a half later. A day and a half after that, Wahlman joined Kasey for a late breakfast at the little mom-and-pop diner across the street from the hotel. A waitress named Justine brought coffee and asked if they were ready to order.

"We still need a few minutes," Wahlman said.

"That's fine," Justine said. "I'll check back in a little while."

She stepped away and refilled the cups at the next booth.

Wahlman wore jeans and a t-shirt and a nice pair of leather work boots, all purchased by Kasey with money her parents had wired from somewhere in Virginia. None of Wahlman's ribs were broken, but they were still very sore. His chest looked like someone had spilled several different colors of ink on it.

"Dad said we can stay at the lake house in Tennessee," Kasey said, tearing a packet of sugar open and stirring it into her coffee. "He said we can stay there as long as we want to."

"I'll have to take care of the situation down in New Orleans first," Wahlman said. "It shouldn't take long, now that the word is out about what was going on. They'll have to book me, but I should be able to get out on bail."

"At least nobody is trying to kill you now."

"Yeah. So I can breathe a little easier."

"A lot easier."

"I couldn't have done it without you."

"I know."

"You're the best thing that ever happened to me."

"I know."

Kasey had provided some of the details behind her experience at the research facility while Wahlman was convalescing in the hotel room. She'd left her car on the side of the highway and had crawled through the tunnel of foliage and had seen that the front gate was wide open and that two vehicles had been parked there—an unmarked cargo van, which meant nothing to Kasey, and a dark green luxury sedan with a small United States Army flag attached to the antenna and a front plate with two big stars on it, which meant plenty. She'd watched from the edge of the woods as four men wearing dirty white coveralls emerged from a metal hatch that was flush with the ground. The men threw some tools into the back of the van and climbed in, and a few seconds later the headlights came on and the van sped away. Figuring that a general and his or her entourage wouldn't be using a grimy service tunnel to get to the green luxury sedan—the only other vehicle in sight—Kasey ran to the guard shack and walked inside and saw the portal to the pneumatic transport system. There was a narrow cot in one corner of the shack with a thin mattress on it. Kasey rolled the mattress up and tied it with a sheet and dropped it into the dark and empty space behind the slot for the PTS capsule and watched it disappear into the blackness. She had no idea what kind of effect the fat cushiony foreign object would have on the system, but she hoped that it would slow the general and his crew down long enough for her to make it over to the service hatch. Of course it had ultimately done a lot more than that. It had caused General Foss and PFC Bridges to be trapped inside the system, somewhere along the transit tube, where they'd remained until the percussive wave from the explosive charges swept by, causing their lungs to slowly and painfully fill with blood.

A horrible way to die, but then they were pretty horrible guys. The only one Wahlman felt bad about was McGaff. He wished it could have gone differently with him.

He thought about it as he sat there in the little mom-and-pop diner and sipped his coffee, and he thought about everything that Kasey had done for him. Everything in the last few days, and everything since the day he'd met her.

"You're amazing," he said.

"I know," she said.

"Will you marry me?"

"I'll think about it."

Kasey smiled.

Wahlman smiled back.

He leaned forward and she leaned forward and they met in the middle and kissed, and they talked some more and drank another cup of coffee and decided to skip breakfast and go on back to the hotel for a while.

Thanks so much for reading THE REACHER EXPERIMENT BOOKS 1-7!

Love Jack Reacher? If so, I think you'll also love Nicholas Colt in AMERICAN P.I.

"This is a character I'm eager to follow through many adventures to come," says bestselling author Tess Gerritsen.

For occasional updates and special offers, please visit my website and sign up for my newsletter.

All of my books are lendable, so feel free to share them with a friend at no additional cost.

All reviews are much appreciated!

Thanks again, and happy reading!

Jude

Printed in Great Britain
by Amazon